S0-AIE-146

Dear Reader:

Lust, Pride, Sloth, Gluttony, Greed, Envy and Wrath. The seven deadly sins, and the seven sections of *Exit* by Phillip Thomas Duck—a fascinating tale of a man who married for money, only to discover that he was the one being used. A man who is addicted to sex and cannot keep himself from crawling inside of the nearest pair of available and willing thighs. A man who is given power, only to have it snatched away by unforeseen enemies in the most unexpected places. A man with no one to trust and no place to turn to, so he…exits.

Have you every thought about vanishing? Simply walking away from the life that you have, without telling a soul? I have often wondered, out of all the people who turn up missing constantly, how many of them actually walked away. I believe that the number is greater than any of us suspect. Sometimes circumstances can become too heavy; sometimes life can become too difficult; sometimes there seems like there is no solution, so you…exit.

*Exit* is intriguing, captivating, and explosive. Duck is a master story-teller with a poetic style of writing that will keep readers riveted until the very last page. With an intricately woven tale and alluring erotic sequences, *Exit* is an excellent thriller, full of suspense. I am confident that you will enjoy reading it as much as I enjoyed editing it.

As always, thanks for supporting myself and the Strebor Books family. We strive to bring you cutting-edge literature that cannot be found anyplace else. For more information on our titles, please visit Zanestore.com. My personal web site is Eroticanoir.com and my online social network is PlanetZane.org.

Blessings,

*Zane*

Zane
Publisher
Strebor Books
www.simonsays.com/streborbooks

# ZANE PRESENTS

DETROIT PUBLIC LIBRARY

0 5674 05400205 0

# EXIT

FRANKLIN BRANCH LIBRARY
16651 E. MCNICHOLS RD.
DETROIT, MI 48205

AUG    2011

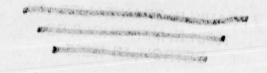

ZANE PRESENTS

# EXIT

## PHILLIP THOMAS DUCK

STREBOR BOOKS

NEW YORK  LONDON  TORONTO  SYDNEY

Strebor Books
P.O. Box 6505
Largo, MD 20792
http://www.streborbooks.com

This book is a work of fiction. Names, characters, places and incidents are
products of the author's imagination or are used fictitiously. Any resemblance
to actual events or locales or persons, living or dead, is entirely coincidental.

© 2011 by Phillip Thomas Duck

All rights reserved. No part of this book may be reproduced in any form or by
any means whatsoever. For information address Strebor Books, P.O. Box 6505,
Largo, MD 20792.

ISBN 978-1-59309-370-9
ISBN 978-1-4516-1717-7 (ebook)
LCCN 2011928019

First Strebor Books trade paperback edition August 2011

Cover design: www.mariondesigns.com
Cover photograph: © Keith Saunders/Marion Designs

10  9  8  7  6  5  4  3  2  1

Manufactured in the United States of America

For information regarding special discounts for bulk purchases,
please contact Simon & Schuster Special Sales at 1-866-506-1949
or business@simonandschuster.com

The Simon & Schuster Speakers Bureau can bring authors to your live event.
For more information or to book an event, contact the Simon & Schuster Speakers
Bureau at 1-866-248-3049 or visit our website at www.simonspeakers.com.

*To Janice Brothers, my beloved Aunt*
*RIP*

*and*

*Ariana, my greatest creation*

# BOOK ONE

# LUST
# SLOTH
# PRIDE
# GREED
# ENVY
# GLUTTONY
# WRATH

# CHAPTER ONE

She caught him completely off guard with her request. *Describe pain.* He frowned for a brief moment. Just a moment. Then his eyes were on her, searching every inch as though it were the first time. She was naked from the waist up. Skin the muted brown of hot chocolate mix. Small breasts with oversized nipples. A gym membership physique, sleek and toned. Beautiful hazel eyes that forced him to swallow every time he looked into them. A smile he'd only ever seen in movies. Always on the face of the bad guys.

Or bad girls.

Her white silk blouse was draped over the back of the lone chair in the hotel room, bra neatly folded over that. She'd eased her peach-colored skirt down an inch past her hips, just as ready as he was to get right to it. But then she'd stopped abruptly. Made her request.

*Describe pain.*

He was already fully naked himself at that point, his penis as erect as a flagpole. He glanced at his watch. Forty-five, fifty minutes tops, then he needed to be back at the office. A half-completed proposal was waiting for him on his desk. There wasn't nearly enough time remaining in the day to finish the proposal before tomorrow's early morning meeting. Responding to her ridiculous request would chop up what little time he did have.

"Why?" he asked her, aggravated. One word, that's all he'd give her. Maybe she'd get the hint, cut this nonsense short. Get to what they both came here for. What they both desperately needed, wanted, desired.

"Haven't heard from you in weeks," she said, softly. Her normal speaking voice was distinctive. Husky. Sexy. Full of something he couldn't ease away from no matter how hard he tried. Which wasn't very hard in most cases. "The time apart has left me... thinking," she continued. "Seems like lately I'm constantly in thought."

"Can't we discuss this some other time?" he asked. "I want to make love to you."

She nodded. "Ditto." And as if to underscore the point she went ahead and eased the rest of the way out of her skirt.

"Damn." He licked his lips, his eyes trained below her waist. "No panties, baby. Damn."

She smiled, repositioned the skirt in front of her like a cover. "I want to do this. You know I do. But I need you to answer me."

"Answer you?"

"Describe pain," she said for the third time.

He shook his head, frowned, sighed, and studied her. She looked about as serious as he'd ever seen her. There was no way beyond this without humoring her. "You want me to describe pain?"

"Yes," she said, nodding vigorously. "Please." She bit her lip. "And I'm very sensual, as you know, so I need to know what it looks like to you. How it feels to the touch. How it tastes."

"This is ridiculous," he complained. "Right now? You can't possibly be serious?"

Her smile said she was and wasn't.

At one time he would have said that pain smelled like coppery blood or musty sweat. That it was colored black, or at the very least a dark, dark blue. That it tasted either salty or bitter. Like gravel to the touch.

"Now," he said, "It's the color of hot chocolate mix."

"Mmmm," she said, licking her lips.

"Smells like Burberry perfume and"—he sniffed the air—"some kind of strawberry fragrance shampoo."

She folded the skirt, turned briefly and draped it over her blouse and bra on the back of the chair. Rotated back facing him with the movie smile in place. He'd always liked her shaved clean. His eyes drifted down. As they say, smooth as a baby's bottom.

He took a step forward, his eyes glazed over like a drunk's.

Her husky voice broke the trance. "Don't stop, please. Go on, continue. Smells like Burberry perfume. Strawberry shampoo. And? How does it feel to the touch? Do tell."

"Soft," he whispered. "Soft as warm butter."

Another step forward.

She took her own step backward, asked, "Tastes like?"

"So good," he said.

She smirked. "I'm afraid that isn't a suitable answer, *Jeremy*."

"It's going to have to suffice," he said, without noting the emphasis she'd placed on his name.

"Uh-uh. I need an answer. If you don't have one…" She started to move toward the chair, presumably to retrieve her clothes. Get dressed. Leave without giving him the pleasure he desired.

"Strawberries," he blurted.

She smirked again, accompanied it with a low laugh. "I'm sensing a theme. You already used that one, chief. Come again."

"Why are you doing this?"

"Come again. I'll pretend I didn't hear that redundancy. Strawberries are stricken from the record."

She was a frustrated attorney in his estimation. Had an associates degree in culinary arts that she didn't use, a decent enough job at the post office, though, but couldn't keep silent during an episode of *Law & Order* to save her soul.

She'd always been more trouble to him than she was worth. And he believed she prided herself on that fact, strangely enough. That it gave her pleasure to know that he'd promised himself, more than once, to leave her alone. And yet here they were. Again.

Another broken promise.

"Tastes like?" she prodded.

"Sweet," he answered. "It tastes sweet. But cut with something..."

She said, "You say sour or bitter, I'm out of here, *Jeremy*."

"Less sweet," he said.

Now she chuckled. "You must want me badly."

Was that correct grammar? Did it matter? Did anything anymore?

"I do want you badly," he said. And this time when he moved to her she didn't back away. She fed him a breast. And then the other. He cupped them both at once. Squeezed them together and deepened her cleavage. Sucked them hungrily, until the nipples were small stones on his tongue.

"I have girlfriends that hate how men fixate on breasts," she managed, her hands on the back of his head, guiding him into her, "and never move on from them. But I love having my nipples sucked. Ten minutes, twenty, it doesn't matter to me one single bit."

She talked too much, he noted.

More trouble than she was worth.

But he lifted her suddenly, carried her to the bed. She would've preferred being under the covers, he knew, but when he eased her knees apart and lowered himself down around her waist the small things were forgotten.

"Baby," she whispered.

He kissed behind her knees. Her inner thighs. Her stomach. Worked upward. Her armpits. The inner bend of her elbow. Her ribcage.

Creative.

"My nipples, baby," she begged, directing him.

He sucked them again, flicked at the hard nipples with his tongue, teased them with his fingertips.

A moment later he moved away. Reached for the nightstand. His wallet on top of the Gideon Bible they left in every room.

"Baby?"

He stopped mid-reach, turned to her, tried to keep his tone neutral. "Yes?"

"I want to *feel* you inside of me."

"I can't do that," he said.

"Why, baby? I'm not sleeping with anyone else. And you—"

"Okay," he cut her off, not wanting to get into *that*. *That* was tricky business.

"Really?"

"Yes."

Another broken promise.

When he eased inside of her, she released a deep, shuddering breath. That released breath was music to his ears. It inspired him. He grunted with each stroke. She moaned with every other. A synchronized duet. A rhythm borne from many sessions of inspired lovemaking together.

It lasted several minutes.

The particulars of their moves didn't matter. Missionary. Doggystyle. Reverse Cowgirl. Insignificant.

They were both satisfied. That's all that mattered.

He lay there afterward, his skin sticky with sweat, a congealed puddle of his semen painting her inner thigh. He'd done his best to pull out. As if that mattered. And to his credit, after, he didn't get up right away. Waited a few minutes. Then it was off for the quickest of showers. Enough to wash away her scent. Burberry perfume, strawberry shampoo. He didn't ask her in with him to shower. That would've defeated the purpose, he supposed. He couldn't afford to carry her scent, to leave with one of her stray hairs.

She waited patiently for him to come out of the shower.

Waited until he had his pants on fully, zippered and buckled; waited until he'd shrugged himself into his shirt, was preparing to button it and dash back to his office.

"Will it be weeks before I hear from you again?" she asked.

"I've been so busy…" he explained, pausing and searching for the right addition.

"Work," they said in unison.

He was smiling at their shared word.

She wasn't.

"It's been a hectic time at work for me," he added.

"And where is work again?" she asked.

He'd never told.

He didn't then, either.

He buttoned his shirt, turned and looked at the one table in the room.

"Looking for your BlackBerry?" she asked.

He didn't answer. Distracted, frowning and continuing to look.

"I have it," she said.

Still, he continued to look.

"Must've left it in the car," he muttered.

"Zero seven, twenty-one," she said, and he turned to her, hearing her finally.

"What?" he said.

"You really shouldn't use your birthday as a pin code," she said, beaming. "I figured it out even though you made it a bit difficult for me. You naughty boy, you."

It took a moment, his face a mask of confusion. But eventually he understood. "You have my BlackBerry?" It wasn't really a question.

"I do, baby." She held it up. He padded barefooted across the carpet, snatched the BlackBerry from her slender fingers. "Not nice," she chastised. "You could've broken one of my nails. Then I would've been *pissed*."

"Don't play games," he said. "I have all kinds of work on that phone."

"Battery's running low," she said. "You have a charger in the Chrysler 300C?"

Their eyes met.

"You never did quite fit with my image of a man that drives a Toyota Camry," she said.

Another lie he'd told her. A pointless lie. But that's how it worked.

He didn't speak.

"MRF provides all of its top executives with a Chrysler 300C," she said, using his company's name, letting him know she knew. "Must be nice. Any other fringe benefits?"

He wanted to say something, but couldn't find the words.

She smiled. "The look on your face is priceless. I'm tempted to snap a pic with *my* phone and text it to Rachel."

Rachel.

His wife.

He swallowed, asked, "Who are you?"

"Karla Savage. Same as I've always told you." She increased her smile, despite the tenseness of the moment. "You, on the other hand, have told one lie after the other. Haven't you...Michael Palmer?"

Jeremy Kitteridge.

The false name he'd given her.

An old buddy from college. Easy to remember.

He asked, "What do you want, Karla?"

Trying to play it cool.

"You," she said.

"You know now that's not possible."

"You mean because of your marriage?" she said, smiling that wicked movie smile. "A snag is all."

"Karla, I'm very—"

"You even think about apologizing now and I will cause you some kind of deep pain, Michael."

"What can I do?" he asked.

"Erase the moment you lied to me about your name. Erase the moment you lied to me about your marital status. Give me back every single moment of these last few weeks that I've spent... mad at you, furious with you, delirious for you to call, desperate to feel you inside of me. Give it all back. Every single moment. Every single thought. Erase every single lie. Can you do that, Michael?"

"Karla..."

"What?" she snapped.

The quickness of her reply took him by surprise. As usual when it came to Karla, he was totally unprepared. "I, I..." He stopped himself, ashamed of the stutter in his voice.

"This is what's going to happen," she said, her voice strong and confident. "I love you, despite it all. I won't pretend that the feeling is mutual. I'm your definition of pain."

"Because you represent my weakness," he said quickly.

"What foolishness are you talking?"

"I have an addiction," he said.

"That's your explanation for us?"

"I don't enjoy lying, Karla. I don't enjoy the deception. The *deceptions* I should say, because they pile up on you rather quickly. I promised myself after our last time together that I wouldn't call you again."

Broken promises.

"Right now I feel remorse," he added. "And not because you've found out I lied. I always feel remorse after I'm with you."

"Ouch," she said in a tone that was truly wounded.

"It's not personal," he said.

"No," she said, speaking in a mocking voice. "Why would I take that personal?"

"It's like I'm in a trance," he went on. "I don't even remember riding the elevator up here."

"You remember riding me, I bet."

"Don't be crass, Karla."

"Certainly," she said, smirking, snickering, "because crass is so beneath you."

"It's not about you," he said, ignoring her tone. "It's about the thrill of all of this. Sex is my drug of choice. My addiction has wrestled the control away from me. It makes all of my decisions for me, and it's dumber than a goldfish."

"Are you trying to hurt me, Michael?"

"Trying to help you understand."

"You love your wife?"

"Desperately," he said. "I can't begin to imagine my life without her."

"And yet you're here with me. Not for the first time."

"Weakness. Sickness. Nothing more."

"Nothing more?" She let the words hang in the air like swamp mist. His words actually hurt more than the actual betrayal. His words would be what she played back in her mind, over and over and over again.

He knew this, and tried to move to her. Apologize with his touch.

"Just go," she said, jerking away.

"Karla, please."

"And you work for your father-in-law," she said. "I'm sure he'd be happy to hear how you're treating his only daughter."

"You've been doing your homework," he noted, nodding, his lips pursed. "If I wasn't involved, I'd be thoroughly impressed."

"I can imagine. Go, please."

"Can I trust this will stay between us?" he asked.

"Don't hold your breath on that, chief."

"Karla?"

She grabbed the Gideon Bible so quickly he couldn't react. Tossed it overhand at his head. The heavy book grazed his temple as it flew past. That would've impressed him as well, if he wasn't involved.

"Go!" she screamed.

"Karla, I need some assurance this will not leave this room."

"Don't worry, Michael. I won't upset your precious lie of a life."

"Why don't I believe you?"

She flashed her smile, let it speak for her.

"I am sorry," he said.

It was genuine. He realized she recognized as much because she quickly turned away from him. He suspected the last thing in the world she wanted to feel was sympathy of any sort for him. In her mind, liars probably deserved absolutely no sympathy.

"Karla?"

She continued to look away. Ignoring him with every ounce of her being.

He gave up after several more attempts, eased the hotel door closed behind him. Out in the hall, and despite the door's thickness, he swore he actually heard her crying on the other side.

# TWO

He was beyond sorry. Sick. Frustrated. Angry with himself. Remorseful. Always, afterward, there was a heavy dose of regret. The most recognized symptom of addiction, he understood, was that it caused the addicted to do things they wished they hadn't done. Many would scoff at his struggle, chalk it up as plain old lust. But it was much deeper than that for him, a severe struggle that cut all the way to the bone. He'd sought treatment from a specialist up in Belmont, Massachusetts. Was prescribed to Prozac and Celexa for a time. But with that controversial drug treatment came a slew of unwanted side effects. Headaches, nausea, dry mouth, insomnia, the occasional bout with diarrhea. Stubborn weight gain. And no wane in his libido. No drop off in his sexual urges. Truth be told, his desires might've actually grown.

It had taken that effort though, to save his marriage. Rachel had discovered one of his earlier affairs, a month-long ordeal with a woman that worked as a manicurist in the salon where Rachel went to have her hair styled. It had been a disaster from the very beginning. He agreed to Rachel's demand that he seek treatment without any pushback whatsoever. Rachel would have left him otherwise. And now, as far as his wife knew, he had gotten a satisfactory handle on his problem. Another revelation of infidelity would topple everything they'd built together. The best thing that ever happened to him would be gone in an instance. Because of an instance.

Fair perhaps.

But not something he could stomach.

Yet another surprise in a day bursting with them. He was somehow three-fourths of the way through his proposal, subsisting on coffee and nerves. His thoughts marred by the confrontation from Karla, uncertain as to whether anything he'd written in the proposal actually passed muster. Whether it was even coherent. Whether it did the job of selling the company's strengths.

Then the surprise came.

Incoming call. Caller ID flashing *Mi Amor* backlit on the screen of his BlackBerry. A Chopin ringtone. One of the composer's twenty-one nocturnes. Very romantic music.

Rachel.

Michael ran his tongue over his teeth, wet his mouth, answered, "To what do I owe this pleasure?" Normal tone. Cheery even.

"Baby?"

Rachel's tone and word choice made him think of Karla, and despite the loveliness of his wife's voice, a voice he'd loved from the very first, he frowned in displeasure.

Regret. Always, afterward, there was a heavy dose of regret.

He managed, "Yes, baby, it's me."

"Expected you home an hour ago," she said, without accusation. "Are you out for drinks?"

He leaned back in his leather chair. The springs sang a sad note. Everything today, from lunchtime on, had a note of sadness attached to it. "At work still, I'm afraid."

"Really?"

"Yes." The pool of light from his computer monitor was the only break in the dark of the office. In the path of the light was a picture frame on his desktop. An 8 x 10. The only personal effect in the entirety of the space. Turned at an angle so he could see it from nearly any vantage. Rachel.

Looking at it now, the rhythm of his heart changed. Picked up its pace. He doubted that would change even fifty years from now. Other women gave him a momentary thrill, certainly. But the thrill of Rachel could only fit inside a box big enough for a lifetime of memories.

"Are you listening to me?" she asked.

He said, "What?" and immediately regretted it. The last thing he needed was for his wife to believe she was secondary in his thoughts.

"I said, 'all work and no play,'" she replied, a song in her voice. This song not the least bit sad.

"Any suggestions to correct that?" he asked, playing along.

"Dinner," she said. He could actually hear the smile in her words. "Our place."

Our place.

Was it still theirs? They hadn't dined there in close to a year. Michael strained to remember his favorite dish. Remembered Rachel's without struggle. Seared yellowfin tuna, dusted with wasabi butter and ponzu sauce. Citrus herb rice and stir-fry vegetables. Then, slowly, his own favorite meal came into focus. Braised short ribs, with creamy mashed potatoes, roasted Farmer's Market vegetables. Everything beyond delicious.

"Will you be done reasonably soon?" Rachel wondered.

He glanced at the computer monitor. Three-fourths completed. Eight a.m. presentation meeting. Arriving at work at his usual time, seven-thirty, would mean disaster. Reprimand. He'd been entrusted with this proposal. Solo work. No one else to blame. No one to point fingers at. Behind because of his proclivities. It would take much more of the evening, working, for him to save face. His broken promises had gotten him here.

"Finished now," he said, using his mouse to scroll to the top toolbar and save the document. "You have thirty minutes to get beautiful for me. That leaves you twenty-nine minutes to just sit on your hands."

That was dusty, too. Covered with cobwebs. He hadn't said it to Rachel in close to a year. At one time it had made her smile. He hoped it still did.

"Michael?" she whispered into the phone.

"Yes?"

"I love you."

And she disconnected before he could reply.

He pocketed his BlackBerry and picked up the picture frame. A smile for the ages. The most beautiful woman he'd ever laid eyes on. "I love you, as well," he whispered to the image.

He meant it.

Two-story Colonial with vinyl siding, jewel-tone colors, modest decorative moldings, exterior spandrels. Rocking chair front porch, hung with flowered pots. A two-car garage, barely.

Rachel was waiting for him by the garage. High school redux. A first date.

She wore a dress that fell to just above her knees. Michael knew it well. Nude color, silky material, it left no mystery to the fullness of her breasts or the width of her hips. Her two-inch heels brought out the definition in her calves. Over the dress she wore a black coat with a furry mocha chocolate collar. The coat hung open like a door with a broken hinge. *Thank God for small miracles*, Michael thought.

Rachel's skin was the color of honey, a perfect complement to the dress. Hair a shade or two darker, streaked with near blond highlights. It trailed down to her shoulders. The only description for the color of her eyes was light. Lighter even than Karla's. Looking into them was like looking into a pool of water. They made you dive in. They made you lose pieces of yourself. Made you think. There'd be things remembered, and a mad dash to add to those memories. There'd be thoughts of things that inspired smiles, and things that had made the tears flow. The full spectrum. That was Rachel's eyes.

They kissed at the passenger side of the Chrysler, and then Michael opened the door and she wiggled inside, a trail of vanilla musk seasoning the air. He softly closed the door and looked to the sky for some reason. Ink black and salted with stars. A bitterly cold day had yielded to a reasonably cool evening. The air smelled the way he imagined peace and calm would.

*Describe peace and calm.*

"An evening with my wife," he said aloud, smiling.

He stepped around the back of the Chrysler and was about to open the driver door. It yawned open before he got his hand on the handle. Inside the sedan, he could see Rachel stretching across the seat to open it for him. He smiled again and settled inside.

"Spoke to a woman about interior aesthetics today," she said at once. "She believes she can redesign the inside of our house and make it more attractive to sellers."

Michael glanced at the T-style FOR SALE sign planted on their front lawn. Eight months on the market. No takers thus far.

One close call that neither of them talked about anymore. Rachel as ready as ever for an upgrade.

"Interior aesthetics," he said, pulling from the curb. "Sounds expensive. And unremarkable."

"My initial reaction as well," Rachel admitted. "But her phone pitch was flawless. After speaking with her for a little over two minutes, I was completely convinced. I'm inclined to give her a chance."

"Someone you found in the Yellow Pages?"

"Actually she found me."

"Yeah…?"

"She combs through real estate listings and calls the homeowners who have had properties listed for some time without a sale."

Michael nodded.

"Maybe it was her voice," Rachel said.

"Her voice?"

"Like a jazz singer's. And she speaks in this melodic way that just…"

Despite himself, Michael licked his lips.

"She spoke about the psychology of beauty," Rachel went on. "In terms of what choices we make for everything. Even toilet paper holders. If we make all of the right choices, the house will lull buyers."

"Sounds sexual," he said without thinking.

Rachel slapped his arm. "You're worthless. Do you know that?"

"Totally," he said, smiling.

Then they fell into silence. A void that was more intimate than any words they might have spoken. His right hand was clasped in her left. She fingered it absently with her thumb. Little circles that were charged with erotic feeling. After a time he heard a low hum in her throat, almost imperceptible. Her spirited mood painted his own dark mood until it was the color of white cake frosting.

How could he have put his marriage in jeopardy again? Why did he continue to break promises he made to himself?

The answer came quickly.

Sickness.

Addiction.

He thought of all the naysayers, realized that even he could occasionally count himself among that number. But there was no other possible explanation for the bad choices he made. Always, afterward, there was a heavy dose of regret. Shame even. A promise to never let it happen again.

And then it did.

And the cycle continued.

Regret. Shame. Promises he'd eventually break.

Candace. Davida. Ingrid. Melissa. The list went on and on.

Hannah. Dawn. Jennifer. Kim.

Kim.

What a disaster that had been.

Their last time together there had been tears and threats. Advil threats. She'd swallow an entire bottle's worth if he broke it off as he was saying he *had to*. She'd wondered why he had to. He'd said because.

Rachel was his because.

So he'd broken it off with Kim and she hadn't swallowed the Advil and life went on.

Then.

There was always a then.

Karla.

After Kim, the K that started Karla's name should've served as a warning, an omen, a harbinger of bad things to come.

But.

There was always a but.

He'd settled into the situation with Karla with such familiarity and ease he convinced himself it couldn't possibly be wrong.

"What are you thinking about?"

Rachel, pulling him from his thoughts.

"The romantic dinner I'm about to have with my beautiful wife," he said without missing a beat.

"Liar."

"I'm wounded." His free hand came off of the steering wheel for a moment, and he pressed it to his heart to illustrate the point.

"An incredibly accomplished liar," she added.

If she wasn't smiling he would've truly been wounded.

The truth hurts.

The fact that she could smile and joke—and about him lying—was a true testament to just how great this woman was. She kept no record of wrongs. She forgave.

"I've lied to you before," he said, serious all of a sudden. "And thankfully you forgave me. It's not something you'd ever have to worry about happening again."

The crinkles at the corners of her mouth nearly broke his heart. She nodded, squeezed his hand and looked out her window.

He thought she might be fighting off tears. He was on the verge of doing so himself.

Instead, he focused on the road. Dark. Back roads. Residential. Sprawling estates that put his own neighborhood, a more than decent one, to shame. English manors and Shore colonials and new constructions. Homes built for New York bankers and industrialists one hundred years prior. On land rumored to have been bought from Native Americans with rum as currency. Most of the homes sat on two or more acres of manicured land. And inside all of the properties were the amenities of the wealthy. Home theaters, wine cellars, radiant heat. Outside: guest houses, pools, brick patios.

Rachel's posture changed. Strength came to her shoulders and the tears from before were quickly forgotten. As they traveled on through the near darkness he could see her eyes focusing, looking beyond the stately gates that fronted most of the properties, through the tall standing trees, straight to the homes built hundreds of yards back from the road.

"Beautiful homes," he said.

Rachel simply nodded, didn't speak.

Two minutes later he'd reached the commercial strip. Bagel deli, brokerage house, two expensive restaurants. He passed them and came upon a traffic light that flashed red just as he approached. He braked easily and looked off to his left. Ice cream parlor, the lot choked with Mercedes and equally luxurious sedans and SUVs. And beyond the ice cream parlor was the Oceanic Bridge. Just before the bridge a handsome structure crackling with activity.

The light flashed green and he turned left.

Salt Creek Grille. The lively structure.

Their place.

A waterfront restaurant. Just beyond it was the Navesink River. A pool of black dotted by the occasional light. At the base of the restaurant were a grove of boats docked to moorings.

Michael turned in, joined a line of cars inching toward the front of the restaurant, valets waiting to take their keys and park their cars for them.

"Our place," Rachel whispered.

Michael squeezed her hand.

"I'm sorry I went silent on you," she said. "I was caught thinking."

"About?" But he knew.

"Selling our home," she said. "Maybe moving to a town like this."

"A town like?"

She smiled. "Okay. Here. I have my heart set on moving to this actual town. There, I said it."

"We'll toast to interior aesthetics," he said. "Maybe your girl will work magic for us."

"Woman, Michael. Girl sounds so chauvinist."

"Your woman," he corrected.

She smiled again.

"You're happy," he said, like a question.

"I am. Thanks to you and—"

"Me, huh?"

"The flowers, of course. The last thing I expected from you today. And then on top of—"

He frowned. "Flowers?"

"White stargazer lilies. Simple but sweet note: 'With love always.'" Her tone softened and then faded completely. She watched him for a beat. "Have I gone and made a fool of myself? You didn't send the flowers?"

"Flowers?" he said again, smiling. "I have no idea what you're talking about."

And he didn't.

But one thing he'd learned well was the ability to think on his feet. Freelance. And do it without missing a beat. "I'd like to know who's sending my wife flowers though," he said. He raised his voice to a deep baritone. "I'll kill him if I find out."

Rachel laughed, punched his arm. "Be serious."

"He'll see just how serious I am," he said, still with the exaggerated voice.

"Whoever he is, it's you that have my heart," Rachel said.

Michael nodded. All he could do. His mind was bursting apart at the seams but he couldn't let Rachel know.

Who had sent the flowers?

Was this some kind of double play? Rachel having an affair and rubbing his nose in it? No. That couldn't be. That wasn't Rachel's makeup. She wasn't anything like him.

There had to be an explanation for the flowers.

He said, "I do love you."

"Took another man sending me flowers to get you to realize?"

"No," he said. "I knew from the first moment I met you. Every day is simply a reminder."

"Oh, Michael."

One car in front of them. He inched forward.

"We'll make the toast right away," he said. "I'm determined to get you the house you want."

Rachel nodded. "To Karla. May she work her magic."

"Karla?"

Surprisingly no hitch in his voice.

"Karla Savage, interior aesthetics expert," Rachel said. "Our savior…knock on wood."

He swallowed and smiled.

Without missing a beat.

There was the explanation for the flowers.

# CHAPTER
# THREE

Trust, but verify.

Reagan, if she wasn't mistaken. Seems as if she remembered those words being attributed to the former president, in some class she'd taken or book she'd read or show she'd watched. Either way, they were certainly words to live by. She'd trusted Michael, but there'd always been something that didn't quite add up, plus an inner voice that told her to verify. And so she had. Discovered more than she ever thought she would. No, that was a lie. Discovered what she'd always feared. Something about the relationship had always rang false.

Married.

She'd traveled that road once before and it wasn't a pleasant journey. Emotional, dark, soul deadening. She'd emerged from that relationship worse for the wear. Left to question her own sanity, and worse yet, her morals, as Patrick went on living a lie with Elizabeth. Elizabeth. In an ugly moment after she discovered Patrick's duplicity, she'd called his house phone, introduced herself to Liz. And was promptly told by Patrick's wife that she preferred to be called Elizabeth. Insisted upon it, actually. Indignant about a name while her husband was out in the world sticking his thing in another woman.

The conversation started out on that wrong note and proceeded to go south. By the end Karla was calling Patrick's wife, Liz, every third word or so just to make the woman crazy. Liz, Liz, Liz. And it worked.

Or did it?

Karla was the one left crying and questioning herself afterward.

And here she was yet again.

Another wife.

Another phone call.

Different tack this time, though.

*Interior aesthetics.*

She smiled at the ingenuity of it all. She'd driven through Michael's neighborhood. Saw the FOR SALE sign on his lawn. A quick Internet search. House had been on the market for over eight months.

Improved interior aesthetics would reverse that bad fortune.

Yeah, right.

She still hadn't settled in her mind why she'd called his wife. Or why she was preparing herself to actually go meet with the woman.

Was it curiosity? See how beautiful Rachel was? She had no doubt Rachel was in fact beautiful. Michael wouldn't settle for less.

Was it more than curiosity?

Was she about to destroy the façade of a happy marriage? Trample it with her pointy heels?

No.

Destroying their marriage wouldn't change a thing.

Just curiosity, then.

She padded out of the bathroom into her connected bedroom, naked, skin damp and warm still from the shower. Never in a rush to put on clothes, the ringing of her cell phone served as a perfect distraction and excuse to remain naked a little while longer.

Karla trapped the phone in her hands, third ring, a caller that wasn't in her contacts. Her generic ringtone.

*Viva la Vida.*

Coldplay.

Chris Martin did it for Karla in a major way. She had an affection for rough-hewn white boys, she supposed.

"Hello?" she said into the phone. Her tentative voice. She'd been told it was beyond sexy. Sexier even than her natural husky voice. An aphrodisiac. Like chocolate.

"Karla Savage?" Tentative himself, but not sexy.

"Yes?"

"Seranne's," he said. "I have a delivery for you. I'm outside your door. Should I leave it or redeliver when you can be home?"

"I'm actually home now," she said. "Just stepping out of the shower."

"I can wait a moment for you to dress."

"I'll be quick," she said in a whisper. Toying with him.

Michael had left her sexually frustrated. She had to work the frustration off some way.

"I'll be here," he said, and clicked off.

Her blue terrycloth robe was spread out on the counterpane of the bed. She put it on, cinched it closed at the waist. A loose tie that fell open after just one step. She retied it in the same loose manner.

Seranne's was a florist, according to the lettering on the side of the white van she found parked facing the wrong way in front of her house. The driver was sitting on her stoop. He hopped up to his feet as she opened the door, smiled casually, a quick glance at the front of her robe followed by a lopsided smirk that made her bite her lip.

He wasn't bad looking.

Square jaw, haphazard tan, a day's worth of beard stubble. Brown hair, blue eyes. Fairly tall. Rough hands held around the vase of the flower in a gentle way.

The tender care he gave to the vase with those masonry hands of his suggested something to her.

"For me?" she said.

He nodded, smiled deeper. "Someone's got some sense."

"You think?"

"Absolutely."

"What are they?"

He told her and she immediately knew who had sent them. Touché.

She didn't know whether to smile or frown. Whether to sign for the flowers or steal them from the driver's hand and send them raining down into the sewer with shards of the shattered vase.

She signed for them.

"Have a great day," the driver said.

She nodded and watched him drive off down the street, the wrong direction on a one-way.

She closed the door behind her, and lagged there in her foyer. Despite her best efforts not to, she held the arrangement to her nose. Fragrant. Lovely. Pretty as well.

Much prettier than they'd looked when she'd ordered the same arrangement online and had them delivered to Michael's wife.

A card rested in the arms of the stems. She plucked it out, tore apart the small envelope, read it over several times. With love *often enough*.

A minute later she had her cell phone in hand. Dialing.

It seemed as though he picked up before one ring had even cycled.

"Sitting by the phone?" she said, laughing.

"Can we talk?"

"I'm listening, Michael."

"I don't want it to be bad between us," he said.

"By definition, lying to me about your wife qualifies as bad, Michael."

"I know, but I still don't want it to be bad between us."

"Worried I'll suggest a burnt sienna color theme for your bedroom?"

Teasing.

She'd bought him a sweater that color. Last Valentine's Day. Months later, he still hadn't worn it around her. She questioned him about the slight, of course. He chalked it up to simply disapproving of the color.

Yeah.

That shirt was in shirt heaven somewhere, or rescued from some garbage can by some other soul, never having made it to the Palmer house for Michael's wife to question.

"You shouldn't have called my wife," he said. "What's happening between us doesn't involve her."

"I bet she'd disagree."

"Leave her out of this."

"A please would be nice."

"Please."

"Too late."

"This ain't a game," he said.

"Ain't?" She tsked. "What would they think at Brown if they heard you talking that way?"

Another tease.

He'd flaunted a Brown pedigree when they first met, but it turned out that he'd actually graduated from a small school in Connecticut. Nearly everything he'd told her in the beginning was lies. It seemed as though he'd carefully crafted together an entirely false second persona.

That qualified him as a psychopath in her book.

"I've made many mistakes with you. Can I apologize once more?" he asked.

What was that?

Actual pain in his voice?

She almost smiled. Almost. Instead, a strange thing happened. She felt some sympathy chirring in her stomach.

"I'm serious," he said, just as she was about to reassure him that he had nothing to worry about. "Leave my wife out of this."

"You could mess up a wet dream, Michael."

"You better listen to me on this, Karla."

"You don't dictate *anything* to me," she said. "You understand?"

"Again, this is a dangerous game you're playing, Karla."

"I could say the same to you, Michael."

"I don't want you talking to my wife," he said. "And I certainly don't want you seeing her."

"Speaking of which," she said theatrically, "I'm running late for that appointment. I want to look my best. I need to go pick out a dress. Something black would probably be appropriate. You think?"

"Forget all about this, Karla, please."

"How much would that be worth to you?" she heard herself say.

Even she was surprised by the words.

"Blackmail, Karla?" His sigh filled her ear. "I didn't know you could stoop so low."

"Tell you what," she said. "I'll hold off on suggesting John Everett Millais reproductions and feng shui to Rachel *today*. But you work up some numbers and get back to me. And don't take long. And the number should have a lot of your favorite number included."

"My favorite number?" he asked, crestfallen, judging by his somber tone.

"Why *zero* of course," she said, laughing. "Being that you are one, I'd think that would be a favorite. Have I misjudged?"

She disconnected the call before he could reply.

Laughed some more.

Satisfied.

Wishing she could have been there to see the look on his face. He could keep his money. She didn't want it. But, boy, would she have loved to have seen his face.

That would've been priceless.

# CHAPTER FOUR

Twelve steps. Each one simple enough to understand, if not execute. Admit that he was powerless over addictive sexual behavior—that his life had become unmanageable. He'd admitted as much many times before, but now, with Karla breathing hot on his neck, he acknowledged it yet again. Next step. Come to believe that a power greater than himself could restore him to sanity. Divine intervention? Yes, without a doubt that was exactly what he needed. Next. Make a decision to turn his will and life over to the care of God. That divine thread again. If he came out of this unscathed, there was no doubt in his mind the praise and thanksgiving would rise to the heavens. "He who finds a wife finds a good thing." That scripture had been written on the wedding invitations. He hadn't forgotten. Next.

A tap at his office door paused his thoughts.

Reflexively, he inched aside the keyboard he hadn't been using, and readjusted the computer monitor he hadn't been looking at. He'd gotten in early that morning, rushed through the rest of the proposal from yesterday, finishing it on time for the early morning meeting. No one had said anything about it being rancid, so he considered that a victory. But it obviously wasn't his best work. Now, burned out, the keyboard was just an ornament on his desk. Beyond it, Rachel's framed picture, her high-watt smile, looked up at him. He cleared something from his throat and gazed over the picture's top edge, to the doorway.

Joe Larkin.

Six-two, about one-thirty. Dark black hair kept several inches too long, probably thinking it made him look cool. It didn't. The top of Larkin's scalp was flaked with dandruff. Michael had two inches on him and inevitably when they bumped into one another, a fate Michael tried his best to avoid, Michael's eyes would fall on Larkin's scalp. Larkin wore yellowed jeans now, a plain white T-shirt under a navy blue blazer. Moccasins on his boat-sized feet. A goatee in need of a matching mustache hid his weak chin. His teeth were as yellow as butter and yet he was forever smiling.

"Mikey," he said, smiling of course. "My tall brother-in-arms, how's it going?"

Joe thought their shared well-above-average heights made them brethren of some kind.

Not hardly.

"Joe," Michael replied.

"Stopped by to see if you could pull yourself away from the work and grab a bite to eat."

The answer, every day, was no. Always.

Step four: make a searching and fearless moral inventory of yourself.

Michael glanced at Rachel's picture again.

*I don't deserve you*, he thought.

"Mikey?"

Admit to God, yourself, and to another human being the exact nature of your wrongs.

Another human being.

Michael looked up. Joe Larkin was already fading away from the doorway.

Another human being.

It was extremely close, but he supposed Joe Larkin fit the bill.

Michael said, "Sure. I'll join you."

Joe nodded. "That's cool, Mikey. Maybe next—" He caught himself, drifted back fully into the doorway. "Did you say you'll join me?"

Michael pushed back from his desk, stood, stretched, and then walked around the desk and across the distance of his office. He clapped Joe Larkin hard on the shoulder. Larkin's mouth hung open.

"What do you have in mind?" Michael asked Larkin.

"I usually grab a couple of hot dogs," Larkin said in an oddly mechanical voice. "There's a truck over by The Galleria. But if you wanted something more—"

"Sounds perfect." Michael clapped Joe's shoulder again.

They made it to the parking garage without much conversation, and were confronted there with their first decision. Which car to take? Michael's Chrysler 300C or Joe's... Michael didn't know what Joe drove, and Joe only knew Michael's car because all of the top execs drove 300Cs. Even Karla knew that.

"Why don't you drive," Michael said. "Since you know where we're going."

"Sure."

A tan Toyota Camry peppered with dents and bird droppings, the back seat overrun with magazines. Michael shook his head and laughed. Nearly slapped his knee, it was so funny.

"It isn't much," Joe protested.

"It's fine. It's not that," Michael said. "Laughing because I've been driving a Camry for eighteen months."

What he'd told Karla.

"What?"

"Nothing."

Michael grabbed a handful of the magazines and brought them to the front seat with him.

"*Wired*, mostly," Joe said.

"Crap. No *Penthouse* or *Playboy*?"

He chuckled as if he were joking.

As if.

"That's at home with my DVDs," Joe said.

"You have a lot of DVDs?"

"No more than normal."

"Yeah?"

"Shyla Stylez, Katie Morgan, Ava Devine…"

Michael wasn't familiar with any of the names. He filed them away in his head.

Porn, surprisingly, hadn't become part of the equation yet.

He wondered why that had been the case. Everything he'd learned about his addiction told him pornography should've been a deeply ingrained part of his fabric by now. Surfing for Shyla Stylez at work.

"…Stormy Daniels. I love the big, fake, unnatural tits. I don't care if they have surgery scars under 'em, don't care if they're so big they're shiny. That's perfect. Just be ginormous and I'm all in. They've got pimples on their asses and stretch marks and faces that look like a shoe imprint in dog poo, I can look right past all of that if they've got big juggs, man."

"I know what you mean," Michael said.

"My girl has big giant knockers, but they're in a frantic race for her belly button. By the time she's thirty, it'll be all over; she gets an itch on her knee, she could scratch it with a nipple."

"But do you have good conversations?" Michael asked.

"You kidding?" Joe said, sniffing through his nostrils. "She was an English Lit major, dude. She finds poetry in everything. One minute she's talking about 'most quiet need, by sun and candle-light.' The next she's down on her knees bobbing for apples."

"Sounds terrific."

"How long have you and Rachel been married?"

Rachel.

"Not nearly long enough," Michael said and fell into a silence that Joe didn't interrupt. The only sound in the Camry coming from Michael turning pages of one of Joe's *Wired* magazines.

The truck was the length of two minivans, white, except for two big words painted on it in a color that resembled raw meat: *Hot Dogs*. It was parked sideways at the end of a relatively small lot, backed up by railroad tracks, and across those, a large warehouse structure that had been cut up into expensive little niche shops. The Galleria.

"Dirty water dogs," Joe said. His voice carried the same enthusiasm as when he said Shyla Stylez, Katie Morgan, Ava Devine... Stormy Daniels.

Names committed to Michael's memory now.

"I take it they're pretty good?" Michael asked.

"Pretty good?" Joe seemed taken aback. "They're amazing, dude."

Dude.

There it was, just one of the reasons Michael had always declined Joe's lunch invites. They were too disparate. Joe looked like a college dropout slacker wired on something that made his metabolism race. He probably subsisted on Ramen noodles and porn on DVDs. A girlfriend with big tits and big everything else likely. Michael was Ivy League suitable, Armani suits and cologne, handsome enough for the cover of a Nora Roberts paperback novel. He had a wife beautiful enough to take your breath away. Literally.

Joe ordered two dogs. Sauerkraut. Grape soda.

Michael ordered two as well. Ketchup only. A Sprite.

A silver and black train rumbled by. They sat together in Joe's

Camry, WFAN sports radio on low. Mike Francessa laying into the Jets.

"Jets or Giants?" Joe asked.

"Jets."

"Yankees or Mets?"

"Mets."

"Knicks or Nets?"

"Vodka," Michael said.

Joe laughed.

A steady flow of cars eased onto the lot. The routine was standard for most. They parked. They ordered their hot dogs. They sat in their cars and ate as the occasional train lumbered past, the brick siding of The Galleria building a canvas to paint their thoughts on.

"You asked before how long Rachel and I have been married?"

Joe chewed, wiped his mouth, then nodded.

"I don't keep track in years," Michael said.

"You guys have your own special lovey-dovey calendar?" He smiled that mustard-colored smile of his.

"Women."

"What?" The smile remained.

"The first year was Candace and Davida. Year two was Ingrid."

"What?" Joe repeated.

"Melissa and Dawn the manicurist, year three. Year four was Jennifer and Kim."

"I'm not following."

Michael nodded. "The past eighteen months have been… slower. Just Karla." He swallowed the last drops of his Sprite. "So to answer your question, we've been married just under six years. We dated for six months before we got married. A whirlwind romance."

"Dude, I'm like, lost. What do the women have to do with anything?"

"You're dense," Michael said hatefully.

Joe frowned.

"My affairs," Michael explained. "Women I've slept with."

"Wait a minute." Joe sat up in his seat. The two paper hot dog trays rained to the floor. "You're saying you cheated on Rachel?"

"Constantly."

"Shit, dude."

"Over and over and over some more. This last one, Karla, has turned complicated."

"Complicated?"

"She's blackmailing me."

"Shit."

"Indeed."

Joe sighed. "Rachel's beautiful, dude."

"Without question."

"Malcolm would flip if he found out."

Malcolm Ferrer. Rachel's father. Michael's boss. "Without question," he repeated.

"According to the mill, you're in line to take over some day. I can't believe you'd risk that, dude."

"Daniel's direct in line," Michael said.

"Daniel?" Joe sniffed out a laugh. "Daniel doesn't know his ass from the end of a water hose. They're both *big* black holes in his mind."

"Colorful description."

"Apt," Joe said.

Michael nodded. "I suppose so."

"Who else at the company knows about this, dude?"

"Just you."

"Shit. This is heavy. Why did you unload this on me?"

"Had to."

"Had to?"

Admit to God, yourself, and to another human being the exact nature of your wrongs.

"Had to," Michael said again.

"How do you know I won't blab?"

"Someone used the computer in the second-floor lounge room to download flash videos of porn," Michael said. "Malcolm was livid, some of our clients are Disney-types, as you know. I remember the name Shyla Stylez from the report. I still think Malcolm has a hard-on to figure out who was doing the downloading on company property. Have any idea?"

"This is ugly business, dude."

"Indeed."

"I regret asking you to lunch all of these times now."

Regret.

Michael asked, "Why did you do it? We're such an odd...couple. I'm in management. You're in..."

"Mailroom operations," Joe said.

"So why did you do it?"

But Joe didn't hear Michael's repeated question. A faraway look found his eyes. His voice softened several degrees. "I should've stuck with Cassie. That was the long route, sure, but I should've stuck with it. She wasn't a bad lay. Gave head like an Oreck."

"Cassie?" Michael figured if he stayed with the conversation he could get it back on track.

Joe nodded. "Cassie Hart."

"Name sounds familiar."

"It should. She works for you, dude."

"Me?"

"Well, I mean, the company. In HR. The dishwater blonde with the really bad skin but big—"

"Juggs," Michael cut in. "Yes, I've seen her. Haven't really acquainted myself. You're in bed with her?"

"Used to be," Joe said, his voice lowering yet another notch.

"Used to be?" Michael's smile was just the right degree of lop-sided.

"Aw, man, we get together maybe once every four or five months. Every time she gets some results with the Proactiv—like her chin clears up or the blisters have less pus—my phone will ring. Maybe three or four times a year. Tops. That hardly counts, dude."

"I agree," Michael said.

"You're mocking me."

"Not at all."

"I'm gonna start packing my lunches. That's what I'm gonna do. Take it back to seventh grade. Peanut butter and banana on Wonder, the crust cut off and everything. That's how you stay out of trouble, dude. And I need to stay out of trouble. Seriously."

"I agree," Michael said, then, "Let me ask you a question."

"I'm scared to say go ahead, but go ahead."

"With such a great girl at home," Michael asked, "why were you involved with Cassie?"

*Why were you involved with Cassie?* Asked in the past tense, because three or four times a year hardly counted.

"Kissing ass, dude. What do you think? I want to move *up*. Ambition's a bitch. But, again, it was moving slow with Cassie, so I thought I'd give you a run. You seemed like an okay dude. Accessible. No gay vibes, so I figured you wouldn't get all weirded out over two bros chilling at lunch. After today, I realize I fucked up. I'm trying to elevate myself, mostly legally, and you're about to sic the Bellatoris on me over some porn."

Sic the Bellatoris on him.

Michael couldn't help but smile.

He could've kissed Joe Larkin. Nothing gay to it, of course.

"Glad you can still find humor in all of this," Larkin said miserably.

Michael didn't hear him.

The Bellatoris.

Thoughts of them consumed him.

# FIVE

*Bellator.*

Latin.

Warrior, fighter, soldier.

Hushed rumors abounded when it came to the four-headed security team for MRF Global, called the Bellatoris by practically everyone in the company, even though that was the genitive singular form of the Latin word.

No one quite knew how the nickname started or where the Bellatoris themselves came from or very much about them because they kept to themselves. A tight circle never broken. And so stories had to be formed from the ground up. Tall tales were told. Rumors were spread. Actual truths were stretched and fabricated to be sexy more so than factual.

And the group itself made this approach easy, each of the four an enigma.

Lukas Doyle, chief of the team, was blessed with the mind of a Hewlett-Packard desktop computer and the physique of an Ancient Roman warrior. Nearly everyone in the company had a Lukas Doyle tale. They'd either seen him adding long streams of numbers in his head or ripping the company's thick phone directory in half with his bare hands. If pressed to come up with a suitable reason for Doyle to have been adding up streams of numbers, none could be given. And MRF's phone directory was easily six inches thick. It was hard to imagine anyone halving it without some kind of tool. Still, the rumors persisted, growing in intensity by the day.

John Namako, second in command, had a disarming smile that didn't match his eyes. Dead eyes that reminded Michael of Lee Boyd Malvo and John Allen Muhammad, the D.C. Snipers. Michael had encountered Namako at the vending machine on the second floor more than once, each time leaving Namako's presence with a longing to take a shower. Something about the man left your skin feeling as if it were coated with grit and dust.

Liz Sutherland, the only woman in the quartet, was attractive and said to be some kind of tech savvy wunderkind. Beauty and brains, every man's fantasy. The third part of the equation was the rumor that Liz was actually the most violent of the four. Her repertoire supposedly included gamesmanship with a stiletto. And not Manolo Blahniks, either. A spring assisted knife with a dagger point blade.

Then there was the fourth, low man in the rotation, Warren Merriman. His wide face was the opposite of Namako's. He wore his frown like clothes. Everything seemed to bring him some measure of displeasure. He was the wild card, the one to definitely avoid, what with his nineteen-inch neck and grapefruit biceps and that look that said *Stand back*.

Enigmas.

As plugged in as Michael was with company happenings, he'd yet to figure the Bellatoris out, either individually or collectively. In fact, he'd done as most had done, avoided them like the plague. Even when he'd had a security breach, the interaction with them was limited at best, nonexistent at worst, a few short emails back and forth with Lukas Doyle, one conversation he recalled dying as quickly as a lit match in a downwind.

But blackmail was serious business, especially considering all Michael stood to lose. He didn't have the skill set himself to handle Karla and her demands. Turning it over in his head, only four names came up that he thought capable of dealing with his thorny situation. That troubled him on nearly every level. The risk of involving them was obvious. They worked for his father-in-law. But the risk of doing nothing was even greater. His contacts were limited. He needed someone capable and efficient. Someone professional. And he needed this someone *yesterday*. Time was of the essence, as they say. So he made a difficult decision to bring his issue to the Bellatoris.

But not all of them.

Just one would do.

But which one?

It didn't take long for him to reach a decision on that. This was Michael Palmer, after all.

The woman.

Liz Sutherland.

# CHAPTER SIX

Wild hair the color of pennies and eyes the color of freshly mowed lawn. Five-seven or eight, strong in the thighs and buttocks, full breasts. A stomach sculpted by a vegetarian diet and an insane amount of daily crunches. Full lips and a soft voice that caused nearly instantaneous erections. Always in gray scale. Either gray pants and a gray jacket or too-short gray skirt and a gray jacket. A white blouse strained against the swell of her perfect breasts. Her eyes framed by cranberry-colored eyeglasses that made her every man's librarian fantasy.

Michael had only spoken to her once. A quick nod and greeting as they passed one another in the hallway.

She hadn't spoken back.

He saw her often enough after that. Not always by chance.

Each sighting a painful reminder of his failure. A painful reminder of his sickness. Every inch of her body called to mind sex. Every inch of his own body wanted to be near her.

Whenever he spotted her, she was alone. With her laptop. Always with the laptop. Often in the conference room on level three, all of the lights in the room turned off, floor-to-ceiling venetian blinds slightly parted to let in stripes of sun, dapples of that natural light painting the room into something psychedelic.

She left a trail of fragrant lilac behind whenever she left.

Michael knew this because he'd stepped into the conference

room after her, more than once sadly, and, with his eyes closed, sniffed the air until his stomach dropped and his head spinned.

Sickness.

Addiction.

He found her there today.

He eased inside, dropped down in a leather chair directly across from her, only the large conference table between them. She didn't look up or acknowledge his presence. Her fingers clicked the laptop keys with surprising speed. Ninety words per minute, easy. Long slender fingers, the nails painted a color to match her eyeglasses.

The air seasoned with that lilac fragrance.

Michael cleared his throat.

Click, click, click, click.

Unfailing concentration.

On her laptop.

"I thought I might have a word with you," Michael said.

Click, click, click, click.

"I won't take up much of your time."

Click, click, click, click.

"I promise." And he smiled. Realized that gesture was inaudible so added a slight chuckle.

Click, click, click, click.

He didn't continue talking. Sat there, unsure of how to proceed. Her fingers came off of the keyboard, and he thought she might finally respond to him. Wrong deduction. She moved aside a strand of hair that had fallen to cover her face, then went directly back to typing.

Click, click, click, click.

How else could Michael feel but foolish?

She caused in him a foreign emotion. Doubt. He didn't like

that feeling any more than he liked his sickness, his addiction.

He pushed back from the table, stood to his feet, paused to study her, shaking his head as if she were someone to feel sorry for when every pore in his body was swollen with personal shame.

Foolish.

And her?

Sexy even in silence. Breathtaking even as she ignored him with professional calm. He could picture her with the rumored stiletto. Could see her using the sharp point to break the skin on his arm. Some kind of erotic play that bordered on being dangerous.

Handcuffs.

Blindfolds.

Fear and heightened passion.

Sharon Stone in *Basic Instinct*.

He'd made it as far as the conference room's door when Liz Sutherland's soft voice pulled him back. He turned, frowning. Imagined? She still wasn't looking up from her laptop. Still had the keys playing a melody, albeit slower.

Click, click.

Click, click.

"You said something?" he asked.

Eyes the color of freshly mowed lawn. Watching him, finally. "Stay," she said, repeating the word he'd thought he'd heard.

"Ready to talk with me now?"

"We must," she said. "I'm afraid."

"You say that as if it's some kind of penalty," he said, smiling.

She smiled, too. Tight smile. Didn't say anything in response to his words, left him feeling foolish yet again.

He dropped down into the chair across from her once again. She closed the laptop, eased it aside, interlocked her fingers and rested her hands on the conference table.

"I don't know where to begin," he said.

"The beginning would work," she said. "I find that usually is a good place."

Michael sighed a deep breath, squared his shoulders, worked to find the introductory words.

None came to mind.

He managed, "Well…" and fell back into awkward silence.

"If only you showed this kind of restraint in your personal life," Liz Sutherland said, some bite in her tone.

"What's that supposed to mean?" he asked, frowning.

Now she sighed. Frustrated with him.

"January eleventh of this year, you met with a Coca-Cola bottler in Georgia. February eighteenth, four days after Valentine's Day, you conducted a thirty-minute PowerPoint presentation to a luxury car sales consortium in Cherry Hill. Three days ago you made a similar presentation to a children's textbook publisher down in Dayton. Do I need to continue? Go back to last year?"

"I'm confused," he said.

"You're messy, Michael. That's what you are. You leave behind a lot of crumbs."

"The more you speak, the more confused I become."

"I would imagine. You're dense," she said, smiling.

"Excuse me?"

She sighed again. "I've been tasked, among other things, with cleaning up your crumbs. I suppose because I'm a woman they believe I have domestic sensibilities."

"My crumbs?"

She tapped the laptop. Tap, tap, tap, tap. Frustration in the movement. "Don't you get it? Your busy schedule."

"Those dates," he said. "I don't recall making those presentations."

"You didn't."

"Then?"

"The days hold no significance for you?"

"None."

"Perhaps that's why your lady friend has grown agitated with you. Your time with her is insignificant except for the..." She reddened. "...intercourse, *of course*."

"What?" He almost stood to his feet again.

"That's why you're here to speak with me, isn't it, Michael?"

"You always speak in riddles?"

"Your lady friend." She tapped the table with the flat of her hand, a drum tap for each word. "Karla Savage. She's sunk her teeth into you, hasn't she? She's got a pretty good hold at this point. Correct?"

Sickness.

Addiction.

Michael said, "Yes," without looking up at Liz. His eyes were on the table surface between them. The reflection in the polished wood absolutely disgusted him.

"Don't fret, Michael. I'll have a word with her. We can end this meeting now."

He looked up. "You will? You'll handle her for me?"

"That's what you hoped for, I'm certain."

"I did."

"Consider it done," she said. "Goodbye now, Michael. I have tasks to perform."

He looked at Liz Sutherland. "Let me give you her contact info."

"No need, Michael," Liz said, smiling.

"You know how to contact her?"

"It's been a pleasure talking with you, Michael."

"Who else knows?"

"Do make certain the door is closed fully. It tends to stick."

"Who else knows?" he repeated.

"No one, Michael. Now good day. I have work to do. Crumbs to clean up."

His shoulders relaxed. He let out a sigh of relief. Liz Sutherland's jaw muscles tensed, her green eyes darkened.

"You don't like me much?" he asked.

"You're a liability to the company."

He nodded. "Take care of this for me. I won't continue to be a liability."

"I'm certain you won't be."

"What do you mean by that?"

She reached for her laptop again. Within seconds was lost to technology.

Michael closed the door fully on his way out.

It didn't stick.

# CHAPTER
# SEVEN

The last Thursday of the month. Every month, without fail. Catered dinner and conversation. Catch up. Thanksgiving twelve times a year instead of just once.

Michael pulled up to the massive home, and let the Chrysler idle in the circular drive centered by an elaborate fountain, his wife beside him in the passenger seat as stiff as plywood.

"Don't know why I let this bother me so," Rachel said, a lilt and softness to her words that made them sound mournful.

"Take a deep breath," Michael replied.

That stock advice the best he could come up with.

"He'd gloat if he knew this affected me so," she said.

Michael eyed the house. It had Nantucket Cedar shingle. A large covered porch with Soundviews, ceiling fans, and stereo speakers. A guest house on the southern side of the nearly two-acre property. Manicured landscaping that receded to a thirty-five-foot bluff overlooking a personal beach. Blue water that washed up on the sand with a sound like music, the water swirled with foam as white as cotton.

"Maybe he does know," Michael said.

Rachel nodded slowly. "Makes sense. That would explain why he makes us do this, month after month."

"Makes?"

She looked at her husband sadly. "Makes."

Michael wished he had an argument to protest with. Instead, he said, "Look on the bright side. Free meal."

Rachel didn't smile. "I wish I could find some humor in all of this."

"I'm sorry. I know this is difficult for you. I shouldn't make light of it."

"Don't be. I'm glad it doesn't affect you in the same way. I envy you."

What could he say to that?

Nothing.

Rachel sighed, undid her seatbelt. "Come. They're all waiting."

Michael cut the engine, moved around and opened the passenger door. Rachel gripped his arm immediately, snuggled close like a frightened animal. He liked that. Her need fed something in him that was too ugly to acknowledge.

They moved up the drive, gravel crunching underfoot, the chirping of some night bird off in the distance.

Michael pressed the doorbell.

Rachel melted further into him.

The notes of "Beethoven's 9th Symphony (Ode to Joy)" spiraled out onto the porch with them, growing louder with each successive note.

Then the door yawned open.

The woman had dark hair, dark eyes, and a face that always wanted to settle into a smile but never did. Her uniform was snug against her curves. She was petite, but in height only. Michael had to convince himself that staring was a bad idea. Inappropriate. Sickness. Addiction.

"*Boa-noite*," he said to the woman.

"*A vocês também*," she replied.

"*Toda a gente está aqui?*"

"*Sim, claro.*"

Michael led Rachel into the house. Exceptionally comfortable radiant heat throughout. Wood floors. Brazilian cherry. A custom-designed five-zone sound system, twenty speakers on wall mounts around the downstairs, voices from what sounded like a commercial. The advertisement delivered by the fifty-inch plasma television in the den.

"*Eles são em studio,*" the dark-haired, dark-eyed beauty said.

"They're in the den," Michael explained to Rachel. His wife didn't reply. Her vacant eyes told him she hadn't even heard his voice.

He, on the other hand, was immediately relaxed. Why shouldn't he be? He had no problems whatsoever.

He thought of Liz Sutherland in the conference room at the office.

Karla.

That crumb cleaned up. Swept away.

Even the prospect of this evening couldn't dim his smile.

He took Rachel's hand in his own, her delicate fingers cold to the touch, and he guided her down the hall and toward the den.

On cue, as they entered the room, the commercial playing on the television ended, gave way to a program.

*Cash Cab.*

A trivia game show conducted in the backseat of a yellow cab.

Rachel's brother, Daniel, turned. He didn't smile, and even if he had, it would have contained no actual cheer. Daniel Ferrer matched the kind of description that was unhelpful to law enforcement: white male, above average height, blond, couldn't tell what color eyes, average build. Anything else? Anything that actually distinguished him? No. Just…so very typical.

"You made it."

Daniel's wife, Soledad.

Her voice was pleasant. In fact, she stood from her seat, rushed over and gave Rachel and Michael both kisses on the cheek. Michael would've preferred the lips. And that wasn't just his sickness talking. Soledad was the kind of beautiful even the most faithful man would have a hard time turning away from. She inspired wicked thoughts and even worse actions.

Raquel Welch.

Elizabeth Taylor.

Scarlett Johannsen.

Megan Fox.

Soledad made a laundry list of women universally recognized as beautiful, look, well, less beautiful. Another great temptation for Michael. His problem, he decided right then, was that he moved in circles where all of the women were model-beautiful. Even the women who answered doors.

"What's happening here?" Michael managed. He always found it difficult to speak in Soledad's presence.

"Daniel's busy shouting out the wrong answers to *every* question," Soledad said, rolling her eyes.

"Give him credit for trying."

"I'll consider it, Michael."

She smiled and Michael's head swam.

"Act as though I'm not even here," Daniel growled.

"Gladly," Soledad said, turning to frown at her husband across the room. "That shouldn't be difficult at all." She turned back and winked at Michael and Rachel. Michael smiled. Rachel didn't. Her eyes were concentrated on her feet.

Daniel didn't shrink away from his wife's challenge. "Hon, why don't you sashay back over here and sit down and keep the couch warm with that big booty of yours."

A real dig. She'd added a high-impact aerobics class to her schedule at the gym. Cursed her Latin roots on a nearly daily basis. Jennifer Lopez's experience hadn't been her own. She'd never embraced her ass, and, in her mind, had never felt anyone else did, either. There were several billable hours with more than one clinical psychologist that would attest to her frailty in this area.

"You're an asshole, Daniel," she said miserably.

Daniel nodded. "So I've been told. But I'm sure my ever-patient sister doesn't appreciate you all up in Michael's face. We all know how incorrigible he can be."

"Incorrigible," Michael said, whistling. "Great stuff, Daniel. I see you've been thumbing through a dictionary. Keep it up and perhaps Malcolm will allow you to start writing your own presentations instead of just reciting mine from PowerPoint slides."

Daniel stood up. White male, relatively tall, blond. "I'd rather not. The work required." He shuddered unconvincingly. "Even if I took those *long* lunches you're known for it wouldn't make up for the *long* nights at the office, away from my wife."

Michael smiled. "I'm sure Soledad wouldn't mind."

"Boys, boys, boys," Soledad said, recovered from Daniel's moment ago insult. "Malcolm feeds us all handsomely, no need to fight like two Rottweilers over one steak."

Malcolm Richard Ferrer.

The family patriarch. Founder and CEO of MRF Global. One of the richest men in the United States. He'd golf regularly with Gates and Trump if it wasn't for his arthritic hip and hands.

He actually entered the room at the mention of his name. Ever the opportunist.

"Did I hear my name?" he asked, amused.

Rachel, up until that moment absent in every way, turned to

the sound of the gruff voice. Malcolm Ferrer had lost inches and weight to age, little more than five-nine and one-fifty now, but Rachel took a step backward as if it were a giant's shadow darkening the doorway instead of a frail old man approaching his mid-seventies.

"Malcolm." Soledad beamed. She left a tattoo of her red lips on his liver-spotted cheek.

Malcolm wore slippers, silk pajamas, and a heavy robe.

Hugh Hefner, the first thought that flitted through Michael's mind. Hosting a party at the Playboy mansion. No surprise Michael's mind would travel there.

Michael moved to the old man, proffered a hand. He was advanced in age, but Malcolm's grip was as strong as black coffee. He clapped Michael on the back after the handshake. Strong in that as well.

"You're well?" Michael asked.

"Very," Malcolm replied.

Voice strong, too.

"Good."

"And you?"

Michael smiled, said, "Splendid," with an accent that would've made Sean Connery proud.

Malcolm moved his head so he could see beyond Michael's shoulder. "And how's my precious little girl?"

Rachel didn't answer.

Later, Malcolm stood at the edge of the bluff looking down at his private beach. The air was seasoned with tobacco. Malcolm's expensive pipe, made of calabash and with a meerschaum bowl, was held firm against his paper-thin lips.

"Dinner was suitable?" he asked Michael. It was just the two of them under a sky as dark as coal.

"As always," Michael said, nodding.

"I noticed Rachel didn't have much of an appetite."

"Veal," Michael said. "She hates it. I thought you knew that."

"I do seem to recall," Malcolm said, humor in his voice. "I'll make note of it again, for next time."

Michael had heard that before. A part of his spirit nudged him to press the old man, move into an offensive that his helpless wife was incapable of, but a greater part vetoed that notion. The old man didn't like to be challenged. Pressure made him hard. Like diamond.

Michael said, "You wanted to speak with me?"

He'd been summoned to the bluff shortly after their dinner. Left Daniel and Soledad bickering with one another in the den, Rachel off in the bathroom with the faucet running.

"Indeed."

"Everything okay?" he asked Malcolm.

"It can be."

Cryptic. But Michael wasn't equipped to spur the conversation in its intended direction. It would get there. Eventually. When Malcolm decided the moment was ripe.

Michael said, "Mmm," hoping that was a thoughtful enough response to move things forward.

"Yes, indeed. It can be," Malcolm repeated.

"Can it be?" Michael said. A simple juxtaposition of the old man's words. At a different point in life Michael would've been ashamed for himself. He had no shame whatsoever anymore.

Sickness.

Addiction.

He'd been robbed of shame.

"Rachel's mother was a beautiful girl," Malcolm said.

Girl.

"I've heard."

"Haitian."

Michael nodded.

"Skin as black as the sky is now," Malcolm added. "More than one soul questioned my sanity for the involvement."

Involvement.

"You were *involved* for how long?" Michael asked.

Malcolm sniffed a laugh. "Long enough for Rachel to be conceived."

Michael cleared his throat. "Rachel has some...concerns about your relationship with her mother."

The closest Michael could come to actually pressing the old man. Not bad.

"My first inclination was to banish the both of them somewhere," Malcolm said, chuckling. "But I didn't."

"Rachel feels as though you practically did," Michael said slowly.

"Daniel's mother," Malcolm said, ignoring Michael's comment, "Now there was an interesting woman."

Woman.

Michael knew more about Daniel's mother than Rachel's. Apparently she'd suffered some kind of mental breakdown.

"Despite the fragments in her thinking," Malcolm said, "it's difficult for me to regret the relationship."

"Especially with Daniel the product of that union," Michael said.

Malcolm snickered. "I must admit your rivalry with Daniel is a pleasure to witness."

"I apologize for my comment," Michael said. "It was uncalled for. I don't want to be petty."

"Oh," the older man said, orgasmic in his tone. "Do be petty. That's something you must be."

"He's your only son."

"I'm afraid I did not pay God enough attention on Sundays," Malcolm replied. "Daniel is my penance."

Wow.

Michael cleared his throat once more. "You wanted me for…"

"These old bones are softening, dear Michael. Shockingly I'm not promised forever."

"What are you saying? Are you ill?" The sudden rise in Michael's voice was a mystery even to himself. He wasn't aware that he cared about the old man on that deep, concerned level.

Maybe he didn't.

Maybe he just realized which side his bread was buttered on.

Malcolm waved him off. "Viagra, red wine, daily walks, and young women—they've served me well, Michael. I'm speaking more of the future. A future that grows less distant with each passing moment."

"You're certain you're okay?"

"Fine," Malcolm insisted. "But it's probable, statistically, that my children will outlive me."

Michael nodded.

"I'm not entirely comfortable with that notion," Malcolm said.

"I don't follow."

"MRF Global is worth a little more than five billion dollars, Michael."

"Sure."

"Rachel's pedigree is suspect and Daniel is an intellectual fly-weight."

Do be petty.

Michael said nothing.

"I love them both, as best as a man like me is capable of. I do hope you understand that, Michael."

"I do."

"But I loathe the thought of MRF in either of their hands. And I'd like the company that bears my initials to continue on long past my death. Legacy, you see." He paused, and Michael held his breath. "That is why I handpicked you, dear Michael."

"Me?"

"To lead, dear."

Waves crashed against the promontory. Off in the distance a bird sang a song. The stars above them were bright, littered the sky the color of Rachel's mother like lawn seed.

"The company?" Michael said, surprised.

"Don't act so shocked, Michael. There have been rumors, of course. And your ambition is what interested me from the start."

"What if I didn't want to lead, Malcolm?"

"Then I will have miscalculated badly," the old man said. "And Rachel will have another reason to hate me."

"Rachel?"

"I assured her of your worth, you see."

"What?"

"Despite her misgivings, I gently explained to her that her only likelihood of ever seeing Ferrer money rested with you."

Michael's mouth went dry. He licked his lips to no avail. "What are you insinuating, Malcolm?"

"Insinuating?" Malcolm chuckled. There was malice in it. "I haven't been clear enough, dear?"

"Say it." Michael's hands were balled in impotent fists.

"Oh, dear," Malcolm said. "Are you just now realizing that your relationship with my daughter is not the great love affair you thought it to be? I do hate that I'm the one to open your eyes. I rather like you, dear."

"I'm leaving now, Malcolm. We'll both pretend this conversation never occurred."

"You reminded her too much of me, dear. She would've never given you a second's glance were it not for my...encouragement."

Michael said nothing.

He didn't move, either, though in his mind he had already stomped away.

"I wish for my name, our great company name, to never lose its sharp edge, Michael. You're my hope. When I'm gone, you'll keep me alive."

"You've hurt me today, Malcolm."

"Certainly not my intention," the old man said.

"Do be petty. Correct?"

"At times a necessary evil, dear."

"I'm leaving," Michael said, and actually started moving toward the house.

"Michael?"

He turned back. Let that gesture imply a response. Didn't speak.

"A little more discretion is all I ask."

"What are you talking about now?"

"Once Sutherland and her three mates have settled your matter," Malcolm said. "Please assure me that she won't have to continue filling in the blanks on your schedule."

Liz Sutherland had lied about who knew about his relationship with Karla. Michael made a mental note to never trust her, or the Bellatoris for that matter, ever again. A corner of his mind reminded him that Malcolm should join that list as well. And Rachel. Rachel.

Michael cast aside that last thought, frowned. At that moment he felt so sorry for his wife. For himself. He couldn't clearly see Malcolm's features in the near dark but he could envision the wicked smile on the old man's face.

He left Malcolm standing there by the bluff.

Quiet.

Neither of them spoke during the ride home. Rachel because her father always put her in a depressed state. Michael because of what had been said at the foot of Malcolm's beach. Once Michael moved beyond feeling sorry for Rachel, all that remained were the old man's words, echoing strong inside his head. They'd managed to do what his infidelities had not. They'd caused a deep fissure in his feelings toward his wife. In a matter of moments Rachel had changed right before his eyes. No. Maybe she hadn't changed. Maybe his love had.

He glanced at her. Sitting, turned sideways, staring out of her window. And not at the houses, either. He doubted she actually *saw* anything.

He did, though.

He saw clearly for perhaps the first time since he'd known her. Thanks to her father. Her hateful, petty, rich father.

It was too much, the silence. Michael jammed a CD in his player. One he'd burned himself. Full of favorite songs. The speakers popped and crackled for a split second, then music filled the car. The Beatles wondering where all the lonely people came from. "Eleanor Rigby." A string quartet backdrop that reminded Michael of Vivaldi. Dark lyrics. He expected Rachel to respond in some way. A glance. A few words. Something.

But she kept up her vigil with the window.

Lonely people.

He'd picked a perfect song.

When the song came to its diminuendo, he rewound it to the beginning. Did that four more times during the lonely drive home.

Home.

They were finally back.

Surprisingly, Rachel sat there and waited for him to walk around the Chrysler and open her door. He expected a smile, a nod, once he'd done so. Yet again he met with disappointment as Rachel moved past him without any gesture. When she reached their back door she stopped again, waiting for him to open it with his key to allow her entry.

He did.

She made it to the bedroom without assistance, pausing long enough to let her pocketbook fall from her shoulder onto their bed, then went into the bathroom just off of the bedroom and locked herself in. The pipes burped and screamed and then eased into a quiet flow of running water.

Michael reclined on the counterpane of their bed, shoes still on, for nearly an hour before giving up.

He hopped up then, went to the closet, pulled down a thick wool blanket from the top shelf, and dragged it, its ends lapping at the floor, out into the living room. He contemplated watching television for a moment, but ended up huddled under the blanket with the room as dark as his mood, staring up at a ceiling he couldn't see clearly.

Ten minutes in, thoughts crowded his head, thoughts so malignant he would've turned on the television then. But the remote was at least eight feet away. Too far for him to reach. And so the television remained black.

Twenty minutes in, he snorted, wiped at his moist eyes. Dabbed them dry with his fingers, convincing himself it was nothing Claritin could not fix. Just allergies. That's all.

❧❧

She came to him without a word. He awakened with the weight of her body on his chest, her hands fumbling at his belt. Despite that, his greater concern was the darkness. He blinked to adjust his eyes. She had his belt undone, leaning over him and scorching his skin with feverish, panicked kisses. Instinctively he wrapped his arms around her, pulled her so she was straddling his lap. Her hair was wet, from a shower, he presumed. Her skin was warm.

No bra.

G-string panties.

He reached down and rubbed two fingers across the crotch of the panties. She moaned and rode his fingers. Wet in a matter of seconds.

He hooked a finger in the material, eased it aside, a second finger slipping inside of her. Her moans increased and so did the bucking of her hips.

A moment later her arms squeezed around his neck in an ever tightening grip. Tight, tighter, tighter. She yelped and her arms fell away. Two seconds of recovery, and she was up, sliding his pants down past his ankles.

She still hadn't spoken. There was so much he wanted to say to her, ask, but he didn't dare halt this pleasure.

She sat on his lap, her back to him, reached down and inched his hardness deep into her own wetness. He stared at the spot where he knew her ass was, seeing it in his mind's eye clearly even in the darkness, so round, so golden brown, so beautiful, as it worked up and down on his penis. His hands were quiet, one on each hip.

Sweat rained off of her.

His penis throbbed like a stubbed toe.

When she began to fatigue, he took his hands from her hips and used them to guide her up and down on his hard shaft.

She came quietly.

In waves.

He came loudly.

In one long rush that left him feeling completely empty, hollow.

"I love you," she said.

The only words she'd say for the balance of the night.

He believed her.

He smiled without expecting anything else from her.

Satisfied.

Content.

## CHAPTER NINE

The contentment lasted less than twenty-four hours. The next morning he sat, under the glow of his ignored computer monitor, a stack of papers he couldn't concentrate on growing like weeds in front of him. Outside of his office he heard the low murmur of workers. Inside of his office he heard a ringing cell phone. It took until the fourth ring for him to realize it was his own.

He frowned at the screen but still answered the call. "What?"

"I'm going to hang up and call back. We'll try this again. If you answer the same way, I'll hang up and make a different call to you-know-who."

"I don't have time for this, Karla," he whispered.

"I don't care," she whispered back.

He wondered then what he'd ever seen in her.

"What can I do for you?" he tried.

"I miss you," she said.

The sudden shift and softness of her tone caught him by surprise. She sounded as sincere as Rachel had last night when she'd said that she loved him. His attitude shifted right along with Karla's.

Sickness.

Addiction.

"I miss you as well," he heard himself say.

"Really?"

He sighed, leaned back in his leather chair, relaxed. "Really."

"Come see me," Karla said.

"Not a good idea, Karla."

"Why not?"

"The things you said when we last spoke."

"Emotions," she explained. "I let my head get the best of me. Just emotions."

"Which are bound to show up again," he said.

"I wasn't serious, Michael. I mean you no harm."

"This call is harming me, Karla."

"Yeah," she said.

The softness again. Sincerity. Vulnerability. All of it making Karla so... He couldn't deny it. His sudden erection wouldn't allow denial. He reached down and touched himself. The pain of needed release had him as swollen as he'd ever been.

Sexy.

Karla was sexy.

"I'm sorry," she said. "I promised myself I wouldn't call. This is so... I'm sorry. I'm hanging up now."

"Karla?"

"Yes."

"Where?"

Silence. He asked a second time.

"Not the hotel," she said. "That's... Bad memories."

"Oh?"

"Five hundred thread-count sheets," she said.

"What?"

"Good sheets. Egyptian cotton, Bellino Italian linen. What we're doing isn't deserving of good sheets."

"Don't beat yourself up, Karla."

Who was this man talking?

"A motel," she said. "That's more appropriate."

"Name the place."

She did. Even the name told him that it would be a roach motel. That their occupancy would be paid for by the hour.

"Karla, that's ridiculous."

"How I want it to be," she said, speaking low. "This is dirty. I don't want to fool myself into believing it isn't."

"We don't have to do this," he said.

"We do."

He knew she was right, of course. It was hard to explain to anyone that wasn't involved, but, they definitely had to do this. This thing was bigger than the both of them.

A sad but true actuality.

"I'll be there," he said.

"Right to it? No more attempts to reroute all of this."

"I think that's best," he said. "Before I change my mind."

"You wouldn't."

He glanced at Rachel's picture on his desk. Then averted his eyes. "I suppose you're right, Karla."

"What are we doing?"

"What we shouldn't be."

"Does it bother you?"

"Yes," he said, then, "No."

"It doesn't bother me as much as it should, Michael. That's terrible to say, but it's the truth."

"Yes."

"Lunch time?" she asked.

He glanced at his watch. Thirty-seven minutes after ten.

He said, "Now," and disconnected the call.

He knew the address but not the directions. He moved his computer mouse for perhaps the first time all day, surfed to

Yahoo. Maps. Driving directions. Filled in the A and B fields and printed the results.

Nineteen minutes.

15.3 miles.

He pushed back from the desk and stood up. Grabbed his light coat off of the back of his chair, and shook himself into it. A song was on his lips as he moved for the door.

Surprise smothered the song.

Liz Sutherland.

In his doorway.

Her ubiquitous laptop, folded closed, under her arm. The sexy cranberry-colored glasses magnifying her eyes. Gray jacket, white blouse, gray skirt that rode high up on her thighs, and then dissolved into her hips.

"Going somewhere?" she asked.

"Yes," he said without missing a beat. He squared his shoulders in a show of confidence. A show.

Liz stepped aside, her face blank. He passed. Didn't look back. Couldn't.

It was different with Karla. Different than it had been the night before with Rachel. Not better. Just different. And this time it wasn't dovetailed with regret. He lay beside her, afterwards, arm in arm, content. Work called his name but the siren of needed rest was louder. Work wasn't going anywhere.

He faded into sleep with Karla's leg crossed over his own.

# CHAPTER TEN

Mall. Early, early morning. Seniors walking the empty corridors for exercise. And red-eyed strippers dressed in major university sweatshirts and sweatpants two sizes too large for their frames. Sneakers on to round out the outfit. Reeboks mostly. Their nails cut surprisingly short, but still painted. Plain candy apple red. And for others, candy apple red with designs.

And one other woman. An anomaly. She didn't belong there at that hour any more than he did. She wasn't old. Attractive enough to have been an exotic dancer, certainly, but without even knowing her, he could tell that would never be her fate. He could tell by the way she moved. With sophistication. She was a woman with class.

She wore a tan raincoat that dropped to just below her waist, affording him a view of her legs. Thin but strong legs. Brown, the calves moving like pistons as she walked on in four-inch heels.

Not walked.

Sophistication. A sashay. Soledad's walk.

He watched her up the escalator, and turned around to follow. In heavy pursuit. When he caught up—and there was no doubt in his mind that he would—he'd say, "I'm Michael Palmer, not Jeremy Kitteridge. And I must be dreaming because you're more beautiful than anyone I've ever seen or could've imagined."

She'd smile.

And then without further pause they'd be fucking. Fucking hard. Their bodies slick with sweat, their sex parts connected as if they'd done it together a million times before. Orchestrated strokes that were more art than pornography. Millais not Stylez.

After they finished, she'd speak and he'd realize those were her very first words. He'd introduced himself, told her he must be dreaming, and eased inside of her naked body in quick succession. "I'd like to do this again," she'd say, her voice oddly familiar.

"You don't know me," he'd say.

"I know your body," she'd reply.

Dreaming for sure.

But he had to catch up with her before any of that could happen. He stepped off of the escalator, on the mid-level, and looked around. Empty corridor the length of his view. No seniors, no strippers. A sunglass kiosk. A *Piercing Pagoda. Victoria's Secret. Foot Locker. Bare Escentuals. Borders. Banana Republic. Bath & Body Works. Pandora.*

The woman gone. Vanished.

The regret and despair were just about to settle in when he spotted her up ahead of him, a tiny dot on the landscape but definitely her. That walk was unmistakable.

Sashay.

She'd shed the raincoat. He spotted a black skirt that fell no more than a hand-length below her waist. So tight she probably had to lie down to put it on, he thought. A top that revealed her sexy brown shoulders.

He was close enough in an instant to see the stitching in her clothes.

Dreaming.

She was in *Bath & Body Works*, unscrewing the spray top on

several fragrances, touching the uncapped bottle to her nose. Her face was obscured from his view. But he knew without a doubt whatsoever that she was beautiful despite his inability to see her face.

She flowed to the back of the store as he weaved through the aisles in her direction. No sales girls around. The store deserted except for the two of them.

No.

A man at the back of the store. He was shirtless, skin the color of shredded coconut. Hair the color of an exotic dancer's finger-nails. Taller than Michael even. More muscular. Skinny jeans clung to his lower body and yet they didn't make him look like a homosexual. They made him look stylish.

The woman fell into the bare-chested man's embrace and offered him a naked breast seemingly in one motion.

Dreaming.

Then the shirtless man was flat on his back on the cleared counter space at the registers, the woman straddling him, whipping her head so that her hair flipped. Topless now herself.

Michael's brain told him to turn heel, leave. He took several tentative steps forward instead.

The lover's moans replaced the music that had been playing. The moans actually piped through the store's speakers.

Michael made it to the counter, right up on them, and tapped the woman on the shoulder. She bucked twice more on the shirtless man, her fingernails digging into his chest, before looking up.

Rachel.

Michael stumbled backward, overturned a display, spray bottles rolling around his feet like marbles emptied from a nylon net bag. He ran. Slipped on a bottle and wrenched his ankle and lost his balance.

Falling.

And falling.

And falling.

He woke with a start. Breathing heavy and confused and alone in a strange bed, the spot next to him warm but unoccupied.

What the…

Understanding met him at the same time as the smell.

Roach motel. Urine?

And the sound.

Squeaking.

He sat up, blinked against the darkness. Squeak, squeak. A figure at the foot of the bed. In a rickety old chair bottomed with casters. He remembered it. An unappealing green color, duct tape bandaging a wound in the seat.

He whispered, "Karla?"

The shadow mumbled, rocked the chair frantically. Karla, bound and gagged just a few feet from him. He started a move in her direction, stopped just as suddenly as he'd begun. From the left came another black figure. A scream died somewhere in Michael's chest, elbowed aside by his heart, beating so strong it felt like a punch to the ribcage.

Another figure swam in from the right.

One over by the door, leaning against the frame. A final one sitting on the small table at the edge of the room. Michael's briefcase was on that table, and for some strange reason he worried about its safety. So much more to be concerned about but that briefcase was on his mind. The aftereffects of shock?

The figure from the left moved closer.

Michael managed, "Who are you?"

The figure said, "An existentialist, are you? I would've never guessed." Chuckled. "Who am I? Who are you? Who is anyone?"

The Bellatoris. Lukas Doyle.

Not a home invasion. A roach motel invasion. On public property.

Still, Michael didn't relax. This might be worse.

He asked, "What do you want?"

"Order."

The figure from the right moved behind the figure in the rickety old chair at the foot of the bed. A slim, tall figure. Liz Sutherland, Michael realized as the smell of lilacs hit his nostrils. Then he caught the glimmer of her knife blade, even in the darkness, and that further confirmed his suspicion.

Or maybe it didn't.

Could he actually see that detail in the darkness?

Maybe he was still dreaming.

"No, you're not dreaming this," Lukas Doyle said, as though reading Michael's thoughts. "Go ahead, pinch yourself."

Michael didn't have to.

"This is criminal," he said.

Lukas Doyle laughed. "I should say so. This place is a bomb shelter in Timor-Leste. My eyes are burning, just from the air. I believed you to be a bit more high-class than this."

"You need to explain what's happening," Michael said. "I'm your superior."

Wrong word choice. He regretted it at once.

"Superior? You're laying there on sheets that were already stained when you got here. Your dick is as soft as a deflated balloon. The stink of Burberry perfume and roach spray on your skin. Your paramour has pissed herself. And you're my superior? Interesting."

Michael swallowed.

"What do you do?" Lukas Doyle snapped.

"Do?"

"Occupation." The four syllables like hammer strikes.

"You know the answer to that."

"I'm armed, Michael Allan Palmer. Humor me."

"I won't."

"That would be a fatal mistake, Michael Allan Palmer."

Fatal.

Had Michael heard that correctly? He was certain he had.

He whispered, "Consultant," in a voice ruined by phlegm.

"Expound, please. The more detail the better."

"What is this?"

"Decision time. Expound."

"I won't do this."

Lukas Doyle turned. "Liz."

Michael heard the blade slice through the air. Actually heard it. Karla whimpered.

"We can cut Karla Renee Savage into ribbons, Michael Allan Palmer. You *decide*."

"What do you want?"

"Consultant...expound."

"Our clients are businesses of every ilk. Fortune 500. Retail, industries, etc. We help them improve their business processes. I manage a portfolio over a hundred companies strong. I perform audits for operational health. I find holes, weaknesses, areas of opportunity and I manage their transition to better practices."

"Improve efficiency?"

"Certainly."

"Sounds like inspired work."

"I'd like to think so."

Lukas Doyle turned back to Liz. "Take the Kotex out of Ms. Savage's mouth. If she screams, the Kotex will come in very handy sopping up her blood. Understand?"

Liz nodded, unstuffed Karla's mouth. Karla took breaths in with big gulps, cursed everyone in the room between breaths.

"I'll chalk your petulance up to nympholepsy," Lukas Doyle said, then quickly raised his hand to silence her. "Don't get yourself unjustifiably excited, nympholepsy isn't what you think. It means a frenzy of emotion for something unattainable. Something unattainable, like the ability to stand up and walk around this room unencumbered."

"Fuck you," Karla said.

"Such a potty mouth," he said, clucking his tongue. "Michael, you should really be more discerning about where you stick your business. You did stick your business in Ms. Savage's mouth, right?"

"Fuck you."

Karla.

Michael admired her for the animus.

"Maybe before this is all over," Lukas Doyle said, chuckling. "If Michael doesn't mind sharing."

"Fuck you," she repeated.

"Say it twice more," Lukas Doyle said. "There are four of us. I'm sure the others would love to join in the party."

She uttered the two words a third time.

Got slapped across the face by Liz Sutherland's free hand. Whimpered.

"And what do you do, Karla Renee Savage?" Lukas Doyle asked.

She didn't reply.

"Liz?"

Michael heard the cut, closed his eyes. Liz smothered Karla's screams with her hand.

"What...Do...You...Do?"

It took Karla a few torturous minutes to answer. United States Postal Service. Clerk.

Lukas Doyle whistled. "Have to watch my back with you. Postal worker…I know you're capable of mass murder then."

"Fuck you!" she screamed.

"Liz, stuff Ms. Savage's dirty mouth with the Kotex again, please. That's if you don't need it to sop up her blood."

Karla struggled, but Liz managed to stuff it in her mouth.

"This is criminal," Michael said.

"Karla's ex-husband, Allan as it turns out, how's that for irony?" Lukas Doyle paused for effect. "Anyway, he's a podiatrist. Very successful. He's *footing* the bill on her home. Drumroll, please." Chuckle. "They still share a bed from time to time. Allan likes to enter his ex-wife from behind, grab hold of Ms. Savage's hair and call her degrading names while he slaps her on the ass. She likes to stick a finger in his ass while she sucks his cock. An interesting couple, those two. More creative now than when they were married, I would wager. Were you aware of any of this, Michael?"

Michael shook his head, slowly. "No."

"You really do need to get to know your whores in more detail, Michael *Allan* Palmer."

Karla rocked the chair. Mumbled through the Kotex.

"Well, this was an easy decision," Lukas Doyle said. "Liz?"

Michael, with his eyes closed shut, counted five neat stabs. Five anguished grunts.

Karla twitched in her chair for a bit, and then fell eerily silent.

Michael's eyes watered.

He vomited.

Lukas Doyle tsked. "Merriman's responsible for *all* clean up. You're not endearing yourself to him, Michael."

Michael retched again.

"I'm a consultant as well, Michael. Perhaps that's why I was partial to your occupation over the former Karla Renee Savage's.

That and the fact that the price of stamps keeps rising. Pisses me off."

Michael said nothing.

"Let me explain how this will go, Michael. You up for an explanation?"

It took a moment, but he nodded.

He didn't dare challenge them.

"Karla will go missing. She won't be found. And you're a part of this so you'd be advised to keep your mouth shut. I'd hate to have to replay your conversation with the former Ms. Savage for the police. The blackmail call. Plenty of motive for you to want her gone. For good. We have that and many other interesting calls on reel. You remember the call I'm speaking of?"

Michael nodded again.

"I'll be watching you. Now we're all going to leave now, absent Merriman. He has to clean up this terrible mess. This situation is perfect for our exit. Fleabag motel. Everyone's too busy fucking and shooting up and picking nits out of their hairs to pay attention to anything else. We'll walk right out of here as if we never existed. You paid cash I'm sure, correct?"

Michael nodded.

"Have to fill out a registration card? Provide your vehicle's tags?"

Michael shook his head.

"Inspired choice, Michael," Lukas Doyle said, chuckling again. "Tell me this wasn't meant to be. It couldn't have worked out more perfectly. Thank you, Michael Allan Palmer. You've been a wonderful co-conspirator."

Michael vomited again.

LUST
SLOTH
PRIDE BOOK TWO
GREED
ENVY
GLUTTONY
WRATH

# CHAPTER ONE

Michael was certain the feeling would never fade. But what was the feeling exactly? Sadness? Despair? Fear? Anger? Guilt? A combination of all those emotions and a million others combined to create a gumbo that he thought of as one singular feeling? He stood under the water flow of his shower, the temperature turned to its very coldest setting, and let the spray massage deep into his muscle tissue. After five minutes, his teeth began to chatter. After ten, his entire body shook violently. By minute fifteen, he was crying so hard the frigid water was practically forgotten. It took restraint he didn't realize he possessed to not call out her name.

Karla.

Nearly a full day removed from the madness in the roach motel, and yet in Michael's mind it had just happened. Karla rocking the swivel chair, trying her best to break loose. And a moment later Liz Sutherland saddling up behind her, knife blade glinting even in the dark. Then Karla twitching like a seizing epileptic. Then Karla still.

Still.

That was an easier concept to grasp than…dead. Michael couldn't wrap his mind around dead. Murdered. Murders only happened in movies and books, and even though Karla had a movie villain's smile, her life certainly wasn't a movie. Nor was Michael's.

Still.

He turned off the water and stepped from the shower enclosure, trailing wet footprints across the tile, room temperature air prickling his skin. It took him forever to towel himself dry. Just short of forever to dress for work.

He moved about quietly, not wanting to disturb a sleeping Rachel. The fact that his wife remained resting was the only thing to happen in the past few days that he could acknowledge being grateful for.

He wished he could sleep as well. Sleep until one day bled into another, and another, and after several cycles of that wake up to discover... What? A Karla that wasn't still.

A fantasy that rivaled *Harry Potter*, *Twilight*.

Karla was gone.

For good.

Never to be found.

That last part he wasn't so certain of, though. He watched *CSI*. Every crime left behind clues. He expected a visit from the police any minute now.

Stop obsessing, he told himself. Go on.

He kissed Rachel's face, softly so as not to disturb her, grabbed his briefcase and headed downstairs. A quick stop in the kitchen for a glass of pink grapefruit juice and a chocolate chip granola bar.

He poured more than half of the glass of juice down the drain a moment later, loaded the glass in the dishwasher. One bite of the granola bar was all his stomach could hold.

The Chrysler 300C's keys were spread like fingers on the island counter. He stopped and avoided them for a beat before scooping them up and heading out. Inside the sedan he remembered stories of garden hoses connected to exhaust pipes and threaded through slightly parted driver's-side windows. A decision that left the car's occupants dead. No, still.

He wasn't quite ready for that fate, though.

He pulled to the end of his driveway, looked to his left, and all clear, pulled out into the street.

Just up the block a woman stood patiently as her Irish setter urinated by the curb. The woman had skin the color of hot chocolate mix. And even inside the car, windows rolled up, Michael could smell the Burberry perfume on her skin and the strawberries in her hair.

He saw the same woman three turns later, down a different street. Same skin coloring. Same fragrances. This woman was bent at the waist, retrieving her newspaper from a wet lawn.

Michael wasn't insane, he didn't believe, but he spotted this same woman several more times on the route to work. Coming out of a 7-Eleven with a Styrofoam cup of steaming hot coffee, placing the cup on the roof of her Toyota Camry and rooting through a large pocketbook for keys. And another woman, later, turning back for her fallen slipper as she attempted to dart across the street to place mail in a blue USPS mailbox.

By the time he realized he wasn't driving to work he'd seen an approximation of this same woman a total of seven times. Skin the color of hot chocolate mix. Burberry and strawberry fragrances. A movie villain's smile. Always in motion. Never, ever, still.

He came to a parking lot littered with broken glass and sand and candy bar wrappers. No other cars were in any of the spaces. He parked at an inebriated angle, the nose of the Chrysler splitting through two adjacent spots. A grayed plankboard walkway built between rows of winter-dead bushes led down to the deserted beach. Surprising, as it was an early Saturday morning. But then again, this beach wasn't very attractive.

He didn't bother removing his shoes and socks, didn't bother rolling up his pant cuffs. He clacked across the plankboard walk, trudged through the sand, and came to the mouth of the water. He paused there, thinking, contemplating, deciding.

Across the expanse of the ocean was a view of the Manhattan skyline that could only be appreciated at night.

The air was colder than his shower. The water sluggishly crashing against rugged rock structures that jutted from the ocean surface.

Michael had never learned to swim. In fact, water was the closest thing to a real fear he'd ever had. He stepped forward until the incoming water rose to a height that wet his pants right above the knees. When the water receded, he took two more steps forward.

The voice was strong above the rolling waves. Surprisingly it didn't startle him. He turned back, walked up toward dry beach, impassive despite the smile on his visitor's face.

"Can it be that it was all so simple then…" Lukas Doyle's eyes sparkled like the broken glass in the lot. "Gladys Knight and the Pips. I love old soul. How about you, Michael?"

Michael didn't answer.

Lukas Doyle nodded as if Michael had, as if they were in agreement on the reply.

"Songs had feeling in the past," Lukas Doyle said. "Lyrics meant something. Nowadays we're fucking our women because they remind us of Jeeps."

He shook his head. A preacher disheartened by the sinning masses.

Michael stood there, looking at nothing and everything at the same time.

"Can it be that it was all so simple then…" Lukas Doyle repeated. "Feeling, meaning. Do you see it?" He cleared something from his throat, hocked it into the sand. His eyes and smile changed when he focused on Michael again. "In the old days I would've snapped your neck and fed you to the ocean. Today, because of all the advances in forensics, and because I don't particularly care to test those advances twice in the same amount of days, I'm simply *telling* you to get your ass to the office, right now, you insolent bastard."

# CHAPTER TWO

By noon the sky outside of Michael's office window was the color of one of Liz Sutherland's outfits. Gray with the promise of a coming rain. With the bleary weather came a bleary attitude. No one smiling in the outer office. No cheery voices floating about. Some would chalk it up to a long six-day workweek, but Michael knew better. Most Saturdays the atmosphere was close to a party. People came in, worked half the day, and collected a full day's pay. Not a bad proposition for most. But Michael sat there in his own office, feeling worse than ever before, in a state greater than depression. Paralysis more apt. Lukas Doyle's appearance down at the beach had shaken him almost as much as the day prior, in the roach motel. Just how far was the man's reach? Michael knew he should be grateful on some level. Karla was gone, never to return, and yet he was still among the living. He'd been granted a reprieve not afforded to Karla. That meant he must live. No use dwelling on what couldn't be changed. He couldn't bring Karla back. But he couldn't shake the feeling of despair, either. Couldn't stop thinking of her. Couldn't help wondering how this all spiraled out of control.

He had to do something, he knew. He'd die otherwise.

And suddenly he had a thought. The prospect made him push away from his desk at noon, blood coursing hard through his veins, with a feeling he could actually describe: anticipation.

He hustled to the elevators, stabbed the DOWN button several times. The car arrived with a bing and he moved inside quickly. On the ride down he almost hummed along with the wordless elevator music.

Second level.

The doors rumbled open and he exited the elevator, pausing just long enough to figure out which direction to turn. Right.

He found the room at the end of the corridor. Its size surprised him. It stretched the length of the building. Lights burned bright inside and the low sounds of competing music—hip hop and something else—wasn't as unpleasant as one would believe it to be.

Large mail carts were butted up next to one another throughout the room. The desks here weren't polished walnut, but rather pedestrian metal painted black or gray. The many file cabinets were largely tan in color. Several overhead bulbs were blown out and still, it was brighter than Michael could ever get his own office to be.

He found Joe Larkin in back, bobbing his head to one or both of the songs playing, hunched over a sloppily made sandwich, newspaper spread out under it all.

"You work Saturdays as well," Michael said. "That dedication needs to be rewarded."

Joe looked up, saw Michael, and sighed heavily.

"Lunch? My treat," Michael said, unmoved by Joe's gesture.

"Already eating," Joe said, stating the obvious.

"Doesn't look very appetizing," Michael said, scrunching his nose. "Let me treat you to something a bit more enjoyable. More dirty water dogs?"

"I'll pass, dude. I'm thinking secretaries might be the move."

"Secretaries?" Michael said, frowning. He moved closer, sat down on the corner of the desk where Joe Larkin ate. Larkin edged aside the newspaper.

"You have a secretary," he explained to Michael. "All the big-wigs have secretaries. I pick the right one and give her the"—he made a fist, slowly punched the air with it in mimic of a piston—"maybe she puts in a good word for me."

Michael smiled. "Not a bad plan, but most of the bosses are sleeping with their secretaries, Joe."

Joe stopped chewing, a disgusted look on his face. He balled the sandwich up in its foil, tossed the misshapen lump into a nearby wastebasket. Balled up the newspaper and did the same with it, too. "You suck the big one, Mikey. Pardon me for saying so."

Michael hunched his shoulders, smile still in place. "No offense taken. Now, come on, let's do lunch."

"You've ruined my appetite."

"I know a spot where the waitresses have big…"

Joe's eyes showed interest. It took a moment, but eventually he nodded. "Suddenly I'm hungry again."

"Hair?" Joe said. The waitress had just taken down their orders. Sandra was in her fifties but looked ten years older, in comfortable tennis sneakers but walked as though she had problems with her feet. Heavy-handed with her makeup, hair styled in a puffy bouffant.

"Sixties theme," Michael said, grinning. "What did you think I meant when I said 'big'?"

Joe made a sound like a muffled firecracker. Michael nearly laughed. If Karla were still alive he actually might have. Finding the strength to smile was a chore but occasionally he mustered the strength for that. Laughing was beyond his current capability.

"Last time I let you trick me, dude."

"Last time I'll try," Michael said, serious.

"So what did you want me here for?" Joe asked. "It's gotta be something. And, knowing you, it's gotta be bad. Let me guess: you gave some chick herpes? Got some chick pregnant? You're paying for her abortion with your floor's coffee money?"

"You have a pretty negative impression of me, Joe."

"Has nothing to do with the fact that the first time we sat down to talk you confessed to cheating on the big boss's daughter for the whole of your marriage and then told me that the newest woman you're laying the screws to is blackmailing you." Spoken in a quick burst, no pause to catch his breath.

"A mouthful," Michael said.

"So what is it? Tell me."

"It's been a difficult few days," Michael said.

"The chick that's blackmailing you?"

Michael wished that were so. Wished that Karla was still here to put pressure on him. He'd sacrifice his own comfort for her life. Probably the most unselfish thought he'd had in years.

And completely worthless.

Karla was gone. For good.

"It's a bit more complicated than that," he told Joe.

"Shit. She *is* pregnant." He eyed Michael, waiting for a response that didn't come. "Don't tell me...herpes?" Nothing. "Damn, herpes *and* pregnant? Say something, dude."

Michael said something.

A request.

Joe shook his head, banged up against the table as he attempted to rise, fell back into his seat, frowning in momentary pain. Michael took the opportunity to pin him in, scooting up beside him.

"I really need your help on this, Joe."

"I'll pass, dude," he said, shaking his head, still frowning from the pain. "First of all, I don't involve myself with *them*. And all the rest that you're asking is…this is some heavy duty stuff, dude."

Michael managed a smile. "Would you expect anything less from me?"

"Why, dude? Why?" Whining.

"I wouldn't bring this to you if it wasn't important, Joe."

There was a jug of iced water on the table. Joe reached forward, poured himself a glass, guzzled it dry in one big gulp. Refilled the glass a second time. Repeated the gulp.

"Will you help me?" Michael asked.

"I don't know, dude."

Hedging, Michael realized. Now was the time to turn that hedging in his favor. He leaned in to Joe, placed an arm on the bony man's shoulder, a smile in place on his handsome face. "You help me and I'll help you, Joe. There's an opening coming up in R&D with your name written all over it." Sad that he could look Joe in the eyes without wavering.

Lying.

Part of his addiction, sickness. It came natural.

Joe sighed, his face a mixture of pain and confusion. "I'd like that, dude."

"It's all yours, Joe."

Joe sighed again. "They are so heavy duty, dude. My name can't be in this. I don't want any trouble from them."

*Them* didn't need any other title.

"No one's will be," Michael assured him.

Joe nodded. "Okay. I'll help you out."

"Eight o'clock. The time is very important. And exactly where I told you. The details are precise for a reason."

"I got it, dude."

"Repeat everything back to me."

"Eight o'clock. At…"

Michael nodded a moment later. "You got it all."

"Can I go now?"

Michael raised an eyebrow. "You haven't eaten."

"Not the least bit hungry, dude. And if I get hungry…I'll pick my sandwich out of the garbage."

"Sounds appetizing."

Joe nodded. "Life is the dumps, dude. We're all picking through garbage, it's just some of us don't know it."

Michael couldn't disagree.

# CHAPTER
# THREE

They were watching him. He was certain of this. They'd been watching him for some time. Months, maybe even years. He was certain of this as well. Armed with the knowledge gleaned from watching him, they'd know where he regularly went, what he did, what he liked, what he didn't. They'd know his habits, his routines. The things that were essential to his life.

In other words, they'd know *him*.

He'd thought of them the entire weekend, wondering where they were in the shadows. Barely speaking to Rachel because his mind was so occupied. And this morning, Monday, he'd watched for them the entire ride to work. They were out there somewhere.

He never did see them.

Somehow sleepwalked his way through the day, leaving at night, knowing they were watching him then.

Monday nights were set on his schedule. Eight o'clock PM, every Monday, he could be found one place. Like clockwork.

Strolling through his local library.

But, even with his extra plans in place, this evening was nearly aborted. On the way in, a few minutes prior, he'd almost lost his nerve. The DVD and BOOK return boxes out front caused a hitch and a stumble in his step. The boxes reminded him of mailboxes. The ubiquitous blue boxes with the USPS seal. And that made him think of Karla.

It was a slight miracle he didn't rush over to the grass and vomit his breakfast and lunch. An even greater miracle that it only took him a moment's pause to recover from the sight of the boxes. Perhaps he was getting better. He'd learned from experience that was the nature of mourning. Each day it got a little bit easier. Each day it got better in inches.

But that wasn't it, the game of inches that recovery was.

He'd lived the past few days under a pall like none he'd ever experienced before. Lukas Doyle tracking him to the beach was the final jolt in what had been a pure nightmare. Now it was time to turn the tables. He'd thought it through as best he could, considering he had zero experience with matters such as this. All of the thinking brought him to one conclusion: he knew of his enemies, sure, but he knew nothing about them.

Time to change that.

It was the anticipation of that change that brought him hope. And with hope came peace.

For the first time in days he felt a measure of peace.

That peace would be short, though, if Joe Larkin didn't come through for him. He almost laughed at the notion. His life in Joe Larkin's hands.

A glance at his watch showed the time as 7:58. In two minutes he'd know whether he could rejoice. Or cry. He couldn't get too far ahead of himself, though. There was still the strong possibility that all of this was a big waste of time. That his plan would fail.

He pulled a book from the shelf, thumbed through the pages, not really looking at them, reading the tightly packed together words but not actually processing them.

7:59.

He swallowed, put the book back on the shelf, and shuffled sideways two steps. Picked a different book from the shelf. Black.

Slim. The vision of a moon over white waters bisected by rough rock. It reminded him of the beach. He paid attention to book covers.

"*Nights in Rodanthe?*"

The soft voice didn't startle him, despite the suddenness of her appearance. She'd eased up beside him so quietly he hadn't seen or heard her entrance. *Perfect*, he thought. He turned, smiling. "Easy reading," he said, acknowledging the slim book in his hand.

"You don't look like the type to read Nicholas Sparks."

"How does the type look?"

She let her gaze travel over his body, head to toe, back again. "Shorter, softer…usually has a pair of tits. Or is it a pair of tit?"

A pair of tits.

She had nice ones herself.

Full inside her white lace bra, stretched tight against her hunter green T-shirt. V-neck front, an impossible line of cleavage. With a glow that made him wonder if she actually oiled them with something. Lotion, Vaseline.

"You're not very discreet," she said.

"Not very," he admitted.

"That's the problem with having these," she said, cupping her breasts. "And a diseased face to boot. Doesn't give men much incentive to actually look me in the eyes when they speak to me."

"I'm sorry," he said, looking up. Red flare-up on her chin, a little less severe on her cheeks. Several cherry-colored blemishes on her lined forehead. A pizza pie.

"Uh-huh, sure. You're sorry. Now go ahead and refocus on my boobs."

Tits, boobs, if she made it to *knockers* he might have to slip one in his mouth. He felt an erection throbbing in his pants. Getting better? Or returning to his old ways?

Sickness.

Addiction.

"Have I gotten off on the wrong foot with you, Cassie?"

Cassie Hart.

Joe's friend from HR.

"I've seen you at work and you've never said two words to me," she said. "*That's* the wrong foot."

"I'm self-absorbed, I'm afraid. I'll make it a point to speak in the future."

She nodded and all seemed forgotten. Her face softened. She looked at him as most women did. With appreciation.

He said, "So Joe spoke with you?"

"I'm out here like Anita Blake, vampire hunter, aren't I?"

"Yes, of course."

"You owe me some money, by the way," she said, touching the brim of a Yankees cap. "I had to spring for this. You wanted a disguise, you got one. No one would make note of a Yankees fan around here. There's only like, what, a gazillion of them?"

He pulled out his wallet, fished out a twenty, held it up for her to take.

She didn't.

"George Steinbrenner's Yankees," she said. "You know? Babe Ruth, Mickey Mantle, A-Rod, Derek-fucking-Jeter. The *Yankees*."

He fished out a second twenty.

She nodded and took the bills from his grasp. Then her eyes were on him again. Ready for business. "As nice as they are, I know you didn't have me come out here to drool over my bazoongas. Why all the secrecy? Clandestine meeting place. Disguises."

"Joe spoke to you about what I wanted to know?"

"He did."

"Well, there it is."

Again she nodded. "Lukas Doyle's a psychopath. In the clinical and legal sense, I'd suppose. Calm and collected. Most bad men are capable of killing you. Pow-bang-boom…to the head." She shook her own head vigorously. "Doyle would lock you in his basement and feed you one M&M a day until you wasted to nothing. A psychopath."

"Liz Sutherland…"

"Makes me ashamed of my monthly periods," she said, smiling.

"Namako has eyes like the D.C. Snipers. Remember them?" Michael asked, joining her in smiling.

"D.C. Snipers? Try again. Those guys had *feelings*. They put down blankets in the trunk of their sniper car to make it more comfortable. Namako wouldn't realize it if he was lying on rocks and broken Heineken bottles."

"And the steroid freak…"

Her smile immediately vanished.

"Yeah, we know they're a scary bunch, but I don't care to spend all evening at the library," she said. "Did enough of that in college."

"Where was college?" Michael asked, trying for rapport. He'd noticed a sudden chill.

"I don't have any information on them," she said, instead. "Other than what you already probably know, from water cooler talk."

"But Joe said—"

"Joe talks too much. Thinks too much of himself. He's come over my place a few times to give me an oil change, and most of the time, after he leaves, I end up fingering myself to finish off what he started and left incomplete."

"Colorful," he said.

"Just letting you know that Joe doesn't have the sway with me that he might have led you to believe…"

*But you're here*, Michael thought.

"...even though I'm here," she said, as though reading his thoughts.

"I see."

"I was intrigued. Figured why not. I've always sort of admired you. From a distance." She smiled sadly. "I wanted to also warn you off of this. It's not a healthy choice asking questions about them."

"I don't smoke and I run several miles a week," he said. "I'm healthy enough to indulge in unhealthy choices occasionally."

"Mmm."

"Men have used you for a long time," he said. "You learned to accept it. Now you actually embrace it."

"Maybe," she said.

"I'm not asking for your help without giving you something back," he added.

She smiled. "Wait, don't tell me. Is there a second top secret biggo-wiggo job opening up in R&D? I can report to Joe Larkin, V.P. of the newest division, appointed personally by Michael Allan Palmer."

"I—"

"Feed that bullshit to an insecure *ass* who'd accept you telling him that the sky is made of cream cheese if that would get him out of the mailroom."

Michael low-whistled. "Which fingers?"

"Pardon?"

"Joe definitely didn't do the work. Which fingers did you have to use...you know, to finish up what he started? I'd like to offer them an apology on behalf of the company."

"Maybe I'm being hard on Joe," she said, smiling. "I'm just now realizing he definitely isn't the only *ass*."

He didn't have a reply to that.

"Look," she said, "there's nothing in any of their files. Okay? Leave this alone. I like you."

"Nothing?"

She shook her head. "Nada."

"That's typical?"

"That's very *not* typical."

"Someone extricated their info?"

"No."

"How can you be sure?"

"I processed their hire."

That short-circuited him. What now? The despair was working its way back. A tingle in his toes, a heated tingle that worked its way up his body, bit by bit.

"Do we know anything about them? Regardless of the empty files?"

"You've heard the talk."

"Besides rumors?"

"No. Leave this alone."

"You're telling me that they were hired without you or anyone in your department knowing anything about them?"

"No."

"No?"

"There are stories about their previous"—she groped for the right word—"experiences. I'm told the stories are quite persuasive."

"Stories? They were hired off of stories?"

"They seem very capable," she said.

He thought of waking in the darkness. Karla bound and gagged in the motel chair. Karla. Still.

Never to be found.

"Sounds crazy to me," he said.

"I was told to hire them and I did," she said. "The directive came from on high. It's not my place to dissent. My name isn't on the building."

Michael frowned. "From on high. You're kidding. I can't believe Malcolm would do this."

"Malcolm didn't."

"You said your name wasn't on the building."

"It isn't."

"I'm confused."

"Malcolm's *initials* are on the building," she explained. "The F stands for Ferrer, if you didn't know. And as hard as it is to believe, Daniel's a Ferrer."

"Daniel was the one?" Michael said, surprised.

She nodded. "Whodathunkit? You're good for more than just drooling over my fun bags. Yes, Daniel was the one."

# CHAPTER
# FOUR

They were watching him. He was certain of this. He didn't care. He walked out of the library with his shoulders squared and his head held high, the Nicholas Sparks romance trapped under his right arm. Couldn't bear the thought of his usual type of book. Crime fiction, mostly. John Sandford's Prey series. James Lee Burke's Robicheaux books. Anything Dennis Lehane. No. Not today. Maybe never again. Fictionalized crime couldn't compete with the thoughts of real mayhem that floated through his mind.

Karla.

All of this was…unbelievable.

He used his key fob to chirp the Chrysler's locks. Looked back at the library as he slid behind the wheel. Wait ten minutes until after I've gone, he'd told Cassie. She'd nodded somberly, those big breasts of hers bouncing with the slight movement. The erection still stood proud in his pants.

Always on, sexually, regardless of the situation.

He pulled from the library lot, moved easily into the sparse evening traffic. Radio on so low he couldn't tell what tune was playing. It didn't much matter. This evening wasn't about music.

It was about action.

Revelation.

And more action.

They were watching him. He was certain of this. He didn't care. One bit.

⊂⊃

Ranch. One-story, of course. Stone and white siding, large front yard. No porch, no guest houses, no private beach. Still, better than Michael's home with Rachel. The inequity had never grated him the way it did to Rachel. Until now. So many changes had and were taking shape inside of him. Changes that actually scared him. A bloom of hate flowering in the pit of his stomach. Never before had there been this kind of anger. He'd always been a lover, not a fighter. A cliché, but it fit him like…a glove. Another cliché. But nothing about him was typical anymore. He supposed that nothing ever would be again.

He parked at a crooked angle in the driveway. Hopped out, engine still running, driver's-side door left yawned open wide.

Stabbed, stabbed, stabbed the doorbell. Chased that with several fists banging on the door.

A light winked on in the foyer. The door opened a moment later. No security chain holding it at bay.

"Michael?" she said, surprised.

"Where's Daniel?" he barked.

A frown knitted her brows. "Hello to you, too."

"Hello," he offered. "Now where is he, Soledad?"

"In the back," she said, not daring to challenge his obviously dark mood.

"Outside?"

She nodded. "Tinkering with his new bike. It'll never run again after he finishes working on it. I won't be the least bit displeased, either." She smiled. "I brought it to his easily manipulated attention it was making a terrible noise, suggested he pull out his tools and go fix 'er up. He probably thinks it was his idea."

Michael left Soledad there, moved around the side of the house, gravel crunching under the soles of his shoes.

Harley-Davidson Fat Boy. Black. Twin Cam engine, satin chrome muffler, narrow seat, low suspension. Front shock covers, floorboards. MSRP over sixteen thousand.

More than Michael would've paid for a car if the company hadn't provided him one.

Daniel stared at the bike, puzzled, parts laying on a drop cloth at his feet. He turned at a sound, spotted Michael nearing him, did a double-take.

"Expecting someone else?" Michael asked. "Someone reporting on my movements maybe?"

"What are you talking about? Wasn't expecting anyone," Daniel said, wiping his grease-stained hands on his trousers. Then bending down in a baseball catcher's crouch to examine the underside of the bike.

"I was wondering if you could explain something to me, Danny."

Daniel looked up. He hated "Danny." It had always been a struggle for him to be taken seriously. Danny certainly didn't help matters. Sounded like the name you'd give a boy with a magic carpet and talking animals as best friends.

"We'll see one another at the office tomorrow, Michael. I'll make it a point to chew down some TUMS and swallow some ginger ale and come find you. *Tomorrow*."

"No. This gets settled tonight, Danny Boy."

Daniel looked at him. "Are you purposely taking an adversarial tone with me?"

"I suppose I am," Michael admitted.

Daniel rose from the crouch, his eyes narrowed, wiping his

hands on his pants again, slowly. "You come to cause trouble? In my house?"

"Technically we're outside," Michael said, and looking up to point. "See, that's the sky."

"Soledad let you in?"

"Again, Danny, we're outside."

"It's been a long day," Daniel said. "I don't have the energy to joust."

"I understand. This probably won't take long."

"That was me warning you off before this turns ugly, Michael, not an invitation to keep this shit going."

"Was it? Communication has never been your strong point, Danny. I'm afraid your warning flew right over my head."

"If it wasn't for Rachel, I would've broken you in half a long time ago, Michael. I want you to know that."

"You mean, tried to."

"I'd like you to leave," Daniel said. "There, I said it nicely."

"No," Michael said. "Also said nicely."

"I don't know what my father sees in you."

"Something he doesn't see…elsewhere."

Daniel nodded thoughtfully. "Notice I didn't say what Rachel sees in you? In this family it's all about what my father wants. You have a job and a beautiful wife and no scratches on you…all because that's what my father wants. Don't get too high on yourself, *Mikey*. You can thank my father for all of that. The great job, the lack of scratches"—he smiled—"the beautiful wife."

Michael was wounded by the words. He couldn't show it, though. The weak exploited the weak in others. That made them feel better about themselves. Michael wouldn't allow himself to be Daniel's therapy.

He said, "The Bellatoris…"

Daniel smiled. "Who? That a rock group or something? Learned about them from one of your party girls?"

Michael didn't take the bait. He remained calm, neutral. "I understand you brought them into the company. They're causing me some trouble now. I'd like you to have a word with them. Shorten their leash. I don't want trouble, with you or them. I just want to live."

"Let's suppose I know who you're talking about. Let's suppose I actually have the power to do what you're suggesting." He paused. "I don't like you, Michael. That's no secret. So what if I took them off of their leash completely? What if I did that instead?"

Michael gritted his teeth. "When you threaten another man, all bets are off, Danny. This is my life we're talking about."

Daniel waved him off, bent back into a crouch, his attention back on the bike.

Michael said, "Malcolm—"

"Won't be around to hold your dick forever," Daniel cut in. "I don't care to hear anything about the old man right now."

"I'm sure he'd love to know your true feelings, Danny."

"I'm sure you'll run off and tell him." He held his hands up in front of his face, examined them. "And look at this, my hands aren't shaking."

Michael nodded. "I was hoping we could resolve this. I see that I have to have this conversation with someone that actually *matters*."

"You stir up my father, Michael, and the both of you will be sorry."

Michael arched an eyebrow. "Is that a double threat, Danny Boy?"

But Daniel was back focused on his bike, his forehead lined with frown wrinkles.

Michael left him there.

# CHAPTER

And went home.

Rachel was awake, in the kitchen by the sink, tap water on and running slow into the neck of a tea kettle. Michael stood in the doorway and watched her admiringly. Her pajama pants rode low on her hips, a glimpse of her panties visible above the waist. One strap of her camisole hung off of her shoulder. She turned the faucet off, took the tea kettle from the sink, and set it down on a lit oven burner, blue flame the color of her top licking at the bottom of the tea kettle. Then she turned back.

Her hard nipples made two impressions in her top.

Michael licked his lips.

She looked up then, spotted her husband. He nodded. She nodded in turn, a small smile at the corners of her mouth.

"What do you have there?" she asked, nodding at the book under his arm.

"Nicholas Sparks."

She frowned, quickly eased back into a smile. "A romance novel? Seriously?"

"Yes."

"Hmm."

"This is the part where I take you off to the bedroom."

"What about my tea?"

"It can wait," he said.

She moved to turn off the flame on the oven, but Michael was on her, taking her by the shoulders, turning her to face him, the flame still burning bright under the kettle.

"I need to turn that off," she whispered.

"Let it whistle," he said, smiling. "We'll find out who is louder... you or the kettle."

"Judging by the look in your eyes," she said, smiling, "I might win that one."

He took her hand, led her from the kitchen, toward their bedroom.

He felt an energy he hadn't had in days. Rachel hadn't even been the last woman he'd made love to. But right now, she was the only woman in the world that he wanted to touch in that intimate way.

The bedroom lights were out. A votive candle flickering on their dresser.

"Romantic," he said. "Expecting someone?"

She bit her lip. "A girl can hope."

His hand fell to the small of her back, guiding her toward the bed. They didn't lay down on it, though. Stopped and faced one another. She stood on tiptoes, and found his mouth. Soft lips. Her tongue easing inside his mouth. His tongue responding. A moist dance.

He gripped her head. She tried to ease away. He held the grip firm, and after a moment she eased her arms around his waist. Suddenly she didn't care if her hair was disturbed, didn't care if Michael dominated her. She was content being enslaved to him.

The strap fell further off of her shoulder. He eased the other off as well. Left her shivering in the cold. Nipples like stones.

He bent just enough to trap a breast in his mouth. Karla loved her nipples sucked. Rachel had always been indifferent about it. But today wasn't typical in any way. Today was a day of revelation. Rachel gasped and moaned like a strong wind as his mouth sucked hard on her breast.

A moment later her hand fumbled at his belt. She managed a hand inside his pants. Gripped his thick erection. Stroked the undershaft at the tip, the most sensitive part, with her thumb.

A room filled with moans.

Then they were on the bed together, both of their pants scattered on the carpet.

His erection grinding the front of her panties. Her panties growing wet in the crotch.

"Finger me," she whispered.

He dipped a finger in her warmth, testing it like coffee. Hot but not scalding.

"Two," she said.

"Beg me."

"Two fingers, please."

He gave her three and she fucked them without complaint, moving her hips up and down as his fingers disappeared in the thatch of pubic hair that covered her vagina.

The finger play lasted just a few moments. She wanted, needed, the real thing. He separated her lower lips with his thick erection. Dipped it deep inside her warmth, her legs spreading wide to accommodate it, her ankles crossed at his lower back to keep them clutched together close. She wrestled like that, lovemaking that was centimeters away from being violence.

Later, her legs propped up on his shoulders, the ceiling appearing to rise and fall from her view. Her vagina pulsing like a beating heart muscle. Each twitch tight around his penis like a fist.

She came hard and long. Screaming out in a voice she didn't recognize.

That seemed to inspire him. He pounded her flesh with all of his strength.

Slap, slap, slap.

And then he was coming, too.

A loud roar ripping from his chest.

He fell away, spent.

Both of their chests heaving. Both of their bodies slick with odorous sweat.

"What was that?" she said in a rasp.

"Passion," he told her. "Passion, baby."

It sounded corny but she didn't shoot it down. She reached over and found his hand, grasped it, squeezed.

"The security team at work…" he said, moments later.

She nodded.

"They're bent," he said.

"Bent?"

"Criminal, crooked, destructive."

"I'm not surprised. My father—"

"Daniel's behind them," he cut in.

"My brother Daniel?" she asked, her tone thick with surprise.

"The one and only."

"I don't believe it."

"Trust me."

"Didn't think he was smart enough to be behind anything."

"They need to be reeled in."

She frowned. "Is this relevant to us somehow? Are they causing you trouble of some sort?"

Admit to another the nature of your wrongs.

"Daniel has it in for your father," he said. "I'm concerned about the old man."

Silence was the only sound for awhile.

Then Rachel cleared her throat. "Talk to him. Have a word with my father."

"I definitely will," Michael said.

"Now," she went on, her eyes sparkling. "Let's use your energy for better use."

"Again?"

She bit her lip, nodded.

That surprised him. A day of revelations.

She was already wet. He edged himself inside of her, more than pleased to do so.

# CHAPTER SIX

Malcolm's top-floor office. A slice of the building too elaborate to describe in detail. In most corporate settings it would have been assigned the duties of a conference room.

Malcolm's secretary greeted Michael with a small nod, clicked a few buttons on her phone, spoke softly into the receiver, and a beat later nodded again. He'd gained favor enough to enter. Malcolm was standing in the center of the floor as Michael walked in. The old man's smile was slightly unsettling, and he didn't offer Michael a seat, but Michael wouldn't be deterred. He stood tall.

Malcolm was dressed to his part. Dark blazer made of a silk patterned fabric. Wool pants. A cotton poplin shirt with microchecks. Silk tie. Black calfskin loafers.

Michael said, "Ermenegildo Zegna. Very impressive."

"I'm paying you to be the fashion police?" Malcolm said, smiling.

Fashion police.

As good of a lead-in as any.

Michael cleared his throat. "Speaking of police. I thought I'd have a word with you regarding the Bellatoris."

"Who?" Malcolm's smile widened.

Michael matched the smile. "Same thing Daniel said when I mentioned them. Like father, like son, I suppose."

Malcolm's smile dropped like sand in an hourglass. "If you're here to insult me, dear, I must bid you adieu."

"Not my intention at all."

"I do hope our vibrant conversation from the other evening hasn't caused any animus."

"I'm animus-free, Malcolm."

"Delightful," the old man said, clasping his hands together.

"About the—"

"I'm afraid I let the cat out of the proverbial bag the other night," the old man said, cutting him off. "Your current salary isn't commensurate with my hopes and expectations for you. That's certainly evident to you, and I can't begrudge you the notion. I'd be thinking the same thing. But it would be a severe tactical error on my part to adjust your compensation package at this point. So, unfortunately, I'm afraid my daughter must continue mopping her own floors and folding her own laundry at this point, dear. You do understand my position, I hope."

"Is every conversation with you a company of one, Malcolm? Do you actually ever hear the other person?"

Malcolm smiled. "On those rare occasions when the other person isn't just making so much noise"—he looked off thoughtfully, nodding his head slowly—"Yes, I've been known to be more engaged."

"Well, this," Michael said, "is one of those moments."

Malcolm's eyes found Michael again, that ever present smile still glowing. "Decisions, decisions," he said, sighing dramatically. "Do I hear you out or ask Celia to prepare me a coffee and Danish?"

"Take this seriously, Malcolm."

"Well, your choice of women does show a strong degree of discernment, dear. I've seen photographs. This latest, Karla Savage, is truly a splendid creature. I truly admire discernment in a man. So, go ahead, dear. The floor is all yours." He held out his arms to represent as much. A showman.

"The Bellatoris…" Michael prodded.

Malcolm took that moment to take a seat. Leather throne chair behind a big polished wood desk. "We had some terrible security breaches, dear. Much worse than just downloaded porn. Daniel happened to be around while I vented my frustrations. My son suggested we hire contractors of a sort to handle our issues."

"Brutes," Michael said, falling into the guest chair directly in front of Malcolm's oversized desk.

"Exactly. Which is why I entrusted the task to Daniel."

"You made a mistake. They're dangerous, Malcolm."

"Where is this coming from, Michael? Upset that they've caught you one too many times with your hands in the cookie jar?" Malcolm smiled. "You are quite photogenic, I must admit. I've never photographed well myself. I envy that in you."

"You're comfortable with having a corporate security team out following your employees? Taking pictures of your employees like private investigators in a sleazy detective novel or something?"

"Very," Malcolm said, nodding.

"They're dangerous," Michael repeated.

Malcolm sniffed, waved his hand dismissively. "Brutes, as you said. But competent brutes. The security breaches have ceased. I rather like them. That Doyle is actually intelligent. I suppose he didn't leave all of his brain cells in the wilds of Ia Drang or wherever it is he came from."

"*You* made a tactical error," Michael said. "You should've never brought them aboard."

"I would tend to disagree," Malcolm said. "And since you aren't speaking in specifics, I'll leave my response at that."

"Daniel has it in for you, Malcolm."

"And I for him," the old man said, smiling.

"He's using the Bellatoris for his dirty work," Michael added. "I fear for your safety."

"Brutes. But harmless to me. I rule this kingdom, dear."

"I've seen them at their worst," Michael objected. "They're far from harmless."

"That Liz Sutherland...magnificent creature, is she not? I'm not even sure the Viagra would keep me equitably prepared for a woman of her great talent."

"You're not listening, Malcolm."

"This conversation bores me, dear. But I'm trying to be polite and not yawn. If my chin hits my chest, do close the door softly on your way out."

"What I'm saying is just noise to you?"

"Of the highest order," Malcolm said. "This is horrid rap music, a jackhammer breaking up concrete, a baby's cry."

"You'll regret this blasé approach someday, I'm afraid."

"Not my only regret," the old man said. "I have"—a smile—"a few."

Michael gave up. Rose from his seat and turned to leave. Malcolm's voice pulled him back at the last moment. He turned back to the old man, his hand on the doorknob. "Yes?"

"Perhaps you'd lower your angst if you approached the... Bellatoris? Latin, correct?" He chuckled. "Perhaps you should consult with Ms. Sutherland. I understand she's adept at...comfort play. And we both know how much you appreciate the comforts of a beautiful woman. You can present me with a play-by-play afterward. I'll live vicariously through you."

"She's adept at a great deal, Malcolm."

Malcolm flashed his teeth. "Well, there you go, dear. I look forward to the blow-by-blow account."

Michael didn't ease the door closed. He let it knock shut of its own accord.

Now what?

He was out of ideas.

# CHAPTER
# SEVEN

An old gray Plymouth, cancerous smoke billowing from the exhaust pipe, the body smeared with white-green bird shit and mud, idled at the curb cut in front of Michael's house. It was 7:36 at night, another long day. This one actually longer than most. It seemed to have dripped by like a leaky faucet. And Michael couldn't remember much of what occurred, after he left Malcolm's office. Entire chunks of conversations he'd had were missing from his memory. He'd worked on a proposal but couldn't recall any of its details.

And here was the gray Plymouth.

"Shit," he said, pounding the Chrysler's steering wheel as he pulled into his drive. Shit, shit, shit. He'd completely forgotten what day it was. Hadn't been keeping his eyes on the calendar.

He sighed, cut the engine, grabbed his briefcase and lumbered out of the car, easing the door shut with his hip.

He walked toward the Plymouth instead of the house, looking back over his shoulder in time to see a curtain part and then flutter closed. Rachel. The passenger window of the old Plymouth was rolled down as he reached the car. He bent and rested on the door's sill, peering in through the opening. The man behind the wheel had skin the color of a Snicker bar wrapper. Close-cropped black hair going white. White, not gray. Bushy eyebrows loosely in the shape of boomerangs. He was approaching his sixty-first birthday yet had the body of a forty-year-old gym freak. Hands like cinderblock. A handsome face not the least bit marred by the two knife scars. One that tracked through an eyebrow. The other that kissed his cheek.

"Michael."

Voice as sharp as a broken beer bottle neck.

"Rid."

Eric Ridley. Michael's uncle in every way but blood.

"You forgot?"

"No, no," Michael said.

"Eye contact wavered for a second," Ridley said. "But that's enough. No need to lie to me, boy."

Boy.

Michael wasn't insulted. "You're right, Rid, I forgot."

Ridley shook his head, went back to sucking on an orange half, spitting pulp out of his window a beat later.

"Why are you sitting out here?" Michael said. "Rachel's home."

Ridley pulled a seed from the orange with his teeth, frowned, bit into it, then spit it out as well.

"Rid?"

"A man shouldn't sit around in another man's house with that man's wife if that man isn't home."

"One of your rules?" Michael said, smiling.

"And you know it."

"A little convoluted. But I get the principle. Still, you were welcome to wait inside. Rachel likes you."

"And I like her," Ridley snickered. "Which is why I kept my ass right out here."

"You're like an uncle to her."

"All uncles aren't created the same, boy. Which type? The one that teaches you how to read the stock market? Or the one that gets drunk and pisses on the grill during barbecues?"

"You tell me," Michael said.

Ridley burped, patted his pot stomach, the only sign of aging on his otherwise lean and athletic body. "Done downed a couple beers today. Sorry 'bout that. Now, you were asking me which type uncle I am?"

Michael smiled again.

How many smiles was that for the day? He'd gotten to the point where smiles needed to be counted. Real progress.

"Give me a minute, Rid. I need to run this inside"—Michael lifted his briefcase—"and give Rachel a kiss."

"I'll be out here," Ridley said. "Wishing I was you."

Michael play-frowned. "On second thought, you're right. It's best you don't go inside if I'm not here."

Ridley laughed. A laugh that started strong, like a bear's growl, almost turned into a whooping cough, and then died almost as suddenly as it sparked.

It was one of Michael's greatest pleasures. Ridley's laugh reminded him of so much that was good. Warmed by it, he moved swiftly toward the house. Five minutes later he was back outside, dropping down into the Plymouth's passenger seat. Ridley was still working at the orange half, most of the juice sucked from the meat. He'd stop when he hit rind.

"Some kiss…" he said.

"Yes, it was," Michael said. "Yes, it was."

Ridley pulled away from the curb. "How've things been?"

"With Rachel?"

"Only thing that matters."

"Good."

"Good. That's all?"

"After all we've been through, good is a minor miracle."

Ridley nodded. Driving one-handed, sucking the orange.

"What about you, Rid?"

"Eating a daily aspirin. Pretending my morning Cheerios are steak and eggs. Damn near shitting my pants every time I smell peanuts."

Michael said, "I think the thing about smelling peanuts beforehand is an old wives' tale."

"I don't think so, boy."

"It sounds quite ridiculous to me. An urban legend. Like Walt Disney's remains being frozen and buried under DisneyWorld."

Ridley reflexively touched his chest, right by his heart, with two fingers. "Hope so. But just to be safe rather than sorry, I've cut the sex back to only twice a week."

Michael tried to smile but couldn't. Truth was they were both scared to death of a heart attack. They'd seen the damage up close and personal. Michael's father. Eric's partner on the force.

"What's the cruelest thing you saw out there?" Michael asked. His voice wasn't a whisper exactly, but neither was it strong.

Eric Ridley didn't have to think.

"Twelve-year-old boy," he said. "Got his hand on a gun the way these young boys do. A Glock. Plastic bullshit that just..." He sighed, turned down a dark road. "Shot his cousin in the face, point blank range. Jealousy."

"Sneakers? Videogames?" Michael wondered.

"Butter."

Michael frowned. "You're kidding?"

"They lived in the same project building. The cousin had butter in his refrigerator. He had a loaf of bread in his. Instead of putting their heads together and making themselves some toast, they..." He let his voice trail off.

"Jesus."

"Yes, sir."

Michael settled into silence.

Ridley turned, studied him. "Something on your mind, boy?"

Lukas Doyle tracking him to the beach. Karla rocking that chair in the roach motel.

"No," he said.

Ridley frowned, his eyes going dark as he concentrated on Michael's face.

Michael pretended not to notice.

Thankfully his discomfort didn't last long.

"Here," he said, nodding up ahead.

Ridley turned to look, nodding himself, swallowing as well. "Here."

The grounds were semi-soft. Mostly dirt, sprinkles of grass. The lot before them was recently blacktopped, fresh white lines painted in to indicate parking spaces. Crickets and birds made competing music. They got out of the Plymouth slowly, moved forward with measured steps. Every foot or so they had to weave around a plot. Then they came to two and stopped. Ridley's breath came in slow rasps. So, too, did Michael's.

Francis Lloyd Palmer.

Frank.

Joan Palmer.

Jo-Jo.

Michael's deceased parents.

Frank from a heart attack when Michael was just seven. His recollections of his father were faded images he worked hard at keeping alive.

And, much later, Jo-Jo from breast cancer. Eight years now but there were still nights when Michael cried out for her.

"Sixty-one really isn't that old," Ridley said. "Yet every day I feel as though I'm running from...something."

"Or to," Michael said.

"To?"

"Life," Michael said.

"It isn't promised," Ridley whispered.

"No. It isn't."

"Complicated."

Michael didn't speak, let Ridley continue.

"Your father was tall, wiry. Muscles like gristle. Hard, tough. He ran at least a mile every morning, for *fun*. No vices." Ridley's snicker pierced the night. "Now me on the other hand, a full balanced meal meant an Old Grand Dad, a Newport, and a bloody rib eye, a baked potato loaded with butter and salt and pepper. And your dad's gone and I'm..."

"He was a good man?"

"You know he was."

"Tell me about him."

"What? We've had a million—"

"Humor me, please."

Ridley nodded. "First word comes to mind is tough."

"Didn't let anyone walk over him?"

"Francis Palmer? No, sir. He didn't invite trouble, mind you... but he sure didn't back down from it when it crossed his path."

"Did that happen often?"

"Most folks could see that Frank wasn't one to trifle with," Ridley said. "He didn't tend to have too much resistance in life. But when he did..." Ridley whistled.

Michael indicated the ground with a nod. "Alright. Go ahead, Rid."

Ridley uncapped a plastic twenty-ounce bottle. Ginger ale.

Schweppes. He poured it slowly, splashing the grave marker, wetting the earth at its base. "To your born day," he said, his voice more raspy than usual. "RIP, brother."

Brother.

Said it like he meant it.

Michael knew that he did.

Ridley recapped the bottle, moved over and ran his hand over the smooth edge of Joan's marker. "Your mother wouldn't tolerate any drinking. That wasn't a loss for Frank. He couldn't stomach anything stronger than that damn ginger ale. They were a perfect match."

"Complicated," Michael said.

Ridley looked over his shoulder. "What's that?"

Michael's eyes were on his mother's stone. "How long after my father died before you started sleeping with my mother?"

Ridley stumbled without taking a step. "Something's up with you, Michael."

"You're saying you didn't?"

"I didn't."

Michael smiled. "I love you, Rid. You've kept my father alive for me. I'd die for you."

"I know, boy, and I would—"

"Your eye contact wavered for just a second. But that's enough," Michael said.

It took a moment.

More than a minute, less than five.

Ridley started to tremble.

His eyes watered.

Michael clapped him on the shoulder. "It's fine. I understand. My mother was as fine a woman as my father was a man."

"That's right, Michael. That's right."

"I want to thank you for reminding me of something very crucial."

"What's that?" Ridley asked, his voice full of phlegm.

"Don't let anyone walk over you," Michael said.

# CHAPTER
# EIGHT

Jade Cassini considered herself Asian. A ridiculous notion, considering that her skin was white as china dishware, her eyes as blue as Caribbean water, and her parents were Rita and Corrado and not Deshi and Bao-Yu. But none of that mattered the least bit to Jade. Her skin *was* as white as china. China. And her first name, Jade, well, you'd be hard pressed to scan the Yellow Pages and not find a dozen Asian restaurants with Jade in their name. So, despite the surface problems, Jade rode her Asian affinity like a calm wave.

She'd bought a book of Sudoku puzzles for the down times at work, times when the phones didn't ring, but even in the silence of those moments she couldn't seem to figure out the number puzzles. She'd half completed one in the EASY section and that amounted to her lone attempt. Still, she didn't blame the Japanese for popularizing something so obviously unsolvable. She loved the Japanese, her sisters and brothers in the East.

Jade was just starting her second month at MRF Global, still probationary, and all in all she had no real complaints. Working the phone system was easy enough; most calls were handled by the automated system, and those that weren't usually were simple reroutes. Human Resources? No problem, hold for one moment, please. The "please" was the most difficult part. The company insisted on courtesy, and even though Jade was practically Asian, courtesy wasn't her strongest attribute. Just ask the creep from

Adrenaline last night. He'd thought buying her Grey Goose and Red Bull mixers entitled him to free touches on her ass and boobs. Wrong. She'd punted his balls with a kick that would've made Corrado proud. A smile would've parted Rita's mouth as well. She might've even paused long enough from cooking—always cooking—to offer her only daughter a nod of admiration.

So…thinking about it a bit more, Jade gave herself the benefit of the doubt. Kicking the guy's balls wasn't necessarily discourteous. He had it coming. She was still practically Asian.

She picked up the Sudoku book, encouraged. Flipped through it a few times and then set it down on the desk again. Studied her nails instead. Short, lavender polish, intricate designs. Done at the Korean shop last weekend. Lunch of seolleongtang soup afterward from Myung Ga's.

Jade supported her community.

She was thinking of that when her phone flashed. She patched in right away. "MRF Global. Quality is our finest quality and we aim to make it yours as well." The tag line didn't seem all that original or inventive to her. American companies, sheesh. Honda wouldn't have some lame tag like that. Neither would Mitsubishi or Sanyo. "How may I help you?"

The voice on the other line sounded muffled. A cloth over the receiver? Jade asked the caller—a deep-voiced male with no accent—to repeat what he'd already said.

"There's a problem in your mailroom," he said.

"I'm sorry." Jade touched her headset out of reflex, adjusted it for the same reason. "What kind of problem might that be?"

"Not a very good one to have," the caller said.

"I'm sorry," Jade said again. Courtesy, see. "Who am I speaking with?"

"Don't send down the lackeys to check on this either," the

caller said. "This is an A-team situation. Get Lukas Doyle on it."

The company had two layers of security. Rent-a-Cops in tan uniforms employed to deal with the usual security problems. And Lukas Doyle's team. Jade knew of Doyle by name, reputation, and rumor. To her knowledge, she'd never seen his face. She'd never placed a call to his extension. She'd been told, at her hiring, that if she ever needed to call Doyle's line that meant al-Qaeda was in the building. Jade had laughed and so had the HR woman. They'd joked about how handsome Bin Laden might be with a thorough shave. He was tall and dark after all. Then the laughter had died and the HR woman had gotten like super serious and whispered Lukas Doyle's name. It wasn't to be spoken aloud at whim. And it wasn't to be shared. Even inside of the company his presence was sometimes thought of as an urban legend. "Don't hesitate to call him if there's a real problem," the HR woman had said. "But be very certain it is a problem. We wouldn't want to disturb him for any old thing."

*We wouldn't want to disturb him for any old thing.* Like he was some old geezer in a nursing home and visits after a certain hour threw him completely out of balance.

"Did you say Luke S. Coyle?" Jade asked into her headset.

The caller laughed. "You were trained well. You should make it through probation without a hitch."

Jade heard herself say, "Thank you, sir. Thank you so much."

Polite and grateful, even in a possibly hostile situation. A credit to her distant ancestors.

"No, I said Lukas Doyle," the caller said. "Esteemed ruler of the mighty Bellatoris," he added in a movie preview voice, following that with a deep chuckle.

"Mr. Doyle is only to be contacted in critical moments, sir. What exactly—"

"Would a bomb in the mailroom qualify?"

"Are you saying you have knowledge of a bomb, sir?" Jade's voice didn't tremble.

"Very good knowledge."

"Would you hold, sir, while I try for a contact?"

"No."

And he was gone.

Jade bit her lip, dialed Doyle's extension.

"Yes?" A voice as smooth as expensive whiskey.

Jade identified herself, name and rank.

"What can I do for you, Jade?" Calm, assured. She fed off of his energy.

"I just received an odd call, Mr. Doyle."

"Lukas, please."

"Lukas."

"Odd in what way, Jade?"

"He mentioned your name personally…Lukas. And he claimed there's a bomb in the mailroom."

"I'm going to disconnect now, Jade. Keep your line clear until you hear from me."

"Okay."

Her headset went to static and then silence. She pulled out her makeup compact, flipped it to the mirror side so she could reapply her eyeliner. Narrowed, her eyes looked like almonds.

Jade smiled at her reflection.

Lukas Doyle wasn't afraid of bombs. He'd disarmed plenty. Most were crudely made, easy enough to disable. A few had required extra care. Military tools such as the Stingray, a barb-shaped charge that transformed forty ounces of water into a deadly blade. Once released, the water did two things: First, it sliced through the exterior casing of the bomb. Metal, wood, plastic. It didn't matter. Second, once the blade of water entered the explosive device, it shred wires, detonators, and any other pertinent bomb parts. So no, Lukas Doyle wasn't afraid of bombs. He had too much expertise and technology on his side.

He ordered the Rent-a-Cops to evacuate the building.

And then he made his way down to the mailroom.

He'd ordered lights out and blinds closed in every office but the mailroom. He ambled into the phosphorous glow of the space. Music blared from a stereo near the door. He volumed it down but didn't turn it off. Didn't want to upset the electrical balance in the office in even the most miniscule way. Doyle didn't have any specifics about the bomb. Where it was planted, or anything of that sort. But, again, he had technology on his side. A pocket bomb sensor the size of the first cell phones. Other than that he was naked. Not in the usual sense. He had on clothes. However, in different circumstances he would've worn a demining apron to protect his front, the apron over a blast-resistant suit. Blast-resistant suits were essential. Helmet, collar, blast plates, overshoes and quick-release straps. Made of Kevlar or some other aramid-based product. Aramid was the generic name for Kevlar. The suits made the task of bomb sniffing much more pleasant. Flame-resistant, tightly woven fabric. They afforded the sniffer a certain amount of comfort; a belief that they would survive if the bomb detonated. A boom wasn't the end of their world.

Most would've focused on the lack of those protections. Lukas Doyle wasn't most, though. He weaved through the aisles created by the hulking mail carts, his sensor device extended out in front of him. Searching for the explosive. Naked of any protection.

"Boom!"

Something careened off of Lukas Doyle's forehead. He touched his skin with his three innermost fingers. Dry as a wood chip. He looked down at his feet. A ball of crumpled writing paper lay by his shoe. Several steps beyond him were the sounds of a chair, its joints in desperate need of oil.

Doyle looked up but nodded down. "Rusty joints," he said calmly. "Sounds like the chair from the motel the other day."

Michael frowned, swallowed, and then quickly squared his shoulders. Lukas Doyle chuckled, set the bomb sensor down carefully on a nearby desk. Bent to pick up the crumpled paper, and tossed it back to Michael. "You're committing Class H felonies now, Michael *Allan* Palmer? Bomb hoaxes are quite frowned upon. 9/11 has made everyone jittery."

"You aren't human," Michael managed.

Lukas Doyle nodded. "Unfortunately…for you…you are."

Michael's nostrils flared. His hate was a palpable thing. It filled the room like the smell of leaking gas fumes.

"Please tell me there was a purpose for this little hoax, Michael," Lukas Doyle said, crinkles at the corners of his eyes and mouth. "I bet you stayed up all night thinking about it. Running it through your little head. It probably invaded your dreams. Rachel's probably at home right now, whistling as she tends to your home, because I know you well, Michael, and I'd just imagine your dick was as hard as Chinese arithmetic last night. The thought of throwing me off balance must've sent your blood coursing."

"What you've done…what you're doing to me. You…you.

You're not going to get away with this," Michael said. Each word was a labor. Like swallowing with strep throat.

"I already have gotten away with it, Michael Allan Palmer."

Michael didn't reply.

Couldn't.

What *had* he hoped to gain with this stunt? At this moment, he couldn't even remember himself. Whatever the goal, it hadn't been met. This was as abysmal a failure as any he'd ever had.

A Class H felony failure.

Lukas Doyle read the worry in Michael's eyes. "This pitifully impotent display will remain between us, Michael Allan Palmer. You have my word as a man and a gentleman."

Despite himself, Michael nodded.

Grateful?

Lukas Doyle crossed the floor, shiny hard cement lacquered gray. He stopped in front of the chair where Michael sat. "A tactical error," he said. "One of many you've made today, I'm afraid. Never put yourself at a vantage lower than your opponent. Now, stand up."

"Opponent?"

"You're right," Lukas Doyle said. "We're on the same team. In this together. Stand up."

Michael stood, expecting the worst.

Lukas Doyle placed a hand on Michael's shoulder. Michael flinched at the movement. Doyle smiled, squeezed and patted the shoulder. "Relax. I don't usually bite."

Michael released a deep breath.

"Better?"

"Yes."

"Good. We need you calm, relaxed."

"I am."

"And Michael…?"

"Yes?"

The punch kicked Michael back into the chair. He almost toppled over it. Breathing became something he had to think about, had to focus on, rather than a natural process.

"Don't ever fuck with me again," Lukas Doyle said. "I don't have the patience for foolishness."

And then he left, Michael gasping for a teaspoon of air behind him.

# NINE

M ichael returned to his office and locked his door and closed his blinds and endured the searing pain that sliced through his abdomen. He pulled his wastebasket near his feet, and more than once retched into it. A string of salty saliva hung from his lips. He wiped it away with the back of his hand. His eyes were rimmed with tears. The physical pain was punishing, but his feelings of foolishness and weakness were even worse. He'd strived to shift the balance of power from the Bellatoris to himself and instead managed to come away even less empowered than he'd been before.

It had seemed like a good idea when he conceived it. Kick the hornet's nest and send the Bellatoris scurrying for cover, and in that chaos, take the reigns in this deadly game.

On the paper of his mind, it was written so beautifully there was no doubt it would prevail. He could stop looking over his shoulder. His fear of sleep would ease. He'd drop down into the driver's seat yet again. In control.

But...

Lukas Doyle was more than he anticipated. If the new rumors were that Doyle was a Cyborg, created in some secret Russian lab, frostbite winds howling outside a smudged warehouse-style window, Michael wouldn't scoff at the notion. Lukas Doyle might not be an actual Cyborg, but neither was he human. He was the stuff of science fiction.

Michael was in over his head. These were people capable of murder. Cold-blooded killers unmoved by the sounds of a squeaky chair, rocking frantically, or the Kotex muffled screams of a dying woman.

Michael couldn't take them on singlehandedly. That was for certain. He couldn't take what he knew to the police either, for all of the obvious reasons. And though the bomb threat hadn't worked, he'd had the right idea.

He couldn't stand by and do nothing. He couldn't imagine looking over his shoulder for the rest of his life. No. Something had to be done. But what?

He took a pad, a ballpoint pen. Items for memos. And he started to write, to brainstorm ideas. A word algorithm to solve the greatest problem of his entire life. Two-thirds through the sheet he ripped it from the pad, folded and folded and folded it. Ripped the folded sheet into confetti and let it rain from his fingers into the wastebasket.

Only one thing to do.

Malcolm.

He had to tell the old man everything. Details about the original meeting with Liz Sutherland in the conference room. Waking up in the near dark of the roach motel to find Karla bound and gagged in a chair at the foot of the bed. The Kotex they stuffed into her mouth. Liz's gleaming blade. Karla rocking the chair frantically while Doyle disrespected her and barked orders.

Then.

Karla. Still.

Never to be found again.

Yes. He'd tell Malcolm and the old man would be forced to do something. It would be out of Michael's hands at that point. He'd tossed a softball at Malcolm the other day. Of course the old man would shrug off any notion that the Bellatoris were a threat. But once Michael gave him the full story…

How could Malcolm remain inert?

He couldn't. He didn't get where he was by remaining still. Still. No, that wasn't Malcolm Ferrer.

Michael pushed from his desk. Fast-walked across the carpet, for his door. Unlocked and opened it. Stepped out, only to have a hand press into his chest and push him back on his heels. The door eased shut. The lock reinstated.

Just the two of them.

⊷

"You want to tell me what you're doing?" Michael asked.

"You want to tell me, Michael?" His voice cracked at that moment, nothing masculine about it. He wrung his hands like a wet mop handle. Paced the pile carpet.

Michael said, "Joe, seriously. I have something to attend to."

"You've attended to enough, dude. You need to explain some things to me. And stop *attending*, please. My bowel movements haven't been regular since our first lunch together. And now this thing is touching other people, too."

"What thing? What people?"

"Cassie, dude. Cassie." Joe rushed over to windows that looked out onto the floor, edged the blinds aside an inch, peered out. His shoulders shook like palsy. He breathed deeply through his nose.

"Cassie…" Michael ventured.

Joe bolted around. "She quit, dude. Her office is empty. Too empty. I've called her cell. No answer."

"Quit when?"

"Supposedly yesterday. Just left a signed resignation letter on her supervisor's desk. I heard some word about it this morning. After our little fire drill." He did something near a smile. "So I went to check. Everyone in her department is puzzled. Meredith is shitting bricks. Cassie left a lot of unfinished work on the table. I'm hearing Meredith's more of a terror than usual. If I thought she wouldn't puree my dick in that blender hole of hers, I might swoop in and…"

Michael plopped down in his chair again. Joe did the same, in a seat directly in front of Michael's desk.

"What are the odds someone in *HR* would quit their job and not give proper notice?" Michael wondered aloud.

"Exactly, dude. And we're talking Cassie here. She counts rubbers."

Michael looked up, frowning. "What?"

"Rubbers, dude. She has a drawer full of them at her place. And she keeps track of the running inventory. Says shit like 'fifty-six, that should last me another month or so.' And then she smiles like it's a big fat joke. But it isn't, dude. Cassie likes order. Thrives on it. She's a planner. She wouldn't just up and quit a job. Too rash."

"What's being said?"

Joe's eyes lit up; he stabbed the air with a bony finger pointed at Michael. "That's the thing. There's a rumor that she was involved in something heavy. That she left the way she did to cut her losses because they were on to her."

"Maybe that's so."

"Uh-uh, dude."

"How can you be sure?"

"Those porn downloads you mentioned…"

"Yeah?"

"Cassie's aware of my uh…affinity…for the art. She confronted me after that happened. Wanted to know if it was me. Threatened to tell someone. I had to swear on a stack of Bibles and my grand-mother's grave that it wasn't me."

Michael nearly smiled. "She backed off?"

"Reluctantly. But I had a dream right after. These dudes, must've been twenty of 'em. They were plowing this broad. Giving it to her every which way but loose. Mouth, the usual spot, her shit hole. And then after they'd all milked all over her...she turned around..."

Michael knew where this was going.

"...and it was my grandmother, dude. I brought that bad mojo on her by lying."

"You're sicker than I am, Joe. I probably shouldn't be around you."

"Point is: I had to lie. Cassie's a serious chick, dude. She has *integrity*."

"So what do you think happened?"

Joe looked at Michael, incredulous. "Are you dense, dude? The fucking *Bellatoris*."

Just what Michael had been thinking.

He swallowed, hard.

There were several people in the corridor of Malcolm's floor, mostly low-level staff. A few men with off-the-rack suits, but custom ambitions. One had the basics of possibility, more than six feet in height. That actually mattered. Very few upper manage-ment types were short. An attractive woman in her early thirties walked the hallway with a clipboard pressed to her chest. In addition to her looks and age, she smelled good. All of that mattered the same as height did for men. She had strong possibilities as well.

Michael strutted past them while they drifted by at the edges of the corridor, close to the wall and highly aware of him. He didn't know any of their names, or their faces even, and that saddened him. He had few allies in the company.

Malcolm.

Joe.

That was the extent of it.

He rounded the wall bend, weaved through a mess of cubicles, and came upon the old man's office. Just outside was Malcolm's secretary's desk. Vera wasn't there. The woman in her place clacked at the keys on a laptop. She looked up as Michael slowed. Smiled.

Gray jacket, gray shirt, white blouse, cranberry-colored eyeglasses.

Michael said, "Fancy meeting you here."

"Fancy."

He moved to pass, but Liz stood and blocked the front of Malcolm's door. "Something I can help you with, Michael?"

He shook his head. "Just need a quick word with Malcolm."

"Mr. Ferrer is not taking any appointments at this time."

"I don't have an appointment."

"Of course not," Liz said. "And you couldn't obtain one…at this time."

"You must not have gotten the memo. Malcolm's my father-in-law."

"Which is why you get those great meals the last Thursday of every month." She smiled. "But today's not Thursday."

Michael inched forward. "Step aside, please."

"We both know I won't be doing that," she said, her hand slipping into her pocket. "And you'd be advised to take a step back."

Michael looked down at Liz's pocket, thought of Karla, her

throat slashed. "I can pull out my cell phone and call Malcolm," he said. "Let him know I'm out here."

Liz Sutherland's smile widened. "I'm pretty certain you couldn't."

"Oh no…?" Michael pulled it out as promised, and dialed. An automated voice informed him that all circuits were busy. He dialed a second time. Got the same result.

He dropped the cell phone back in his pocket.

"Don't tell me," Liz said. "A problem with the line?"

Michael said, "Cassie Hart."

"Cassie Hart? Can't say I know the name. It does sound familiar, though. Actress? Singer? I'm really not up on pop culture."

"Cut the bullshit, Liz. I believe you and your gang have done something to her."

"How did you develop such a negative impression of me, Michael?"

Her hand had slipped out of the pocket. He glanced at it. Empty. No stiletto. He made some mental calculations. He was taller than Liz, undoubtedly stronger. It was lunch hour, so virtually all of the cubicles at his back were unoccupied. No witnesses then.

"Thinking about rushing me, Michael?"

He didn't respond.

"You might want to look over your shoulder before you do," she said.

Reflexively he did.

Namako, the D.C. Sniper, was fast-stepping this way. A scowl etched into his face. A posture that spoke of bad intentions and endless pain.

Michael said, "You won't get away with this."

"Experience says we will."

Experience. Her word choice wasn't lost on him. The Bellatoris had done this kind of thing before. Michael hadn't. The realization made his shoulders slump, but to his credit, he immediately straightened his posture.

Namako had reached him, the heat from the big man's skin warming Michael's back like a lamp.

Liz's face softened. "I have a feeling your cellular service will be operational later this evening. You can call Malcolm after seven and speak about whatever your little heart desires."

The defeat wounded him, but Michael had no choice but acknowledge it. He turned, slowly, brushed past Namako. That was the closest contact they'd ever had. Namako smelled of soap and sour milk. Sweat coated his forehead. His eyes, dead.

Michael couldn't beat them. They were always two steps ahead. They also had the obvious advantage in numbers and experience with this sort of thing.

He left Liz and Namako there, content with the fate of the moment. But tonight, come seven, he'd call Malcolm and speak his peace.

Six calls.

All straight to voicemail.

Anxious, a little before nine o'clock that evening, he warmed up the Chrysler and drove by Malcolm's house.

All there was quiet. No lights burned from any window. The doorbell went unanswered.

Tomorrow he'd reach the old man, by hook or crook. For now the Bellatoris had another victory.

# CHAPTER
# TEN

t was a scene from a horror movie. Rain pattering the roof as skinny tree branches pawed at the windows. The sky dominating the background a black curtain, void of stars. The air colored by a stench that smelled curiously like scorched electrical wire. And down in the house itself, a haphazard old basement that resembled a makeshift Radio Shack. Gadgets and such, many in unworkable condition, scattered all about. A satellite dish propped against the brick wall in one cobwebbed corner, several AM/FM radios, a camcorder mounted on a tripod, a DVD player, compact discs strewn about in jewel cases, a cordless telephone base, and a Wii game system, its green POWER light burning bright as a bulb.

A mouse skittered about frantically inside the walls, imprisoned between two support beams. Music blared from some unknown place in the dusty basement. Jay-Z's "99 Problems." Mindy McCready's "Guys Do It All The Time." Competing sounds of hip-hop and country and western.

At the rear of the basement a *thwack thwack thwack*. Thwack thwack thwack. A tennis ball punching holes in the brick wall, spitting up red dust on contact. Lukas Doyle, covered in sweat, a racket in his hands. Doyle stopped abruptly, wiped at his forehead using the wristband on his wrist, and let the yellow tennis ball bounce to a stop at his feet.

"Shrouded forms that start and sigh as they pass the wanderer by," he exclaimed in a booming voice with echoed off of the brick walls. Edgar Allan Poe. *Dreamland.*

Then laughter.

Lots of slow, calm, maniacal laughter.

And the scene fading like a drawing on an Etch-A-Sketch.

Michael had two more dreams. Driving in an ice storm, sharp blades of ice making spider webs in the Chrysler's windshield, the glass leaking blood from the cracks in its surface. And the second, making feverish love to a woman with no eyes, nose, or mouth.

The sound started low, like the echo of a moan, and then it became something bigger. Later, Michael would recall that it broke for a time, and then started up again. On the edge of sleep, he heard his wife's voice, moments after she'd shifted positions in the bed beside him. The comforter pushed off of her, Rachel sitting up in the bed now, wiping at her eyes, coming awake herself, her back against the headboard. That's how Michael envisioned it in his half-sleep. His mind busy playing its little tricks while his body fought for more rest. His mind toeing between a return to the naked woman with no features or a full wake.

Full wake won out, as Michael's eyes opened. He blinked, tried to adjust to the darkness.

Beside him, Rachel was on the phone. She shifted when she

noticed Michael awake and the sleep left her voice. It went from raspy to its natural form. She moved from stutters of "okay" and "uh-huh" and "okay" again to asking questions. Full sentences.

"What are they saying?" she spoke into the receiver.

Michael heard the tinny reply from the phone receiver but couldn't make out the words. He stretched his tired muscles. He glanced at the digital clock on their nightstand. Glowing numbers. 3:26. A.M. The backyard beyond the bedroom window as black as tar.

"Should I come down there?" Rachel asked.

Another tinny reply.

"Okay," she said, sighing, "just give me a little bit of time to wash my face, get my bearings."

Tinny reply.

"I'll throw on something," she said, impatient, edgy. "I'm coming. I'm coming."

She placed the phone on its cradle, not quite carefully. Rubbed her eyes with her hands, inhaled, then exhaled. Phlegm rattled in her nose. Sinuses always an issue for her.

"What's happened?" Michael asked.

Rachel looked over at him. "I didn't mean to wake you. I'm sorry."

"What's happened, Rachel?"

She sighed once more, hard. Pursed her lips and shook her head for a time. Then she steeled her shoulders and smiled. The smile didn't have the warmth of her normal smile. "Feel like getting dressed and taking a ride with me? I hate driving in the dark."

Michael tried a different tact. "Sure. Where are we going?"

"Hospital," she said. "My father seems to have had himself a stroke."

"What?"

She stood without a further word, stretched, walked slowly across the bedroom, disappearing into the light of the bathroom. The door eased shut and a beat later there was the sound of running water.

Stroke.

The old man.

Michael took a deep breath. "Jesus."

Daniel and Soledad were already at the hospital. In a small waiting room with couches and a limited vending machine. No one else in the room. Soledad was sobbing softly. Daniel was calm but disheveled—wrinkled clothes, red eyes, hair askew. He looked up as Michael and Rachel entered the room. He didn't speak. Soledad stood instantly, rushed over and hugged the both of them at once. Her tears were warm on Michael's shirt.

"Can we see him?" Michael asked.

Soledad shook her head. "We're waiting on the doctor. I know one of the nurses, I asked her for real details. She said…"

"Yes?"

Soledad shook her head, started sobbing once more.

Michael left the women there, moved over by Daniel. He put a hand on Daniel's shoulder. Daniel started to quiver, but held his jaw tight. Michael moved his hand away after a time and just stood there by his brother-in-law, completely unsure of what to say or do. They'd never been close, and, even after this, probably wouldn't be. A tough call on how to handle the present situation if there ever was one. So awkward silence filled in.

The awkwardness of the moment didn't last for more than a few minutes, thankfully. The doctor entered the room. Indian, female, her name littered with a string of A's and Y's. Skin the color of salted cashews. Black hair tracked with strands of a brilliant gray. Something attractive about her even though she was far from beautiful.

Daniel stood to his feet, shoulder-to-shoulder with Michael. "Is he..."

"We're trying to understand the damage," the doctor said.

"The damage?" Daniel managed. "Will it be much?"

Doctor AY smiled carefully. "Let's hope not."

Daniel sighed, plopped back down on his chair.

"We discovered Norketamine in his urine," Doctor AY went on.

"Which is?" Daniel asked, looking up from his seat.

"A pharmacologically active metabolite that confirms the presence of Ketamine."

"Ketamine?" Soledad wondered.

Doctor AY nodded. "Used primarily as anesthesia for animals. Less commonly for humans."

"So why is this...Ketamine. Why is it in Malcolm's urine?" Soledad again.

Doctor AY sighed. "It can be used—abused rather—as a recreational drug. It has dissociative, hallucinogenic properties."

"Are you suggesting my father's a druggie?" Daniel barked.

Doctor AY smiled. A disarming smile. "Point five to five milligrams per liter of blood is indicative of anesthesia levels. It would take one to two milligrams to impair a person's driving. An acute fatal overdose would be at the upper limits, likely six to twenty."

"My father...?"

"Sixteen," Doctor AY said.

The air left the room.

"The most common method is insufflation."

"English," Daniel ordered.

"Inhaled," the doctor explained. "But your father's nasal passages are undisturbed."

"Which means?"

"I understand your father smokes tobacco…in a pipe."

"He does."

Doctor AY nodded, pursed her lips.

Soledad said, "That's significant? The pipe?"

"It is," Doctor AY said. "I believe Mr. Ferrer has been the victim of malicious targeting."

"You mean…" Soledad let her words trail.

"Yes. Mr. Ferrer has an enemy. And it's someone close to him."

Michael moved from Daniel's side, went over and leaned against the vending machine. Soledad took up the void beside her husband, placed an arm around Daniel's neck. Daniel bowed forward, buried his face in his hands. Rachel hadn't yet spoken and didn't look as if any words were imminent.

Soledad looked down at her husband, said, "You need to make some calls, honey. Make sure things are in order."

Michael muttered, "I can guess who the first call will be to. Let them know mission accomplished."

Daniel looked up, his eyes narrowed in anger. "You have something to say, Michael?"

"I said it."

"Sounded like an accusation of some sort."

"Lukas Doyle," Michael said.

"What about him?" Daniel asked, frowning.

Michael waved him off. Rachel sat down on one of the couches, detached. Doctor AY cleared her throat.

"So what next?" Michael asked the doctor.

"Mister Take Charge," Daniel sneered.

Michael turned back to him. "Somebody competent has to."

"Now is not the time, Michael."

"Too upset about your father?"

"What do you think?"

"I think if you are, it's because Malcolm wasn't finished off in one shot."

Daniel shook in anger. "Let that be the last thing you say to me, Michael."

Soledad rubbed Daniel's head. After a few rubs he jerked away.

Doctor AY cleared her throat once more. "We're doing our best to stabilize Mr. Ferrer. The next twelve hours or so are critical. We'll know more by—"

Michael whipped around, his brow furrowed, took a hard step toward Daniel. "What did you say?" he screamed, spit flying.

Daniel frowned. "I didn't say anything. You're hearing things."

Michael had heard Daniel. He was certain. Sounded as though Daniel had said Karla's name under his breath.

The anger rose up in him before he was able to understand it. Therefore he had zero chance of harnessing it. He'd crossed the floor in the small waiting room before an eye blink.

His first punch landed square on Daniel's jaw. His second grazed Daniel's temple. Doctor AY gasped, bolted from the room and out into the hallway to yell for assistance.

Third punch to the top of Daniel's head. That was the one that would swell Michael's knuckles. Daniel fell off of the plastic chair, a heap on the cold floor. Soledad standing by, helpless.

The fourth blow wasn't a punch. A hard kick to his downed brother-in-law's ribs.

The guards, two of them, had Michael by the arms before he

could inflict more damage. Breathing heavy, Michael looked around. Soledad with a horrified expression on her gorgeous face. Daniel, on the floor, breathing heavy himself, looking up, eyes wide. Doctor AY studying Michael as if he were an entry in *Gray's Anatomy of the Human Body*. And Rachel. Gone was the impassive mask from earlier. Her mouth hung open a slight crack. Her eyes were painted in disappointment. Her gaze stripped Michael of all his clothes.

He said, "Rachel…"

She looked away, shaking her head.

Doctor AY said, "This is an incredibly stressful experience, I know." She paused long enough to clear her throat yet again. Long enough to gain Michael's full attention. "Tense. But it's also important that the hospital remains a…place of comfort, safety."

Michael swallowed. Both of his elbows remained in the strong grips of the security guards. "I'm unsafe?" he asked.

Doctor AY smiled with her cheeks and eyes, no teeth. Michael surveyed the room again. Judging by all the assembled faces, not one soul had any charitable feeling for him.

Soledad was probably the closest. The horrified expression melted into one of morbid fascination. She might've been watching a four-car pileup on the interstate.

"See that Rachel gets home," Michael said to her.

Soledad nodded.

"Well, gentlemen," he said, turning his attention from one guard to the other. "I'm ready to be escorted on my way so that you can return to continue keeping the hospital a place of comfort…and safety." A sad smile accompanied his words.

The guards wordlessly ushered him out.

At least, he reasoned, they weren't the Bellatoris.

That would've been infinitely worse.

# CHAPTER
# ELEVEN

The cold air outside slapped his face. At the same moment an understanding set in. Michael sighed in realization. He'd messed up. Big time. Story of his life. What must Rachel and the others be thinking about him now? He couldn't bear to speculate. Instead, he squinted his eyes against the cold, biting wind swirling and looked hard in the direction of the hospital building. It was a well-lit structure, its ubiquitous glass windows seeming to gleam like the surface of an expensive diamond. Lively looking despite the despair and illness that was housed inside its walls. Michael sighed, flexed the fingers of his right hand. Already the fingers throbbed.

No use dwelling on that, though.

He changed focus, fished in his pants pocket, came out with his BlackBerry. He tumbled it end over end in his hurting hand. Call her? Ask her to come outside and talk? He stilled the phone so the screen was upright in his hand. Stared at it. Impotent. Unable to move. But that was an exercise he couldn't engage himself in. He had to do something. Inaction was death. Literally. The best he could come up with, though, was a deep frown and a head shake, those gestures followed up by him easing the cell phone back in his pants pocket.

There was no point in continuing to look at the building, so he ignored it completely as he used his key fob to unlock the Chrysler.

He fell in behind the wheel and got it started immediately, turned the heat on to full blast, pulled from his spot and out onto the road without adjusting his rearview mirror. Without looking back.

No point in looking back.

A moment later, Howlin' Wolf's rough voice broke through the quiet in Michael's spirit. "Moanin' at Midnight," and, right after that song, "Killing Floor."

He replayed "Killing Floor" twice more on the way home.

It wasn't quite four-thirty in the morning by the time he made it home. The sun was contemplating its rise. But the house before him was dark, lonely. The opposite of how the hospital had appeared. The windows here smudged, and holding no noticeable gleam. Howlin' Wolf his only company.

The tears came sudden. For Malcolm, and for himself. He lived with the emotion for a moment, then snickered in embarrassment and gathered himself and moved for the house. Walking quickly through the sheet of cold. Inside the house, he avoided the bedroom and stopped in the kitchen instead. Searched around until he found a metal bowl in a cabinet above the sink, a dried leaf corner of Romaine lettuce stuck to the inside curve of the bowl. Inadequate dishwasher. Not the only inadequate thing in Michael's life. If he were standing in front of a mirror he could see in his reflection the definition of inadequacy.

*Don't do this to yourself*, he thought.

He removed the dried lettuce with a fingernail, flicked it in the sink, trudged to the refrigerator, and pulled out an ice tray. Twisted the tray until cubes of ice rained into the metal bowl. He took a deep breath and submerged his badly swollen hand in the ice.

The kitchen wasn't oppressive, so he left and found a seat in the den. Left the lights off and plopped down in the seat, his hand buried to the wrist in the metal bowl.

He fell asleep before the thoughts could come.

When he awakened hours later, morning sunlight painted the den. The ice cubes had melted into water, and the metal bowl had somehow been turned over during his nap. The front of his shirt and pants was close to soaked. He picked at his shirt and patted at his pants, frowning in disgust. No point in getting upset, he told himself. An easy enough fix. A change of clothes and he'd be back to normal. He reached inside his pants pocket and pulled out his BlackBerry. No missed calls. Disappointment sat like a stone in his stomach. He shook it off, made it to his feet on the first attempt and toured the house, flipping on lights in every room. Empty throughout. Not one room occupied. There was only one thing he could think to do. He took a deep breath and readied himself for work.

He drove to work in complete silence.
No Howlin' Wolf.

Was he up to working? The thought didn't come until he'd actually arrived at work, as he sat in the idling Chrysler looking at nothing. He was in the process of willing himself through a drive back home when a jarring sound came from his right. Clunk, clunk, clunk. He turned to see Joe Larkin, frantically worrying the Chrysler's door handle. Michael wiped at his eyes and disengaged the locks. Larkin fell inside and slammed the door behind him. Breathing like he'd run a sprint. He closed his own eyes and slammed his head against the seat rest over and over again. Having some kind of breakdown?

"What's going on?" Michael said, in a measured, calm tone.

Joe's eyes remained closed.

"Joe?" Michael touched his shoulder. Joe flinched in surprise. "What's going on, Joe?"

"This is so heavy, dude. God, God, God."

Michael squeezed the shoulder. "Tell me."

"Drive, dude."

"What?"

"Drive, dude. Away from here. Let's get out of here. Go, dude. Go."

"Joe—"

"Go," the mailroom clerk barked.

"What do you have there?" Michael asked, nodding at the manila envelope in Joe's white-knuckled grip. His tone was calm, relaxed. A much needed approach considering how wired Joe Larkin appeared to be.

"Dude, go," Joe shouted.

Michael nodded and eased from his parking spot, nosed his way from the garage, out into the flow of traffic. "Now," he said, "talk to me, Joe. What's troubling you?"

"What are you doing, man?" Joe asked.

"Driving apparently."

"That's not what I mean."

"I don't know *what* you mean," Michael said. "You aren't being very clear."

"The Bellatoris! The Bellatoris!" Joe yelled, waving the manila envelope.

"Joe—"

"I don't want to hear it, dude. This whole business is a big ball of dog poo."

"Dog poo?" Michael didn't think he was capable of amusement. Leave it to Joe Larkin to dispel that belief.

"You laugh. Always. Shit is so funny with you, dude." He pitched the envelope at the dash, double-punched the air.

"Joe…"

"Cassie tried to help you and…"

"Joe?"

"…disappears for her trouble."

"Joe?"

"The big boss is crazy if he gives you the keys, dude. I'm sorry."

"That probably won't happen," Michael said. "The big boss is in the hospital."

"What?" Joe calmed, looked at Michael.

"Stroke," Michael explained. "It looks like tampering of some sort. They found a…a drug in his system that—"

"Ketamine," Joe whispered.

Michael slowed the car but didn't come to a complete stop. A car behind him honked and blasted around him. A frown etched his eyebrows. "How do you know that?"

"This is bad, dude. This is so bad."

"How did you know about the Ketamine?" Michael repeated.

"God…this is…dude, let me out." Joe reached for the inside handle, jiggled it. Michael hit the child safety switch.

"How did you know about the Ketamine?" he asked Joe.

Joe sighed, and released the door handle. "Dorothy LeMay."

"Who?"

"*Memphis Cathouse Blues, Taboo II, Night Dreams…*"

"What?"

"...*Bad Company, Garage Girls.*"

"You have to help me out here, Joe. I don't know what you're talking about."

"Dorothy LeMay, dude. Porn actress from the 70s, 80s."

"Okay..."

"Cassie knows how much I appreciate the history of the art."

"Right."

"We got a letter in the mailroom. It just sat there because we couldn't figure out who to deliver it to. Chick's name wasn't in the corporate directory. No one knew who she was. It took me awhile to put it together." He paused. "Dorothy LeMay," he said, picking the envelope from the floorboard. "Don't you get it? This letter's from Cassie."

Michael's heart started to pound. "A secret message, you're saying?"

"Yes, dude."

"And Cassie mentioned something about Ketamine in the letter?"

"Yes, yes. I didn't get it. The letter wasn't making much sense. It started out as a confession. It turns out she's been doing the horizontal tango with 'Roid Rage from the Bellatoris."

"Merriman?" Michael couldn't hide his surprise.

"Yeah, dude."

"Go on."

"Dude's balls are like marbles, she says."

"I don't care about Merriman's testicles, Joe."

"As if I do?"

"Go on, please."

"Anyway," Joe continued, "she confesses to that. Then she warns me about how dangerous they are. 'Roid Rage is talking a lot of jazz to her about some brilliant plan."

"Plan?" Michael said.

"Yeah. And she says if anything happens to her, I should warn you."

"Wait a minute." Michael pulled to a sudden stop. Then eased to the side of the road. More cars honked as they swerved around him. "If anything happened to her? She goes from confessing a relationship with Merriman to worrying about her own safety?"

Joe nodded. "Three-page letter, dude. First page was black ink. Next two were blue. I think she wrote 'em at different times. By page two she was sounding paranoid."

Michael nodded. "Warning me…"

"That you're part of the plan. They're gunning for you, dude."

Michael licked his lips. "Okay."

"You're taking this pretty light, dude."

"Thinking," Michael said.

"*Thinking*?" Joe said, with a rise in his voice. "I *think* you're forgetting something?"

"What?"

"The Ketamine, dude."

Oh, that.

"What about it, Joe? What did Cassie say?"

"That's what messed up the big boss?"

"Yes."

"Cassie said that was part of the plan but she wasn't sure how."

"Okay."

"You're still not getting it, dude."

"Help me out, Joe. What am I not getting?"

"The warning. Cassie said they'd pin the Ketamine on you. Something about invoices with your signature. A trail with Accounts Payable. I didn't know what that meant."

Michael didn't hear another word.

Pinning the Ketamine on him.

Shit.

He glanced at Joe, tired, disturbed, resigned to his fate, sure for the first time of what had to be done, what steps to take. He said, "I have to get something from your car."

# BOOK THREE

LUST

SLOTH

PRIDE

GREED

ENVY

GLUTTONY

WRATH

# CHAPTER ONE

The house was a modest wood-frame with faded yellow siding. The metal fence that bordered the property was painted in a black powder-coated finish the manufacturer claimed resisted chipping and fading. Pure propaganda on both fronts. At the street side of the property was a stamp of dry lawn hardened by the cold. And beyond that, on the house itself, two mismatched window treatments. One with a dirty shade pulled down. The other with blinds snapped closed. Three dented garbage cans set by the concrete steps that led up to the front door. Last year's Christmas wreath still nailed to that door.

An old Plymouth in the driveway.

Michael climbed the steps, opened the screen, rapped hard on the wood door.

Morning birds propped themselves on the branches of bare trees and sang in a chorus. Other than that, pure silence carried on the slight breeze. The street was only a few hundred paces long. Three other houses on top of one another. One the victim of a relatively recent fire. All of the houses dark inside. All with empty driveways. Empty curb the length of the block other than Michael's Chrysler and an orange Dumpster used to remove debris from the burned house.

The door Michael knocked on opened a crack. No security chain held in place. One dark eye peering up at Michael from the cover of darkness.

Michael said, "I'm sorry. Is Ridley in? I'm—"

"I know who you are," the dark-eyed person said. A woman. She opened the door all the way, flicked on a switch in the hallway. The lights flickered and then went nearly bright. The woman's hair was the color of rum, her skin the color of condensed milk. Her eyes dark, of course. Heart-shaped lips. Small in stature but thick in the breasts and hips and thighs. Probably in her fifties but she could easily lie a decade or more off of her age.

She was wearing a man's dress shirt and no pants. The shirt reached down to just above her knees. Nice, toned legs. She wasn't wearing sunglasses but she wanted to be.

"You're Michael," she said.

He nodded, smiled. Didn't speak any words out of awkwardness. Who was she?

"Wondering who in the hell I am?" she said, crinkles at the corner of her eyes.

Michael nearly winced. "Am I that obvious?"

"Not at all, honey,"—she shook her head, smiled—"yeah, pretty obvious."

"You and Ridley must get along just fine," Michael said. "He can read people pretty well, too."

Her smile held. "We have our moments, Ridley and I. Sometimes it gets wild. I'm Jacqueline, by the way."

"Pleased to meet you, Jacqueline," Michael said.

"Likewise," she said, and started walking.

Michael closed the door behind him, locked up, and followed Jacqueline through the small kitchen into an equally small living room. An entertainment center for Ridley's television and a tattered couch were the only furniture.

"*Price Is Right*'s on," she said, plopping down on the couch, remote control in hand. "I might like to catch it. Ridley's in the bedroom. You can go right on in."

Michael nodded and turned to leave. The bedroom was right off of the living room. Several pictures hung on the wall outside of it. Snapshots of Michael from adolescence to adulthood. A picture of Michael's father in uniform, shoulder to shoulder with Ridley. A picture of Michael's mother and father, taken at a picnic of some sort. Michael's parents smiling bright for the camera. Michael paused on that one, swallowed.

"He sure enough sticks to type, doesn't he?" Jacqueline called from the couch.

Michael eyed his mother in the photograph. Light skin, hair the color of rum. Heart-shaped lips.

"I suppose he does," Michael admitted.

Jacqueline snickered.

Michael eased the bedroom door open, stepped inside, closed it tight behind him. Flicked on the lights.

Ridley lay sprawled on the mattress, forearm covering his eyes. Pajama bottoms, naked from the waist up. Soft in the middle, a forest of gray hairs on a muscle-hard chest. Breathing somewhere between easy and labored. That is, in the split second before the light surprised him. He shot up then, startled. Breathing heavy. Definitely heavy.

"It's me," Michael said. "Sorry."

Ridley touched two fingers to his chest, probed the area, all the while nodding. It took a moment but the rise and fall of his chest calmed. His shoulders relaxed. So did his face.

"Sorry to disturb you," Michael said.

"You'd've come in fifteen minutes ago you would've disturbed me," Ridley said.

The room smelled heavily of sex.

"Took your aspirin?" Michael asked.

"I did."

"You look spent."

"I am," Ridley said. "Reason I limit this to once a week."

"Jacqueline doesn't look like the type to be satisfied with that for too long."

Ridley smiled. "Okay, you got me. Twice."

Michael arched an eyebrow.

"Thrice. I swear 'fore God on that. With a day in between for recovery, like lifting weights and whatnot."

Michael nodded. Sat down heavily on the corner of Ridley's bed. Ridley scooted up on the mattress, touched at his chest again, by the heart, with the same two fingers, a frown on his face.

"You'll live into your nineties if I know anything," Michael said.

Ridley didn't speak.

"When did you have it?" Michael asked.

"What's that?"

"Your heart attack."

"Boy, I ain't never—" Ridley noticed the look on Michael's face, probably, stopped cold and sighed. "How'd you find out?"

Michael shook his head, and then shrugged his shoulders. "My awareness is sharpening, I would suppose. It just dawned on me right now, actually. I've noticed little things that went beyond you just having concerns because of my father's heart attack."

"I've slowed."

Michael nodded. "Some. When did it happen?"

"Three years now," Ridley whispered.

"Why didn't you tell me? I should've been there to help you through it."

"You were still dealing with your mother's… And things weren't too great with you and Rachel then, either."

"Doesn't matter," Michael said. "Don't ever go through something like that alone, Rid. You hear?"

"Yes, sir," Ridley said, nodding slowly. "Yes, sir."

"There any worries about...another one?"

"Worries? There's always worries. But I take better care of myself now than I ever did before. It was a wakeup call."

Michael nodded, retreated into silence.

Ridley gave it a moment. Then: "Tell me, boy."

Michael looked at him. "I'm in trouble, Rid."

"I see that. Rachel?"

"No, no. Not that." He sniffed out a near laugh. "Well, actually, probably a bit of that, too. But my trouble is bigger than that even."

Ridley frowned.

Michael formed a brave smile. "Was reading this article in *Wired* magazine, about a guy trying to get away. It's hard because everything is electronic nowadays. We leave footprints everywhere. I envied the guy. Think maybe that would be the move for me."

"This trouble got you thinking about running away?"

"Yes," Michael admitted.

Through an ever deepening frown, Ridley said, "Tell me."

Michael cleared his throat. "I believe I've mentioned the security team at work. Everyone calls them the Bellatoris..."

"This Cassie girl just sounds like a flake that got burned out," Ridley was saying a moment after Michael had told most of the details. "She'll turn up."

"What about her claims that they're out to get me?"

Ridley shook his head. "I don't see it. You're valuable to that company."

"Malcolm's stroke is no accident. I heard what the doctor said."

Ridley played at the gray hairs on his face. "That *is* troubling. But..."

"But?"

"Those rich folks are some deeply troubled people, boy. It ain't beyond the realm of possibility the old man was putting a lil' something sweeter than tobacco in his pipe. Rachel's the only sane one of the bunch. And they've done their best to even make that not so. The way she's been treated."

"I'm worried."

"Keep your eyes open, is all." Ridley paused, chuckled. "You're getting pretty good at seeing the unsaid."

"They're dangerous, Rid." Same words he'd used to forewarn Malcolm.

"You talk about 'em like this is some back alley bullshit. I can't see them shooting up the corporate offices. Cordite rising above the cubicles and whatnot."

And just as he'd done with Malcolm, Michael elected to keep a crucial factor of the equation to himself. He'd personally witnessed the Bellatoris' brutality. He'd seen them kill without provocation and without any seeming guilt. Cold-blooded killers they were.

"They're dangerous," he weakly repeated.

"So is crossing a busy street, but usually we make it across."

Michael's shoulders went slack.

Ridley sighed. "I know some of the newer blood on the force. You want me to see if I can find out anything? If the hospital suspects some kind of foul play, the law is bound to get itself involved. I can see what's happening with it. That'd ease your mind?"

Michael thought about it. Nodded. "What do I do in the meantime?"

Ridley smiled. "Now that's an easy one, boy. Go get in at least one of *your three* with Rachel."

# CHAPTER
# TWO

Michael moved from Ridley's house moments later, calmed by their exchange. Rid was likely correct in his belief that Michael was a bit paranoid. After all, Michael had been in the motel room with the Bellatoris. He'd witnessed them at their absolute worst. Why would they intentionally antagonize someone with that knowledge of their behavior?

They wouldn't.

The pressure they'd been applying was understandable when Michael really thought it through. They needed to keep him in line. They needed to make sure he didn't crack. They needed to keep his mind off of roach motels and creaky chairs and serrated knives and blue mailboxes. Why would they set him up when he could turn around and point a finger of his own?

They wouldn't.

The streets that led from Ridley's quiet little neighborhood fed into a highway route littered with commercial businesses and state troopers hidden in the brush with their speed radars cocked. Speed traps. Michael slowed the Chrysler as he eased onto the highway, powered up his CD disk changer and listened to the Beatles and Howlin' Wolf and Coltrane.

Calm.

He pulled off of the speed trap route fifteen minutes later, winded through another quiet residential area. A two-lane. One lane for each direction. The back way he often took home from Ridley's. He slowed again. Relaxed and at-ease. Glancing at the homes at the side of the road as he passed them. Making mental notes of the different styles of architecture he had fondness for. Then quickly erasing those mental notes. The house hunt would be Rachel's department. No use in fooling himself. He'd be lucky if she allowed him input on what decorations to hang on Halloween and Christmas.

He smiled at the thought.

The vehicle pulled from a side street, nearly colliding with the front end of Michael's Chrysler. A bulky black SUV. A Yukon, Michael believed. Michael mashed down hard on his brakes, turned the Chrysler's nose toward someone's lawn. The black SUV that had caused the near accident stopped dead ahead in the roadway, straight across so it blocked the entire lane. Michael looked over there, a frown of disgust masking his face.

The frown remained as the other driver opened his door. The frown deepened as Michael took in the form emerging from the vehicle. Thick neck. Big hands. Powerful build from head to toe. Biceps like grapefruit. Michael swallowed as the driver smiled.

Merriman.

The steroid freak in the Bellatoris.

Michael struggled to shift the Chrysler in reverse. His hands trembled like a washing machine. His heart hammering his chest as the Chrysler's tires fought for purchase with the roadbed. His heart continuing to hammer as he finally righted the Chrysler, and, its tires squealing, sped a wide circle around Merriman's black SUV.

Heart hammering away as he glanced at his rearview mirror and saw Merriman back behind the wheel of the Yukon, giving chase.

∽∾

Michael was familiar with the roads but the anxiety of the moment erased the physical map from his memory. He struggled to work his way through the fog, eyes narrowed, teeth gritted. A fork at the end of this road, left prong leading to roads he'd never traveled. Right prong leading to… Think, think. A small bridge, he believed. Then a right turn to more roads he'd never traveled. Or a left into a maze of winding roads he'd traveled often.

The Chrysler's tires ca-clunked as they hit the start of the bridge. He crossed it at a dangerous speed. Made the left into the maze of roads just as the Yukon reached the mouth of the bridge.

There were signs that warned of deer. Signs that warned of concealed driveways. Yellow in both cases. The color of hazard.

Hazard, for sure.

He blew past everything, taking curves with reckless abandon.

For a moment he didn't spot the black Yukon in his rearview, but his heart still didn't settle down. It tapped at his ribs like a hammer driving a nail through pitted wood. His mouth was dry as well. He licked his lips, coaxed up enough spit to try and chase away the cottonmouth. And no sooner than he'd done that, a moment before he would have truly relaxed, the black Yukon filled his rearview mirror again. He groaned and pressed down the gas, sinking it to the floor.

Merriman must've done the same because the Yukon ate up the distance between them. The sights at the side of the road, sights

Michael had been enjoying minutes before, were now blurs. Political lawn signs, roadside mailboxes with engraved family names, the houses themselves—Michael took none of it in.

A beat or two more and Merriman would be right up on him, bumper kissing bumper. Or, bumper punching bumper probably more accurate. Michael pictured himself buried deep in the woods somewhere, his steadily decaying flesh making the soil all the more rich.

Spurred by that dark vision, he eased off of the gas, pulled his wheel hard to the right. If he wasn't mistaken this road cut through the last bit of residential area and fed into another commercial strip. Six or seven streets crisscrossed it, and the speed limit fell to twenty-five. But it was a chance he had to take. If he could make it through and out to the main road, there'd be hope.

He glanced in his rearview again. Merriman was still on his trail, traveling slow as well to adhere to the neighborhood.

Michael passed the first parallel street. Either five or six more to go. The interior of the Chrysler was all silence, even the rush of heavy pulse had left Michael's ears. His concentration was on the road and nothing else. He gritted his teeth as he passed the next street, looked behind him.

The black Yukon's headlights were eyes of menace. Its grill a mouth of gnarling teeth. In a black frame that spoke of doom. Not to mention the man at the wheel. Doom personified.

All the inspiration Michael needed to escape.

Streets three and four were memories. Street five was marked with a STOP sign. Michael braked and looked both ways. All clear to his sides, if not behind him. Merriman was less than a football field away. Michael tapped the gas and started rolling again. He spotted Merriman's head making the same side-to-side survey behind him.

The temptation to speed through the rest of the street was strong but the fear of causing some innocent child harm was greater. Michael kept his speed at an even twenty-five. Merriman seemed to operate with the same restraint, as the black Yukon hadn't made up any of the divide.

Street six was also marked by a STOP sign. But all Michael cared about was the roadway about eight hundred feet ahead. Cars whizzed by at speeds nearly three times his current pace. The main road. He exhaled and inched past the STOP sign, glancing back to see Merriman just approaching it.

Then he turned back, his eyes on the road again.

And had to hit his brakes. Hard.

The roadway blocked.

By a second bulky black Yukon.

And Merriman easing to a stop behind him, bumper kissing bumper.

Shit.

Lukas Doyle shot his cuffs as he exited the front Yukon. Michael licked his lips and considered his options, clicking his door locks as Doyle started a slow stroll in his direction. Even walking slowly it only took Doyle ten seconds to reach the Chrysler. He tapped the glass and motioned for Michael to either lower his window or exit the vehicle. Michael did neither. In his sideview mirror, he spotted Merriman making his way toward them as well.

Doyle stepped away and had a quick conference with the steroid freak. Michael was boxed in by the two Yukons, otherwise he would've taken that moment to make a run for it. Instead, he strained to hear them. A futile effort. Their voices were hushed by the glass. After a beat, Merriman retreated to his Yukon and Doyle retrained his attention on Michael.

Dignity.

It meant something to Michael.

He clicked his locks, paused a beat before opening his door, shot his own cuffs as he made it to his feet, shielded from Lukas Doyle by the car door only. He squared his jaw and steeled his shoulders, staring at Doyle wordlessly. Every bit Doyle's match in his mind.

"When exactly was your brain put into a blender?" Doyle asked.

"I'm not afraid of you," Michael said.

"Oh no?" Doyle smiled. "That just serves to bolster my hypothesis about your brain. Pure mush at this point." He took a step toward Michael and stopped. "You should fear me. I'm H1NI, bed bugs, HIV all wrapped into one. I'm not suggesting a paralyzing fear, but a respectful one would certainly be prudent. The pangs every man should feel when he gets that first colonoscopy at fifty. You should respect that I could very well mean your end of times."

"Any harm that comes to me," Michael said, "Won't go unpunished."

Doyle laughed. "Jacqueline's much too polite to let Ridley know that his erections are as weak as goat's milk. If he represents the entirety of your threat of retribution I like my chances."

Michael shifted his weight. Doyle's reach was beyond scary. Was there anything this man didn't know about Michael's life?

"I know everything," Doyle said in answer to a question that hadn't even been asked aloud.

Michael's jaw muscles churned.

"Thinking about rushing me?" Doyle asked. "You *are* dumb."

"I'm bigger than you."

Doyle nodded. "You are indeed. But now isn't the time for steel.

That should have occurred earlier in your evolution. This new-found courage doesn't hold much sway in my mind."

"I won't be intimidated."

Again Doyle nodded. "I'd guess as much. You're much too stupid now. Brain's a smoothie."

"Insult my intelligence again and…"

"I won't go unpunished," Doyle said, nodding. "I got you." He took another step toward Michael anyway. "Personally I'm offended at drawing the assignment to chase you down. So much I'd rather be doing."

"Well, now you've caught me," Michael said through gritted teeth. "Take your best shot. And make it your best."

Doyle sighed, chuckled. "Is that Ray Liotta? Or Bobby De Niro?"

"Fuck you."

"Joe Pesci?"

"Fuck. You."

"Tempting offer but I didn't stalk you for extracurriculars, Michael Allan Palmer. You're wanted back at the offices."

"Wanted?"

"Yes, you insouciant fool."

"For what?"

"I'm just the messenger," Doyle said. "Why don't you head on back and find out for yourself." And noticing Michael's hesitation, he added, "Your call."

Michael still didn't speak or respond in any noticeable way.

Doyle shrugged, moved on, back toward the Yukon.

Michael watched Merriman, and then Doyle, take off.

Wanted. Back at the offices. Something to do with Malcolm, no doubt. His stomach seized up as he considered the possibilities. The old man, dead. Terrible news.

He headed back.

# CHAPTER THREE

ilacs. Liz Sutherland's scent heavy in the conference room, peppering the air, soaked into the furniture and the walls and the carpet it seemed. Michael had come full circle, back where he'd first foolishly approached Liz about his problems with Karla. He would've orphaned his firstborn for a do-over, a rewind, but life was often too stingy for second chances. Definitely in this case. Karla was gone forever and there was nothing he could do to change that. Besides, the present situation was critical enough to wipe away any thought of what was. It was a moment swollen with uncertainty of what was to come.

Michael's familiarity with several people in the room was largely by name only. He recognized just two faces—Hank Geathers and Benjamin Wallace—but his past dealings with both of those men were cursory at best. The only person in the room with which he had any intimate knowledge was Daniel. And Daniel's glum demeanor, even more broken than usual, confirmed Michael's worst fears. Malcolm was indeed dead.

Still.

"Malcolm's died?" Michael asked miserably.

"Have a seat, Michael."

Michael looked at the man who'd spoken to him. "And you are?"

"Eli Catena," he said. Michael knew the name. A bloodhound from Legal.

Michael nodded. "You didn't answer my question. Has he?"

"No," Catena said. "Now have a seat. Please. I'll explain everything."

Michael fell into a soft leather chair, the far end from Daniel, relieved in his spirit. He couldn't deal with another loss. "What's the meaning of all of this?" he asked, swiveling his head to take in all of those present. Key board members, several company lawyers, and Daniel.

Catena was obviously the appointed spokesman. He tapped a small stack of papers into a neat pile, leaned back in his chair, rocking it gently.

"Would you not do that?" Michael asked.

"What?"

"Rock your chair. It unnerves me."

Catena regarded him curiously for a moment. After a beat, he calmed the chair, picked up a pencil and tapped it against the table instead. A bundle of nervous energy.

"You said you would explain," Michael said.

Catena sighed in a way that Michael suspected had been decided hours earlier. "Succession planning is almost as vital to a business as its purpose for incorporation."

Michael nodded. "Okay."

"There needs to be a clear and visible transition plan for leadership and management. Accountability both during a transition and for the long term." Catena actually ticked items off with his fingers. "Financial planning for buy-outs." Tick. "Employee retention bonuses." Tick. "Clear plans for client retention." Tick. "Comprehensive buy/sell agreement." A tick and a wide smile. "I won't bore you with all of the particulars. Just understand how crucial a good succession plan is."

Again Michael nodded.

Catena stood to his feet. About six feet tall. Trim and tanned. Cornflower blue eyes. Brown hair streaked with premature gray. A handsome young face absent of any age lines. Dressed in a short-sleeve Polo shirt and khaki pants. It was too cold for golf but he had the air of a man disrupted from nine rounds on yielding greens.

Michael glanced at Daniel. Daniel's eyes were on Catena. He looked on the verge of rushing the young lawyer.

Catena settled down on a corner of the long conference table. He wrung his hands like a wet mop. Cleared his throat and began again. "This great organization is well prepared for the tragedy that has suddenly befallen us. I'll take it that everyone in this room is now aware of Malcolm's precarious health?"

Nods all around.

"Daniel's just come from the hospital and he informs me that Malcolm is not responsive but fighting just the same. As we'd all expect of course."

He hopped off of the table, moved to the other end, repeated the earlier ritual. Sat down on a corner, wrung his hands.

"A good succession plan isn't static," he went on. "It's proactive. It's governed by clear goals and metrics. Specific, measurable, appropriate, realistic, and timely goals."

"Transparent?" Daniel called out. "Public. Right, Eli? Isn't that a condition of *good* succession plans?"

"Usually," Catena said, nodding. "Certainly, Daniel."

"Well, great," Daniel replied, throwing his hands in the air dramatically. "Usually, but not always."

"There are certain circumstances where the kind of transparency you're suggesting isn't prudent, Daniel."

"Like in this case. Right, Eli?"

"I've looked at our succession plan with a very critical eye, Daniel. It's solid."

"Our?" Daniel sniffed a laugh. "You mean my father's, don't you? There was no inclusion whatsoever in this process. Don't kid any of us."

"Malcolm thought it best that he handle the particulars, Daniel. He understood how delicate this all was. I can't say that I disagree with his approach."

Daniel rose to his feet, looked around the room, flashing on every face for a few seconds, a sneer curling his lips. "Make sure you grease the skids, gentlemen. Makes it a lot easier to accommodate the shaft when it's drilled into you."

He slapped his chair aside and stomped across the carpet, ignoring Eli Catena's plea for him to stop. He paused at the door though, looked back over his shoulders, his eyes trained on Michael.

"Rot, my friend. Rot," he said.

And then he stepped through and slammed the door behind him.

A low murmur floated through the room. Eli Catena released another prepared sigh, chased it with a rehearsed head shake.

"He's feeling some stress," Michael said.

"More like envy," Catena said. "Misplaced and altogether oppositional with the best interests of this company."

"Envy?"

"I suppose his spirit is tweaked that Malcolm's plan initiates you as our interim CEO."

Michael's mouth fell open into an uppercase O, but no words came. He was much too shocked to respond.

# CHAPTER
# FOUR

Michael was still trembling hours later, adrenaline coursing through his body like oxygen-rich blood. Interim CEO. The promotion had required a move to a bigger office. Not Malcolm's, but damn close in both extravagance and square feet. Polished wood everything, a chair comfortable and large enough to sleep in, carpet so plush it swallowed his footsteps. Wall-mounted speakers. Satellite radio or his own personal CD player, the controls for both enclosed in a glassed-in case he was told was made of ivory and inch-thick glass. Jazz playing softly from the wall-mounted speakers. Miles. "Sketches of Spain."

For the better part of the morning, Michael had been intimate with a company paperweight he'd found on his new desk. MRF Global chiseled on the top of a square of smoothed amethyst rock. Michael twirled it in his fingers now, nodding to the melody of the music, enthralled by nothing.

A buzzing sound crashed through his thought. It took him a moment to locate its source. His desk phone. A different tele-communications system from his old office.

He picked the phone up, pressed buttons until his new secretary's voice feathered his ear.

"Mr. Palmer, I'm sorry to trouble you."

"It's okay"—Melba, Maureen? Something with an N instead? Noreen, Nancy?—"What is it?"

Her voice softened even further, into a whisper. "Perhaps I should have just called security. I'm sorry, Mr. Palmer."

"Is there a problem?"

"A young gentleman… He works for us. I verified as much. I believe I've seen him around before. He works the mailroom, according to our directory." Another notch fell off of her voice. "He's in a very agitated state. He insists on speaking with you personally. I've tried to explain to him that your schedule doesn't allow spur of the moment visits but he persists. I can call security, if you'd like. I truly do apologize, Mr. Palmer."

"Send him in," Michael said.

"I beg your pardon?" she said, her voice rising now.

"Send him in. I have an open door policy for all employees."

"Very well," she said, sounding discouraged nonetheless.

Moments later Michael's office door opened, and closed right away.

"She needs to put her diaphragm in the microwave or at least leave it out on a counter until it gets to room temperature. I mean…damn."

Michael smiled, said, "You look like shit, Joe."

And he did.

Unshaven. Dark circles under his eyes. Hair unkempt. If his pants were light colored there might've been an indeterminate stain in the crotch. A street bum for all intents and purposes.

"At least I'm living," Joe replied. "Which is more than I can say for Cassie, dude."

Michael sat up straight. Was it happening again?

"What are you talking about?" he asked.

"She's gone, dude. Poof. Right after you started asking questions about the Bellatoris."

"Haven't we had this conversation?"

"I been by her place, dude. No one's seen her in days. Something's awry."

"Awry? Shit, Joe, why do I feel like I'm watching bad programming on BBC?"

"Joke around, dude. That's your M.O. Meanwhile Cassie's all fucked up in your bullshit. Can't believe you don't care. This is all your horseshit fault, dude. I blame you."

"Have a seat, Joe. And lower your voice, if you would."

"No. And no."

Michael sighed and stood to his feet, moved around his cavernous desk, met Joe in the center of the floor. It was awkward positioning, standing there that way, but Michael didn't dare mess with the dynamics. Joe seemed on the verge of unraveling.

"I'm gonna take Cassie's letter to someone," Joe said. "I'm gonna explain how she's gone missing."

"Someone? You mean the police?"

"If I have to."

"That would involve me, Joe. I can't be involved."

"You *are* involved, dude. Just 'cause you get to play Bill Gates until the old man's able to eat solid foods again doesn't change that."

"You should watch what you say, Joe."

"Why? You gonna get the Bellatoris on me like you did Cassie?"

"You know I didn't *get* them on her."

"Didn't you, though?"

Michael sighed again. Risked a hand on Joe's shoulder. "You're emotional. I understand. But I really believe Cassie burned out. She's somewhere sipping drinks with umbrellas in them right now, while you...and I sit here and worry unnecessarily."

"That's not what you thought the other day."

"Cooler heads prevail."

"You're so busy sucking the company's tit right now you won't even admit the obvious."

"Which is?"

"The Bellatoris have done something to Cassie."

"What are you? Auditioning for a John Grisham novel, Joe? Just full of conspiracy."

"Don't talk down to me, dude."

Michael said, "The CIA shot Kennedy and crashed Junior's plane. Elvis is alive. He and Michael Jackson are somewhere fighting over who gets to play cards with Tupac Shakur and Princess Di?"

Joe was a whirlwind of gestures and emotions. He poked out his mouth, frowned, took a step toward Michael, fists balled, took a step back, relaxed his hands, sighed, cursed, grabbed at his unruly hair, released it from his grip and punched the air, bit his lip. Cried.

"Joe?"

"They did something to her, dude," he said through a veil of tears.

"I don't think so, Joe."

"Sure you do. But you're all set in your own situation, so everything is copasetic in your world. Fuck Cassie."

Michael pursed his lips. "I appreciate you, Joe. I really do. And the good thing is I can really help you now. I'm in a position to enact some real change in your life, Joe. Say goodbye to the mailroom."

Joe took out his laminated employee ID. Turned it over and over in his hands. Then handed it to Michael. "You're right, I'm saying goodbye to the mailroom. But I don't want any help you'd give. I quit."

Michael shook his head. "Wrong move, Joe. You're being way too emotional right now."

"And you're being too emotionless. You know deep in your gut something's happened to Cassie. This isn't all some great big coincidence. And you..." He waved his hand dismissively. "I've said all I have to say. I gotta go, dude. Love, peace, and hair grease." He walked for the door.

Michael called out, "Quitting? Without two weeks' notice, Joe? I'm sure your supervisor wouldn't approve. Don't burn bridges."

Michael's words turned Joe around. His eyes were unreadable. "You really are deceived, dude. Really. I feel sorry for you. The fall's gonna be a bitch."

"I don't plan on falling, Joe."

"Of course you don't. That'd be foolish. But that's what will make it all the more tragic."

"I never took you for the glass-half-empty type, Joe."

Joe's face moved into the approximation of a smile. "Deceived."

"Let me help you," Michael tried once more.

Joe sneered. "I never ride the bum horse."

"I'm the bum horse?"

"Somebody needs to shoot *you* up with Ketamine," Joe said.

He turned to leave.

Michael let him go.

# CHAPTER FIVE

Dusk.

The air smelled like refrigerated fruit. Carried a chill that easily worked itself deep into Michael's bones. His jacket, a thin fleece with a marred zipper, wasn't close to sufficient. He jogged from the building for his car, and halfway to it, gave up the jog and fell into a full sprint. Shuddering like a wet dog as he eased behind the wheel and quickly worked the heat system to full blast. Waving his hands in front of the vents so he could get the circulation necessary for a drive home.

After a few minutes he was comfortable enough to leave. He pulled from the garage and blended in with the traffic. Music was the last thing on his mind, so the stereo and CD player remained turned off. Day one as interim CEO had tested him in ways he wouldn't have thought possible.

Decisions.

Crisis management.

More decisions.

So much for his belief that the real work happened in the trenches of mid- and lower management, and that Malcolm's role was little more than director of a corporate orchestra.

Throw in the tension with Daniel, sudden envious whispers that Michael wasn't up to the task of CEO, and Michael's own feelings of inadequacy, and, well, suddenly his own ambition felt completely misguided.

Careful what you wish for.

All of these thoughts crowded his head on the drive home and before he realized it he was pulling up to his house.

Lights burned in the window that fronted the living room.

And suddenly he had another concern.

Rachel.

He hadn't spoken to her all day. They hadn't shared a word since the debacle at the hospital earlier that morning. Michael had no idea what kind of spirits she was in. Taking her temperature was priority number one. If she blew lukewarm, he'd move in and tell her about his day. Cold or hot would get an identical response: a quiet retreat to the couch. Live to fight another day.

Michael found her watching *Deal or No Deal* on their sixty-inch television. Wearing a halter top and short shorts. Sexy. He thanked the heavens for house heat.

At that moment, seeing her dressed that way, he automatically chalked her down as lukewarm.

"Baby," he said.

She looked up but didn't speak. He stepped into the room, stopped a few feet short of her, blocking her view of the television.

She muttered something and got up from the couch.

"Rachel," he called as she reached the door.

She turned back. "What?"

"It's not healthy for us to ignore one another."

"You've been ignoring me?" She raised an eyebrow. "Thought it was just me pretending that *you* didn't exist. Now I don't feel so bad."

"You've been feeling bad?"

"Figure of speech," she said.

He smiled, licked his lips, let his eyes trail over her body. "Speaking of figures..."

"That would be your response. Typical."

"Shoot me." He shrugged. "I love making love to you."

"You love making love," she corrected.

"To you," he said.

"If only that were fully true," she said, sadness crawling up from her mouth to her eyes. "If only it were just about me."

"What are you insinuating?" he said, wondering if Daniel had somehow gotten to her.

She left without answering. He followed her to the bedroom.

She plopped on the bed, crossed her legs, noticed Michael's eyes studying her thighs, uncrossed her legs. Couldn't keep her hands quiet, and so she smoothed the counterpane on the bed. Michael grabbed the television remote from off of the dresser, pointed it at their bedroom television, flipped to one of the digital cable's music channels, then crossed the room, slowly, destined for her. She looked away, touched a hand to her throat, resisted the urge to hum the music playing softly from the channel he'd turned on.

Michael reached her.

Her head was still turned away.

He ran his fingers through her thick hair. Her mane biracial in texture, tangled, strong, scented with coconut oil. He twirled it, worked the hairline with a feathery touch of his thumb.

She looked at him finally.

"You were brutal and unkind, dominating simply because you could be. You exploited a broken man in a difficult situation. My brother hasn't been a brother to me, ever, but I hated to see you treat him in that way. Reminded me of my... And you were so triumphant about it. Gloating. Reminded me of my... And now you hold his title."

"You heard?"

She nodded. "I heard."

What else had she heard?

"Interim," Michael said, then, "but you're right."

She frowned in surprise. "I'm right? About?"

"All of it. Everything you said."

"How should I take that?"

"My dominance? Exploiting someone weaker? My triumphant demeanor?"

She nodded, used his words. "All of it."

He stood above her, the crotch of his pants near her face. "Dominance. Exploitation. Triumph. You make it sound dirty. It doesn't have to be, Rachel."

She licked her lips, eyes on his crotch. "It is dirty," she said.

"Does dirty have to be bad?"

She looked up, whispered, "You'd like me to be dirty, wouldn't you? You enjoy dirty?"

He nodded. "I do."

Sickness.

Addiction.

"I can't involve myself with you now, Michael. Too many emotions and thoughts in my head."

"I'm sorry, Rachel. I was wrong at the hospital. I'm sorry. How often have you heard me utter those words?"

Hardly ever.

She smiled. "You're horny. You'll say anything when you're that way."

He nodded. "I mean it, though. I am sorry. And, well yes, I'm horny as well. I have a beautiful wife."

She leaned forward, kissed him at the front of his pants, then leaned back and regarded her work as though it was brushstrokes of art. His erection was a thing of pride.

"Happy now?" she asked. "I'm weakening."

"I make you weak?"

"Always," she whispered.

"Wet?"

She shook her head, said, "More like soaking, gushing."

"You've always had a way with words."

"You've always had a way with…" She reached forward, undid his belt, popped the one button on his pants, urgently dropped them down to his ankles, pulling his boxer briefs along with them. Michael stepped out of the tangle of clothes, his erection waving.

"Jesus, Jesus," she whispered.

"Take off *your* clothes," he whispered back.

She did it slowly. A striptease. Twirled the last article, her panties, on her finger like a parlor trick. Her smile made Michael want to fuck her. Not make love to her. That was too neat, too dignified, too restrained. He wanted to get dirty, needed to. Fuck her. Fuck her until the smile turned to a frown of pain, a frown of pleasure. Fuck her until she offered every inch of herself to him.

He took the panties from her finger, tossed them to the floor. She gazed up at him, batting her eyes, the smile remaining in place on her striking face. Trying her best to keep the power, but the swell of her breasts, the fast rising and falling of her chest, betrayed her.

He held all of the power.

He dropped down on bended knee, roughly parted her legs.

She pushed him away, roughly as well, closed her parted legs.

He smirked, stood, shrugged when she looked up at him.

She grabbed him by the waist, pulled him close, forced him down on bended knee again, parted her legs, and eased his head in her valley.

"That boat has sailed," he said, easing his head back out.

"Why do you do this?"

"Beg me."

"What?"

"Beg me," he repeated.

"Beg what?"

"You want your pussy licked, Rachel. You and I both know that. Beg for it."

She sniffed. Looked away. Touched her neck. Looked back. Looked away. Looked back.

"It's real simple, Rachel. Say please, please, please lick my pussy, Michael."

"I will not."

"*Eat me*, then. That's easier for you to manage?"

"Dream on."

He laughed, took his eyes off of her, stared at what she wouldn't beg him to lick.

"Michael...stop that. It's perverted."

She didn't close her legs or cover up, he noted.

"I mean it, Michael."

"Lick my pussy," he whispered, still staring at it.

Silence.

For long seconds.

Then.

"I hate you sometimes," she said, without feeling.

He waited.

For long seconds.

Then.

"Lick my pussy, Michael."

"Please, please, please."

"Lick my pussy. Please, Michael."

"That's two *pleases* short, baby."

"Please, please, pl—"

He started in on it before the words left her mouth. Flicked his tongue at it. Licked it like a bowl of ice cream.

Moved away.

"Please, please, please," she begged.

A quick study.

He returned, feasted on it, pausing every so often to kiss the inner thigh of her left leg and her right leg, getting a deep shudder from her each time.

He whispered, "You like this?"

"Yeah, baby," she moan-growled. "Fu-uh-uh-uk."

Coming in waves.

Pausing long enough to catch her breath, then forcing him to his feet, pulling him to her face, inhaling his manhood. Taking it deep throat.

"You're...so...Jesus, Rachel."

Lathered in her spit, his penis punched the inside of her jaw. All tongue, no teeth. Great technique.

Moments later.

The bed rocked. The music played. She cried warm tears that washed his naked chest.

Then he turned her over, pushed her ass up, crushed her face into the pillow with his energetic thrusts. Moving in and out. In and out in a hard rhythm that made another kind of music as the headboard slapped the wall.

He turned her over again. Face to face. Pinched her nipples and made her moan. Eyes open, watching her face. Her eyes closed, head turned sideways on the pillow.

"Open your eyes," he said.

She did.

"Beg me."

"For *what* now?"

"I'll stop doing what I'm doing if you don't beg me."

"Dick me," she moaned. "Please."

"Beg."

"Give it to me, baby. Please, please, please."

"Beg."

"Oh, God. Stick it in me, Michael. Damn."

"Beg."

"That big dick…"

"Beg."

"…deep in me."

"Beg."

"Fuck me."

"Beg."

His rhythm got faster, harder, more fierce.

"Fuck me. Please, please, please."

He put her legs up, an ankle on each shoulder, and he thrust as deep into her as his genetics would allow. Plenty deep.

"Shit, baby," she moaned.

"Rub my nipples," he said. Begged.

Tables turned.

She fingered his nipples and he thrust even deeper.

She moved her ass, up down up down, in rhythm with him. Tomorrow her legs would be sore. Raised above his shoulders in such a…

…it didn't matter.

Pleasure was the moment.

The moment was pleasure.

She came once more. In waves that made her eyes water. An orgasm so strong she feared she might've wet the bed.

He made one last hard thrust.

Held her there, legs up on his shoulders.

Growled.

Came hard.

Fell away.

# CHAPTER
## SIX

When Michael awakened, they were still in one another's arms, Rachel's head resting on his chest. Outside their bedroom window, the motor of a car in serious need of a tune-up was a vibrating note that wouldn't cease. A strong wind walked the neighbor's garbage can across the asphalt. The sun was absent, its usual light, peeking through the slats in the blinds, very much missed. A day painted gray by winter's chill and unyielding bleakness.

Michael eased Rachel's arms from around him, carefully settled her head down on a pillow. She didn't wake.

Later, as he prepared to leave for work, she finally opened her eyes, caught a glimpse of him with briefcase in hand.

"Leaving?"

"A CEO's work is never done," he said, smiling.

"Have a good day, baby."

"Call me if there's any word on your…" He couldn't finish the thought.

"I will," she said, smiling now herself. A tight, courageous smile.

The goodbye kiss was one that neither of them wanted to end.

⊂⊃

"Hey there." The tap on the door came after the words. Michael glanced up from his desk, at the figure in his doorway.

He nodded instead of speaking.

"What do you have there, Michael?"

Michael regarded the stack in front of him. A color brochure, several loose sheets of paper, the pages crowded with numbers.

"Stock prospectus," he said. "For Sarfocure."

"Inspired reading?"

"They specialize in intratracheal suspension," Michael said. "What do you think?"

"Sounds boring as all hell. I wouldn't want your job." Smiling.

Michael frowned. "What did you need, Daniel?"

"We have a meeting."

Michael's frown deepened, and he looked down at the full calendar on his desk top.

"Emergency gathering," Daniel said. "It wouldn't have made it to your planner."

"Emergency?" Michael's voice caught in his throat. "Has Malcolm…"

"Kicked the bucket? Not as of yet."

Michael felt his shoulders relax into the leather of his chair. "Meeting?"

"Same conference room as…" Daniel cleared his throat, forced another smile. "The large conference room we used when you received your executive appointment." He tapped his watch. A Movado. Expensive. Black face, no numbers, a diamond in the twelve spot. "We're convening there in ten minutes. Sharp. Be there or be square."

"And this meeting includes who? And is about?"

"Same attendees as yesterday," Daniel said. "Loose ends and knickknacks from what I'm told."

"Knickknacks?"

"Loose ends."

Now Michael cleared his throat. "About the hospital… I wanted to apologize to you for my behavior. I was completely out of line."

Daniel nodded. "I suppose we'll never point out the spinach in one another's teeth but at least we should be able to work together for the good of MRF. I know I can do that, at least."

"Agreed."

Daniel tapped his watch again. "Ten minutes."

Michael continued to look after him even after he'd left the doorway.

All nine members of the board were arranged around the enormous conference table. If that wasn't odd enough, the room had been completely silent as Michael neared the door. No chatter whatsoever inside. Usually there'd be a low hum like the drone of a light fixture. All eyes were on Michael as he stepped inside, and following him as he made his way past the table for the head seat. He managed a bright smile as he fell into his chair.

"Gentlemen," he said, and looking to his left. "And lady."

Mary Hendrickson.

She was an old bird with liver-spotted skin that bruised easily and was thin enough to showcase the network of blue veins beneath it. She dressed in handsome skirt suits, the hems nearly touching the floor, and carried herself with the straight posture of a concert pianist. She was also childless and carried an odor that was like basement mold. Depression Era, the stereotype of a spinster. Michael was certain she'd never had sex in her seventy some odd years of existence.

Mary, through her past comments, clearly assumed he'd had too much.

They'd never truly gotten along.

And now he was in power.

The distaste on her face, a curl at the corners of her wrinkled mouth, a frown dancing in her eyes, caused Michael to smile. Triumphantly. Goading. He supposed he'd never learn.

"Michael," several of the room's occupants murmured.

Catena, the young bloodhound from Legal, sat surprisingly still in his seat to Michael's right. Catena's gaze held steady on something unseen by anyone else that rested on the table's surface in front of him.

Mary Hendrickson unnecessarily scooted her chair forward. "Shall we begin, gentlemen?"

More murmurs.

She trained her eyes on Michael. "We have an unfortunate problem that begs to be addressed."

"Problem?" Michael's smile had yet to diminish. "I haven't heard of any issues. Am I aware of this problem?"

"I'd think so."

"You'd think so?"

"Yes, Michael."

"I'm afraid I'm a bit confused," he said. "What exactly is the issue here, Mary?"

"You," she said matter-of-factly.

"Me?"

She glanced down at a spiral notepad flipped open in front of her. Used a shaky finger to navigate through what looked like a column of scrawled words. "Candace McCullough, Davida Williams, Ingrid Christensen, Melissa Wright, Dawn Hirsch."

Michael swallowed. Licked his lips and resisted the urge to loosen his collar.

Mary looked up. "Do any of these names hold any significance to you, Michael?"

"In what way would they?" he heard himself say.

Mary's smile was an ugly thing. Grayed, too-small teeth, and dark diseased-looking gums.

Daniel shifted in his chair. The rattle of its casters got Michael's attention. Daniel's smile wasn't as ugly as Mary's but it was a million times more hateful. Lopsided and unrelenting. Smug.

"You're denying a relationship with these women?" he asked Michael.

"I haven't denied anything," Michael said. "I was asked a question and I, in turn, asked for further clarification. In what way would these women be significant to me?"

In his mind he thought, *Do not let them see you sweat, Michael.*

Make them doubt themselves from the very beginning. Make them question what it is they believe that they know. Shatter their onslaught before it begins completely.

Mary Hendrickson said, "I would hope the women you've slept with hold some significance for you, Michael."

"As the men you've slept with hold significance for you?" he quickly shot back.

Her wrinkled neck colored but she didn't back down. She glanced at her spiral notepad, started once more with the women's names. "Jennifer Kelley. Kim Cooper."

"This is ridiculous," Michael barked. "No one in this room has made a vow of celibacy. We're all adults. As long as our relationships are consenting in nature…" He paused, thought, struggled to find the correct words. "He who is without sin cast the first stone."

Daniel chuckled. "Is that before or after the scripture about not cheating on your wife?"

Michael didn't have a comeback.

The room went quiet except for the quiet tick of the clock on the wall.

"I've made my share of mistakes," Michael said in a whisper after a time. "I'm sure I'm not alone in that regard. Rachel and I have made peace with my failings. Our marriage is as strong as it's ever been. I don't see why any of this is company concern."

"Karla Savage," Mary Hendrickson said.

"What?" Michael's heart exploded in his chest. Immediately, his head ached.

"Your latest mistress," Daniel said. "I'm not so sure my sister has made peace with this one. In fact, I'm of the impression she isn't even aware of it. Maybe we should give her a call to *clarify*."

Michael's nostrils flared. He turned his focus on his brother-in-law. "You're scum, Daniel. You're excrement. Somebody should've flushed you down the drain a long time ago."

Daniel nodded, smiled. He seemed to grow bigger right in front of Michael's eyes. And, by contrast, Michael felt himself growing smaller by the second. Frustrated, he looked away. Looked for something to grab, throw. For something to punch, kick, pound.

Mary Hendrickson resumed the conversation. "Back to this latest…matter. It grew contentious and complicated, did it not, Michael?"

"You tell me," Michael said, without looking at her.

Mary nodded. "It did. Apparently Ms. Savage grew uncomfortable with her role. She wanted more than rushed hotel visits during your lunch. So she blackmailed you."

Michael remained silent.

"And you apportioned company funds to ensure her silence."

"What?" Michael's head swiveled, his gaze focused back on Mary Hendrickson. A stare-down. When it became obvious Mary wouldn't blink first, Michael pushed back from the large conference table, and stood to his feet. "This has certainly crossed a line."

"You crossed the line," Daniel said. "Over and over and over again. My sister's blind and emotionally crippled to begin with. My father sees himself in you. But I'm not blind or impressed by you, Michael. I believe the board agrees. You're not fit to lead."

"You son of a bitch." Michael's attempt to round the table and get his hands on Daniel's neck was immediately thwarted. It took three board members to hold him at bay.

"Ringling Bros.," Mary Hendrickson muttered aloud. "A circus. I never thought it would ever come to this here. I'm highly ashamed to be in your company today, sir."

Sir?

A show of reverence while they took his head off at the shoulders.

"Lies," Michael screamed. "I did not use company funds to pay any women."

"Not women," Mary agreed. "*Woman*. This Karla Savage individual. Three checks in quick succession. Twenty thousand dollars each."

"You must have liver spots on your brain as well," Michael said.

"We have copies of the checks, Michael. Plus several back and forth emails between you and Accounts Payable in which you misrepresented the payee on those checks."

"Ridiculous."

"And sordid emails between you and Ms. Savage. Including several thanking you for the funds."

"The smoking gun," Daniel said.

"Is this the Bellatoris' doing?" Michael asked him. "It is, isn't it? You put them up to this."

"What are you talking about now?" Daniel asked, smiling. "Bellatoris?"

Michael looked around the room. "This isn't as it seems, gentlemen. I assure you it isn't. I've been set up."

"The great conspiracy," Daniel said. "John Grisham. Michael's own private Pelican Brief."

A suggestion Michael himself had made, to Joe. Did the Bellatoris have him bugged as well?

"Son of a bitch," he said.

"Go ahead, Michael," Daniel said. "Continue. The name calling really distinguishes you as a leader. And then when you're done with that, physically attack me as you did at the hospital. I suppose you'll deny that as well?"

"You won't get away with this, Daniel."

"That's what you should've told yourself when you decided to steal company money."

Michael made another lunge for Daniel. Was held back yet again by the three board members.

"You've finally gone and stepped in it, Michael. I can't say I didn't see this coming. You've always struck me as unduly reckless."

"Fuck you."

"Eloquent as always."

Michael nodded knowingly. "Why don't you tell everyone what you had the Bellatoris do to Karla, Daniel? Tell them how you've had the Bellatoris following me. Harassing me needlessly." He looked around again. "This is all a rouse. I assure you."

"Who are the Bellatoris?" Mary Hendrickson asked.

"Daniel's own handpicked security team. Headed by Lukas Doyle."

"Bellatoris?" she wondered aloud. "Greek?"

"It means *warriors*," Michael said, nodding. "And they are. They're...brutes."

Brutes. Malcolm's word.

"You sound absolutely crazy," Daniel said. "I'd refrain from speaking if I were you."

"Tell everyone you didn't see to their hire, Daniel."

"Of course I did. They're highly experienced and qualified security professionals. We've had breaches, as your own misappropriation of company funds confirms. I hired them to stop the breaches. To eliminate them completely. And they have done so."

Michael noticed several heads in the room nodding. He was losing this battle. Fast.

"I! Took! No! Money!" he shouted.

"Evidence says otherwise."

"The Bellatoris."

"Right." Daniel smiled, looked around himself. "My very own corporate A-Team. Face, BA—"

"They killed Karla and you know it."

"What?" Daniel stopped sudden, frowning. "Killed her?" The frown looked real. An actor. And a good one at that. Michael would've never guessed.

"Are you suggesting foul play of some sort?" Mary Hendrickson asked.

Michael had spoken too much. He fell silent.

After awhile, Daniel, sober, said, "I request a motion for dismissal of Michael Palmer's CEO duties."

Nods all around.

# CHAPTER
# SEVEN

It was a low building with a flat roof. Barnyard red siding, set at the back of a large lot just off the main stretch of road that led to the area's shopping mall. Poor lighting in the lot, but still it was choked with cars. Inexpensive models with high mileage and serious body wear, for the most part. A few pickup trucks with exaggerated tires, and flames and such painted on their rear panels. Rich Kubiak parked his Toyota Camry in one of the few available empty spaces. The Camry's interior smelled strongly of motor oil and acetone, of McDonald's' hamburgers and spoiled milk. Work and family odors. Kubiak shut down the Camry's engine, hesitated briefly, then went ahead and got out and walked over a carpet of crushed beer cans and see-through beer cups and a used rubber or two. Headed for the building.

The building was fronted by a neon sign, several of the letters blown out. Below the sign was a light-colored awning with the shadow pictures of two crossed champagne glasses and the silhouette of an extra curvy woman. The awning was bordered with a string of unlit light bulbs. The building's two front-facing windows were completely covered over with beer posters and old football schedules for the Jets and Giants and Rutgers' Scarlet Knights and flyers for one-night dancing engagements from porn stars. Kandy Kupcakes' poster was bisected by a tear that trailed all the way from the header to the footer. The tear had been repaired with strips of Scotch tape, and was so old it would have to be scraped off the glass with a razor if Cheaters was ever shut down and turned into a Domino's Pizza or a Burger King.

None of this stopped Rich Kubiak.

He walked inside.

First thing he saw was a guy as big as the building itself, sitting comically on a barstool that looked moments away from disintegrating into fine wood dust beneath his considerable bulk. Second thing was a chalkboard advertising a menu of hastily scrawled offerings. VIP Champagne Room. Lap dances. Twenty dollars for four minutes. One hundred and twenty for fifteen minutes. Two twenty-five for a half an hour. Kubiak made a quick decision, paid the cheap cover and moved inside through a curtain of smoke.

A DJ was spinning records from an elevated cubby at the far corner of the room. The music vibrated the organs in Kubiak's chest and rumbled the hard floor beneath him. Reminded him of the subway system in the city. Lots of bass in the song of the moment. That he-she-it freak that improbably got the hot girls. Marilyn Manson. *Beautiful People.*

To Kubiak's left was a long bar area. Each of the eight stools in front of it was occupied. The bartender was a college-aged girl wearing a generic sports jersey, the material tied in a knot that touched the underside of her heavy breasts. Her navel was pierced. She wore enough makeup for two women. She was a blur of constant movement.

Straight ahead of him was several small tables built for two at the most. And beyond the tables was the main stage. Two dancers were doing a lesbian tango on the stripper pole. An Asian girl with a cookie sheet ass and watermelon tits. A Caucasian girl with small natural breasts and a thick bottom, ass and thighs, that wasn't in proportion with her smaller upper half. Her tongue was pierced and buried deep in the Asian girl's mouth. Their hands were busy. They were massaging one another without lotion or oil.

It didn't look like an act.

Kubiak smiled, a rarity for him these days, and fell into a velvet chair at one of the tables. His eyes were riveted to the UN sex thing happening on the stage in front of him.

Another girl glided over near him, stopping just off to the side of his table so he could still see the action on stage. He looked down at her feet for rollerblades. She wasn't wearing any. The stage was that quickly forgotten. He let his eyes travel her frame. She wore tight boy shorts and a top like the bartender's. Block sports-styled numbers stitched across her chest.

"*Ocho cinco*," he said, nodding at the numbers, eight and five, on her jersey.

"I preferred Chad Johnson," she said back.

His eyes lit up. "You know sports?"

Her smile matched his eyes. "Among other things."

The DJ had switched from Manson to Def Leppard. "Pour Some Sugar on Me." Kubiak was thinking, pour some cold water on me. He desperately needed to cool down.

He said, "I like a woman that can enjoy herself some sports."

Her smile didn't falter. "You're built like a football player yourself. You play?"

"Does fantasy count?"

"Fantasy is good, baby."

Her smile had him erect. Her words strengthened the erection. He said, "You dance?"

"In the shower," she replied, letting a sliver of tongue slip from the crack in between her lips.

At first he thought she meant the privacy of her home, but then he noticed her gaze trail to the stage. In one of the dark back corners there was a makeshift glass stall, a showerhead and a spotlight directly above it.

"I'm on in twenty minutes," she said. "I hope you can stay and watch. I'll be rinsing milk off of me."

"Milk?" He noticed the catch in his voice.

"It does a body good."

He turned his attention back on her. About five-eight. One forty. Toned from gym workouts. Big-chested, and wide-hipped. Dark hair. Arresting eyes that looked to be light blue under the dim lighting. A wet mouth that was composed of sensual bee-stung lips. That smile.

"What's your name?" he asked.

"Scarlett."

"Pretty name."

"And yours?"

He told her.

"Lovely name, that," she said. "If I were you I wouldn't say it too loud, though, these other money-hungry bitches will come running over, taking the name literally."

Rich. Taking it literally. He liked Scarlett. A lot. He said, "I'm satisfied with what I've got right now."

"Speaking of *got*," she said. "We have a two-drink minimum. What are you drinking?"

He smiled. "Multitasking, Scarlett?"

She nodded. "Earlier, I insinuated that I had many talents. Guess you didn't believe me."

His smile widened. "You insinuated?"

"Yes, sir. Now, your drink?"

"How about a Knobs Creek?"

Scarlett nodded. "Sure thing. A warm Heineken, coming right up."

Rich was still smiling as she glided away, in the direction of the bar. Again, he looked down for rollerblades. White knee-high hooker boots instead. Damn, she was sexy.

He turned his attention back to the stage. The Asian girl was out of her top. Her nipples were hard and long. The Caucasian girl was down on her knees, her head buried in the Asian girl's crotch.

"I like Chinese food but that's ridiculous."

He turned. Scarlett. Back already with his warm Heineken.

"Drink it fast," she said. "And it'll seem like expensive whiskey."

"Will you join me?"

She was sitting on his lap, an arm around his neck, before he got the words out. "Plumber, carpenter, or mechanic?" she asked.

"What?"

She said, "Rough hands, a little dirt under the fingernails, and your skin's stained. I figure mechanic."

"Close," he said.

"How close?"

"Close," he repeated.

"So if I asked you about torque power and broken window regulators, you'd be able to give me good credible advice?"

"Not a lick," he admitted.

Their shared laughter was music.

"Haven't seen you here before," she said a moment later.

He frowned. "This is about to turn into a scene in a Humphrey Bogart movie, isn't it?"

She made a crooked mouth, spoke in a gruff voice. "Of all the strip joints in all the towns in all the world, he walks into mine."

An interpolation of a line from *Casablanca*. Rich's smile nearly matched hers. His eyes crinkled at the corners.

"I did a little film school," she said, reddening.

"Did any film work?"

"You might could say that," she said.

"Hmm."

"Hmm, indeed."

"What's your story?" he asked.

"My story?"

"We all have one."

She touched a finger to her chin, looked up at the rafters. "Hmm, let me see." Then she dropped the finger and looked back at him. A deadly serious expression on her pretty face. "My stepfather…"

Rich tilted his head. "Yes?"

"Never touched me improperly," Scarlett said.

"Okay."

"Cocaine…" she went on.

"Yes?"

"Never much interested me."

Rich smiled, nodded. "Alright."

"I've never been raped," Scarlett said. "They might not look it but my boobs are real. I don't suffer from low self-esteem. I considered film school, like I told you, but no, I'm not dancing my way through school. I don't already have a master's degree, either, and I'm not doing this for some undercover exposé article I'm writing for *The New York Times*."

"Okay."

"You're wondering what I'm doing here then?" she said.

"There's that thought," Rich Kubiak acknowledged.

Scarlett smiled mischievously. "Why I'm giving you a lap dance, of course. Silly boy." At that, she grabbed Rich's hand and pulled him toward the VIP Champagne Room.

Rich Kubiak had *nothing* to lose.

He didn't resist.

∽

"This usually happen?" he asked a while later, glancing down at his crotch, then around the room for a napkin.

"Mostly," Scarlett said. "I'm told I'm pretty good."

She'd grinded her ass against his erection in an unbelievable flurry of rhythm. He'd felt his penis burrowing into the crease of her buttocks. At home. Warm. Safe.

And then he'd ejaculated as the sounds of AC/DC's "You Shook Me All Night Long" leaked into the private room.

A deep release that made him growl and sit up straight as plywood, holding Scarlett tight to him by the waist as he emptied. Surprised by the intensity of the climax.

"I wouldn't have believed it possible," he said.

She smiled.

"What do you do when you're not working?" he asked.

"I fill my time *not* dating the guys that come into my work," she said, still smiling.

"Oh?" He couldn't hide his disappointment.

She nodded. "And whenever I get free time, I spend that time *not* dating married men."

Now he was smiling, sheepishly.

"Glove box?" she said.

He touched his wedding finger. Bare. A thin band of discoloration where his ring should've been.

He nodded.

"In the pouch where you keep your insurance and registration cards, right?"

He nodded once more. "You're something else, Scarlett. I might be in love. Seriously."

"Beth," she said. "Donna Elizabeth."

"What?"

"Scarlett's my stage name."

"Are we having an intimate moment?"

She nodded again, too. "You had me at hello. Don't know what it was but…"

"So what now?"

"Tell me about your, um, mechanic work and then ease into talk of your wife," she said sadly.

"It's pretty boring stuff."

She half-smiled. "You're paying for another thirty minutes"—glanced at his crotch—"and it'll take nearly that long before you're ready for another lap dance. So we have time."

"My story?" he said.

She nodded.

He relaxed and told it.

Six Heinekens later.

Which really wasn't shit. But Kubiak wasn't a drinker. He realized that as he tried to bring the room back into steady focus. As he tried to decipher if the curtain that gave him and Scarlett privacy from the outside was burgundy or red, or, shit, black even.

"You okay, Rich? Your eyes are rolling like marbles."

He smiled stupidly, burped loudly, punched his chest with a weak fist. "I'm cool."

"Not much of a drinker, are you?"

"Frankly, Scarlett, I don't give a damn."

She frowned as he giggled. "Please don't vomit," she said, wide-eyed. "They make me clean it up."

"Jill of all trades," he said in sing-song. "She skates over and takes your drink order. She rinses milk off of her body in the shower. She gives lap dances. She uses big SAT words. She *insinuates* that she's done some movie work. She…"

"Rich, baby?" Ever since he'd told her his story, her tone had changed, become motherly.

"Especially masterful at the lap dance," he said, not listening to her. "Like a Broadway production. *Riverdance*."

He muttered more nonsense she couldn't make heads or tails of. Something about some guy named Michael Flatley, who she took to be the lead of Riverdance. And then the Michael talk became something else altogether. Michael, Michael, Michael. Kubiak singing mournfully that he was a deep pool, that dark spring, warm with a mystery he'd reveal to her.

She wondered if the chemo drugs and alcohol were a bad mix. Touched Kubiak's shoulder and tried to relax him that way. It didn't work at all. He got even more restless, anxious.

"I should call Loretta. She's probably worried sick."

"Rich, that's probably not a good idea right now. Do you realize where you are?"

He fumbled in his pocket anyway, pulled out a cell phone, one of the prepaid cheap ones, frowned and glanced at the monitor that was nearly as big as the display on a Kindle e-book reading device. "Look," he said, waving the phone for Scarlett to see. "Six missed calls. All from Loretta. My long-suffering wife that won't have to suffer much, much, much longer, see."

Six. The same number of Heinekens he'd consumed. Symbolism of some sort? Maybe. Probably.

"Rich, baby?" Scarlett's tone was small, tentative.

Again, Rich wasn't hearing her. "Let's give her a ring, Scarlett, shall we?"

"Rich, baby?"

Without thinking, he dialed the number. Loretta picked up on the third ring. Calm, but just over eleven years of marriage had taught him to recognize the rising anger at the corners of Loretta's voice.

"Hunter fell asleep crying for you," she said.

"Low blow, Loretta. Using a five-year-old to make me feel guilty."

"Nothing else seems to work."

"Sure enough."

"You've been drinking?" A statement more than a question.

"I have," he said. "Knobs Creek aka warm Heineken."

"And it's loud wherever you are."

"AC/DC," he said.

"Strip club?"

"Certainly, Loretta."

She was crying softly a moment later.

He didn't expect that. It sobered him some.

"Shit. Loretta…"

"You've given up," she managed.

"You heard the doctors, Loretta. I'm not winning this one. We have to prepare you for…life without me."

"Hunter is—"

"Gonna grow up without his dad," Kubiak cut in.

Now he was crying as well. He quickly wiped the tears away with a hand as rough as Emory paper.

Scarlett squeezed his shoulders. He'd forgotten about her.

"Come home, please," Loretta whispered. "We'll get through this if you don't give up."

"I will," he said. "I'll come home. Gotta kill a guy first, though."

"What?"

"Don't wait up, Loretta. It's pointless."

"Richie…"

He disconnected the call.

∾

"Did I hear you say you were going to kill a guy?" Scarlett asked as soon as Kubiak pocketed his cell phone.

Kubiak looked at her. Low-cut top. Clinging boy shorts. That smile. That personality. Intelligence and quick wit to boot. Life was too damn short, for sure.

He nodded, said, "Daniel Ferrer. Some guy works with him named Michael Palmer hired me to do the dirty deed. I'll make a whole pile of money and leave it for Loretta and Hunter. It won't replace me, but...it'll certainly help. They won't be eating Ramen noodles for breakfast, lunch, and dinner, for at least five years if she's smart with the money. And Loretta's pretty good with money. Keeps everything budgeted pretty tight."

Scarlett frowned. "You're scaring me, Rich. You sound serious."

He smiled, said, "Serious as cancer."

"You're drunk," Scarlett said, shaking her head unbelievingly. "This is alcohol talk."

Kubiak stood up. "You're right. Pay me no mind."

"Where are you going?"

He smiled. "*Not* to kill Daniel Ferrer for this Michael Palmer bozo, that's for sure."

"Stay," Scarlett said, grabbing his wrist, caressing it lovingly.

"And burn through all the money I'm making *not* to kill Daniel Ferrer for Michael Palmer? That wouldn't be wise."

"I don't know what to say."

"Goodbye," he said. "That's the word of the moment when it comes to me. Goodbye."

"Rich..."

He took her hands in his own, looked her deeply in the eyes. Light blue; he'd been correct. "Don't know what I was expecting when I stopped and came in. But it wasn't *this*. I really want to thank you. You've made a dying man very happy in his last days."

"Rich…"

But he was moving away from her.

Then gone.

She watched the curtain flutter behind him.

The *burgundy* curtain.

Sad to see him go.

# CHAPTER

# EIGHT

The sky outside Michael Palmer's office window was white, full of wind that rapped the glass like the bump of hard knuckles, the sun as dull as an old light bulb. Earlier, on his way in to work it had been squint-bright, yet useless in warming the chilled air. Michael was dressed both for the weather and the fashion runway. A long, gray tweed overcoat. Dark corduroy pants. A stiff dress shirt. Heavy leather shoes. A muffler. A hat. His jaws and neck gleamed from a fresh haircut. He smelled faintly of expensive cologne and fragrant soap. Altogether representative of a CEO.

How could they take that away from him? He was the right man for the position, without question. He understood the complexities of the business better than anyone except Malcolm Ferrer himself. MRF Global was in good hands with Michael at the helm. And yet it was being snatched away from him.

He turned from the window, paused and looked out over the expanse of his new office. Loneliness. That was the sensation of the moment. He was alone in this fight. No allies. No friends. No shoulder to lean on. The feeling squeezed in on him, the emotion of it all causing an actual physical awareness. He had to leave before he passed out. Before he started to hyperventilate. Had to go. But where could he turn? And who could he turn to?

He rushed from the office without an answer. Ignored the

hushed whispers and quiet murmurs that greeted him in the outer office. Ignored his secretary—Maureen or Noreen?—as he bolted past her desk and she called for him, one dainty finger upraised in the air.

Where to?

He reached the bank of elevators. Didn't have an answer as he stabbed the DOWN button. No answer when the elevator doors binged open. Stabbing the button in the car, still without an answer. Falling toward the ground floor, no answer. The door binging open on the Atrium level.

Michael stepped out.

Finally with an answer.

He'd done it just once before. Hadn't felt good about himself immediately after. Unable to scrub away the stink of it all for days. Weeks. Months. Realizing then just how sick he was. How deep his addiction ran.

Just once before.

Miserable and full of pity for the longest time after. He'd immediately deleted the number from the contacts in his phone. But he hadn't erased the number from his memory. The fact he remembered a number he'd dialed just once, that spoke volumes.

Sickness.

Addiction.

He retreated behind a potted palm tree in the lobby, its fronds still and tall enough to shield him from view.

And.

He dialed that remembered number.

∞

Michael had stripped down to Perry Ellis boxers and a Hanes wifebeater undershirt by the time she arrived at the Marriott. She entered the room in a flourish, brushing crystals of rain off of her waist-length black coat. They spoke to one another with their eyes, and then she smoothly shrugged out of the coat, carefully laid it across the back of a chair, lit a long Virginia Slim with a Zippo lighter, and took a soft pull on the cigarette. She didn't bat her eyes, but the soft way she released the smoke, puckering her lips as she did so, was alluring enough to make Michael erect. Her attire was professional and entirely complementary to her curvaceous body. A cashmere sweater molded to the shape of her ridiculously full breasts. Tight, dark gray dress pants with subtle vertical stripes that lengthened her already supermodel-long legs. Black cutoff boots with three-inch heels. Eyes the color of coal. Thick lashes. Smoky eyeshadow makeup. A thin, straight nose, bee-stung lips. A tiny mole just above the upper one. Deeply tanned skin. A stunning brunette. Prettier than Eva Mendes and Cindy Crawford, but similar to them both in look.

"Usually save the smoke until after," she said, in a rich raspy voice that reminded him of Karla. "But I can see you're…sizable… so I'll partake beforehand if you don't mind. Clear my head and get myself ready for what is sure to be some vigorous action."

"Whatever makes you comfortable," Michael said.

"I was born comfortable, sweetie."

He didn't doubt it.

He patted the spot next to him on the bed. She took another pull of her Virginia Slim, snuffed it out with her fingertips, dropped it in the wastebasket next to the lone desk in the room, and took her place next to Michael.

They watched one another for seconds.

Then she said, "This isn't low rent, sweetie. We don't haggle over blow jobs in some alley behind Jade Garden. I'm a high-priced ho. So treat this as close to normal sex as possible."

Michael frowned.

"Meaning," she said. "Ease back the collar of my sweater and kiss my neck."

He did.

Kissed her there. She took in a deep breath. Inhaled him like Virginia Slim smoke. Michael eased her hair out of the way, held it at the back of her head, sucked right below her ear, and down the length of her neck. She leaned in to him, moaning softly. He ran his left hand under her sweater searching for a bra. Found nothing but naked flesh. Round and firm breasts above a washboard stomach. Her skin feverish to his touch. His own skin heating as well. At first he touched the breasts softly, carefully, but something in the way she carried herself told him she preferred a more cavalier touch. He kneaded them, pinched the nipples. Her moans increased. She searched for his lips. Locked them in a kiss too intimate for the circumstances.

Their tongues danced.

He tasted mint on her breath.

"You eat pussy?" she asked, breathless.

"No."

"Shame."

"You suck dick?" he asked.

"This is real sex, sweetie. Inspired lovemaking. We're not in the backseat of a Civic. Creativity rules the hour."

"That a yes?"

She narrowed her eyes, offered him a crooked smile. Eased a hand in the opening of his boxers. Gripped his hardness with one fist. Turned and twisted it until he turned and twisted right along with her. It hurt so good his eyes watered.

"You eat pussy?" she asked again, raspy, through gritted teeth.

He heard himself say, "Yes."

"Take off my pants."

He did.

Pants and her G-string panties. Took them both off.

Her pubis was shaved clean. The texture of her skin like silk on his tongue a moment later.

Both of her hands on his head, guiding him deeper into her core. Flicking his tongue over her swollen clit.

She panted and slid across the mattress. He growled and chased her. Flipped her over. An ass as round as her breasts. One of those Brazilian asses. Pure perfection. He kissed a cheek. Then the other.

Then.

Spread them wide with his hands and leaned inward to lick her asshole.

She muttered something unintelligible.

He eased a free hand under her, fingered her clit at the same time he ate her ass.

Sickness.

Addiction.

Taking this sex to places he'd never been before.

Her juices were a fountain on the spread below them.

He turned her over roughly, stuck his tongue in her pussy again. Licked around the folds until she pushed him away.

"Fuck," she muttered, and like a professional, didn't pause or hesitate, changed positions so that she was between his legs.

She took his length deep in her throat. Plenty of spit in her warm mouth. The head of his penis seeming to touch the walls of her esophagus.

Inspired lovemaking.

Creativity.

He was emptying out, in her mouth, before he realized what was happening.

The release greater than any he'd ever had.

He wanted to fall asleep. Drift off to a place far from here.

But she straddled him, somehow worked his flaccid penis into the opening of her vagina.

No rubber.

Sickness.

Addiction.

Over the line.

She moved her hips. Up, down, up, down.

And he felt himself growing.

Getting hard.

Within moments of the fullest release he'd ever had.

Amazing.

She grinded on his lap.

His dick throbbed.

Solid as rock.

He flipped her, fell out, just as quickly put himself back in.

Pounded her flesh.

Fucked her pussy as hard as he could.

Breathing heavy.

Legs aching from the stress.

But fucking it as hard as he could.

Gripping her ass as she gripped his.

Her ankles locked at his back.

A fight. His thrusts versus her locked-in position.

He won.

She eased her ankles apart. Opened her legs wider. Gave him full access of her flower.

He watered it with his semen.

A deeper release than the first time.

Rolling over on his back after.

Breathing extra heavy.

"Shit," he managed.

A revelation.

A change.

The regret he always felt immediately afterward…absent.

She said, "Should I shower now or wait?"

He said, "Wait. We'll be getting dirtier in a little while."

He couldn't see the smile on her face as much as sense it. Two kindred spirits. Intent on inspired lovemaking. The creativity of sex.

"I've never enjoyed myself more," she said. "I mean it."

He nodded.

"Got caught up in the moment," she added. "Not using protection was pretty reckless."

"It was," he agreed.

She studied him a moment, then said, "This is you."

"Me?"

She nodded. "I've helped you find yourself, I think. Sex. This is your thing."

As much as he wanted to, he didn't disagree.

Couldn't disagree.

It *was* him.

He was home.

At last.

CHAPTER
NINE

The television mounted high up on the wall was tuned to MSNBC. Volume on low. The host of the current program, Chris something-or-other, had perfectly coiffed gray hair and wore an understated but finely cut dark suit, all the while discussing the machinations of some ambitious political mover and shaker. The civic talk was completely lost on Daniel, though. The only things he heard were the occasional clicks and whirs of the intravenous contraption that fed liquid life into his father's veins, and the intermittent little bleeps and blips of a second machine that measured that fragile life, one drip of a heartbeat at a time.

Daniel crossed the cold tile, stopped at the window looking out on the street. The glass was slightly frosted by the chill on the air, but Daniel could see just clear enough. Several stories below, a man, comforted in a heavy goose-down coat, sold cut flowers from a cart on the corner, the flowers submerged in dirty water in equally dirty white painter's buckets. The opposite corner was manned by an even bigger cart, a yellow Sabrett's hot dog umbrella stapled to it, its proprietor rubbing his hands together and doing a little dance similar to the one Daniel did in front of his wood-burning fireplace.

Daniel gazed from one cart to the other, totally enthralled by the vendors' every movement. Better to focus on them than what lay ten feet behind him, give or take a foot.

His warm breath further fogged the windows. He resisted the urge to wipe the window clean with his gloved hands.

He resisted the urge to take off the gloves.

Or his heavy tan coat.

This was to be a short visit. He couldn't bear the sounds, the smell of urine and weak bowels and coppery blood and antiseptic cleaning solutions and the muted lights in the room and the hallway and the squeaking wheels on the food trucks that delivered trays of meals unfit for an animal. He couldn't bear the thought of his father in this state.

Unmoving.

Unresponsive.

He touched the glass finally, with one gloved finger, and drew a shape in the dew that could've been a million different things. A fist. A lump of misshapen clay. A heart.

And just as quickly as the shape took form, he wiped it away with the side of his hand. Juvenile. He had to pull himself together. He took a long breath, and then another. And turned back.

His father still lay in the bed, unmoving, unresponsive.

And Soledad was in a chair next to the bed, a tray table with a toothpaste bin and an empty water pitcher atop of it crowded by her, one leg pressed under her Indian-style in the chair, the other tapping the floor in some kind of rhythm, quietly flipping through the pages of a magazine she'd taken from the visitor's lounge. *Cosmopolitan.* Find the Perfect Gift for Anyone. How to Look Hot When the Weather Sucks. Craziest Wedding Dresses Ever.

Daniel looked at her instead of his father.

She must've felt it, because she looked up from her pages. Smiled.

He nodded back without smiling.

Malcolm's hospitalization had taught them the fine art of silent communication. Surprisingly, these silent exchanges were more intimate than any words they'd ever spoken to one another. Daniel's love for his wife had grown exponentially in the past few days.

"You look tired," she said. "Exhausted, actually."

He nodded.

She stood, stretched, yawned herself, and then tapped the armrest of her chair.

Daniel shook his head when she looked his way.

"The visitor's lounge?" she said, frowning slightly. "They had that long couch in there. You could stretch out much better."

"Home," he said. "We have that nice bed in our bedroom."

"Doctor should be in soon," she said, still frowning. "Didn't you want to have a word with her?"

Daniel sighed.

Soledad pursed her lips. Then: "Why don't you go down and stretch out in the car then. You can turn on the heat and relax. I'll sneak you a text when the doctor comes in."

He didn't smile exactly. But close.

She called for him as he neared the exit door of the room.

"Yeah?" he said, turning back.

Her sigh was almost imperceptible. The emotion Daniel read on her face wasn't at the corners of her mouth, but at the corners of her eyes instead. The look broke his heart.

He said, "What is it?"

She sighed again, this one more auditory. "I'm sorry."

"You don't have to be," he said, without pause, without knowing what she was sorry for. Whatever the sin, it was forgiven. That's how much he loved her. And always would.

"For everything," she said in an explanation he didn't ask for, didn't need. "For being so hard on you all of the time. For your relationship with your father. For how everything is going at work. I'm sorry for it all. You're a good man, Daniel. I mean it."

His own emotion *was* at the corners of his mouth. *And* his eyes. He'd always been an emotional soul, but the latest with his father just magnified what was inherent to him. He quickly sniffed his rising emotion away, which served to make it imminently worse.

"I love you," Soledad said quickly. "Now go get that rest."

Saving her husband from embarrassment.

Daniel's smile told her that he loved her as well.

Weary, he left the room and his loving wife and sleeping father behind.

Moments later, he was down in the hospital's immense parking garage, inside his Chrysler 300C, the heat turned up way high, his driver seat craned back flat, his eyes closed tight, a forearm resting across them for extra emphasis. Sleep was only but a beat away. He was both pleased and displeased by the prospect.

Tired, for sure. Exhausted, actually.

But afraid he might dream.

Soledad sat on top of him, took his hardness in her hand, and eased it deep inside of her, a wet sucking sound reverberating in an echo that bounced off of walls he couldn't find. All around them was a vacuum of incredible whiteness. White sheer curtains on a canopy bed. White floors. White walls he sensed but, again, didn't see. The bed they lay upon, a hospital bed as it turned out with a remote controller that changed its positions, the bed made up with thin white linens. Soledad leaned forward with her arms propped on the headboard behind him so that her breasts hung near to his face. She breathed fast, moaned loud, a patina of sweat covering her warm skin. Daniel took a breast in his mouth. Sucked it until Soledad's nipple hardened. Then the other breast and a second stone nipple. Her breaths came even faster. The sounds of their flesh slapping together drowned out the other sounds Daniel heard, somewhere in the distance. Clicks and whirs. Bleeps and blips.

Soledad came like a wild beast. Whipping her hair and thrashing.

Daniel emptied himself inside of her quietly.

Opened his eyes and noticed a shadowy figure at the head of the bed, the only break from the whiteness around them.

The figure stepped forward.

Michael Palmer.

Daniel waved at Michael, said, "Come on in, brother. There's plenty of room."

Soledad eased aside the covers so Michael could join them. Michael moved forward, naked from the waist down, his penis swollen and stretched to its full length. Soledad clapped her hands in joy. Daniel reluctantly mimicked his wife's ecstatic clapping. The bedsprings cried out as Michael fell in with Soledad and Daniel. Within seconds they were a tangle of limbs and naked flesh under the thin white sheet.

Then another figure broke through the whiteness. A slump-shouldered figure.

Malcolm Ferrer.

He, too, was naked from the waist down. His erection was as strong as Michael's, the penis of a man taller and younger. Malcolm took steps toward the bed, the erection pointing his way forward. Again Soledad clapped ecstatically. Daniel didn't this time. He grunted in severe disapproval, then said, "You'll have to wait a minute, father. We're not quite ready for you, yet."

Yet meant *never*. They'd never be ready for him. There wasn't enough room for Malcolm in the bed with the rest of them.

But Daniel wouldn't say that.

He rolled over instead, watched Michael Palmer stick his tongue deep inside Soledad's mouth.

Daniel clapped, slow and steady.

Three competing sounds that weren't bleeps and blips or clicks and whirs lulled him from his dreams. The parking garage was built in a circular fashion, six stories high, open to the elements on each level but clothed in a stainless steel scrim. It had started to rain. A hard driving rain abetted by strong easterly winds that smelled of salt and dead fish. Either the rain or the wind or both tapped a rhythm on the steel. The sound managed its way inside the Chrysler's interior. In addition, a plane in descent flew overhead, leaving behind a loud rumbling roar that seemed to ripple through the concrete like it was water. Lastly was the whoosh of heat from the Chrysler's vents.

Daniel Ferrer yawned and stretched, reached down to his left and blindly found the lever to raise his seat to an upright position. The digital clock on his dash told the story of a nearly one-hour nap and yet he still didn't feel refreshed. No matter. He had to go back inside. Soledad waited, and, though his father was unresponsive, he felt Malcolm waited as well.

He was out of the Chrysler in seconds, stretching once more, then locking up with a button on his keychain fob.

Fourth of the six levels, the hospital's entrance door all the way across the expanse of the level. Story of his life. Never one to get the space closest to the building. Always stuck out somewhere on the perimeter.

All of his thoughts were inane, purposely to avoid finding some context for his eccentric dreams.

He started walking.

Halfway across the level he spotted the front wheel of a bike, peeking beyond the nose of the Accord parked next to it. Silly, but his heart quickened a bit. So did his pace.

He reached the bike, a Suzuki Boulevard C90, MSRP over eleven thousand, and was about to bend and rub his hand across the floorboard-type footrests, when he realized he wasn't alone. A man stepped from the shadow behind the bike, a cigarette dancing between his lips, an orange and black ember working its way toward ash at the tip. The man dropped the cigarette to the oil-slicked pavement, and ground it out under his boot. His face was weathered beyond his years and though he was solidly built there was something unhealthy about him that Daniel couldn't quite put his finger on.

"A beaut, isn't it?" the man said, rubbing his hand over the seat of the bike.

Daniel nodded. "Yours?"

The man hesitated. "Yup. One of my more reckless purchases but"—and he smiled—"you only live once."

"Exactly," Daniel said, same thing he'd argued to Soledad when he bought his bike.

"You ride?" the man asked.

Daniel half smiled, nodded. "Yup." He couldn't recall ever using the word before but something about the man was magnetic. Something about him pulled Daniel right in.

The man moved forward another step, just a few feet separating him from Daniel now. His right hand opened and closed at his side. His upper lip was wet with perspiration. He closed his eyes ever so briefly, his lips moving in a whisper that looked prayerful. Then he opened his eyes again, smiling. Daniel noticed a chipped tooth in his lower row.

"Diarrhea," the man said.

Daniel had heard him clearly but still asked, "Excuse me?"

"Got to a point where my bowels just never felt completely empty. Always with the gas pains, cramps. Drank lots of milk to try and ease it but..." The man sighed, shook his head. "Then one day there's blood in the seat of my underpants."

"That's a tough tale, friend," Daniel said, finally noticing something sinister in the man's tone. He stopped, looked at the expensive watch on his wrist. "Well, I better get on inside. I'm hoping to speak with my father's doctor."

The man sucked his teeth. "I'd prefer you didn't."

"What's that?"

"I'd prefer you didn't," he repeated.

"You'd prefer I..." Daniel didn't finish it, just shook his head and took a step toward the entrance.

The man rushed ahead, blocked Daniel's way.

Daniel stopped. "You're troubled, friend. But there's nothing I can do to help you"—he rerouted, reached a hand in his pants pocket and fished out his cell phone. Concentrated on the phone, not even looking up. The strange man reduced to less than a threat. "Tell you what. Why don't you give me your number, friend? Maybe we can go riding together sometime." Fingers hovering above the keys, waiting for the digits to add to his contacts list.

"They call it distant when it spreads, turns metastatic. Ain't nothing *distant* about what's happened to my liver. Ain't nothing distant about the time I have left, either."

Daniel looked up then, his cell forgotten. Something in the man's tone...

The sound that leaked from Daniel's mouth would have embarrassed him if he had the wits to process it. As it stood, he didn't. His cell fell from his fingers, clattered on the hard pavement. Didn't break into pieces.

He took a hard step back, raised his hands.

A nine-millimeter automatic trained on him. And the man's hand wasn't shaking.

Daniel realized fear would get him killed. The last thing he could do was allow fear to seep from his pores like stale sweat. He had to bluff courage if necessary. He believed he could. He was Malcolm Ferrer's son, after all. Courage ran in his blood. He swallowed, managed, "What's your name, friend?"

"Rich Kubiak." No hesitation. Not a good thing. If the man wasn't concerned about Daniel knowing his name then...

"What do you want, Rich Kubiak?"

"A smile."

"Pardon?"

Rich let out an exasperated breath. The gun still didn't waver. "Could you smile for me?"

Daniel frowned. "Smile?"

Rich nodded. "I'll be seeing you in my dreams, what little time I have left. Least you could do is smile so that'll be the lasting image."

Daniel's frown deepened. "You're drunk?"

Why hadn't he realized that earlier?

Rich smirked, made a teeter-totter gesture with his left hand. "Ooon po-keet-oh."

Un poquito. *A little.* Bad Spanish.

"Let's start with you putting that away, Rich Kubiak," Daniel said.

"I was supposing I'd *end* with putting it away instead, Daniel."

Daniel cocked his head to the side, his eyebrows knitted. "You know my name?"

"Yes, sir."

Daniel processed what that meant. Then: "This about money?"

Rich nodded. "Loretta and Hunter need to eat, *friend*."

"Loretta? Hunter? Wife? Kid?"

Rich nodded.

Daniel smiled weakly. "How long you been married?"

Rich smiled strongly. "Appealing to my human side, Daniel? Pretty smart. I bet in most cases it would probably work."

"Just letting you know," Daniel said, his hands still upraised, "I mean you no harm."

Rich chuckled. "Course you don't. I'm the one with the piece."

And he fired it twice to illustrate his point.

One shot punched a hole in the knee of Daniel's pants. The second ate a chunk of Daniel's neck as he fell in a heap. He landed hard on his stomach, crawled a paintbrush stroke of blood along the dirty ground underneath him. His moans sounded oddly sexual.

Rich slow-strolled along behind Daniel as he crawled for his life. It didn't take much effort to overtake Daniel. Daniel was in the narrow corridor between two cars, still on his stomach, weeping softly, exhausted, the still ground like a treadmill below him.

Rich bent down, grabbed Daniel by the collar of his shirt. Daniel cried out, warm tears spilling down his cheeks and into his mouth. Rich turned him over by the captured collar. Gently.

"Aww fuck," Rich said, eyeing the gaping wound in Daniel's neck. Raw shredded meat, whorls of smoke rising from it. "This is some ugly business, friend. I'd no sooner been involved in it. God awful shit."

Daniel's eyes were closed in pain and confusion. His weeping was near hysterical.

Rich said, "Shh," and kissed the business end of his gun against Daniel's forehead.

Daniel muttered. God, Jesus, Lord.

Rich shook his head. "You talking to the Lord now, Daniel? Tell Him I wasn't too keen on the prospects of a colostomy bag, but I would've adjusted my thinking if He'd've just given me the chance, righteous mother—"

The nine-millimeter barked twice more.

Daniel's brain matter was warm, lumpy oatmeal on the pavement.

"Aww fuck," Rich repeated, sighing.

He stood to his full height, knees cracking with the effort, almost toppling over because of those weak joints and his silly overindulgence of alcohol, blotches of Daniel's dark blood and pieces of Daniel's pinkish flesh splattered over his face and hands and clothes. He looked down at the broken shell at his feet and shook his head. Life was a miserable, miserable thing. And it never ended well because it always, always, always ended in death.

Somebody in the distance broke those thoughts, a loud yet hesitant voice yelling at Rich Kubiak. No, more than one voice. Several. A mob maybe. Set to confront the madman shooting rounds in a public parking garage. The hospital. Oh, the irony of it all.

Rich pocketed the nine-millimeter automatic and turned around to face them.

His own hands upraised now.

# CHAPTER TEN

It wasn't just sex. They'd talked as well. Once the line had been crossed, once Michael had entered her without protection, all the walls had tumbled down. Their exchange turned into something more intimate than paid-for intercourse. A date almost. That, Michael realized, was a more egregious sin than the actual infidelity, than the unprotected sex with a stranger. And yet it didn't bother him.

In the process he'd discovered himself.

Who he was.

Who he wasn't.

He left the hotel moments after her, content, at ease. Warm still from a steaming hot shower, her scent scrubbed off of his skin but ever present in his nostrils. The *Sweet Pea* fragrance from Bath & Body Works, she'd told him. His fingertips tingled with the remembrance of her soft flesh, the sexy curves and contours of her body. The muscles in his groin, loose, relaxed. He chirped the Chrysler's locks with his keychain fob, fell in behind the wheel, released an audible breath that banished the ounce of guilt trying desperately to attach itself to him. An ounce being a generous portion with which to measure the guilt, because, truthfully, he was as at peace with his actions as he'd ever been.

Did he have a problem?

Certainly.

Could he overcome it?

Well, yes. He'd overcome it today in fact, by not fighting it. By allowing his inner desires to have their way. And he'd discovered that he didn't love Rachel any less afterward. She was still the woman of his dreams, and he'd do his best to let her know that as often as he was capable. He'd given too much power to the sickness, he now realized. He'd always looked at himself as having two options: either he beat the sickness, or it certainly would beat him. But now he understood that didn't necessarily have to be the case. They could coexist. He'd satisfy his desires and go on loving Rachel deep in his soul.

He'd placed the key in the ignition and turned it, and had his hand on the rearview mirror, adjusting it, tilting it just right, when he noticed the dark figure in his backseat.

His yelp was smothered by a different sound as a hard blow struck his right ear. A devastating blow that echoed through Michael's head and shoved him forward into the arms of darkness.

Water splashing his face, swimming into his nostrils, threatening to drown him. A rough hand slapping him to consciousness. A relentlessly harsh light following the frenzied path of his squinted eyes. Thick rope biting into his wrists and ankles. The squeaking sounds of the chair he was strapped to reverberating through the space as he struggled, to no avail, to free himself.

"Experience should've taught you the futility of that exercise," a voice called from the gloom.

Michael quieted himself as the source of the voice stepped into view. Lukas Doyle's shirtsleeves were rolled up past his elbows. A green garden hose was threaded through his hands. The look in his eyes made Michael swallow.

"Insouciant," Lukas Doyle said. "I've used the word to describe you before. Do you have any idea what it means?"

Michael's mouth was stuffed with rag, duct tape circled from his lips to the back of his head. Yet Lukas Doyle looked at him as though he expected an answer. And quick.

Michael struggled to supply one, his words muffled by the duct tape.

Lukas Doyle's jaw muscles churned, his nostrils flared, eyebrows knitted by a deepening frown. "Carefree, unconcerned, light-hearted," he said in an even voice as he moved closer. From experience, Michael knew how quickly Lukas Doyle's calm could turn into searing fury so he turned his head slightly, not wanting spittle to spray his face when it happened. Merriman stood in view, not five feet from him, thick veins roped across his swollen biceps. He worked the palm of his left hand with the fist of his right. Pounding it over and over again. Poised to hit something else with his sledgehammer strike. Michael frowned and turned in the other direction, spotted the dead eyes he associated with the D.C. Snipers peering at him from the shadows.

Boxed in.

No choice but to look Lukas Doyle in the eyes. Doyle was the unquestioned leader of the Bellatoris, he'd expect Michael's undivided attention. There would be no proceeding until he received it.

Michael turned back, and gave it to him.

Lukas Doyle nodded. "*What joy when the insouciant armadillo glances at us and doesn't quicken his trotting across the track into the palm brush. What is this joy? That no animal falters, but knows what it must do?*" He inched even closer and Michael flinched. The fearful gesture seemed to wound Doyle in some way. His eyes appeared to soften and so did the hard mask that covered his stone face. "That's from a poem entitled 'Come into Animal Presence.'

Denise Levertov. She was born in Essex, in the U.K. Her mother was Welsh, her father a Russian Hassidic Jew. When she was twelve she sent a poem to T.S. Eliot. He sent back a two-page letter of encouragement. She went on to publish her first poem at the age of seventeen. Are you familiar with her work, Michael?"

Michael mumbled words into the duct tape again.

"No?" Lukas Doyle said sadly. "That's too bad."

He struck Michael sudden and fiercely with the back of his hand. Two of the chair's casters lifted off of the ground but quickly touched back down again. The chair didn't topple over. Michael's eyes watered and his nose burned. He labored to breathe.

"I've failed you," Lukas Doyle said. "Failure makes me miserable, you understand."

Another sound. The harsh light in Michael's eyes dimmed. He took the moment to further survey his surroundings. Wide open space. Dirty concrete flooring. Smudged windows angled above him. Ceiling that was at least thirty feet high in his estimation. The air was dank, carried the smells of basement mold and engine oil and a million other unpleasant odors he couldn't quite place. A warehouse of some sort. Old and abandoned.

Liz Sutherland's heels clicked the concrete as she stepped forward. The heavy industrial-strength flashlight she'd had trained on his eyes in one hand, the gleaming point of her infamous knife in the other. Michael searched her face for emotion. Blank.

"I'm afraid I've allowed you to remain unconcerned," Lukas Doyle said, breaking through Michael's concentration on Liz Sutherland. "I've allowed your carefree attitude to foster itself into the ugliness that it now is. I take full responsibility for doing so; you're completely absolved of any guilt in the matter, Michael." He paused, allowed an unpleasant smile to flitter across his face. "You aren't absolved of abusing the charity I've extended to you, though." He shook his head. "That I'm afraid you must pay for."

He struck Michael again, backhanded as before. The chair tipped sideways and righted itself.

Liz placed the flashlight at her feet and walked wordlessly in Michael's direction, disappearing behind him. Michael strained to look over his shoulder. Couldn't, of course. A moment later the cool kiss of metal was on his ear. Then just as suddenly it was gone.

*They'll torture me*, he thought.

He felt something rooting through his hair. He closed his eyes. Tight.

Pressure on the back of his neck. He kept his eyes closed. Liz Sutherland's sharp blade edged under the tape at Michael's neck. It chewed through the duct tape without concern. An *insouciant* cut. Michael wondered how much of his hair had been shorn off.

Lukas Doyle moved to him and, in one swift movement, ripped the frayed duct tape from Michael's face. The skin burned like a raw wound. Michael spit out the rag and coughed and gasped for air. Liz was still behind him and the fear of what she might do next was almost too much. He shivered and searched the distance for some hope. None presented itself. None existed. A hopeless situation if there ever were one. His shoulders sagged.

After a moment, he focused his eyes on Lukas Doyle. Better to die with some measure of dignity.

"You've graduated to prostitutes," Lukas Doyle said, shaking his head. "Again, I feel responsible for that cavalier approach."

"Fuck you," Michael managed.

Lukas Doyle nodded. "I figured that was coming. Your problem is one of perspective, Michael Allan Palmer. You lack the proper context of thinking when it comes to practically everything."

Michael remained silent. He'd said all he would say.

"You seem to always align yourself with the wrong individuals,"

Lukas Doyle continued. "Loose women, both those you've paid for and those you've acquainted through traditional means. Incompetents in the mailroom...and with Human Resources." Lukas Doyle smiled. "Corrupt former police officers."

Michael's eyes sparked alive.

Corrupt former police officers?

Lukas Doyle's smile widened. "A nerve has been touched," he said. "Your surrogate father, Ridley, isn't quite the decorated individual you believe him to be, Michael Allan Palmer. You asked him to turn over some rocks and trample through my life...?"

It wasn't really a question.

"...leaves me no choice but to trample through his. You've now involved him. Just as you involved the others. And again, you aren't the blame, Michael. I'm afraid I allowed this all to occur. This has gotten out of control. I take responsibility for the collateral damage that must occur."

Only one word floated through Michael's mind.

*Corrupt.*

Lukas Doyle read the questions in his eyes. He said, "That surprises you? Ridley, corrupt? You don't know the details, do you? That figures, an individual with your lack of discernment. Well, let me enlighten you about the great Ridley, Michael Allan Palmer."

Lukas Doyle smiled and enlightened Michael.

# CHAPTER
# ELEVEN

t was grunt work, pure and simple. There was nothing romantic or glamorous about it. And worse, it afforded those that took on its many challenges with little in the way of respect from those that didn't. The brave men and women that took the oath to protect and serve were, in many minds, individuals that lived somewhere in the margins, distant from the neat little writing lines. Maybe all of that was the truth. Maybe it wasn't. Whatever the case, the work never left you. Ridley's heart still quickened at the sound of an alarm. In restaurants he insisted on tables that gave him a clear vantage of the front door and entire dining area, and his eyes rarely stayed on his food or his dinner companion, instead in constant observance of everything around him. Instinctively he measured people by their height and weight, their hair and eye colors, any distinguishable gestures and marks. His blood always was and always would be a dark shade of blue.

He'd made peace with this fact.

Everyone didn't understand it. Couldn't understand it. It made relationships a difficult proposition. Jo-Jo obviously had a deep understanding of the phenomenon, and so they'd taken to one another without any glitches. Jacqueline was similar in so many ways it was eerie. He thought he might actually ask her to marry him one day soon. An old timer like himself, married. The thought made him shake his head in astonishment.

She'd left, but he could still smell her scent in the air.

He'd yet to tell Jacqueline, or admit to himself, how lonely the house became when she left.

He shuffled into the kitchen, opened the door that led down into the basement. The door hinges were rusted and didn't allow for an easy opening. He had to jiggle it a bit and put some weight into the effort. The hinges cried as it finally yawned open. Ridley sighed, shook his head, felt along the wall at the top of the stairwell, found a switch, flipped it up. Muted yellow light focused a path down creaky wooden stairs. Cause for another sigh, but he didn't bother. He simply took the steps, one at a time. Slowing as he neared the middle, practically crawling near the bottom. Breathing heavy.

His slippers scratched the basement floor as he touched down on cold concrete the color of raw pottery clay. He paused and leaned against the stairwell wall, touched his chest with the two familiar fingers, a pulse that seemed to skip and jump just beneath his clammy skin. Clammy skin. Poor circulation. Imperfections in his heart rate. *Ba-bimp. Ba-bimp. Bimp bimp bimp...bimp. Ba... Ba...Bimp.* Who would have ever predicted this?

Another heart attack waiting to happen.

He was certain of it.

No, no, no. That was defeatist thought. Ridley was a great many things but defeated wasn't among the number. Yet he had to really work to refrain from the negative thoughts that seemed to plague him the last few years. Had to make sure he didn't let the thoughts cripple him where his body, or heart more aptly, had not. Remember, he had to tell himself, you've been knocked down but not completely out. A vast difference between the two. It wouldn't be easy moving forward, for sure. But nothing ever was.

He pushed off of the wall and scratched his way across the

basement, stopping at the back of the space, near a ragged brick wall that shed red dust on the regular. He looked at the head-high glass case butted up against the brick wall, and, directly to the side of the case, a long foldable picnic table. The glass of the case was Windex cleaned. The top of the table covered with old newspaper taped down with masking tape so that the sheets didn't shift out of place. An ancient wood chair with soft cushioning was situated by the table, a duplicate chair beside it, the second chair's seat filled with a square box-shaped device, a power cord trailing like a snake toward a nearby wall socket.

Uniden police scanner.

Ridley turned it on, adjusted it to the proper channel, his old Precinct's. It coughed static and then burped out several calm voices in the midst of a major crisis.

*Report of two victims and multiple people barricaded in the basement.*

Ridley paused to listen.

*Respond to Broad and Spruce Streets, their stage. We have a shooting on West Front Street, but we need to stage at Broad and Spruce.*

Ridley reached for the glass case, managed the door open, eased out a bolt action rifle, laid it down carefully on the picnic table. His eyes never leaving the police scanner the entire time.

*Notify EMS to stage at Broad and Spruce.*

*Staging EMS Broad and Spruce. 10:38.*

Ridley bent at the waist, his eyes still trained on the scanner, and rooted through a sagging cardboard box under the table. Pulled out a cleaning kit he kept in a leather bag styled like those used for bank deposits.

*Students in the basement were in classes that were being held in basement classrooms.*

*10-4. If you can communicate with anybody from them, have 'em lock their doors.*

Ridley scooted the empty chair up to the table and sat down heavily in it. It took a bit of effort to remove the rifle's bolt. To do so he pulled the trigger and pressed a lever. The bolt clattered like ice in a glass as he dropped it on the table. Sweat prickled his back, molded his T-shirt to his skin.

The scanner squawked.

*226, I have information. Suspect described as an Asian male, wearing a dark jacket, likely black, black glasses, in his 20s. Vehicle is Bravo Whiskey Echo 7823. '94 Buick Century. 4-door green, to a Henry Woong. Whiskey Oscar Oscar November Golf, 8 Grove Street, East Orange. Date of birth 4/12/61.*

*Copy. Broad Street and Spruce shut off and also North.*

Ridley removed a collapsible ram rod from the leather pouch, fitted a small folded cloth through a hole in the rod's body. Opened a container of nitro solvent that released a strong chemical odor.

*Black jacket, black glasses, stands between 5'8" and 6" tall. There is a male down on the ground in front of the reception desk and a female with an abdominal wound on the first floor under one of the desks. Most of the subjects so far are in the basement, about 20 of 'em, unable to barricade that door, there's no furniture.*

*10-4.*

*Do we believe him to still be in the basement at this time?*

*The first floor. And he did enter the building alone.*

*10-4.*

Ridley dipped the cleaning pad in the nitro solvent and pushed the ram rod down the rifle's throat, back near the firing mechanism where he'd pulled out the resistant bolt.

He worked through three pads before one came out completely clean. At that point he put the ram rod and solvent back in the kit. Took out a larger cloth and gun oil and dipped a corner of the cloth in the oil. Used the corner to wipe down the metal parts of the rifle.

Sweat flowered on his forehead and he realized he wasn't breathing as smoothly as usual. He paused long enough to hand wipe sweat from his brow and take a couple of deep breaths.

Then back to it.

He wiped down the wood of the rifle with the dry portion of cloth. The scope lenses were smudged so he wiped them down as well.

*Bryant, I know you're busy. Ask Hill if they want some kind of perimeter set up or what they want from us.*

*Copy, 13. 10:43.*

Done.

Ridley carefully packed everything away, cleaning kit in the sagging cardboard box under the table, the rifle in the Windex cleaned glass case, and pushed back and up from the table, satisfied. He stood there a moment more, listening intently to the scanner.

*C106 will be there momentarily to assist closing that down and then you can slide down to 3s location.*

*Copy Bryant.*

That was *done*, too.

He turned off the Uniden scanner, pivoted stiffly and moved toward the steps, paused there at the foot of the stairs with one arm propped against the wall. The rise and fall of his chest was obvious. Which, in his mind, wasn't a good thing. Normal breathing should be a natural, unthinking action. It shouldn't be obvious unless you'd really exerted yourself, which he hadn't. It shouldn't take any noticeable effort to simply breathe. If it did, as was the case now, then you had yourself a major problem. Ridley shook aside those thoughts and headed up. He was toward the middle of the stairs when he heard it.

The cordless Vextra in the kitchen.

He picked up his step just to prove to himself that he could, and had the receiver in his quivering hand by the fifth ring.

"Hello," he answered, nearly breathless, the word hacked up into more than its normal two syllables.

The work never left you.

"Rid," the voice on the other line said. It was an unmistakable voice. A symphony of deep notes mixed with comically high ones. The voice of a boy struggling through adolescence. The voice of a ghost.

"McNutt," Ridley said to the cop son of an old colleague. Everyone called him "Nuts" as they'd done with Daddy McNutt years before, but in the case of this younger carbon the nickname wasn't quite endearing. Ridley remembered junior from Daddy McNutt's funeral a few years earlier. His shirt darkened in the underarms with sweat that smelled like sour cream and onion potato chips. A walk that made you think of the Tin Man in the *Wizard of Oz*. Awkward in every way a human being could be judged. But an incredible cop with a real nose for the law. Ridley's kind of guy.

"You staying warm?" McNutt asked.

Twenty-six degrees that felt at least ten below that. Nobody was staying warm. Awkward small talk.

Ridley said, "Hell of a situation you got on Broad and Spruce."

"You heard about that, huh?" McNutt said without emotion.

"Was hearing it happening on the scanner I got for a retirement gift," Ridley said. He looked out of his kitchen window. An orange Dumpster the length of two Cadillacs resting along the curb across the way. The burned frame of a duplex on the lot behind it. The shingled siding interrupted by scars of charred brown-and-black and what looked like ripped foil paper. Plywood instead of wood covering most of the windows in the window frame cutouts. Eleven Mexicans misplaced by the fire. Ridley had sensed something in the air the night of the fire and looked out his window. Spotted the flames licking at the duplex's cheap wood structure. Called it in to 9-1-1 and walked outside in his slippers and pajamas. Even today, three months removed from that day, he could still smell the wood barbecue in his nostrils. He shivered, turned his attention back to the caller. "We got it buttoned down yet, Nuts?"

We.

The work never left you.

McNutt let out an inappropriate laugh. "You know how it goes. We're all over it, Rid. Weapons and Tactics is in on it now. Those trigger-happy fucks will make wonton soup out of Hostage Boy he doesn't give it up real soon."

"These are the breaks," Ridley said. Then: "But you didn't call to see if an old fool was listening to the scanner."

"No," McNutt said. "No."

"You find out something about the security over at MRF for me?" Ridley asked.

He'd called in a query after Michael left, at Jacqueline's insistence. If it weren't for her, he would've probably let it sit for awhile. Michael struck him as paranoid. He couldn't believe that a corporate security outfit was as bent, and dangerous, as Michael wanted him to believe. Now, though, hearing McNutt's disturbed voice on the line so quickly after his call, he wondered if he were wrong. Thank goodness for Jacqueline.

McNutt cleared his throat in the receiver. Rustled his chair as he readjusted his body positioning. "My old man—God bless his soul—he always said you were stand-up, Rid."

"Nuts was a good man hisself," Ridley said.

"Sure enough," McNutt said. "What he actually said about you was 'Rid's dick is harder than the skulls on these knuckleheads we have to yank back by the collar.' I'll never forget those words. In a way, they're very profound. You know what I'm saying?"

"No," Ridley said. "Why don't you take the mashed potatoes out of your mouth, Nuts, and get to it?"

"Mashed potatoes?"

Ridley said, "Been reading a lot of James Lee Burke. 'Bout as close as I get to the action anymore. Books and my scanner."

"I like that Lee Child myself," McNutt said. "My old lady does, too. She'd sit on the oven burner to keep her sweet spot warm for Child's Jack Reacher. Meanwhile, I have to manage a twenty point vig with MasterCard to get her excitable. But, like you say, these are the breaks."

Ridley said, "Nuts?"

McNutt lived with several coughs for a beat. "Sorry about that," he said afterward. "Trying to quit the damn cigarettes. They're killing me slowly. I've moved over to the Marlboro Lights, but, well…"

"Nuts?"

McNutt sighed. "We caught ourselves a body down at the hospital yesterday. Multiple GSW's. One of the girls at Cheaters had an interesting perspective on the situation."

Ridley said, "Cheaters? That one of them titty bars?"

"And ass," McNutt said. "Can't forget the ass."

"Okay?"

"Scarlett, that's her name, claims a guy came in, got himself in an inebriated state, and then started yapping about how he was going out to kill somebody, *for somebody*. A hired hit, in other words."

"Our body at the hospital?" Ridley said.

"Yes."

"Okay?"

"Rid, listen. Like I said, my old man had every kind word regarding you."

"You'd like I'll see if I can scare up some of them old S & H Green Stamps we used back in the sixties," Ridley said. "Might have some packed away still in my basement. We can lick 'em together and keep reminiscing about the good old days."

McNutt sighed again. "I couldn't tell you shit about Pearl Harbor or Hiroshima or fucking Paul Revere, but I know my history. My *cop* history."

"This gonna conclude at some point, Nuts?"

"The body turns out to be Daniel Ferrer."

Ridley straightened and exhaled loudly. Immediately the rhythm of his heartbeat changed. Surprisingly, he didn't track it. "Shit," he said. "The family's been notified?"

Thinking of Rachel, of Michael.

"Soon," McNutt said. "A few extraordinary things have occurred that kind of took precedence."

"That so?"

McNutt sighed again. "Look, Rid. I'm not gonna sit here and blow smoke up your ass. I respect you too much for that."

"Okay…" Ridley said in a measured tone.

"Thing like this, a rich guy like Ferrer involved, you know the brass gets a hard-on to get it all figured out pretty quickly. We've been on it pretty hard for the little while since it crossed our desks."

"I'm sure," Ridley said.

McNutt sighed once more. "Scarlett claims the guy doing all the talking while she was doing the cha-cha on his lap was hired out to do the hit on Daniel Ferrer by your old partner's son. Michael Palmer."

"What?"

"I know, Rid, I know."

"His brother-in-law," Ridley said. "His wife's brother. Are you serious?"

"Word is they weren't raising their hands to be one another's Secret Santa any time soon. Lots of issues at work. Personality conflicts. Public disputes. Apparently they got into it at the hospital when the old man had his stroke. You're aware of all of this, or I'm giving you new news?"

"Murder is serious business, Nuts."

"It is."

"It takes a special kind of person to plot something like this."

"Agreed."

"Michael Palmer isn't your guy. I can vouch for him. Trust me."

"Not on this one, Rid. I'm sorry. We have some solid intel."

Ridley turned his eyes away from the charred house across the road. He sat down in a mismatched kitchen chair hemorrhaging foam stuffing from a rip in the seat. "We're listening to strippers now, Nuts? I never met a stripper or a hooker couldn't tell a good story. Most of 'em could knock *Twilight* and James Patterson off the fucking *New York Times* list if they could keep their drawers on long enough to focus and get the shit down on paper."

"We got the shooter, Rid. A Rich Kubiak. Black coffee is the drink of the Gods. His head's cleared up quite a bit and he's sticking to the story he told Scarlett. Judge Fitzgerald let us creep Kubiak's BOA accounts. Twenty large in one of them. Wired in from Palmer's company. We made an inquiry with Accounts Payable at MRF Global first thing this morning and they're not sure about the payment. Lotta *hmm's* and *well geez's* 'cause now they realize something's hinky with how Palmer asked them to code the payment. But, bottom line, Rid, Michael Palmer authorized the payment. That's solid."

Ridley closed his eyes, breathed through his nose, dropped his head and rubbed at the closed eyes. After a beat he said, "This Kubiak fella says Michael? And you believe him?"

"He does. And the trail's warm as Scarlett's love box. We got this thing now called electronic footprints…"

Ridley noticed a severe weight on his chest. He touched by his heart with the two fingers. *Ba-bimp. Ba-bimp. Ba…Ba…Ba…bimp.* "I appreciate the call, Nuts," he said, cutting it short. "And I understand fully. You do what you have to do. I won't interfere."

"We're holed up outside Palmer's place, and at the MRF offices, but so far he hasn't shown himself either place. Soon as he does we're gonna grab him and have a word or two. Thought you'd wanna know, Rid. I'm sorry I had to be the one to tell you."

"Again," Ridley said, "I appreciate it. I won't interfere."

Ridley set the cordless gently back in its base. One, two, three beats, a quick split-second decision, then he picked the cordless up again and dialed the familiar numbers slowly. His heartbeat matched the rings cycling in his ears, sluggish and drawn out.

He contemplated hanging up, unsure of what he'd say.

The call dropped into voicemail. Michael's professional voice came on the line. A refined, educated voice. Definitely not the voice of a man who'd orchestrate a killing. Ridley pictured Michael as a young boy, then as a young man, and finally, now. Married, a respectable member of society. Smart enough to be the CEO of a major corporation. Frank would be incredibly bothered by the trouble that seemed to be dogging his boy.

*Leave a message.*

Ridley managed, "We need to get together, son, posthaste. Make that your number one priority."

Breaking his word to a brother in blue.

Interfering.

# CHAPTER TWELVE

Merriman and the one with eyes like the D.C. Sniper's were directed to leave. A moment later, Michael heard old-fashioned freight elevator doors bang shut off in the distance. And after that, the whir of hardworking cables as the rickety elevator plummeted toward the bottom level. A settlement of water collected in the eaves fell in a loud splash on the concrete flooring. Michael's breaths coming with the rapid thrush sound of a panting dog.

But other than those sounds the warehouse was silent.

Michael stared straight ahead. Lukas Doyle wouldn't meet his gaze. What to make of that? Could anything positive come out of Doyle's sudden detachment? What did it mean?

Michael swallowed, fearful he knew what it meant. His moment of reckoning had finally arrived.

Doyle's nod was slight, nearly imperceptible. Liz Sutherland moved from the shadows at Michael's back, heels clicking, gleaming blade in her hand. She traded a silent communication with Lukas Doyle, and paused there, her back to Michael, as Doyle retreated the way Merriman and the one with eyes like the D.C. Sniper's had gone. When the freight elevator's doors banged once more, she turned back to Michael, smiling, her knife hand raised.

He risked a glance in his rearview mirror. A breath caught in his throat and died. Both of his nostrils were caked with dried blood. Bottom lip bisected by a split that burned like fire every time he frowned from the pain embedded in his muscles. His left eyelid a swollen, plum-colored mess, the eye peeking through a slit the shape of a mail slot. Still, he felt fortunate. The whisper of death had seemed inevitable. And, before that final mercy, a long difficult torture that would send him to the grave broken, bruised, battered.

None of that happened. The surprise still had its arms around him. He glanced back at the warehouse. A dark, foreboding structure that seemed to lean with the strong swirling winds. His hands shook as though overcome with palsy but he willed his key in the ignition. *Get away before she changes her mind, and comes to cut you into ribbons.*

He allowed the engine to warm for just a few seconds, and took off. Two turns later he pulled over on a quiet street and sobbed.

Later.

He listened to the voicemail message twice, unable to read Ridley's tone. There was something both unemotional and emotional at the edges of Ridley's voice. A contradiction for sure. Perhaps Ridley had discovered something about the Bellatoris, just as Michael had discovered something about Ridley.

Corrupt.

It was still hard to swallow.

Despite the oddity of Ridley's message, Michael decided returning the call would be another injury he could ill afford to contend with. He flipped his BlackBerry on the passenger seat and continued driving.

Headed for the warm comforts of home.

Home sweet home.

Michael braked to a stop. Up ahead a car idled at the curb directly across from his house. He spotted a light bar mounted in the rear window, the car's wheels painted black, a divider between the front and rear seats. A Chevy Impala, not the Crown Vic from movies and books. But obviously an unmarked police car. The guys inside, both who appeared to be white, both with close-cropped hair, seemed particularly interested in what was happening inside Michael's silent, dark house. Their eyes were riveted in that direction, seeing nothing else. *Rookies*, Michael thought, *sent to do the scut work*. Good thing, otherwise Michael was sure he would've been spotted by now. He pulled into a drive several car lengths behind them, reversed out easily and turned the way he'd come.

Safely away, he reached over and plucked his BlackBerry from the seat. Dialed one-handed. Ridley answered in the same unemotional and emotional tone as the voice message.

Michael said, "We should meet up."

The ground was hard. Mostly dirt, sprinkles of grass. The lot had recently been blacktopped, but the white lines painted in to indicate parking spaces were already fading. A flutter of soundless birds swooped across the sky. Ridley slowly eased himself out of his old Plymouth, made it to his feet, and closed the driver's-side door behind him. Michael mimicked those movements as he made his way from the Chrysler 300C. They converged at the grille of Ridley's Plymouth. A frown creased Ridley's face as he noticed the damage to Michael's. Michael didn't explain, and Ridley didn't ask. Instead, they moved without speaking toward the gravestones. Every foot or so they had to weave around a plot. When they reached the two they cared about they stopped. Ridley's breath came in slow rasps. Michael's own breathing was even, measured.

Francis Lloyd Palmer.

Frank.

Joan Palmer.

Jo-Jo.

Michael's deceased parents.

Ridley's eyes watered as the cold slapped his face. He buried his hands deep in his coat pockets. Michael seemed unaffected by the frigid temp in comparison. He wasn't squinting. The leather gloves he'd worn earlier were stuffed in his pockets instead of on his hands. He looked up and over the headers of the gravestones, focused on something far off in the distance.

"It was her eyes that got me," Ridley said.

Michael didn't ask whose eyes.

"And her smile. Like a fireplace in the winter. It had a warming effect. Worked its way from your toes and made it all the way to your head. She was simply a beautiful woman, inside and out. And I know that's something people say all the time, but in her case it was true."

Again Michael nodded.

"Of course I knew it was wrong me feeling that way, and so I tucked it away. Safe and sound, so to speak."

"But…" Michael said, moved finally to speak.

Ridley hocked phlegm, spit it on the cold hardened ground, a distance from the grave markers. Respect. That mattered to him. Always had. "Your father pulled me aside one day. Real serious-like. I could tell something heavy was on his mind. Frank was always serious, mind you, but that day even more so."

"Okay."

Ridley glanced at Michael, breathing hard through his nostrils all the while. The air like ice cold water circulating in his lungs. "He had a couple scares before…"

The heart attack. The BIG one.

"Scares?" Michael asked, oddly detached, his eyes not once settling on Ridley.

"I don't know the details," Ridley answered, shaking his head. "He was pretty guarded about it all. As we tend to be. But whatever it was, it opened his eyes to his own mortality. 'We ain't promised forever,' he told me."

"That we're not," Michael agreed, thinking about himself tied to a chair, duct tape covering his mouth, in some old abandoned warehouse out of a horror movie.

Ridley frowned. "What's troubling you, son?" Pausing, waiting for the confession.

None came.

"Continue your story," Michael said.

Ridley hesitated, sighed after a moment. The sigh like a dying man's last breath. "He asked me to look after you…and your mother. He kept saying, 'She's a beautiful woman, Rid. And young enough still.' That's as close as our type would ever come to granting permission. You understand?"

He let the words settle before risking another glance Michael's way. For his part, Michael finally showed the first signs that he respected the bitter cold. He had his hands together and pressed to his lips as he blew on them, his shoulders hunched forward in his coat.

"You heard me?" Ridley asked.

Michael nodded, toed the hard ground with his shoe. So many thoughts trapped inside his head.

"He was giving me permission, boy."

"Did you need it?"

Ridley considered the question for a moment. "Made it easier," he answered truthfully. "But I would've been there for Jo-Jo either way. I would've done anything for that woman."

"I see."

"I was the one that noticed the swelling in her arm, Michael. I'm the one that made her go to the doctor."

Swelling in her arm.

Yellow pus leaking from her nipple.

Stage IV before she knew what hit her.

Spread to her lungs and liver.

"I bought her the wig after her treatment."

"I remember it," Michael said. "I didn't care for it much."

Ridley frowned, hocked more phlegm, spit it on the ground. Near to Michael's feet.

Michael looked up. They locked eyes.

Ridley said, "You've gotten yourself in a whole heap of trouble, boy."

"Oh yeah?"

"Interesting response."

"I bet," Michael said.

"I'm responsible for you," Ridley said. "I promised your father I'd look out for you."

"A man of honor," Michael said, spitting the words.

Ridley frowned again. "You have a problem with me all of a sudden?"

"Tell me about your pension," Michael said.

Ridley's frown deepened. "That's a curious request."

*Describe pain.*

"Tell me," Michael said.

Ridley shifted, winced, then settled himself. "It's handsome enough," he said. "I'm paid in eight and a half percent. 'Tween that and my Social Security, I get by."

"And if you lost it?"

"Can't see how I could. I put in a lot of blood and sweat for that money. Put my life on the line every time I hit those streets."

"And if you lost it?" Michael repeated.

"I'd be in trouble," Ridley admitted.

Michael nodded, looked away.

"Say it," Ridley said.

Michael didn't hesitate. "George A. Eugenides."

Ridley swayed, caught himself. "What are you saying, boy?"

"There was a motorcycle accident, the summer of '02. Mr. Eugenides, the county district attorney, out on his Harley, blowing off some steam. Turns out Mr. Eugenides mixed up a few words… mistook 'above the law' for 'uphold the law.' An easy enough oversight, I suppose." He paused, watched Ridley. The older man's face looked ready to crack. Michael's stomach rumbled, but he kept on. "Eugenides found out he was the target of an investigation involving the cover-up of his motorcycle accident and he—"

"Stop right there," Ridley barked. "I don't like where this is going."

"You were close to retiring."

"Stop, Michael."

"Mr. Eugenides asked you to testify." Again Michael paused for effect. "Or better still, his sister Jacqueline asked you."

Ridley turned to leave. Michael grasped his shoulder, easily turned him back. The old man had no resistance. "You gave false testimony."

Ridley hung his head.

"You also started up with Jacqueline," Michael said. "And if my math is correct, that would've been the time my mother was losing her battle."

Tears flowed from Ridley's eyes.

"Corrupt," Michael said.

"Where'd you hear about this?" Ridley whispered, his gaze on the ground.

"The Bellatoris," Michael whispered back. "They found out I'd asked you to check up on them. Apparently they have connections down at the Precinct. They weren't happy about your snooping. They confronted me earlier."

Ridley looked up. "Your face?"

Michael nodded. "Old warehouse. Tied me to a chair. Duct-taped my mouth closed."

"Jesus, what kind of—"

"Dangerous," Michael cut in. "Just as I told you. Worse than I told you. I've personally witnessed them kill."

"Kill?" Ridley's voice died on the wind.

Michael's turn to look away, to hang his head. "I'd been having an affair. Another one. The woman, Karla, learned I was married, made noise that sounded an awful lot like blackmail. I asked one of the Bellatoris for help with Karla. The woman in the four, Liz Sutherland. I thought she'd put a small scare in Karla, make her back off. They killed my problem for me. I was there. A broken down roach motel. Karla called and wanted to get together again. I was, am, weak when it comes to that sort of thing. Karla insisted on somewhere dirty because what we were doing was dirty. I woke up to darkness, Karla tied to a rickety old chair.

They cut a second mouth out of her throat." Not quite sobbing as he told it, but close.

"Jesus," Ridley whispered once more.

"Before I came to you, I asked the girl from HR I told you about, Cassie, to tell me anything she could about them. As you know, she's gone missing now."

"Jesus."

"You're not to ask any more questions about them, Rid. Or else your life will become as complicated as mine. I'd hate for you to lose your pension...or your life. They're capable of making either of those things happen. But they're my nightmare. I don't want to see anyone else hurt."

"Michael—"

"But I do have one last favor to ask."

"Name it," Ridley said, his voice hoarse.

"There were some police stationed outside of my house. It was pretty obvious they were looking for me. Can you find out what they want?"

"Daniel Ferrer."

Michael frowned. "What?"

"You know a man named Rich Kubiak?"

Michael shook his head, still frowning.

"Daniel's dead, Michael."

"What?" Michael asked, stumbling back.

"Murdered."

"When?"

"Yesterday."

"My, God. Rachel." He moved to leave.

"The Kubiak fella claimed you hired him to do it," Ridley called.

Michael stopped, turned back slowly.

"There's record of a payment to Kubiak through your company. Your name's all over it."

Michael sighed. "I'm in trouble?"

Ridley nodded. "Deep."

"What do I do?"

"Get away," Ridley said. "Let me try and sort some of this out for you. Remember the article you were telling me about?"

Michael nodded. One of Joe Larkin's *Wired* magazines. A lengthy piece about a contrived manhunt. Could someone actually disappear in this age of electronic footprints? The writer tested his savvy against a slew of other online competitors. Him versus them.

"A blueprint," Ridley said.

"That's ridiculous," Michael replied.

Ridley nodded. "All of this is ridiculous. Something out of a novel."

"I need to be with Rachel."

"You go back to the house, you won't be."

"How did this all happen, Rid?"

"I aim to find out, boy."

"Rachel."

"I'll look after her."

"Been doing that forever, Rid."

Ridley nodded. "Sometimes better than others."

"I understand about my mother," Michael said. "She wasn't going to make it. You had to move on, for sanity's sake."

"Appreciate you saying that, boy. But I don't understand."

They stood there with their silence.

After awhile Michael cleared his throat. "So I just go?"

"Yes, sir."

"Now?"

"Right now."

Michael looked off in the distance again. Stood there, shrouded in the cold. Thinking. A beat later he took a deep breath, turned to Ridley, offered a hand. Ridley pulled him into a full embrace. No words spoken as they released one another. Michael attempted a smile and headed off, weaving around plots.

Ridley watched him go.

Watched him exit.

LUST
SLOTH
PRIDE
GREED
ENVY
BOOK FOUR
GLUTTONY
WRATH

# CHAPTER
# ONE

They were watching him. He was certain of this. They'd been watching him for some time. Months, maybe even years. He was certain of this as well. Armed with this understanding, he realized that he couldn't travel to or from the graveyard in a linear fashion. No, that wouldn't do. His drive was full of quick turns and double-backs and abrupt stops and sudden takeoffs and more turns and more double-backs. As circuitous a route as he could manage. And altogether atypical for him. Throw them for a loop with behavior out of the norm. He was pretty confident it'd worked, that he'd lost their tail on the way to the cemetery. But he took the same precautions now, upon leaving. The road behind him black as pitch, empty. No headlights. No cars with the headlights darkened that he could spot, either. He relaxed, his heartbeat falling into a smoothed rhythm, everything settled now, and so, all of his anxiety leeched away. Both calm and clear.

Ready to run.

But first...

☞☞

The angled parking spot was facing the rear brick wall of a wireless cell phone carrier's building. He nosed the Chrysler within a foot of the wall, a strip of retail stores lit up brightly at his back. One storefront dominated his rearview mirror. Large blue Plexiglas signage centered with seven familiar white letters, red trim border below it with more familiar letters. The company logo on the sign, a tilted square, half of it a red domino with three pips on its face, the other half blue like the larger part of the sign, those seven familiar white letters again. Recognized the world over. Domino's. *The Pizza Delivery Experts.*

Michael scanned the lot before sliding his key from the ignition. He exited the Chrysler and headed straight for the pizzeria. The counter-girl at the front wore a baseball cap and the standard uniform. Her high-watt smile did nothing, though, to distract from a complexion that reminded Michael of Cassie, pockets of inflamed red acne covering an otherwise attractive face. Ironic, he supposed.

He ordered a cola, added, "And Cheesy Bread," with a smile to match hers.

"Sure thing," she said. "It'll be a minute. I just finished baking some."

Michael turned and looked through the window to outside while he waited. Red and white flashes of brake lights and turn signals created a light show in the lot. Cars fought for spots or waited calmly to change places. Lots of traffic for a bitterly cold evening.

"Keeping your delivery guy busy?" Michael asked, turning back to the counter-girl.

"Yeah," she said, half-smirking, rolling her eyes. "And out of my hair."

Michael nodded knowingly.

She glanced at the once-white wall next to the checkout area, settling her gaze on a black and white clock. "He'll probably be back any minute. I'm sending him right back out, too." Smiling but meaning it.

Michael smirked. And a beat later she handed him his full order, something extra in her lovely eyes and her equally lovely voice when she said, "Hope you enjoy. *Come again*."

"I will," he said.

Her last smile invited him to do exactly that.

He shook aside erotic thoughts and stepped outside, the door sounding as he exited the store. A cursory scan of the lot didn't reveal any issues, so he crossed it and fell back behind the wheel of the Chrysler, glancing back at the Domino's once, the counter-girl a small blur. He sighed, half-laughed. Bad skin, but sexy in some way. Typical he could travel to that place of thought. Typical that he could find something erotic in any occasion.

Sickness.

Addiction.

The root cause of everything he now faced.

The engine remained off as he pulled apart the Cheesy Bread, mozzarella and cheddar singeing his fingertips. Hot. The way he liked it. The way he liked *everything*.

A gray Buick backed out of the corner-most spot facing the strip stores. The spot went unoccupied for several minutes before another car pulled into the space. A tan Toyota Camry peppered with dents and bird droppings, the back seat overrun with magazines. Exhaust funneled from the car's rear as a tall thin man hopped out. He carried a red-colored hot bag under his arm like an artist's portfolio case. His uniform matched the counter-girl's. Michael smiled and shoveled the last bites of bread in his mouth as the delivery driver rushed inside the Domino's.

Two swallows of soda and Michael was exiting the Chrysler,

chirping the locks with his keychain fob. Moving to the cover of shadow created by a stone pillar next to the Camry.

He started a count at one, made it to eleven. The Domino's driver hustled back out into the cold, holding the hot bag more carefully now, oblivious to his surroundings. *I used to be the same way*, Michael thought. Those days were gone forever now. Never to return.

He came out of the shadows, moved past the rear of the Camry, had the passenger door open and was plopping down into the seat just as the driver reached for the transmission tree.

Michael eased the door shut beside him.

"What in the..." the driver blurted, clearly startled.

Michael smiled like a man whose life hadn't completely come apart at the seams. Clapped a hand on the driver's shoulder. "Good to see you, Joe. I was wondering if you'd like to go shopping for me?"

# CHAPTER TWO

She spit out stray strands of her long dark hair without losing her rhythm on his lap. Bucking wildly, her skin oiled with a thin sheen of exertion sweat. More hair fell into her face. This time he grabbed it, the bunch of it in his strong fist, and held it like that just over her bare shoulder. The gesture forced them even closer, her thick breasts smashed into his chest. The headboard clanged the wall. She reached forward and held on to the top of it, that slight movement raising her breasts to his mouth. He let her hair fall free, gripped her by the waist, worked her up and down and up and down on his hardness, the erect nipple of one of her breasts painting brushstrokes on his lips.

She moaned loudly.

He was eerily silent in his pleasure.

She came with a torrent of sound and movement.

He came holding his breath, his face scrunched in a painful-looking grimace.

She fell away, landed crosswise on his lap. Their dance was well rehearsed. He knew his steps. On the nightstand next to the bed sat a long-stemmed wineglass. Red wine. A soft Shiraz, even though he preferred a burgundy or Chianti. He reached for it, took the sip she insisted he take, and handed it to her. She leaned up and doubled his sips, then fell back flat again, the glass held at a precarious angle in one hand at the rise of her breasts. He knew his steps. He eased the glass from her slender fingers, took another sip, and set it back on the nightstand. They sat there unmoving for a while before he patted her stomach so she'd roll over. He hopped out and stood by the side of the bed, rolled off the condom, knotted it tied, handed it to her to place in the ripped condom foil tossed on the nightstand with the red wine.

"One of these days I'll ask what you do with it," he said, realizing then that he'd never seen her discard it in the wastebasket next to the bed. The fear of an unwanted pregnancy stick-up didn't grip him. He'd gladly have a baby with her. He might even work at being a good father to their child.

"I send it to the lab for testing," she said, smiling. "Figure I can make some money if I find out what's in it that makes you so…" She let the thought flitter, glanced at the digital clock across the room on his dresser. "We started at seven thirty-two," she said, frowning. "Goodness. Forty-two minutes?"

He smiled. A gesture that didn't come easily for him. Usually. "Seven twenty-one. Fifty-three minutes. Don't cheat me the foreplay."

She licked her lips suggestively, looked at him through sexy narrowed eyes. "You're so right. Those eleven minutes certainly weren't forgettable. I apologize for the oversight."

He nodded. "Apology accepted."

"Once more in a bit?"

Again he nodded.

"You're a marvel of nature, Lukas."

"L-Arginine," he said.

"Which is?"

"Your thirst for knowledge, I'm sure you'll find out."

"One of twenty amino acids," she said, smiling. "A building block for protein. A male performance enhancer."

He studied her through a playful frown. "Playing me?"

"Always," she said. "Have to remind you from time to time that I'm not one to take lightly."

"I definitely don't take you lightly."

"Have to keep you on your toes, then," she said.

"Speaking of toes…" Grabbing at her feet, nail polish as red as the lipstick he'd kissed off her full lips earlier.

She wiggled away, laughed in a reserved way that stoked his fire.

He prepared himself to chase her across the mattress. Another anomaly, just something he didn't do. Usually. But his phone interrupted the play, the ringtone chiming loudly from the nightstand. "Sympathy for the Devil." The Rolling Stones. She picked the phone up, considered the screen, handed it to Lukas, a wide smile on her beautiful face.

He sighed upon seeing the caller ID. Pressed the green icon anyway. "Liz."

"We have a problem, Lukas."

Tight, buttoned up, repressed, the opposite of the naked woman on his bed. Liz's laughter wasn't reserved. It was nonexistent.

Lukas Doyle cupped the phone to his ear and stepped across the room. "A problem, you say?"

He turned suddenly, without hearing Liz's response, at the sound of his bedsprings yielding. Watched as naked beauty approached him. An assured, confident strut. When she reached him she stood on tiptoes, kissed him deeply, red wine on her tongue. Slapped his naked ass before disappearing in his bathroom.

He watched the door close.

"Lukas?"

"Yes." His eyes still on the bathroom door.

"Did you hear me?"

Finally his gaze left the door. "I'm sorry. Repeat, please."

"Michael Palmer's out of our sight. Namako and Merriman lost him."

That gained his complete attention. "Lost him?" he said, through gritted teeth. "How?"

"Palmer must be reading Sun Tzu to hear Namako tell it. Made a lot of quick turns and such."

"Not like him," Lukas Doyle said as the bathroom door opened again. Naked beauty standing there framed by a filter of light, her shaved pussy an open invitation.

"Not at all," he heard in his ear. "What do you think it means?" The voice growing fainter with each word as his focus shifted to the naked woman.

"We'll discuss it later, at the meet," he said. "Keep me posted, Liz."

"Keep you... Is someone there with you, Lukas?"

He disconnected without responding.

"Aren't you going to answer that?" Naked Beauty asked, smiling mischievously while nodding at the phone chiming in his hand. "Sympathy for the Devil," once more.

His own crooked smile answered *that* question.

# CHAPTER THREE

A barrage of questions:

"What are you doing here, dude?"

And.

"How did you find me?"

And.

"What do you want, dude?"

Then a couple of statements:

"Don't say shit about the uniform. I don't want to hear it. It's a temporary situation until…"

And.

With suddenly upraised eyebrows.

"You're in some stink. That's it. No, dude, I'm not letting you crash on my couch."

Michael waited it out, then, smiling, said, "I'll explain everything while you drive. Meantime, you should probably get moving. You've only got thirty minutes."

The eyes under the upraised brows widened. Joe took a torturous deep breath. "Shit, dude. What trouble are you bringing my way now? I can't escape it, can I? Thirty minutes for what? You gonna tell me the Bellatoris are gonna come looking for me?"

Michael's smile widened. "Thirty minutes to deliver that pizza."

Joe's shoulders relaxed, his face turned back neutral. "Funny."

"I'm glad. Drive. I'll explain."

A moment's pause, and then the clear understanding that this wasn't going away, it never did with this dude, it was best to just go ahead and get it over with, whatever it was, and Joe switched the transmission to DRIVE.

"Now start explaining," he said.

Michael did.

# CHAPTER
# FOUR

Lukas Doyle arrived more than five minutes late for the meeting. The rest of them were already out at the end of the wooden pier. Merriman propped up on the rail with his back to the water. Namako sitting, yoga-style, on the pier floor itself, crushed into the corner bend where two of the sides met. Liz standing in the small space between the two of them, her heels clicking like computer keys, her beautiful face pinched ever so tight as she examined her watch, and then, noticing Lukas' approach, examined it once more.

The water beyond the pier was a sheet of marbled ice, white foam frozen in swirls that made the lustrous surface look pretty enough to walk or ice skate on. However, signs planted near the water line warned the hazard of such activities. Bitterly cold, but still not cold enough to freeze the water through and through. A thin layer of ice that would crack under little weight. Provocatively innocent-looking, inviting, yet altogether dangerous.

In the other direction, at an approaching Lukas' back, the land sloped upward forming a hill that made the area a park. Replete with an impressive gazebo, a sandbox playing area with swings and jungle gyms, and two twin clay tennis courts. On the Fourth of July holiday, a large barge docked out in the water and spit fireworks into the sky. A display watched by so many the surrounding streets had to be blocked off with wood barricades.

Liz turned over her wrist, examined her watch once again as

Lukas reached the end of the pier. He ignored that but simply couldn't ignore how she fingered a stray tress of hair from her face. That subtle gesture brought about memories from hours earlier.

Naked Beauty.

"How did we lose him?" he asked, getting right to it, disarming the group with the *we*.

"You're tardy."

Liz, of course.

Namako inquiringly looked up at her from the pier floor. Merriman, he of the perpetual curious glower, watched her as well, appearing more perplexed than usual by her sudden outburst. Liz's eyes were on Lukas, as dark as the sky framing a half moon.

"He gave you the slip?" Lukas asked, ignoring Liz with all his might.

"Exactly," Namako admitted, his eyes back on Lukas. "It's embarrassing, I know."

Lukas looked out over the railing, speaking in his measured but calm voice. "If this were the times in those history books you favor, you'd be due several lashes, Nam."

Namako nodded, dropped his head.

"Oh, now this is important?"

Liz, again.

Lukas turned to her, expecting her to capitulate. Instead, she crossed her arms over her chest, tilted her head ever so slightly, dark eyes unblinking, pointed chin up.

Lukas sighed, looked off to his left. A man in the distance, a rolled newspaper in one hand, directing what looked like a Labrador on a leash that glowed fluorescent green. The dog scuttled under a bench despite its owner's best effort to keep it from under the shelter, sniffed the ground, and backed its rear against one of the bench legs. A beat later, the owner crouched down, shaking his head and unrolling the newspaper. To Lukas' right, a seafood restaurant jutting out over the water, built on stilts. A marina right beyond that.

"Your attention is easily divided today, I see, Lukas."

He nodded, sniffed through his nose. Of course Liz was right. What he had to tell them, and the fact he'd been sitting on the shadowy knowledge for hours, fully supported her argument.

"We have ourselves an Enron-size problem," he said.

Liz's head tilted again.

Namako sat up bolt straight.

Merriman didn't move the slightest.

"Daniel Ferrer was murdered," Lukas said.

"What?" came from three harmonious voices.

"When?" Liz asked. "There's been no mention."

"Delicate situation," Lukas said, sighing. "Malcolm's on death's bed. Michael soon to be relieved of his interim responsibilities. Daniel was the obvious next in succession. There'd obviously be a great deal of panic now if this were common knowledge."

"Shit."

"Plus," Lukas added. "The murder has some prickly…variables."

"Like?" Liz demanded.

Another sigh from their leader, altogether atypical. "Daniel was shot. The police have the trigger man in custody. And testimony from a stripper that personally heard Mr. Trigger premeditating the murder."

"Damn."

"Mr. Trigger has also given a full confession."

"It's settled then."

Lukas shook his head. "Mr. Trigger and the stripper both say he was hired out for the job."

"You're shitting," Merriman said, finally in.

"I'm not shitting."

"Who?" Liz asked.

Lukas looked at her. A face that would look even more beautiful if she were to ever smile, laugh. "Michael Allan Palmer."

Silence settled over them.

"He's run off," Liz whispered, after a moment.

"I suspect," Lukas agreed. "Perhaps his buddy, Ridley, caught wind of Mr. Trigger's capture and accusation and warned Michael off."

"The police have anything else?"

"Mr. Trigger received a twenty thousand-dollar stipend from the company's coffers. Evidence shows that Michael initiated the payment."

Liz frowned, looked hard at Lukas.

He focused on Namako and Merriman instead. "We need to find him before the police do."

"Who cares?" Merriman said, waving it off.

"*We* should care," Lukas Doyle said calmly. "I can imagine if they catch him, he'd trade Ridley's heart for a chance at freedom."

"And?" Merriman asked, shrugging.

"Or the knowledge of some dirty business that took place in a certain roach motel," Lukas said, slowly, instructively.

Merriman finally understood. Realization made him hop down off the rail. "Shit."

Lukas clasped his hands, rubbed them together for warmth, offered a weak smile. "No more talk. Let's go catch our fish." The overall motif of the park and its surrounding water, obviously influencing his metaphors.

Liz asked, "When did you learn all of this, Lukas?"

Hours ago. But he was intrigued by the fragrance of something that smelled so much fresher than this, so intrigued he didn't react. Couldn't react. But now he was reacting. They all were. Four more than capable souls out to track down one in-over-his-head man.

"Lukas?" she said.

Lukas turned away, walked off without answering.

# CHAPTER FIVE

Twenty-six minutes, smartass. Four pizza deliveries spread out over a seven-mile radius in three different towns. The last, a hot little MILF on Cambridge Street right here in town, opened the door wearing cream-colored shorts and a halter top, one of the straps falling off her shoulder, no bra, didn't need one, either, an extra large with sausage—yeah, *sausage*—delivered HeatWave piping hot right to her front door exactly twenty-six minutes, according to Joe's Swatch, from the very moment he'd pulled from the lot outside of Domino's. There's your thirty, dude. With four minutes to spare. Beat that.

Not that it mattered one bit to Joe what the hell Michael thought. Major pain in the ass, that guy. Nothing but trouble from the very first. Joe's bad for ever wanting to get close to the dude in the first place. Thinking Michael would help him on the come-up. Joe sniffed a laugh at the idea now.

Wrong as fat girls in spandex.

That got another laugh out of him. Nearly a third of the girls he'd gotten Joseph-from-the-Bible with had BMIs like the Dow Jones on its worst day. Not that Joe was counting.

"Did you need some help finding anything?"

Joe jumped, startled out of his thoughts, a hand to his chest. Some lady all up in his space, crowding him.

"Sorry," she said, wincing. "I didn't mean to sneak up on you like that."

He smiled to set her at ease. She smiled back, teeth like Seabiscuit. A bit square-shaped in her black pants and blue Walgreen's polo top, but something frigging enticing about her just the same. He could work a few of those excess pounds off of her with his own personal workout plan if it came to it. Bent-over rows and whatnot. She really wasn't bad. Definitely could put her to some use, he decided, nodding, leaning against what he took to be wall, knocking over a box of *Nature's Valley Sweet & Salty Nut* peanut bars from the carefully arranged display for his trouble. A lesser dude would've fallen with the box.

"Shit stains!"

He bent in disgust, the lady as well, just an inch of separation keeping their heads from clashing.

"I got it," she said, a hand on the box.

"No, let me," he said, a hand on the opposite end.

She relented, obviously smitten, falling into the awareness that everyone eventually fell into that Joe was cooler than X-Box Kinect. Cooler than the Black President. Cooler than tit rings and navel piercings.

"So," she said. "You've found everything OK?"

Back on her feet, hand-pressing her black pants.

Wanting to keep the convo flowing. At all costs, probably.

Must've been some iron at her core, he thought. Another one pulled to his magnetism.

He had no trouble reading the header signs over each aisle. But he also had a responsibility to the ladies of the world. Disappointing this one, any one, would be like milking his jerk log to a chick-with-dicks flick.

An epic fail.

He smiled at Miss Walgreen's 2010. "Hair dye? Clippers?"

She turned and pointed at an aisle, third from the end.

"Ah," he said, laying it on thick. "Thank you, love."

She frowned, nodded, moved away, traveling backward.

Look into my eyes. Another one entranced by the spell.

Join the line, *mama*.

He took the walk to the hair dye aisle, smiling, shaking his head.

If it were his show, he would've gone with a *Splat Rebellious* Lusty Lavender. But Michael the Mad Puppet Master had been anal-specific: *Just for Men*. Shampoo-in, dark blond 15. Whatever.

The clippers gave Joe more latitude for choice. He went with a marked-down set with all the attachments.

Wielding that control, baby.

Yeah, sure.

He sniffed out Miss Walgreen's 2010 three aisles over, stacking a firewood display with six-pound bags of *Pine Mountain*.

"Come on baby, light my fire," he sang out. Not quite Jim Morrison but pretty damn close.

She turned slowly, her eyes closed for a second. Then her eyes opened and a smile painted her face.

Go on, mama, get yourself composed.

"Yes?" she said.

About one word was probably all she could manage. Entranced. Totally.

Joe went ahead and offered her the deadly Tom Cruise smile. The one that made *them* jump up on couches. He said, "Pre-loaded Visa gift cards? Non-prescription eyeglasses?"

"There," she said, pointing toward the front checkout area.

One word.

Entranced.

Totally.

# SIX

Rachel filled two thermoses with black coffee from a glass carafe, a pocket of hot steam rising up into her face. Most days she'd pause, close her eyes, and drink up the aroma. Dean & Deluca, Napa blend. Wine-like notes of fruit and berries. She paused and hefted the twelve-ounce bag of ground coffee she'd used to brew the pot, a collapsed lung with a half measure of the adequate air. She'd have to order some more. She didn't close her eyes, didn't take the time to appreciate the rich caffeine smell permeating her kitchen.

The two full thermoses were soldiers abreast of one another on the island counter, their lids screwed on tight. Rachel left them there and walked out and down to the foyer, eased her jacket off of the coat tree, shrugged it on. She'd spent the past few hours shrouded in the darkness of the front house, but now flicked a switch on the wall. And a twin switch beside it. Bright light winked on in the hallway, and out on the front porch. She unfastened the front door's locks, yawned the door open a half foot, moved back to the kitchen.

A moment later, a thermos in each hand, she eased the door open further with her hip, released the latch on the outer screen with an elbow.

The air outside was cold, thick as chowder. The street dark but for the low wash of a streetlight and the muted beam of the moon.

Silent but for the low hum of a car engine. A Chevy Impala, its wheels painted black, a partition separating the front and back seats.

Rachel looked both ways and crossed the street. The driver's-side window snaked down just as she prepared to tap it with one of the thermoses.

The driver had a military cut, and even in the near dark she could tell his eyes were light. He didn't bother smiling, but his partner did. Same military cut, same light eyes. Rachel mirrored the driver, not smiling.

"Brought you coffee," she said, handing them the thermoses through the window cut. "Thought you might be cold."

"Spotted us," the driver said, taking the thermoses anyway. He didn't look happy about being spotted. The smile drained from his partner's face as well. Then they took long sips of the coffee, and their faces relaxed in a way that was almost sexual.

Rachel didn't say anything. Whatever she said would make a bad situation infinitely worse. Better to let them orchestrate the conversation from this point forward.

"I'm Officer Brenner and this is Officer Campbell," the driver said, reaching for his badge.

"No need," Rachel told him.

His hands fell back, one propped on the door, the other clasped around the thermos.

Rachel waited him out.

Despite wanting to, she suspected, he didn't sigh. A quick glance at his partner, unspoken communication, and then his eyes fell on Rachel again. "When exactly are you expecting your husband home, Mrs. Palmer?"

Putting all the cards on the table. No pretense. Familiar with her name. Aware of her marital status. Wanting to speak with Michael.

"Three hours ago," she said.

That wrinkled his brow. "Have you spoken with him?"

"Four…" Her voice fading as she looked up the street, the direction Michael normally came from. The opposite direction these gentlemen were facing. Conventional wisdom justified their positioning, a well-lit road with businesses that way, but Michael liked the quiet comfort of the back route home.

Rachel realized the officer in the driver seat, Brenner, was speaking.

"I'm sorry?" she said.

"You've spoken to your husband four times?"

"Left four voicemail messages," she whispered, hugging herself against the cold.

Brenner and Campbell glanced at one another again, silently communicating once more.

"Excuse us a moment, Mrs. Palmer."

"I'll be inside," she said. "Door's open. Just announce yourselves when you come in."

Officer Brenner nodded. What she suspected as rare emotion flitted across his face. Sadness? "We'll just be a moment, Mrs. Palmer. I appreciate your patience. And the coffee."

Rachel nodded and crossed the street, turning back as she reached the curb cut in front of her house. Officer Brenner's eyes were closed in concentration, a cell phone pressed to his ear.

Inside, Rachel closed her eyes as well, leaned against the foyer wall, a dull ache in her chest.

Just a moment ended up being a little more than twenty minutes. The voice announcing itself upon entry was neither Brenner's nor Campbell's. A woman's voice instead.

A black woman.

Rachel hated her immediately. The move felt patronizing in some way.

"Detective Monroe," the woman said, offering a slim brown hand.

Rachel ignored it. "What's your first name, Detective Monroe?"

Monroe frowned. "Ericka. Fredericka, actually. But Ericka goes down a little more easily."

Rachel nodded. "What has Michael done?"

Monroe's eyes sparked. "You believe him capable of *doing* something?"

"You'd have two guys on my house for hours with my husband wrapped around a telephone pole somewhere?"

Monroe offered up a small smile. One of respect. "Ever heard your husband mention the name Rich Kubiak?"

"Never."

"You're certain?"

"I am."

Rachel was aware of Detective Monroe's breathing. The rise and fall of the woman's chest. "This is difficult for you," she told the lady cop. "How about I make it easier? I'm sitting down. I'm incredibly strong. I've had hours to come up with a myriad of possibilities. Some more creative than others. Just tell me."

Monroe nodded. "Your brother, Daniel, was discovered yesterday. The victim of a homicide. I'm sorry."

Rachel felt the room tilt. "And Michael?"

"We have reason to believe he hired the job. I'd love to have a word with him. Again, I'm sorry."

The tilt increased.

Rachel fainted.

# CHAPTER
# SEVEN

Smooth ride. He'd had beaters before, old cars with engines he was imminently aware of the moment he started them. Bald tires and large tanks that seemed to soak up fuel like a sponge. He'd lived in apartments where he had to close his eyes and count to some distant number in order to drown out the patter of a neighbor's feet above him. It took this moment, running away from his present life, to spark the memories of that unpleasant past.

How had it come to this?

Take any thirty-minute block from the day and it was sure to be more than most would ever have to endure. Michael tried it. Let his mind tick back over a thirty-minute chunk. No doubt about which chunk to choose. Surprising Joe at the Domino's Pizza. Answering a million questions while convincing Joe to do some shopping for him. *Best Buy, any pharmacy, and you can go back to your life…dude.* Speak the other guy's language. Joe turning to mush at a pal's plea, agreeing to the shopping. And after the shopping was completed, a soft, miserable, pitying look in Joe's eyes when they finally parted company. Turns and double-backs and more turns and double-backs as Michael made his way to the Parkway. Traveling south, the Chrysler chomping up highway miles as Michael fought a deep urge to call Rachel. Rachel. Oh, the thoughts that then dominated his mind. She'd find another lover. In no time flat she'd forget the shape of Michael's face and the feel of his touch. It had taken Michael great effort to shed those thoughts, but eventually he had.

Focus.

Focus was the criteria of the moment. Without it he'd be caught. Caught before Ridley could piece this all together.

Focus.

He'd stilled his shoulders then and come to a decision. Rachel was the weak link. She was the tether that kept him from escaping. The weight on his back that made what had to be done all the more difficult. A chain around his wrists and ankles. He had no choice but to banish her from his thoughts.

It hurt to do so.

It pained him in a way he wouldn't be capable of describing if pressed.

But...

Focus.

Now, so many minutes later, he settled in for a smooth ride. No thoughts of Rachel. No thoughts of what he was giving up, losing. Just, focused. Warmed by the thought he could get it all back.

Exit 74.

Forked River.

He knew the motel, had been there before. A comfortable, pleasant place. More than capable of providing him with what he needed.

He slowed as he exited, found the shoulder of the road, pulled over. Took a deep breath. *This is the true beginning.*

He pulled out his BlackBerry. It had chimed several times over the past hours. He glanced at the screen. Missed calls. All Rachel. Multiple voicemail messages indicated.

Listen or ignore?

Without much thought, he chose to listen, a decision he would probably come to regret. By her third message a film of tears blurred his vision. He deleted the rest without listening. Pulled out the BlackBerry's battery and held it for a time and then chucked it out the window. They couldn't find his location with the phone dead. Something about triangulation.

He popped his trunk. Pulled his E-ZPass transponder from the windshield and tucked it under a pile of things in his hatch. They couldn't find his location with the E-ZPass disabled.

The man at the motel was Indian. Pleasant beyond measure. Acted as if he remembered Michael from the other times. Michael told him exactly what he needed. The Indian nodded. Michael paid him.

Cash.

# CHAPTER
# EIGHT

lick, click, click, click. Several dead ends so far. No activity with Bank of America. No cell phone calls. Liz frowned, bit her lip, her eyes straining against the glare of her laptop screen. Click, click, click. Email clean as hospital linens. Click, click, click. Think, think.

She looked up at the sound of a different click. Her front door. Then came the soft swish of shoe soles on her laminate floor. Familiar footfalls. She relaxed, realized she'd done so, and went rigid again. Was frowning by the time he made it to her bedroom door. An arrogant smile on his face. Leaning against the frame as if he owned the world and everything in it. The air suddenly spiced with bergamot and white pear, cashmere, wood and vetiver. *Bvlgari Man*. An elegant and sensual fragrance topped only by her lilac. His eyes narrowed, studying her with an intensity that nearly crossed the line to harassment.

Liz wrinkled her nose. "Why do you bathe in that cologne?"

He stepped into the room, smiling. Sat on the corner of her bed, directly at her back. A small reach forward and his strong hands would be on her shoulders. The cold finger of a chill ran up her spine. She shivered, then quickly settled herself down again, swiveling her chair so that she was facing him. "Why don't you sit in the chair so I can see you? I hate talking over my shoulder. And it slows me down to keep turning back."

One chair in the room. Just beyond the doorway, butted against her dresser. Several feet away.

"This suits me just fine, Liz," he said, bouncing on the bed, his smile widening, tapping the mattress with a strong hand to show his approval. "Nice and firm. But still soft. Just how I like my—"

"Suit yourself, Lukas." She turned away from him, feigning indifference, her back exposed.

Click, click, click, click.

"Any luck?"

She shook her head. Click, click, click.

"What have you tried?"

Swallowing before she could get the words out. Overheated all of a sudden. Sweat trickling down her neck, her back. She eased her fingers from the keyboard, blotted at her brow. "Monitored whether there have been any Bank of America transactions," she said.

"And?"

"None recently. He did take out a sum of cash a few weeks back, a little more than fifteen hundred, but I can't imagine he was planning ahead for something like this."

"What else?" Lukas asked.

All business. She envied him that.

"I've checked his cell phone call history a few times."

"And?"

"No outgoing calls since earlier. And that was just to his MRF voicemail."

"Triangulate the phone. That'll tell us where he's at."

Liz turned, frowning. "That's not as simple as you make it sound. But the possibility hasn't been lost on me. I'm working on it. It's going to take some time."

"Time isn't a luxury we have, Liz."

"Who was at your place, Lukas?"

"What other thoughts do you have?" he asked. "Any other ideas?"

"You're avoiding the question," she noted.

"If I answer that, you and I will never be the same, Liz. The mutual respect we now have will be a commodity I appreciate only in the past tense. I've never known you to be anything but focused on the task at hand. Let's keep it that way now. It's very sexy."

Throwing that last bit in to fuck with her.

"I'm a woman," she said. "I can handle split focus. Now, answer the question, please."

He smiled. "Split focus. Now there's something I *can* appreciate."

She felt her lip tremble, wondered, judging by the sudden look on Lukas' face, whether her eyes were watering.

Turned away from him. Click, click, click, click.

Work. She had to focus on work. Behind her, Lukas made a noise that sounded like celebration, victory.

Click, click, click, click.

Ignore him.

But then his hands were on her shoulders. Just what she'd feared. "You're on to something," he said. "I just noticed a change in your movements."

"Take your hands off of me, please."

Squeezing, massaging her needy muscles instead. Parting her hair, kising her neck.

Click, click, click, click.

Her eyes closed. Fighting off a shudder. Losing that battle. Angry at herself for the weakness.

His hands, his warm lips, they both came off of her. She heard him recline on the bed, the clump of his shoes as he toed them off.

She'd shuddered.

He'd won.

In his mind, she knew, there was no further need for him to touch her. A psychologist would have a field day with him. There had to be some scientific name for the complex that plagued him. Asshole.

He yawned.

Despite the anger bubbling inside of her, she wouldn't lose focus on the task at hand. Doing that for herself, not because it was what he expected from her. "Bingo. Got him."

Another dance from the bedsprings as Lukas bolted upright.

"What is it?" he said. At her shoulders but not touching them.

"E-ZPass," she said, tapping the screen with a sharp fingernail. "He went through the Berkeley toll not too long ago. Typical man."

"Meaning?"

"I'd bet that he's down in Forked River."

Lukas frowned but remained silent.

"Where he once rendezvoused with Karla Savage. Exit 74 on the GSP, South. The motel's right off of the exit. Hidden by trees, though. Easy to miss. Some kind of sick nostalgia for him probably. A sexual reconnection, so he can think clearly. Typical man."

Lukas smiled. "You're a genius."

"Who was at your place, Lukas?"

He stood, eased his feet in his shoes. Patted her shoulder. Like you would a puppy.

"Lukas?"

"I'll summon the others," he said. "Be ready to roll in ten minutes."

Off and walking.

She called for him. "I won't stand for you continuing to ignore my deeper questions."

Click, a moment later.

Not her keyboard. Her front door.

# CHAPTER NINE

Let it stand five minutes. Followed by a rinse and shampoo. Bare-chested, his hair coated with dye that went darker by the minute, his eyes squinted against the smell, his image blurred in the motel mirror. A scene in an action movie. Michael couldn't believe this had become his life, but was intent on making it work nonetheless. His 20/20 eyes cloaked in nonprescription glasses. Subtle changes were the most effective, he'd learned. A quick study, he'd sit on this for a few days and then he'd shave his head completely bald, lose the glasses. Subtle changes. Feeling better instantly, he smiled at the blurred reflection in the motel mirror. Bent over the sink basin to rinse out the dye. Then ready the shampoo.

The Virgin Mobile wireless card was a pure gold nugget in his fingers. He tumbled it end over end. Thinking. Planning. In his head, writing the ad he'd soon place on Craigslist. Smiling once more as it all coalesced into shape. He sat down in a chair with a flowered throw across its back, a circular wood table before him, a hole cut in its center, a lamp growing from the hole. Laptop computer opened on the desk. He tapped the SPACE bar, brought it to life. Clicked the Mozilla Firefox shortcut icon. An Internet browser opened.

Showtime.

Most of the pieces had been moved on the board. Chess, not checkers. A yawn fought its way from deep in his chest. He parted the curtains, looked outside. The same few cars in the lot that were there when he checked in. No new arrivals. He settled the curtains back in place. Tired, exhausted actually, he figured he'd earned the right to rest. Despite a few crumbs of remaining anxiety, he decided to answer the deafening call of a deep sleep. Paid up for two days. Maybe he'd slumber through one of them. Starting…right now.

He lay on the mattress, shoes on, eyes closed, visualizing the Bellatoris. Fully aware of what they were capable of. But not worried in the least. A whistle of air passed his lips a beat later. A snore rumbling from his nasal passage.

Asleep.

# CHAPTER
# TEN

ncreasing night and a dramatic weather shift. Ancillary factors in the Bellatoris' effort to recover Michael Palmer. The sky couldn't meet the description of any color, just dark, and a cataract of rain battered their black SUV. Yet as inept as Michael Palmer had proved himself to be, time and time again, his retrieval was most certain to be ugly and unpredictable. So the compromised visibility of the night and the weather was an ally the Bellatoris actually welcomed. How many witnesses would be out braving the punishing rain?

They traveled in silence. One SUV. Lukas' insistence. Merriman at the wheel. Liz brooding in the passenger seat beside him. Namako at the rear, behind Merriman, eyes closed, head tilted back, lost in a visualization exercise. Seeing it all before it actually happened. Michael Palmer's bones snapping like dry twigs under the sturdy soles of construction boots. Wails of pain. Then silence. Walking away as Merriman, the cleaner, turned the rifled motel room as antiseptic as it was the day the outdoor pool was filled for the first time.

Mission accomplished.

Lukas sat directly behind Liz.

"Could you stop that?" she said. First words spoken by anyone for several mile markers.

"Stop what?" Lukas asked. No doubt her complaint was directed toward him.

"Kicking my seat."

"Did I?" His voice as harmonious as the rain. This thing swaying to the juvenile side. "I'm sorry."

Merriman took his gaze off of the road, glanced at Liz. Then the rearview mirror. Didn't return Lukas' smile or head nod. Turned his attention back on the road instead.

Not his concern, whatever was happening between Lukas and Liz.

"He'll be in a room at the back of the lot," Liz said, moving things forward. "Second floor. One room over from the end. His usual room. The motel never has even close to half occupancy. He's gotten that same room every time."

"Predictable," Lukas tsked. "Typical man."

Again Merriman's gaze drifted to the rearview mirror. Namako was nearly catatonic in his stillness. Lukas smiled like a man with a secret. Liz's breathing the only sound in the SUV.

They all fell back into an edgy silence. Liz's breathing and the patter of rain on the windshield and SUVs body. Nothing else.

Merriman eased down on the brake, gently took a tight curve off of the parkway a while later. Exit 74. Forked River.

A quaint little motel hidden by trees. Romantic even. Twenty-two units on two levels. All of the units with outdoor entry. The outdoor pool covered with blue tarp frosted white by winter condensation.

Merriman passed the Check-In office, an Indian man busy watching television behind the counter, and crept off to the back lot.

"Don't see the Chrysler," Lukas noted.

Liz leaned forward in her seat for a closer look-see. She didn't speak.

Namako's eyes opened like window shutters. He surveyed the entire lot with a barely noticeable head swivel.

"Back into that space by the building," Lukas said, indicating a particular spot with a head nod. "I'll have a go look. Keep your eyes open while I'm gone."

"We should all go," Liz said.

Lukas smiled. "Don't trust me, Liz?"

Again, she didn't answer. Turned her attention to Merriman, her hand already on the door handle, her body tilted toward the door. "I'd shut off the engine. You should probably stay at the wheel. Namako, myself, and Doyle can go and have ourselves a look."

Doyle?

Merriman bypassed the rearview, looked over his shoulder. Lukas shrugged, that stupid smile still in place. Plastered on or something.

Liz opened her door, stepped out, closed it carefully behind her. Two more doors opened and closed. Their shoes making crunching sounds as they walked across a stamp of gravel sprinkled on the ground a few feet before the building's cement welcome pad. The metal stairs sagged and cried out as they climbed them a beat later. Soaked with rain, all three of them, that quick. Namako *appeared* unfazed. Lukas *was* unfazed. Liz fussed at her ruined hair as they made their way down the second-floor landing.

They made it to Michael's room of choice. A light burned through the thin curtains in the windows. The blue glare of a television flickered from time to time.

Lukas put a finger to his lips, stepped quietly toward the door, Liz and Namako at his back.

"I'm going to knock," he whispered. "Pay careful attention to what voice answers."

He fisted his right hand.

Raised his arm to knock.

The door shot open.

"Perdo!"

A little Indian man with an aggravating accent. Dark skin, dark eyes. A smile like he'd just jumped out of a cake.

Perdo.

Latin.

To make away with, destroy, ruin, squander, dissipate, throw away, *lose*.

Lukas turned to Liz. The smile on his face finally dulled. "Women," he said, "and your rash conclusions."

# ELEVEN

What made an office space attractive to buyers looking to lease? The parameters were pretty straightforward. One hundred and seventy-five to two hundred and fifty square feet of usable area per person. On-site parking. No restrictions on signage. Reception services.

"You can park your car up the street. Make sure you lock your door."

Michael nodded at the woman. Candace something-or-other. Von-something, the more he thought about it. A royal surname that fit her like two left shoes. Her skin was marred by age lines that competed with the wrinkles in her clothes. Looked as though she'd applied her makeup left-handed in the dark. Breath smelled like Cool Ranch Doritos and Boone's Farm.

"Looks like there's two phone lines but that one doesn't work," she added, pointing at a jack in the far corner of the office. "Something with the wiring. I covered it with duct tape but the last guy peeled that off. Five months behind when I was finally able to get him out of here. Bitter as a whiskey sour. He was probably hoping the next guy would plug in and go kaboom like the Fourth of July."

"Thanks for the warning," Michael said.

"I wouldn't want trouble for you any more than I'd want it for myself."

"I won't be any trouble."

"You have the cash?" she said.

Michael dug in his pants pocket. When he'd first called she'd insisted on a bank cashier's check. It took him a minute to edge her off of that square. At a premium of five hundred dollars. Money well spent as far as he was concerned.

Her eyes widened and she licked her fingers as he pulled out the wad of cash, a stack as thick as one of Stephen King's lighter novels. She flipped through it, counting out loud.

"It's all there," Michael said.

"I'm sure. Eight hundred and eighty. Nine hundred..."

Michael left her to that, walked the perimeter of the office. Cigarette butt burns in the carpet. Ceiling stained yellow by the same cigarettes that had burned the carpet probably. One corner of the ceiling stamped by a brown water mark. A leak. Heavy as it was raining Michael would soon find out if the roof was a faucet. Either way, he'd set up his laptop in the opposite corner.

"It's all here," Candace Von-whatever called.

Michael nodded.

"What kind of business did you say you ran again?"

"I didn't say."

She lingered long enough to process that remark, sort of laughed to herself, then gave Michael the front door key. "Here's hoping your first year's in the black." She stopped, frowned. "Or is it red?"

Michael's hand found her shoulder, the flesh like a mudslide. "Thanks again for taking a chance on me. I'll think of you while I'm framing my first dollar."

Easing her toward the door.

"You have all of my contact info, if there's a problem?"

Again Michael nodded.

Eased her through the door.

"It's been a pleasure conducting business with you," she said.

"You as well."

"If you—"

One good thing Michael could attribute to the space: a thick soundproof door. He leaned against it, smiling as he took in the office. A three-month lease with an option for more.

That thought made his smile widen. He stepped from the door, raised his arms, completed a full circle spin. Damn near giddy.

Slow yourself down. Lots of work ahead.

Another selling point for the place: it had the necessary connections for a laptop. An amenity he'd made sure of before extending his offer. Internet connectivity was the most vital piece of the equation.

He tore open the box from Best Buy. A Hewlett-Packard netbook. A quick, easy setup.

After, he paused long enough to take it all in again, the laptop resting on the threadbare carpet in the corner. The balance of the room bare.

And, smiling, he left.

# CHAPTER
# TWELVE

*Thou art the ruler of the minds of all people,*
*Dispenser of India's destiny.*
*Thy name rouses the hearts of Punjab, Sind,*
*Gujarat and Maratha,*
*Of the Dravida and Orissa and Bengal;*
*It echoes in the hills of the Cindhyas and Himalayas,*
*Mingles in the music of Jamuna and Ganges and is*
*Chanted by the waves of the Indian Sea.*

The Jana Gana Mana. National anthem of India. First sung at the Calcutta Session of the Indian National Congress in 1911.

Prakash Sinha sung it now in a throaty, accent-heavy voice. Over and over and over again. Sung it and thought about the Bengal tiger and the Indian Peacock and the dolphin and the lotus flower and mango fruit and the Saka calendar. Agrahayana, his birthday month, the equivalent of America's late November, so very close at hand.

And so far as well.

A strong wind drove the rain into his face. He didn't bother blinking it out of his eyes. They were closed tight. Clamped shut. Surprisingly he wasn't feeling dizzy any longer. He'd already vomited on the weather-beaten grass two stories below.

"You have a polished voice. But I do need to ask you those questions."

The American who looked like a Wall Street broker.

Bernie Madoff, but handsome.

Crouched down and speaking through the bars of the rail right at Prakash. The one with voodoo eyes held Prakash upside down by the ankles. The woman down below, as some kind of punishment, carefully avoiding the vomit, her arms down at her sides, not even spread out halfheartedly pretending she'd catch Prakash if the voodoo one released his hold. Or if the rain proved too slippery.

"Are you ready to talk?"

*They pray for thy blessings and sing thy praise.*
*The saving of all people waits in thy hand,*
*Thou dispenser of India's destiny*
*Victory, Victory, Victory to thee.*

"Just a few questions and I'll be on my way. You can change your soiled pants and have the rest of your evening."

Something about those words pulled Prakash from his song. He ended it as easily as he'd begun. Had he really soiled his pants?

"Or?" he asked the Wall Street broker.

"Your fate lies in the arms of the woman below."

An odd angle, but even upside down Prakash could see that she wasn't paying much attention to what was happening above her. Her first instinct upon hearing Prakash's scream would be to jump aside in surprise. Caught completely off guard.

"What is your question, sir?"

"Questions," the Wall Street broker said.

"Very well," Prakash said.

"*Perdo,*" the Wall Street broker said.

"It is Latin."

The broker nodded. "Of course. Tell me about the man who told you to use the word."

Prakash described him.

"His name is Michael Palmer," the broker said.

Allowing Prakash into the circle.

Meanwhile, Prakash felt himself lower. The voodoo one starting to tire. Just an inch drop. But obvious to Prakash just the same. His life was now measured in inches.

"Could we continue this discussion in the room?" Prakash asked.

The Wall Street broker attempted a sad face. A face of empathy. Prakash had seen sad, empathy. This wasn't it.

*They will drop me on my head.*

"Reconstruct your conversation…"

"Prakash Sinha."

"Prakash, reconstruct your conversation with Michael Palmer."

"It is not very significant, sir."

"To me it is, Prakash."

"You would kill me for the words?"

"No," the broker said, shaking his head. "I would kill you for not divulging the words. Make this simple for yourself, Prakash. Reconstruct the conversation as best you can. Think."

Prakash swallowed.

The ground drew an inch closer.

"This man say four would come. Four. Black SUVs. Perhaps just one with four inside. Woman in gray. Say Perdo to them, he tell me. Give me two hundred American dollars. My brother and I, we are happy to have it. Business not so spectacular. This Michael Palmer say it is great fun for you all if I say 'Perdo.' So I sit in the window and watch the rain and wait, sir."

"Intent on actually earning the two hundred dollars?"

"Always," Prakash said with pride.

Dropped another inch right after.

"Did he say where he would go next?"

"No, sir."

"What was he driving?"

"I don't know cars, sir," Prakash said.

Rain water in his mouth and eyes. His legs cramping. Getting dizzy again. Spoke too soon before.

"Except black SUVs," the broker said. "You know those." Angry.

Prakash worked some spit into his dry mouth. "Sir, he leave going right."

The ramp for the Garden State Parkway North required a left turn out of the motel. New York. Connecticut. The New England states to Maine. Canada even. Right led South. Delaware. Maryland. Virginia. All the way to the tip of Florida.

Something to go on at least.

"Thank you for that information, Prakash," the Wall Street broker said.

"You are very welcome, sir."

"Anything else, Prakash? Think."

"I have told you all of it, sir."

"I believe you, Prakash."

"Thank you, sir."

"Have I spoken with you?" the broker asked.

"Sir?"

"Tonight. Have I spoken with you? Did the black SUV you were looking for ever show?"

Prakash understood. He was being offered a reprieve. "I watched the rain from the office, then went to bed in the back, sir. The black SUV never did arrive, sir."

The Wall Street broker crinkled his nose. "Showered and then went to bed."

The soiled pants.

"Of course, sir."

The broker stood from his crouch. All Prakash could see were his shoes. Nice leather shoes. Probably expensive. He looked like a man with expensive tastes to Prakash.

After several agonizing seconds Prakash felt himself being lifted back over the rail. When his feet touched the landing he began to sob. Strange it would hit him then.

"You're making me regret setting you loose, Prakash. Stop that."

"I'm sorry, sir." But the tears still flowed.

The broker sighed.

Prakash's sobs intensified as he watched them leave.

# CHAPTER
# THIRTEEN

The streetlight illuminated her perfectly. Red high-heels. Fishnet stockings. Dark-colored boy shorts. A top with a plunging neckline. Waist-length fake fur. Her ass as creamy as morning oatmeal. Big tits that could've stood a lift. Braving the rain, which had lessened quite a bit in the past hour but was still a fine mist.

She walked the same tight circle, up to the corner, around the trash receptacle, stepping off the curb at that point, and back the way she'd come from, resting, finally, under the wine-colored awning for a gold-buying outfit. A cigarette or two there, then back up to the corner and the circle around.

Michael let her play the routine three times, anticipation building with each second, before he winked his headlights on and rolled the Chrysler out from the darkness of the unlit cross street.

She walked toward the car as his window rolled down. A little aged when you got up close, surprisingly little makeup, big doe eyes, brown. One of her teeth capped silver, her smile stirring something awake in Michael.

"Date?" she asked, leaning down through the open window slot.

"Raisin," he shot back.

"What?" The confusion in her eyes excited him all the more. The dumb ones were softer, more pliant, in his experience.

"A little play on words," he said. "Never mind me."

"Nervous, baby?"

"Not in the least."

"You're educated," she said, stating her observation.

"Aren't most of your...dates?"

She smiled again. "Lawyers, stockbrokers. Doctors. Last one talking some nonsense about he was fixing to bruise my esophagus. I didn't know what that meant until he explained it. He gave it the old college try, little as his thing was, I'll give him that much." She narrowed her eyes, smiled deeply. "Now, you, though. You got some size on you."

Michael wanted to clone her, stick her facsimile in his laptop case.

"How much?" he asked.

"What's your pleasure?" she shot back, the tip of a finger in her mouth, going for old school sexy.

Michael eyed her red lips, the finger in her mouth, the cigarette smoke clinging to her clothes and out of her pores. "You have an oral fixation?"

"What's that?" Her eyes dim again.

"You like things in your mouth," he said.

"Oh." She actually smiled.

"Guess what?"

"What's that?"

"Your oral fixation," he said. "I think we might be a perfect match."

That got another smile from her.

∞

Later, she raised her head from Michael's lap, wiping at her mouth with the back of her hand as he zipped up. Bills were on the dashboard. She reached up and took them.

"Anything else I can do for you?" she asked.

Like he was at McDonald's. *Yeah, I'll have a Quarter Pounder with cheese and a Coke.*

"As a matter of fact, there is," he said.

"Name it," she said, smiling, lipstick smeared on her teeth and cheek.

Michael named it.

She studied him for a moment. Deciding. Then: "You need to speak to Dark Child for something like that."

"Tell me where?"

She told him.

Dark Child came by the name honestly. Skin the color of newly laid asphalt. About five-foot-six, with no facial hair, and nothing in his soft build that suggested the possibility of his growing any. A tiny barbell-shaped piercing was threaded through his left brow. Black polish coated his fingernails. His clothes, baggy jeans and a long-sleeve T-shirt, were a full two sizes too big, even for Michael. He held a fat spliff to his meaty lips, squinting hard in a cloud of smoke. The woman standing next to him wore a turtleneck sweater and painted-on jeans. She was nearly a head taller, even without her heels.

Heels.

Whereas Dark Child wore multicolored suede bowling shoes.

A little more than half of the bowling alley's lanes were occupied. Lasers and other arcade sounds peppered the air. Pizza and beer the predominant food and beverage smells.

Michael eyed Dark Child's spliff.

A public place and Dark Child treated it like his back porch. Definitely the right guy for what Michael needed.

The little man tapped the woman's side. When she bent, he whispered in her ear. Michael noticed a flash of disappointment in her face but then she plastered on a smile, straightened, rubbed her hands over her jeans, and moved to leave, glancing Michael's way as she passed.

A plastic cup of beer and a plate with a half-eaten slice of pizza on it were on the counter where Dark Child stood, a gleaming lane at his back. Michael made his way over, stood on the opposite side of the counter, facing Dark Child.

The little man pulled on his spliff, grimaced.

Michael said, "You're Dark Child?"

"That a question or statement?"

Michael nodded. "My name's—"

Dark Child's hand rose. "No names, star."

Again, Michael nodded.

Dark Child sighed. "What kind of trouble Apple involved me in now?"

"Apple?"

Dark Child smiled. Oversized teeth and pink gums. "Your date for the night."

Michael flushed.

"Got that name on account of her ass," Dark Child explained. "Think her government is Thelma or some shit. Might even be Wilma, come to think about it."

Another nod from Michael.

"So what Apple send you my way for?"

"I told her a problem I have," Michael said. "She suggested I come see you."

"Apple thinks I'm Barack or Biden or something. I got to help solve all the world's problems. By the world, I mean our little slice of ghetto heaven."

"She said you could take care of anything."

"See." Dark Child shook his head, moved the spliff to his lips again. Savored the smoke.

"If you can't—"

"This problem have felony implications?" Dark Child asked, cutting Michael off.

Michael didn't answer.

Dark Child's chest expanded. He let out the air in one long rush. "It gonna prevent me from getting dick-deep in some fresh pussy in about an hour's time, star?"

Michael straightened. "You'll be nutting before the night is out, and I'll be a memory."

Attempting to speak Dark Child's language.

The little man frowned.

Michael feared he'd gone too far. But then the frown turned to a smile.

"Nutting, huh?" Dark Child said.

"Yes."

One beat, two, three.

Then: "What you need, star?"

Michael exhaled. "Need to get rid of my car."

"Kinda car?"

"Chrysler 300C."

Dark Child whistled. "Ghetto Rolls-Royce Phantom. New?"

"Yes."

"You must've fucked up and good."

Michael thought of Rachel, MRF Global, the bowling alley he now found himself in.

"How much you need for it?" Dark Child asked.

"A few thousand."

Dark Child laughed. "Yeah, you fucked up. You got papers on this vehicle?"

Michael's turn to squint. "It's owned by the company I work for."

Dark Child shook his head. Studied Michael for a moment. "This some stinky shit, star. This toddler shit."

"Agreed."

"Used to," Dark Child said.

"Pardon?"

"You said the company you work for. Change that shit to 'used to work for.'"

Michael pursed his lips. Slowly nodded. "Agreed."

Dark Child's gaze suddenly drifted past Michael's shoulder. He lifted one finger to signal he'd only be another moment. Michael turned back. The woman from earlier, an impatient look on her face.

"I can't lock my hose off," Dark Child confided a moment later. "She's heard stories about how I get down, wants her back realigned. Don't have insurance for a chiropractor and shit." He laughed. "And I'm aiming to help her out. You know what I mean, star?"

Michael nodded, watching her walk back toward the arcade. Another one that could be named Apple.

"I'll help you, star."

Michael turned back. "Really?"

Dark Child nodded. "Feeling charitable tonight. Give you four Gs for the Ghetto Phantom. Thatta do you?"

"More than generous."

Dark Child nodded, his gaze still focused on the arcade room. "Dick-deep."

Michael hated to do it, hated to interrupt the moment. But it had to be done. "And I'll need one other thing."

Dark Child's eyes were on him again. The little man sighed. "Okay…"

"A ride to the Greyhound station."

One beat, two, three.

Then a machine gun blast of laughter. "Yeah," Dark Child managed. "You fucked up good, star."

# CHAPTER FOURTEEN

"Michael?"

Early twenties, pounds and pounds of baby fat still, disheveled hair he undoubtedly combed with his fingers peeking out from under the bill of a train conductor cap, a serpent tattoo on the top side of his wrist. Dressed in insulated brown overalls and Timberland boots. A smile with something sexual at its center.

Managing to lift his head, a crook in his neck from the Greyhound ride, Michael took the guy in. The little time Michael had been on the road, days and not years, had already hardened him, made him wary and untrusting, slow to react with generosity of spirit. Different.

"You placed a Craigslist ad," the guy said. "Looking for a traveling band you could ride with. We spoke on the phone."

Michael continued chewing his food. Fried pork chops. Fried potatoes with onions. Dulled eyes looking up at the guy.

"No?" the guy said.

All the details correct, the Craigslist ad and all, and still something made Michael hesitant. "Band?" he said, frowning.

The fewer words the better.

"Jacaranda," the guy said.

Michael's frown deepened. "That's a kind of wood, isn't it?"

The guy shook his head, smiled. "It's a kick-ass groove, my man."

Nearly verbatim what he'd said when Michael called with his

prepaid cell phone. Same voice inflection as well. Still, a negative thought nagged at Michael's conscience.

Could be a decoy sent by the Bellatoris.

"Where you headed?" Michael asked.

"Where the wind blows," the guy said.

The band had a definite itinerary they kept updated on Facebook but the guy on the phone had warned Michael that inspiration traveled no set route. Changes were inevitable.

Michael relaxed, nodded to the other side of the booth. The guy fell on the cushioned bench seat, sighing with the effort.

"Twix," he said, extending his hand.

Michael accepted the hand, gave it a firm squeeze.

"You always so careful, Michael?"

*No. It's the road getting to me. Already.*

"Yes," Michael said.

"I can dig it," Twix said, nodding.

Dark Child.

Twix.

Michael craved some normalcy.

A Joe. A Sue. A Robert.

A Rachel.

"So," Twix said. "How do you like Suffolk?"

Virginia.

Red Apple Restaurant.

A truck stop diner and Greyhound drop-off next to a Hess gas station. Colorful locals and out-of-towners entertained by good food and Bluegrass music the second Saturday of every month. Rock and Roll and country the third. All of the women Michael had encountered so far had cigarette smokers' skin and coughs that sounded like an engine throttling.

"When do we leave?" he asked Twix.

Twix laughed. "Finish your meal. The others are out in the van. I'll introduce you later."

Amanda and Alexa. Lead vocal and keyboard. Russell. Drums. Twix. Guitar. And *Amanda and Alexa*. Michael wasn't sure he could even pretend to care about Twix and Russell after meeting the two attractive blondes. Amanda was the taller of the tandem. The only way he could see to tell them apart. Both had eye-popping tits, bodies that turned their thrift store outfits into Kate Spade. Standing by the side of the Econoline van that served as their tour bus while Amanda finished her cigarette, he couldn't help but wonder if the road wasn't so bad after all.

"I'm allergic to latex," Amanda said, out of the blue, between puffs.

"What?" Michael asked.

She tossed her cigarette to the ground, looked down at her T-shirt, plucked it from her breasts to examine it further. Army green, a few light green splotches that hinted at too much bleach during a wash. "Why I don't wear bras," she explained, letting the material fall back snug against her massive breasts. "The latex makes me break out."

Two hard nipples left impressions across the chest of the T-shirt.

Michael said, "Didn't know bras were made of latex."

Amanda looked at him, penetrating blue eyes like Katy Perry. "Shit. You're right," she said. "I get mixed up sometimes. I was a real riot in school...when I went. Never could remember half the shit. Ritalin didn't help much." She smiled. "Just raised my appreciation for...pharmaceutical enrichment."

Michael nodded.

"I don't wear bras," she said, "because I have really, really, really nice boobs."

Michael had been somewhat transfixed by her mutant nipples. He nodded.

"Can't even notice the surgery scars," she noted with pride. And to prove her point she lifted the T-shirt completely up off of her breasts this time. Perky round orbs.

Michael felt a strong erection growing in his pants. He nodded. "No scars."

"They're there," she confessed, "Just done well. So they're not very noticeable."

Twix was in the van behind the wheel, his seat reclined, resting with his forearm across his eyes. Alexa and Russell were inside the Red Apple diner. Looking for OJ and burgers to-go, if possible.

Michael said, "Very well done."

Amanda nodded, pulled the T-shirt back down. Michael's erection throbbed.

"You mentioned a latex allergy?" he said. Anything to get his mind traveling in a different space.

"Yeah," she said, lighting another cigarette with a cheap fluorescent pink lighter that required several tries before it set the Marlboro aflame. She took a drag with her eyes closed. An orgasmic look on her face.

Michael swallowed.

Her eyes opened. She looked at him, deep. "I don't mess with *condoms* because of the latex allergy. Told you I was a big ol' goofball-head. Always mixing things up."

Michael swallowed again.

Amanda pulled on the cigarette once more, and then spoke, her voice pinched.

"What was that?" Michael asked.

"Blow jobs," she said. "You like having your cock sucked?"

No hint of anything extraordinary about what she'd asked in her tone.

He managed a nod.

"Cool," she said. "Sit in the back row once we get moving then." She looked toward the diner, her face as pinched as her voice had been a moment before. "I'm gonna go check on Alexa and Russell. They've probably made it to the bathroom for some doggy-style action. Freaks."

Michael watched her go.

Chuckled, shook his head, and took a seat in the van.

Back row.

# CHAPTER
# FIFTEEN

Above them, in the distant sky, the sun was a soft sphere of blinding light. Totally useless against the bitter cold. But beautiful. A stark contrast to the alley teeming with cats and vermin and rotten food smells. Cardboard boxes were leaned against the brick building, broken down and tied together with twine. They stood by a Dumpster large enough to shield their black SUV from the street at the mouth of the alley. Lukas had his full-length coat buttoned tight, keeping him warmer than the others. His greatest attribute: preparedness. Namako's face was as serious as ever, his eyes their usual dead cast, but his shoulders trembled ever so slightly. Liz's cheeks were the painful red of some apples. Even Merriman was prisoner to the cold, bouncing ungracefully from one foot to the other.

"Merriman, you stand here with your eyes and ears open and the engine running," Lukas said. "Namako, you carefully stroll the street in front of the building. We'll meet you in"—he raised his arm and glanced at his watch—"ten minutes at the corner. The liquor store. Elizabeth and I will pay a visit inside."

Military precision.

Quiet nods and they all fell into place.

"Ladies first," Lukas said, raising an arm to offer Liz passage.

Her eyes were as hard as the ground as she took off. Lukas smirked and followed. She could be moody. Dramatic. Emotional, even. But there was no doubt about her talent. Talents, actually, for she had many. She'd clicked, clicked, clicked at her laptop until Michael Palmer's trail warmed.

Facebook.

He'd logged into Rachel's seldom-used Facebook account several times over the past twenty-four hours. Liz was able to work her mojo and map the IP address to a physical location.

Here.

Warm air kissed their faces as they stepped into the building. Liz grunted her approval. Lukas merely checked the building directory.

"206," he said after a moment.

The only suite on the board absent a business registration after the numbers.

New tenant.

They took the stairs, Liz leading.

"Don't call me by that name ever again," she called, and, gaining no response, "Lukas?"

"Huh?" he said.

"Are you not listening to me?"

"Too busy studying your ass."

She stopped abruptly, two steps from the apex of the stairwell. "You'd better stop."

"Make me," Lukas said, smiling.

"I'm learning to hate you."

"Pity."

"Who was at your place?"

He glanced over her shoulder at the wall, squinted to make out the lettering. "206 is that way," he said, pointing to his right.

"Why are you doing this?" she asked.

He brushed past her, in the lead now.

She sighed but followed.

The office held no furniture and smelled like tobacco. Ruined carpet and yellowed walls. A laptop on the floor, attached to a modem.

Liz crouched to touch the spacebar. Lukas crouched beside her, grabbed her wrist before her slender fingers reached the keyboard. She frowned and tried, unsuccessfully, to wrestle free.

"Look," Lukas said, nodding at the monitor.

Liz relaxed and looked.

A scrolled screensaver.

*How many Bellatoris does it take to screw in a light bulb?*

Lukas sighed. "He's gotten cute."

# CHAPTER
# SIXTEEN

I n no time the dynamics were firmly established. Michael lay across the back bench seat of the van, Amanda's head on his chest. Russell was in the passenger seat up front, Alexa on his lap, facing him, her arms around his neck. Twix had slammed the driver door behind him as soon as they'd reached the rest stop, disappearing out into the shadows.

Something Russell was saying was hysterical. Alexa's cackles filled the interior. For not the first time, Michael wished he were back home. With Rachel.

He hadn't thought about her in…

He simply hadn't thought about her and he wouldn't now either. To do so would be opening the door to a dark corridor overcome with the smells of pain.

And yes, pain had definite smells.

He could describe them without pausing.

*Describe pain.*

No. Rachel mustn't be thought of.

"Twix okay?" he asked Amanda.

She raised her head from his chest, searched the darkness beyond the van. "He'll be alright."

"You two were involved," Michael said, stating a fact, not asking a question.

"Sure," she said.

"Think he might be upset about me edging in now?" A question this time.

"I can't imagine so. We all kinda, you know, get it on. His season's passed. He has to understand that."

So matter-of-fact.

So nonchalant.

Something ached in Michael that he actually couldn't describe. Not pain, then. But what? Something worse?

"So what's your story?" Amanda asked.

"What's yours?" he asked back.

The redirection wouldn't have worked on most. Amanda wasn't most.

"Same shit, different day," she said. "Moms always at work. Nurses' Aide. Acted like she was a damn RN. Worked every shift they'd give her. Smart in every way except when it came to men. Half of her boyfriends were worthless. The other half I fucked."

So matter-of-fact.

So nonchalant.

Michael waited.

"We didn't get along," she said, almost wistful. "I decided to cut out before we hurt each other into comas. Noblest thing I've ever done." Crying softly, a vein opened.

"What's your story?" she asked again through her tears, a moment later, surprisingly remembering she'd started this thread.

Michael edged her aside. "Be right back."

She didn't protest. He eased out of the Econoline van. Walked up a path that fed to restrooms and a cubby with vending machines. Twix was propped up on a bench at the end of the walk, just before the restrooms, his feet on the seat, butt on the backrest, looking up at a chunk of moon. Michael's footsteps must've alerted him. He looked down the path, smiling as Michael approached.

"Michael," he said, that one word the note of a song on his lips.

Michael stopped, out of respect, focused on the moon himself.

"Nice to have someone else in the mix," Twix said. "I tire of the same voices and body odors day after day."

Michael said, "Amanda just told me that you two were involved."

Twix looked at him. "We've had our moments. Yeah."

"I didn't know. I'm sorry."

"Don't sweat it. Amanda doesn't realize she's supposed to have groupies instead of being one. That girl's confused as soon as she wakes up in the morning, my man. Enjoy it for the moment. And don't have hard feelings when she's sucking the skin off of my dick later this week."

Michael half-laughed.

"Besides," Twix said. "I should be the one offering you an apology."

Michael frowned. "Me? For?"

Twix sighed, shook his head. "Damned if I don't feel as though I'm helping you run from somebody that's pretty special."

Michael matched his sigh. "You write the bands' music, I bet."

Twix smiled. "Guilty as charged."

Michael refocused on the moon.

Feeling something worse than pain.

Something he *wouldn't* describe.

Ever.

# CHAPTER
# SEVENTEEN

"He masked the IP address with a program called Tor," Liz explained. "Just to make me work a bit."

"So you'd pat yourself on the back once you broke it," Lukas said.

Despite the thing going on between them, she didn't disagree. "And he logged in remotely," she said. "Through a website called logmein.com."

"Catchy."

"He's gotten cute, like you said."

Agreeing with Lukas' assessment, and not seeming pained by the accord.

"Obvious question is how?" Lukas said.

"Like he's being directed."

"Eric Ridley?"

She shook her head. "I thought of that. Did some checking. Not likely. Ridley's yet to figure out his microwave."

"Someone else?"

"Has to be."

"The mailroom guy at work? Joe Larkin?"

"A fraud," Liz said. "Subscribes to *Wired* because he thinks it's cool probably. His only real interest in the computer is online porn."

"Michael Palmer is making a fool of us. We need to find out how."

"Help," Liz said. "We find out where"—she stopped, frowning—"Shit."

"What is it?"

*Click click click click.*

"Liz?"

*Click click click click.*

"Liz?"

Lukas gave up, let her lose herself in her work.

More than five minutes but less than ten. "That little shit," she said.

"What is it?"

"*Wired*," she said.

"Wired?" Lukas wondered.

"Guy wrote an article about the difficulty of becoming anonymous with all of the electronic footprints we leave behind. He took part in a challenge to see if he could become invisible so to speak."

"Okay."

"Michael's following the article, like some blueprint."

Lukas straightened. "Blueprint. Where's the next wall to be built?"

Liz smiled. "Let's see, shall we?"

*Click click click.*

Lukas frowned as a page loaded in her Mozilla Firefox browser. "That what I think it is?" he asked.

She nodded. "Craigslist."

# CHAPTER EIGHTEEN

The club had the charm of a FEMA trailer. A wedge-shaped building of white brick, storefront windows painted black. A large deli sandwich sign serving as marquee, the performing bands' names advertised in red letters that didn't glow after sunset. Inside, the ceiling was surprisingly high open rafters. The floor uneven, checkerboard design. One long stage. One long bar. A dance floor cut up by support columns every twenty feet or so.

"Darn it," Amanda said theatrically. "You mean to tell me there's no Mosh Pit?"

Twix frowned but kept silent.

"You updated our status on Facebook?" she asked him. "Let our many loyal fans know we'd be here?"

He started a nod, realized she was making fun, stopped, said, "You get ugly when you've been drinking, girl. You might wanna consider giving the alcohol up. Seriously."

"Ugly?" she said. "You're talking?"

Michael contemplated stepping in between them, decided just as quickly not to. Along for the ride only. Nothing more. He certainly wouldn't embrace the role of mediator.

Alexa brushed past him, Russell on her heels, the drummer balancing a wobbly armful of music equipment.

Jukebox.

The place had a jukebox and a dart board as well. A gaggle of college kids were involved with John Lee Hooker, beer, and bull's-eyes. They paid no particular attention to Jacaranda. Wouldn't know Jacaranda if Jacaranda was right in front of their noses.

"Another waste of my time," Amanda complained. "I should crash the dart game."

"Why don't you?" Twix said. "Alexa can handle vocals."

"You're an asshole, Twix."

Her lip quivered, eyes glistened.

Michael noticed Twix softening, tension slipping off of his face, his shoulders relaxing. Twix must've recognized it in himself as well. He hardened just as quickly.

"An asshole," Amanda screamed.

She took off for the door they'd just come in, fumbling at her pack of cigarettes as she moved. The front door banged shut behind her. The college kids were too busy enjoying the transition to Bob Marley on the jukebox to notice.

"Shit," Twix said.

Michael looked at him but kept silent.

Twix sighed. "I'm fucking up. I know it. It won't happen again. Go talk to her."

"Me?"

"You gave the girl her last orgasm," he said miserably. "That's the short straw, my man."

Michael frowned, then went the way Amanda had gone.

She was leaned against the street sign on the corner, shivering, smoking her cigarette. She turned as Michael approached. He smiled. She didn't.

"His dick's practically the length from my elbow to my finger-tips," she said. "But other than that he has no redeeming qualities."

"That's exactly what I came outside to hear," Michael said, easing beside her.

She smiled finally, looked down at his crotch. "You hold your own. No need for Joe."

"What's that?"

"Joe," she said. "J.O.E. Jealous one's envy."

Michael nodded.

Her voice went extra soft. "Speaking of sex, come with me to the van."

Michael arched an eyebrow. "Were we speaking of sex?"

"Always," she said, taking his hand.

He didn't resist.

Amanda didn't speak or even moan while they fucked, just moved in a rhythm that suggested a song only she could hear, rising and falling on Michael's lap, man-made boobs not bouncing, eyes closed tight, face pinched. Silent at the end as she shuddered.

And then her rhythm changed.

Quickened.

She wanted him to come, Michael realized.

He did, a long moment later.

She fell away from him at once, wiggled into her T-shirt, pulled up her panties, and slid inside her jeans. Looked out the window as Michael adjusted his own clothes.

"Ever been in love?" she asked.

He looked out the same window, saw the same things she saw, things only the two of them could see. "A couple times," he answered.

"Sucks, doesn't it?"

He thought of Rachel. "Yes, it does."

"I try to keep my life on a strictly fucking basis," she said. "Just so I don't complicate shit for myself."

"That works?"

She laughed without humor. "Hell no."

"You trying to tell me you're in love with Twix?"

She turned to Michael, looked him in the eyes.

It took a moment.

He said, "No," stretching the one-syllable.

She smiled without joy. "I better head inside."

Michael nodded. "I'll be in shortly."

"Lots to think about," she said through that sad smile.

Again, he nodded.

She eased from the van. Ten steps into her journey back toward the club she turned and, inexplicably, smiled and waved. Michael returned the wave.

She went inside.

He sat there with his thoughts, watching the club.

Later, recalling the next moment, he'd give thanks for his indiscretion. For once his unfaithfulness served a greater purpose.

It kept him alive.

His mouth went dry as soon as the black SUV pulled slowly to the curb just beyond the club, under the dark cover of a blown streetlight. His heart hammered in his chest as they stepped out, one by one.

The steroid freak from behind the wheel.

The D.C. Sniper from the seat behind the steroid freak.

Beautiful Liz Sutherland from the passenger seat.

Lukas Doyle in a long elegant coat from the back, behind Liz.

Doyle paused and glanced the surrounding area. Michael ducked, and a moment later, peeked out again.

The Bellatoris stepped inside the club as if they owned it.

Michael fumbled with the Econoline van's door handle. Got it open and stumbled out into the cold night. Breathing like a rabid animal, he hurried up the block, careful to keep himself hidden wherever there was a blanket of darkness. Walking fast, then trotting, then running.

Running.

Again.

# NINETEEN

Rachel dialed the number once more. As it had for the last few calls, the exchange dumped her directly into voice-mail. Phone turned off. She sighed and disconnected. Sat there on the bed for a beat. Thinking. Then she pulled back the covers and fell into the warm embrace of her comforter.

Crying a moment later.

Surprised to find herself doing so.

Ridley studied the charred house across the street from his own. Jacqueline had called, wanting to come over. He'd deferred until another day. The waiting was the difficult part for him. The waiting and the wondering, actually. He left the window, moved toward his bedroom. The picture of Michael's parents stopped him dead in his tracks. He touched the picture frame, ran his fingers across the glass. "God bless you, boy," he said aloud.

LUST

SLOTH

PRIDE

BOOK FIVE

GREED

ENVY

GLUTTONY

WRATH

BOOK FIVE

# CHAPTER ONE

It took him several days to make it from a certain hell to paradise. Homes there were the color of the sea and the sky. Blue-green, white and beige, soft azure and pink. Filled with evenings that smelled of love, night-blooming jasmine and plumeria mixed with the briny Gulf breeze. Calm and tranquility. Pelicans perched on aged dock pilings and shoreline jetties. Egrets swallowed up by forests of mangrove trees and seagrape plants. Paradise.

The domain of the rich and no longer working. Waterside mansions, golf resorts, four-star restaurants, a thriving art community. Tennis and sailing, and on days that the wind proved itself to be uncooperative, parasailing. License-free fishing off of the long pier. Absolute paradise.

He wore an olive Guayabera shirt, khaki shorts, and amaretto boat shoes. Aviator shades pulled down over his eyes. Head shaved bald. Tufts of dyed blond hair a public garbage with rotting food and crushed containers. His movements hindered by a barely noticeable limp because his muscles were fatigued and tense.

He bypassed the sidewalk cafes with ivy-covered walls and wrought-iron balconies for an impressive crab shack restaurant. Shack being a misnomer for the modern Mediterranean-influenced architecture that housed the eatery. He sat on a bench directly across from it, shaded by a sparsely flowered Royal Poinciana tree out of its peak season, a bed of hibiscus surrounding it.

Several rings cycled in his ear before the line he'd dialed picked up. A twin prepaid cell to his own.

"Michael?"

There was hesitation, relief, and a myriad of other emotions in that one word. Michael understood. He breathed in the various night smells before answering, "Ridley."

"I want to ask where you are," the older man said.

Michael smiled across the miles. "You've spoken with Rachel? How is she?"

"Good. Considering. She knows you're safe, at least."

"Joe got you the phone," Michael said. Small talk. The answer already known.

"Left it outside the library, behind the book return box. Just where you told him to."

Michael nodded. "Good man."

"Yes."

"You've been careful to make sure they haven't been watching you?"

"They haven't," Ridley said. "Focused on finding you, I'd imagine."

"You can't be too careful with them."

"Understood."

Silence settled between them awhile before Ridley finally cleared his throat. "You're doing okay, boy? Bundled up nice and warm? It's gotten awful cold here."

Michael smiled and didn't answer.

"Not much happening on this end," Ridley said, trudging on. "They like you more and more for…the thing happened to Daniel. I've been speaking pretty frequently with the detectives working his…case."

Michael squeezed his eyes shut behind the shades. "Keep working it. Find me a life vest, Rid."

"Doing all I can, boy."

"Keep working it," Michael insisted.

A moment of silence. Then: "I will. Of course."

"I appreciate everything you're doing, everything you've done," Michael managed, his throat suddenly gone rogue with phlegm.

"What do I tell Rachel?" Ridley whispered.

"Nothing," Michael said. "I'll be in touch."

He disconnected before Ridley's reply. Sat there and sighed. Even paradise had its downturns, its valleys.

But inaction would cause him to rethink his steps, so he made it to his feet and headed straight for the crab shack restaurant. It was obviously a successful business, but still had the small touches and little charms of a mom-and-pop. A framed photo in the vestibule of the husband and wife owners and their daughter. A hostess at the podium with a smile as warm as the evening.

"I'm looking for work," Michael heard himself say.

The hostess' smile didn't dim. "Let me go and get Cameron. She'll talk to you about that."

Michael licked his lips, his breaths suddenly shallow.

"Are you a fisherman?" the hostess asked. "I know they're looking for one."

Michael nodded, not trusting his voice.

"Cool." Her smile actually brightened. "I'll go get Cameron."

He turned and looked out the window at the palm-lined street. An active fountain across the way. Michael imagined dipping his toes in it, then submerging his entire body below the cool water. If, in fact, the water was cool.

Her voice was a soft finger tapping his shoulder and breaking his thoughts a long moment later. Delicate as a flower petal. He turned back slowly. The daughter from the framed photo in the vestibule. Dark olive skin that nearly matched his shirt. Large, smoldering eyes made up with smoky eyeshadow. Lips painted a pale pink that didn't distract from the loveliness of her hue. Long black curls of hair reaching down past her shoulders. Womanly, with the severe curves and shape that Hollywood was slowly learning to appreciate. Of all the beautiful things he'd witnessed in this paradise, her smile was undeniably the greatest. She had a hand outstretched for a shake. He slid the aviator shades off. He couldn't imagine what his eyes registered. Hers were in a state of paralyzed shock and dismay.

He smiled, butterflies in his stomach. "Cameron."

Her mouth was slightly parted, but no words came.

Amanda from Jacaranda had asked him if he'd ever been in love. *A couple times*.

Rachel, of course.

And this woman before him now. His first love. The genesis of the emotion.

# CHAPTER TWO

Regrouping. They'd abandoned the road several days ago. The fate that had come of the four band members of Jacaranda forgotten. The charred Econoline van with human bones toasting inside the shell never to be spoken of again. Yet, despite the comfort of that release, a hard line of strain still separated each of them from their desired self. They'd failed miserably. More than once, as it turned out. They never failed, ever, and so the harsh reality of these latest efforts wouldn't sit right with any of them until corrected.

Lukas Doyle had his shirt cuffs unbuttoned, the sleeves rolled up to his elbows. His long jacket tossed across the back of the same chair they'd used to question Michael after his dalliance with the prostitute. Gone were Lukas' careful, graceful movements. His footfalls echoed through the cavernous warehouse.

"Nothing, Elizabeth?" he shouted. "Nothing?"

"I've asked you not to call me by that name," Liz said.

He wheeled around to face her. Jaws churning, eyes hard. Namako and Merriman stood on either side of her with military stillness. Three impotent souls. The misery was evident on all three faces, and mirrored on Lukas'. "Don't call you by that name?" he barked.

The anger was evident, too, in every word, every syllable. It was there in his hardened eyes. In his hands, held as tight fists by his side. Liz swallowed, nodded.

"Michael Allan Palmer has slipped through our grasp more than once. Taunting us as he does so. And you're concerned about a name?"

"Lukas…"

"A…fucking…name."

"Lukas…"

He laughed without humor. "A name."

"We're all tense," she said. "Frustrated. Let's relax and put some thought into this."

"Shut up."

Liz's face reddened from the slap of Lukas' words. The injury made it all the way to her eyes. She didn't speak further. Couldn't.

Lukas stepped closer to her, just a few feet bridged between them. The careful, graceful movements returned. Gone was the simmering anger. A smile lit his face. He spoke in a near whisper. "I'm not Daddy Sutherland taking his only daughter for a supposed camping trip. The zipper of your tent isn't snicking open to announce my unwanted entry…"

Liz slipped a hand in her gray jacket pocket. Her body had started to tremble.

"…I'm not touching you in places I can't even confess to the Fathers."

Her hand tightened around a smooth Zytel handle, fiberglass-filled thermoplastic. Cool to the touch. The beginnings of tears forming in her eyes.

"…you don't have to navigate through feelings of confusion. *It's wrong, but it feels so good.*"

Her hand tightened even more around the Zytel handle.

"…so yes, *shut up* about a name. And find me passage to Michael Allan Palmer's soul." He paused, widened the smile. "Elizabeth."

Her stiletto was out.

But Lukas' hand was raised as well. A FN 5.57-caliber pistol in his firm grip. A handgun favored by the Mexican drug cartels. Known as *asesino de policia*, "cop killer."

Smiling, he said, "Rock, papers, scissors. I believe I win, Elizabeth."

She hesitated for a beat, then relaxed, dropped the stiletto back in her pocket. Let her gaze fall off of Lukas' face. Heels clicking like laptop keys as she exited. Merriman and Namako looking on silently at Lukas as the distant elevator whirred alive.

Lukas' smile went lopsided as he regarded the two men. "Bitches. Can't live with them. Can't live without them."

# CHAPTER
# THREE

They didn't come with their flashers swirling but Rachel sniffed them out just the same. She was at her front door, yawning it open halfway, just as the cop prepared to knock.

"Officer Fredericka," she said, her tone pure acid.

"Mrs. Palmer," the lady cop replied, nodding. Another cop was at her back. Purely an ornament. He didn't speak. Rachel didn't acknowledge him in any way.

"You've tracked down Michael? You've found my husband?"

"We—"

"I'll file a lawsuit if you're here to tell me you've harmed him in some way," Rachel blurted. "Michael wouldn't resist. Despite what you believe about him, he wouldn't."

"Can we step inside, Mrs. Palmer?"

"Why?" Rachel demanded.

Behind her the trill of her house phone sounded. Rachel thought she noticed the lady cop's eyes brighten. She tightened the cinch on her robe and stepped outside, easing the door shut behind her. The sound of the ringing phone disappearing.

"Tell me whatever it is you came for right here," Rachel said.

"I don't wish to be the villain, Mrs. Palmer," the lady cop said. "I'd like to think of myself as an ally."

Rachel sneered. "What did you need to tell me, Officer Fredericka?"

Another phone ring. This one from the deep pocket of Rachel's robe. She'd been in the robe for days. Her cell phone an arm's reach away. So far every time it rang she was disappointed.

"You may answer that if you'd like," the lady cop said, nodding at Rachel's robe pocket.

"Oh, may I?" Rachel smirked now. "So generous of you."

The rings faded, started up again right away.

Rachel stood there, unmoving, unblinking. The lady cop matched her intensity. Again the rings faded and started up once more. The lady cop arched an eyebrow. Rachel's nostrils flared as she reached into her pocket and fished out the phone. More disappointment. But an edge of relief as well.

She answered. "Soledad?"

Listened in silence for a moment. Then: "I have the police here with me now, Soledad. I suspect that's what they came to talk about."

She disconnected and pocketed the cell phone. Squared her shoulders. "Well?"

"Your sister-in-law?"

Rachel didn't answer.

The lady cop sighed. "I'm very sorry, Mrs. Palmer. I truly am."

Rachel considered nodding, but fought it.

The lady cop cleared her throat. "We'll be charging your husband with a second homicide. Have you spoken with him yet?"

A second homicide.

Rachel's father. Dead. The lion silenced. Too much Ketamine in his system. Suspected tampering.

"Mrs. Palmer?"

Rachel stepped back inside the house.

Closed the front door on them.

# CHAPTER
# FOUR

"You're even more beautiful than I remembered, Cameron."

She'd rushed from the crab shack restaurant, out past the splashing fountain, down, down, down the street, running out of steam in front of a museum a while later. Mexican art and the work of American masters from the early- to mid-nineteen hundreds were displayed inside, Michael knew. A huge red, tentacled glass form was positioned outside. The large sculpture would've captivated his interest were it not for Cameron's presence. She looked exquisite in a sundress that hugged her curves like a lover. A bed of snapdragons directly in front of her, at her feet. Michael crouched and touched a petal.

"Asians call them 'rabbit's lips,'" he said. "The Dutch prefer 'lion's lips.' But when you squeeze the blossom"—he did so—"it opens up into something that resembles a dragon's snout. Thus, snapdragon."

"You've come here to tell me what I already know," she said bitterly. "This is my home, Michael."

He stood, smiling. "I always did like my name on your tongue."

"Why are you here?" she demanded.

"I noticed your parents' picture on the restaurant wall," he said. "I'd like to meet them."

She squinted against a nonexistent glare. "I recall you having the opportunity to do so," she said, "and not finding the idea that attractive at the time."

He nodded.

"You loved me," she added. "But not the realities of my life."

"The inconsistency of youth," he said. He didn't dare cheapen the moment with a smile, even though the muscles in his face wanted to settle into one. Cameron Dias, "with an S and not a Z like the actress" she'd pointed out those first moments after their initial meeting those years before, had stirred in him something he thought impossible. Love.

His first taste of it.

A taste that lingered to this day, he realized in a moment of clarity.

College sweethearts.

Her dream was to own the same little piece of Southwest Florida paradise her parents already claimed. To cultivate it right alongside her mother and father. A simple dream.

Michael's dream was to own the world.

"I'm sorry," he said.

She nodded. "For years I looked for you to come. Like a romance novel. You'd walk in the door of my parents' restaurant and tell me you loved me and all you wanted was me and what I wanted. I made wishes under countless banyan trees, Michael. Many."

Indigenous to Asia. Sacred to the Hindus. The trees were believed to represent eternal life. A wish under a banyan tree was certain to be granted.

"I'm sorry," Michael repeated.

"That wish, that desire," she said. "It died a long time ago, Michael."

"I'm in trouble, Cameron. Please. I have nowhere else to turn."

That sounded incredibly selfish, came out completely wrong. He regretted it immediately.

She smiled a smile that wasn't one. "I don't doubt it. Trouble seems to follow you."

"Speaking of countless," he said, recovering, "I've thought of you innumerable days."

"Before, after, or while you were making love to your wife?" she asked.

His turn to be shocked.

Her smile turned to a real one. "And how is work? CEO yet?"

"Cameron…" Using her name as a placeholder, unsure of how to proceed but also aware of the damning judgment that silence would sentence him to.

"I never aimed to stand between you and your dreams, your ambitions, Michael. Those people made me feel cheap. They destroyed everything I believed in. That alone is enough for me to never forgive you."

Michael frowned. "I don't know what you're talking about, Cameron."

"The Ferrers," she said.

Michael was suddenly aware of his heartbeat. He whispered, "The Ferrers?"

"Malcolm Ferrer came to see me right when you were deciding whether to leave that company you were working for up north and join me down here. I admit, he was quite charming, despite his motives."

"And…"

"He expressed how much he wanted you to move over to his company and work for him."

A time of indecision for Michael. He'd been working for a corporation in New York, while longing for Cameron, frustrated by their long distance romance, not believing in its stability. On the verge of chucking his dreams to go ahead and join her. Then came the odd recruitment from MRF Global. He'd done work with them, had lengthy involvements with the old man. Obviously impressed him.

The great Malcolm Ferrer. The courting was more seductive than anything Michael had ever experienced before. They'd shared expensive drinks over numerous discussions. Malcolm had surprised Michael with an exotic beauty content in giving mind-numbing pleasure. On some days Michael still could *feel* her warm mouth enveloping his penis. So had begun his dance with the devil.

"But I told him I was coming here," Michael said. "And then shortly thereafter you broke things off with me and..."

"I don't know about any of that," Cameron said. "But I do know he offered me a substantial amount of money to push you away."

"Money? You're kidding?"

"And when I shredded his check to pieces, he later sent his daughter to gloat that you'd taken to her bed and were getting married. She sickened me with specifics about your...attributes. So don't deny it. There's no doubt she'd been intimate with you, Michael."

"That's ridiculous," Michael screamed. "I do deny it. Rachel and I didn't start dating until some time after I took Malcolm's offer. I didn't even know Rachel then."

"Rachel?" Cameron frowned.

"Malcolm's daughter. My wife," he admitted.

"What kind of game has this been, Michael?"

"What?"

"The daughter that came to see me," she said. "Her name wasn't Rachel."

Michael's eyes tightened in confusion. "Malcolm has only one daughter. What was the woman's name that came to see you?"

Cameron studied him for a moment. Then: "Soledad. Her name was Soledad."

# CHAPTER
# FIVE

Awake, but dreaming. Walking, but floating. Michael hovered above a trolley car as it sputtered by. A white ibis parked itself around a banana tree, its severe, curved orange beak burrowed in the soft dirt at the tree's base. A man and woman flirted under the cover of an umbrella at an outdoor table of a bistro. Oleander blossoms seasoned the air. White, pink blossoms against the dark green leaves. Easy on the eyes, but their oils were a skin irritant. The hem of Cameron's sundress rose and flapped as she walked. The strong legs of a gymnast or ballerina.

She stopped as they reached the fountain across from the crab shack. Michael no longer dreamed or floated. His legs felt heavy, though, weighed down by emotion he couldn't quite finger. Betrayal or one of its cousins. Soledad's long ago deception was a hot coal in the pit of his stomach. Malcolm's interference a thorn impacted in his side.

"I can't imagine the gossip," Cameron said, looking over at her family's restaurant. "I hurried off rather quickly."

"Run away with me," Michael heard himself say.

Cameron Dias smiled. "Make that wish under a banyan tree."

"Cameron…" A placeholder.

"I'm heading back inside, Michael. By tomorrow I won't allow myself to even think your name. By next week this time I will have convinced myself you never came. Six months from now I'll likely have to run through the same exercise again. And again, six months after that." She paused, took a deep breath. "You've changed my life. Twice. Please don't make this harder than it already will be. Leave at once. And don't return."

"I'm at the Inn on Fifth Avenue South," he said. "Room 129. They have the Caribbean restaurant attached to the Inn. Come have a quiet dinner with me and talk."

She left him there without a goodbye. That hurt as much as the revelations about Malcolm and Soledad from moments before.

Could it possibly get any worse?

Of course it could, he realized. He sat down heavily on the bench, dialed with his prepaid cell.

"Michael? I was going to call you."

Michael sighed. There it was. It was about to get worse. "Let me speak first, Rid," he said.

"Go ahead."

"I've directed your attention in the wrong direction," he said. "I need you to reroute. Regroup."

"What's going on?"

Michael told him what he could. Without mentioning Cameron's name.

"How did you come to suspect Soledad?"

"That doesn't matter," Michael said. "Will you keep an eye on her for me?"

"Of course."

"Be discreet."

"You know who you're talking to, boy?"

"Sorry," Michael said. "Now what did you have to tell me?"

Ridley sighed. And told Michael all of it.

They disconnected the call once he'd finished.

Could it possibly get any worse?

Michael didn't bother speculating.

Two homicides on his head now.

# CHAPTER SIX

*My God, I am sorry for my sins with all my heart.*
*In choosing to do wrong and failing to do good,*
*I have sinned against You whom I should love above all things.*
*I firmly intend, with Your help, to do penance, to sin no more,*
*and to avoid whatever leads me to sin.*
*Our Savior Jesus Christ suffered and died for us.*
*In His name, my God, have mercy.*
*Amen.*

The prayerful words of the Act of Contrition left her moist lips the moment she crossed the hotel room's threshold, a smile growing with each recited word. He listened quietly with no expression. Just as she said her Amen, like a scene from a movie, the sequence transitioned with the ringing of his cell phone from across the room.

"Sympathy for the Devil."

"How's that for irony?" she said, starting to slowly work her buttons as he stared at her and ignored the ringing cell phone. It was a long warm-looking coat. Wool and nylon and cashmere blend. With a polyester lining. "You should answer that," she added, when the cell phone rang again a moment later. "Otherwise, it might continue to ring and cause coitus interruptus, which we'd both hate, I'm sure."

"You use the term incorrectly," he said.

She smiled, worked another button undone.

He swallowed and decided he needed a diversion, turned to retrieve her wineglass from the nightstand. Red. Shiraz. Her usual. The carpet swallowed his footsteps as he padded across the room, and hers as well, so he didn't hear her easing up behind him. *Shouldn't be here as if this is some great celebration*, he thought. *There are still loose ends untied. Where is your focus, man?*

And then he turned back with her wineglass in hand...

His next breath caught in his chest. She held the long coat open wide, bunched at her hips by each hand. A model's pose, executed to near perfection. He eyed the ultra sheer, stretch mesh chemise underneath the coat. Thong sold separately.

"I'd imagine you're cold in that," he managed.

"Actually I'm quite warm," she said, with plenty of eye contact. Reaching for the wineglass. Taking a long sip with her eyes closed once she had the glass secured in hand.

Now he had a choice of his own to make. The Glenlivet 21. Amber-colored with copper shades. Oak, cinnamon, ginger on the palate. Or, his personal bottle of red wine. Not Shiraz, but the Chianti he preferred. A squat bottle enclosed in a straw fiasco basket.

Either way, he needed a drink himself.

Badly.

"Sympathy for the Devil" chimed again while he considered his options. Once more, he ignored the phone, poured himself a glass of Glenlivet and took a careful sip. A soft knock at the door interrupted his next sip.

"There's an interruption we both will enjoy," she said, smiling wickedly. "Three's company."

She handed him the glass, shrugged out of her long coat and dropped it on the back of a chair. He watched her naked ass through the sheer chemise as she moved to answer the knock. A sashay that made him hard at his core.

Another woman stepped inside the room, tentative, ill at ease. Not nearly as relaxed as all of the other times. He wondered why that might be as she removed her coat and handed it to the first woman. No lingerie underneath. Turtleneck sweater, and fitted business suit pants.

He wouldn't allow that to disappoint him.

"Quite overdressed," the first woman said, and turning back to face him, wicked smile still in place, "Wouldn't you say we should immediately correct that, Lukas?"

He nodded. Words simply wouldn't come.

The second woman raised her arms, allowed the turtleneck sweater to be eased off. Wiggled her hips a beat later and allowed the pants moved down off of her hips.

Ten minutes.

Within ten minutes they were to it. Sweaty naked limbs tangled. Mingled sex odors. The second woman down near Lukas' waist, his large dick disappearing and reappearing and disappearing and reappearing from deep inside her balmy, wet mouth. His dick covered with much saliva and making sucking sounds as it disappeared and reappeared and disappeared and reappeared inside the vacuum of her jaw. The first woman moaning as Lukas feasted on her shaved pussy, licking her swollen clit with practiced expertise. She came a long moment later, in waves, and redirected the scene. Easing down on Lukas' thick erection while the other woman played with his nipples. And another long moment later, the scene changed yet again. The second woman at the side of the bed, bent forward across the mattress, Lukas' penis crushing through the folds of her slick vagina. Gone was her apprehension from earlier. She cried out in a way that motivated his efforts.

Moaned as though life was close to a sorrowful end. The first woman played with her hair, tossing and twirling it as Lukas rammed in and out in and out, the music of flesh slapping against flesh causing a satisfied smile to paint her beautiful face. This was a perfect scene. An absolutely perfect scene. No, much more.

A celebration.

# CHAPTER
# SEVEN

The dawn of a new day. Soft azure and pink sky. A cool Gulf breeze. The sand on the beach a brilliant white brightened by the new sun's glare. The water was blue-green, calm, schools of jellyfish and stingray and loggerhead turtles living just below the surface. Michael spotted Cameron in her usual morning location, at the far end of the boardwalk right before it curved through a thicket of mangrove trees and seagrape.

Even in his own mind, his appearance felt like an intrusion. Not because she'd expressly asked him to stay away, but because she was deeply lost in thought, focused with still concentration on a brown pelican perched on a piling planted out in the water.

She didn't blink when he eased over. Just continued to look out into the panorama.

Michael settled silently beside her. To speak first would be a second intrusion. Instead, he took her in without staring. No sundress today. A peach-colored blouse tucked into the narrow waist of form-fitting cream shorts. Strapped sandals. Her hair tied back in a severe ponytail. Face scrubbed of any makeup. A spritz of cheap perfume on each wrist. The hint of mint on her breath.

Like a blind man, his senses were greatly heightened in her presence. The polish on both the thumb and index fingers of her right hand slightly chipped. A neglected piercing high up on her left earlobe near to closing. The skin at the nape of her neck as warm as the alabaster sand on the beach.

Greatly heightened.

"Stop staring," she said.

"Was I?"

"Yes."

"I'm sorry."

"You've been watching me, figuring out my routines," she said. "And you called the restaurant the other day, asking after me."

He touched the prepaid cell phone in his pocket, nodded.

"You shouldn't have done this," she said.

And then they both fell silent again. Silent as more of the sun exposed itself over the water. Silent as fishermen arrived and scuttled past with determined anticipation. Silent as two lovers strolled by, hand in hand. And then the two lovers paused for a kiss that stretched across time and space.

"One of the most romantic places in the world," Cameron said, finally. "I'd take it here over Paris any day."

"You always said so," Michael replied, nodding. "I can't disagree after experiencing it for myself."

How different might life be if he'd listened to her those years before? If he hadn't allowed Malcolm's courting to seduce him?

Cameron's hand was on the railing. Michael covered it with his own. Surprisingly, she didn't flinch, didn't ease her hand away.

"Tell me about your wife, Michael."

"Thought you wouldn't allow yourself to even *think* my name today," he said, smiling sadly.

She didn't respond.

Michael sighed. "She's beautiful and tortured."

"Tortured?"

"Her father. Brother." He paused. "Me."

"You?"

"I haven't been faithful to her," he admitted. "From the beginning."

He'd been faithful, always, to Cameron.

Until the exotic beauty Malcolm had handed him with no strings attached.

There were always strings attached, he realized now.

"Why the need to cheat?" Cameron asked. Asking it for Rachel and for herself.

"I thought it was because I have an addiction, a sickness," he said.

"Sex addiction?" she asked, her voice inflected. "Like David Duchovny? Eric Benet?"

"That's what I thought."

"But…"

"I realize now that I was wrong."

"Oh?"

He squeezed Cameron's hand. She didn't flinch. Didn't ease her hand away.

"I was searching for something, Cameron." Another sigh. "Something so easy to find it shames me now. I've caused my wife a great deal of undue hurt. I've harmed myself and…"

She turned facing him. Eyes that absolutely broke his heart.

"…you," he finished.

Her tears were subtle. His less so. Time had healed most of her wounds. Time had only hid his.

"I waited a long time for you to come," she said.

He touched her face. Soaked up a trail of tears with his finger.

"I couldn't appreciate the beauty of a place this small," he said. "The thought of settling in down here felt so constricting. I had such great ambition about how my life should turn." He sniffed at the thought now.

"It's paradise here," she said.

"I know that now."

She saw the look in his eyes, said, "Now's too late for us, Michael."

The kiss was soulful. It also stretched across time and space, like the lovers' on the beach earlier. Cameron had dreamed of it for so long. Michael had refused to let himself rest for so long. Resting would've moved him to dream about her. Beautiful wife. Great job. His life had been settled. Dreaming was hazardous.

Cameron broke the kiss and looked at him, chest heaving. "It's too late, Michael."

"That kiss says otherwise."

"It's too late."

"If this is about my wife—"

"It's about your wife," she said. "And it's about me."

"Cameron…"

"I lost both of my parents a few years back," she blurted.

Michael frowned. "I wasn't aware. I'm sorry."

She nodded. "I'm not the same woman you knew, Michael. I've changed."

Now her tears weren't so subtle.

"The only thing constant is change," he said. "Allow me the opportunity to relearn you."

She shook her head. Several quick times in succession. "It's too late."

And took off.

He was prepared to give chase, but like a scene in a movie, his prepaid cell phone chirped, transitioned the action. He couldn't forget that he was on the run, that his life hung in the balance. He watched Cameron disappear in the distance and answered the call.

"Ridley?"

Ridley's tone stopped Michael cold. Ridley's words turned Michael's legs to water. Michael sat down hard on the boardwalk and listened to it all, every terrible word.

This time *his* tears were subtle.

# EIGHT

She sat curled up in the dark, skin still warm from her latest shower, breath tinted mint from her latest mouth-wash gargle. Sat waiting. Patient. Knowing somehow deep in her bones that today would be the day. Today he would call. Infused with the stirred spirit of her dead mother, a spirit of premonitions. A spirit in concert with *Bondye*, the creator of everything. *Erzulie Freda*, the spirit of love, whispered in her ear, promising a call soon.

It came after she'd drifted to sleep. It took her a few rings to get her bearings. A few rings to ease away from the nightmare that invaded her dreams. The taste of *Them* on her tongue. The smell of *Them* in her nostrils and on her skin. So strong no amount of showers could wash *Them* away.

She fumbled in her robe pocket, came out with her cell phone, answered quickly.

Unfamiliar sounds in the background. Trolley car? The persistent keening of an exotic bird?

"Are you safe?" she asked, nearly breathless though she hadn't moved.

"Very."

She hesitated. Something cold in his voice, despite her suspicion that he was in a warm place.

"That troubles you?" he asked, breaking the silence.

"That you're safe? Why would it? I'm happy you are."

He didn't respond.

"Malcolm passed," she said. "My father's dead."

"I heard."

She frowned. In a matter of days she'd lost the art of conversing with her husband. The days had stretched a divide between them she wasn't certain she could cross. "Ridley's called several times to check in on me," she said. "His calls have kept me sane."

"Sick with worry?"

"Of course," she said. "What's wrong with you, Michael?"

"I've never gotten a chill when you said it," he replied, almost wistful.

"Said what?"

"My name."

"What are you saying?"

"That I've been sleeping with the enemy from the very start."

"I'm your enemy now?"

"From the very start," he said. "When Malcolm was seducing me to come to MRF. When he was offering Cameron money to disappear. When Soledad was pretending to be his daughter, feeding Cameron lies."

"Michael—"

"Our marriage. The whole thing has been a lie. I can't figure out why, though."

"Michael, I'm confused. Who's Cameron?"

"You should be careful what you do in public, Rachel."

"I should be careful?" she said. "You disappear without a word. The only way I knew you were alive is because Ridley assured me you were. He couldn't give me a means of contacting you, though. Then the police come looking for you. My brother's dead, and they suspect you, Michael. Did you know that?"

"Very careful," he said, minimizing all she'd said.

"You call me rambling nonsense," she added. "Meanwhile our lives are falling apart."

"Very careful what you do in public…"

She hesitated again. Then: "Must you keep saying that?"

"You were seen," he said.

"Seen?"

"I can't imagine what actually happened *in* the hotel. But I'm told you put on quite a show outside of it."

Her heart hammered.

Realization took hold.

"Oh, my God," she said.

"Understand now?"

"Michael, let me explain."

"I couldn't trust anything you said to me right now, Rachel."

"Michael, I love you, please…"

The call disconnected without warning.

Her tears were as warm as her skin. She looked at the phone in her hand. Dazed by it.

The Haitian voodoo spirits were conspicuously silent.

# CHAPTER
# NINE

She arrived late for the meeting. Lukas Doyle and Soledad were already out at the end of the wooden pier, huddled close, talking in intimate whispers, unaware of her approach. The water beyond the pier was a sheet of marbled ice, white foam frozen in swirls that made the lustrous surface look pretty enough to walk or ice skate on. However, signs planted near the water line warned the hazard of such activities. She felt the weight of the world in her legs as she moved forward. By the time she reached Lukas Doyle and Soledad, tears streaked her cheeks.

"Guys," she said, announcing herself.

Soledad turned, smiling, and looked into Rachel's face with a puzzled expression. Lukas Doyle grit his teeth.

"I understand your husband contacted you," he said irritably.

Rachel nodded, wiped at her moist eyes.

Why didn't Soledad move to console her?

"What did he have to say?"

"He knows about us," she confessed. "The three of us." That proclamation started the tears flowing again. Heavier than at first.

Lukas Doyle grunted. "Where is he?"

"I don't know," she managed.

Why was Soledad more interested in the moon than her?

"You don't know?"

"That's what I said," she barked.

"What *do* you know?" Lukas Doyle asked.

Again, she wiped at her eyes. "He mentioned a woman named Cameron. Who is she?"

Lukas Doyle shook his head. "No idea."

Soledad turned, smiling once more. "Did you say Cameron?"

Rachel nodded. "Who is she?"

"A ghost from the past."

"Why don't I know about this ghost, Soledad?"

Soledad's face eased into the tender smile Rachel was used to. Tenderness and something else.

Pity?

"Another time, honey," Soledad said. "I think I know where he is now."

"You do?" Lukas Doyle asked. "Where?"

Soledad nodded. "He who forgets the past is doomed to repeat it."

"Where might that be on the map?" Lukas Doyle said.

Soledad's smile widened, as Rachel cried softly. "Southwest Florida. With his ghost, I'd wager."

LUST

SLOTH

PRIDE

GREED

BOOK SIX ENVY

GLUTTONY

WRATH

# CHAPTER
# ONE

It hurt to think. But Drake No Last Name Given expected an answer. And soon. Michael borrowed himself some time with a weary smile as the young man hovered impatiently above him. Drake didn't return the warmth. Just on the north side of twenty, of average height, thin but hard-bodied, cursed with a receding hairline and cheekbones like a Doberman Pinscher, warmth undeniably wasn't Drake's strongest trait. He smelled of soap and seemed uneasy in the starched khaki pants and short-sleeved polo all of the servers were required to wear. He didn't tap his foot but Michael was sure he wanted to.

Questions, questions.

Grilled? Fried? Blackened? Did Rachel perform fellatio on Lukas? No, fuck that, did she suck his dick? Coconut? Buffalo? Scampi? Did she love him? Peel & Eat? Boom Boom? Whatever that might be.

Then there was the portion choice. Half pound? One pound? How long had they been fuck buddies? Was she the impetus for the Bellatoris' harassment? One and a half pounds?

And which two sides? Fresh cut French fries? Baked beans? Did she ride him? Did he pound her doggy-style? Fresh cole slaw? Garlic mashed potatoes? Fresh veggies? Garlic bread? Whose head was buried in whose muff? Hers in Soledad's? Soledad's in hers? Applesauce?

A soup or salad add-on for an additional $3.99.

Live music from a band stationed out on the patio making it even harder for Michael to concentrate. Calypso music. Trinidad and Tobago a mere footsteps away.

Michael glanced up finally, his breath spiced with Red Stripe beer. "I'll go with coconut."

"And your two sides with the shrimp?"

Questions, questions.

"How about...garlic mashed potatoes. And...fresh Rachel."

"Pardon?"

"Fresh veggies, I mean."

Drake nodded, scribbled on his pad. Michael handed him the menu.

"Another Red Stripe, sir?"

"I'm okay," Michael said, pausing for the next part. The crucial part. The real reason he'd come. "By any chance, is Cameron in?"

Drake frowned. "Is there a problem, sir?"

Michael smiled. "I complained about the grouper tacos last time I was in. Too much mango sauce. She was very pleasant, handled my concerns very professionally. I wanted to thank her again."

"I'll let her know."

"I'd like to thank her myself, if you don't mind?"

Drake's frown deepened. "I'll let her know you're asking to speak with her, sir."

"Thank you."

Michael watched him disappear into the kitchen. He took a swallow of his Red Stripe and worked it all out in his mind. *Those who failed to plan, planned to fail.* Winning Cameron over would be no easy task. It would have to happen in increments. Ask her to Mexico or the Bahamas or wherever she wanted to go for a few days. Then ask her to spend the rest of her life with him.

Where he'd get the money for the trip was of yet unsettled.

What he'd tell Cameron when she asked the inevitable questions about Rachel wasn't quite worked out in his mind either.

Cameron's reaction to love with a fugitive was sure to be interesting.

It really, really, really hurt to think.

But thought must not be avoided.

He couldn't tackle any of his problems or order any of his future steps arbitrarily. He couldn't allow the bitterness he felt from Rachel's shocking betrayal to season his experiences. What was done was done. Over. Already old news. Now came the challenge of moving forward.

"I understand there's a problem with your grouper, sir?"

A distinguished voice, the hint of Ivy League in every word. It pulled Michael by the collar, wrestled him away from his deep thought. The guy was on the north side of fifty, of average height, thick but hard-bodied, graying hair slicked back in a way that highlighted his receding hairline, cheekbones like an angry Doberman Pinscher. He smelled of *Eau de Cartier Concentrée* applied liberally, and seemed completely at ease in a steel gray Armani suit with a white shirt, no tie, a pair of dark sunglasses hanging in the V of the shirt neck. Michael didn't actually dislike him until noticing the platinum bracelet on one wrist and the Rolex on the other and the chunky onyx ring on a long thick finger.

Showy.

"A problem with the grouper?" the man repeated.

Management the world over knew now was an instance to smile, but his mouth was a tight line and his forehead was creased.

"I'm fine," Michael said.

"Drake says otherwise."

"Drake is mistaken."

"It's my understanding you asked to speak with Cameron."

There it was.

Cockblocker.

Cameron's uncle?

"Funny, you don't look anything like a Cameron," Michael said, smiling.

The guy smiled back. "Not on my best day."

"Is she in?" Michael asked.

"She is."

"I appreciate your efforts, but could you send her out instead?"

The guy's eyes went dark. He shook his head. "No can do, chief."

Chief?

Michael straightened in his seat. "Who are you exactly…*sir*?"

The guy straightened, too. "Renaldo," he said. "Owner of this fine establishment. Drake's father. And Cameron's husband."

*Describe pain.*

Michael could.

A million different ways.

# CHAPTER TWO

Blankets of sudden rain during the summer months. Pleasing oleander blossoms that irritated the skin. The smell of salt on the searing air. Preying osprey birds nicknamed "fish hawks." Alligators. The absence of a true winter, the lack of fluffy white snow.

Some paradise.

Michael's face gleamed from a fresh shave, and after a long shower his skin was as warm as just laundered clothes. Clean but he felt muddied. As though he'd been trampled on. In bad spirits.

He took the rubber band off of a cylindrical *Wall Street Journal*, but gave up reading after just one inch of the first column.

In bad spirits.

The call of television was so faint he ignored it without much effort. His stomach growled but the thought of breakfast nauseated him. His eyes burned from a sleepless night. The four walls and ceiling offered no new secrets, no new revelations, and no solutions either. Crying was a consideration but he couldn't muster the necessary strength to shed the first tear. In bad spirits.

And then came the knock at his door.

Six days a week she watched the sunrise at the end of the boardwalk. One day a week she ran barefoot through the warm sand until sweat prickled her skin and her breaths grew inchoate, stopping and starting, never quite finding an easy smooth natural rhythm.

Today was a running day.

Spandex shorts that revealed the shape of her sex. A T-shirt darkened under the armpits with her perspiration. She was breathing heavy as she stepped into the room, but not from the run.

The slap came out of nowhere, nearly knocking Michael off of his feet. He rubbed at the sting in his cheek and kept silent.

"How dare you," Cameron said.

"Stick my face in the path of your hand?"

"Be cute," she said. "I'm not above slapping you again."

"What is it exactly that I've done?" Michael asked. Genuinely curious.

"Upset my life," she muttered, dropping down on the bed, letting her face fall in her hands. "Upset my life."

"Glad to see you could still find your way to my room through the upset."

She didn't respond.

He could ease into it.

Or.

"Are you referring to my conversation with the husband I didn't know you had?"

She looked up, eyes narrowed. "Years I waited. Despite everything that happened. Despite how those people made me feel. That woman talking about the length and girth and color of your penis..." She swallowed. "I won't allow you to make me feel guilty."

"Where's your husband now?"

She frowned. "He travels all the time, for business. You happened to catch him in town. Today he's off again."

"And you're here," Michael said.

"Talking this through," she noted.

"Run away with me."

"You're delusional."

"Why won't you?"

"Do you hear yourself?" she asked. "You're serious? You show up after all of this time and expect…" Letting her words trail off, shaking her head.

"It's the stepson, isn't it? You want to see Drake married with a family of his own before you'll be comfortable leaving."

"This is not a joke, Michael."

He sighed. "You love him? Your husband?"

Her gaze dropped as she gathered her thoughts. "My father got it into his head that he should be a pilot. Bought himself a Piper Saratoga. Took Mama into the clouds with him. In one night my life changed, Michael. Neither of them returned. I was going mad trying to maintain the restaurant and cope with the loss at the same time. Renaldo was an established businessman down here. He helped me. Comforted me."

Michael smiled. "Not gifted in the art of conservation, are you? All you had to say was no."

She looked up again, eyes trained on Michael. Unblinking. "You'd prefer all love affairs were like yours and Rachel's?"

Michael's smile dimmed. "What would you have me to do?"

"This is my home," she whispered.

"You have rights to the entire land?"

"What trouble are you in, Michael?"

"More than when I first arrived," he said.

"That's not an answer."

"I believe it is."

"My husband asked me questions I was afraid to answer last evening, Michael. I gave him answers I'm ashamed to admit to right now. That's never happened before."

Michael let that settle. Then: "Do you love me still?"

"Yes."

Both the answer and the swiftness of it surprised him.

She responded to the look in his eyes. "I always will, I'd imagine. But you're married, and you're in trouble, and I'm married, and—"

"In trouble as well," he cut in.

"Committed," she said. "Faithful. I made a decision to honor my husband and I won't turn away from that decision for a stray that wandered in off of the street."

"I'm a stray?" Michael said, a catch in his voice.

"I came to ask you to leave," she said.

"I'm a stray?" he repeated.

"I love you with all of my heart, Michael." She paused. "But I hate you with all of my *soul*."

He nodded, biting his lip. "Then it's settled."

"When will you leave?"

"I'm paid up through two more days."

She reached in her bra, fished out several damp bills, pressed them down on the mattress.

Michael smiled again. "If I didn't know better I'd swear you wanted me to leave at once."

"Twenty minutes ago would've been nice."

"Ouch."

"We know you let me down," she said. "And the fact that you're here, trouble or not, clearly shows that you've let your wife down as well." She hesitated. "Do I love my husband? Yes. And I'm aware of all the reasons why I do. Do I love you? Yes."

"Why?" Michael asked.

She smiled sadly. "Because for once in your life I know you'll do the right thing and take this money and leave."

Ouch.

He nodded. Took his eyes off of her. Moved to pack.

"Where will you go?" she asked.

Not with tenderness. Not with regret.

Pragmatic.

She wanted to be certain he was a great distance from her life. He could hear that in her tone.

Smiling bravely, he said, "Wherever the wind blows. *After* I find the nearest banyan tree."

She nodded, left him to pack.

LUST
SLOTH
PRIDE
GREED
ENVY
GLUTTONY
WRATH
BOOK SEVEN

# CHAPTER ONE

I t was a nice home. The kind that garnered lots of attention in a real estate listing. Minutes from the beach. Minutes from all major shopping and restaurants in the heart of town. Twenty-nine hundred square feet. Three bedrooms, two baths. Family room with fireplace. In-ground caged pool. Two-car garage. Huge backyard. On more than an acre of land. Property taxes under six thousand annually. An attractive property.

More than attractive.

Every night she mentioned the home in her prayers. *Gracias, Dios.*

This night was different in that her lingering thoughts were not of her home but of Michael Palmer. She woke up twice through-out the night, panting, sweating, ultimately grateful the spot beside her in bed happened to be vacant. Renaldo would've undoubtedly asked if she'd been dreaming. And what were your dreams about, *mi amor?*

More questions she couldn't answer.

Or would have to lie in response.

Now, waking up for the third time. The bedroom cooled by her open window. The smell of the Gulf heavy in the air. That point of night when the darkness was at its peak.

And yet still she noticed the shadows in her room right away. Four of them. One directly at the foot of her bed. She gasped without making a sound.

"Cameron Renee Dias-Santiago?" the shadow asked.

Cultured, the tone very relaxed despite the mouthful of words, and more interestingly, despite the felony breaking and entering he was presently committing. Cameron nearly groaned, heard herself rasp, "Yes."

Stay calm. Stay composed. Don't give them reason to hurt you.

"Good," the shadow said. "All the necessary parties are in place except for one." He clasped his hands together as if this were the boardroom of a Fortune 500 company, the meeting agenda carefully laid out. "Do I need to introduce myself by name or are you comfortable with your own gloomy imagination, Mrs. Dias-Santiago?"

She shook her head, said, "I'd assume you're Michael's trouble."

"Ah," the voice said, entertained and more than pleased.

Cultured.

t hurt to pretend. But that's exactly what Rachel had been doing for as long as she could remember. At six years old, her thick curly hair and almond skin were instead bone-straight blonde tresses framing a face best described as pale pink in hue. Her mother had been born in the Port of Marseille instead of Port-au-Prince. Her father's greatest joy was balancing her on his knee while he read her innumerable Aesop's fables from a broad leather-bound volume embroidered with intricate gold print. By the time she reached ten, Daniel was old enough himself to treat Rachel like a dog bone that could be thrown and fetched and gnawed and played with in any way he saw fit. Rachel was forced to convince herself that the subhuman treatment was cute and endearing, and that Malcolm's blind eye was in fact a deep measure of quiet love. When she started developing in her early teens, the looks in the boys' eyes was respect and admiration. The comments they made when they pawed at her breasts and ass weren't the least bit offensive. And again, Malcolm's lack of response was, in fact, quiet love.

As an adult, married by this point, Michael's infidelities were a personal indictment of her own failings more so than his frailty. Not pretty enough. Not sexy enough. Not smart enough. Not sophisticated enough.

Rachel should have taken up knitting because she was the Queen of Nots.

Knots.

Her stomach was tied up in them now. She'd allowed Soledad and Lukas to confuse her priorities. Her sister-in-law had manipulated every situation in a way only a cold, heartless bitch could. And Rachel had completely fallen for it. Hook, line, and sinker.

Sinker.

The ship was definitely sinking. Malcolm gone. Daniel gone. Michael gone.

Just Rachel and Soledad remaining.

Countless millions for the both of them. A wealth of riches equaled a wealth of happiness, she reminded herself. Just what you've always coveted.

It hurt to pretend.

Rachel picked up the phone, dialed.

Several rings cycled in her ear.

Then came the connection from the other line.

Rachel took a deep breath, then cleared her throat. Now or never, as they say. "Officer Fredericka?"

# CHAPTER
# THREE

There was many miles of road between Southwest Florida and Michael's current latitude slash longitude on the globe. He sat with his eyes closed in a window booth of a retread diner.

For two hours.

There was only one other patron in the place. An old guy that looked like a homeless Ernest Hemingway. The air in the diner smelled like grease and lemon disinfectant. When Michael had first come in from the road, the diner was crowded by locals with hearty appetites. At that time the place smelled only of fatty grease. Lucy Holiday, one of only two waitresses, an old bird who surprisingly moved as though caffeine flowed through her arteries, seated Michael by the window and took his order and had it set down on the table in front of him all seemingly in one fluid motion. He'd eaten with the same unbroken spirit.

Then he'd closed his eyes.

Now it was beyond lunchtime. That void in the day where the diner nearly emptied out.

Michael heard dishes clink somewhere off in the distance, then the jingle of the bell over the diner's entrance door. He opened his eyes to see a police officer entering. An unsnapped holster fitted around his nine millimeter. An ex-military stride in precision and detail.

Michael picked up his glass and took a long swallow of what had been iced water before the cubes dissolved. Without making it obvious, he followed the officer's every move. The man leaning over the front counter near the kitchen, whispering something to Lucy, his peripheral focus firmly on Michael.

Not nearly as inconspicuous as Michael with the sly look.

Michael pulled out a twenty and trapped it under the water glass. Eased sideways out of the booth and walked down the aisle as if he owned the place. Determined not to appear unsettled. He'd made it as far as the diner's front door, actually had his hand on the crossbar, when a voice pulled him back.

The officer's.

A smile on the man's face that many would mistake for goodwill. But eyes that had seen the worst the world had to offer... and enjoyed every single bit of it. Eyes that reminded Michael of Namako.

"Yeah?" Michael said.

"The Buick," the officer said. "Parked on the corner with the busted taillight. That happen to be yours?"

Michael swallowed. A junk heap he'd purchased for one hundred dollars even. No papers on it. No use lying, though. "Yes," he answered.

And waited for the bottom to fall out from under him.

The officer's hand eased toward the lining of his jacket.

Slo-mo. Michael's muscles tensing with each millimeter of movement. His heart seized in the grip of fear.

So this is how it ends?

The officer's hand came out of his jacket a moment later. A square white paper between his thumb and forefinger. "It's leaking oil something terrible. You should go see Carl over at Fix-Um's Garage." He paused long enough to smile. "Full disclosure: he's my wife's little brother. This card'll get you ten percent off."

Michael took the card wordlessly. Nodded his thanks and headed outside. The sun on his face was perhaps the greatest feeling he'd ever had. It represented his current freedom.

The feeling lasted little more than thirty seconds. About the time it took him to walk the distance from the diner to the hundred-dollar beater.

The prepaid cell phone ringing in Michael's pocket. It startled his heart.

He answered out of breath, expecting Ridley. Was surprised further to hear Cameron's unsteady voice. The frays at the edge of her tone immediately put Michael on alert. The quiet fear that inflected her every word could only mean one thing.

"Put him on the phone," Michael said.

Rustling in the background. Then: "You're proving to be quite elusive, Michael Allan Palmer. I'm quite inexperienced with being two steps behind."

"Get used to it."

"I'd rather not," Lukas Doyle said. "But, by the same token, I must admit I'm growing to doubt my own capabilities."

"Must make you mad."

"Furious, actually."

Silence settled between them.

Lukas broke it by clearing his throat. "Rather than risk the chance of embarrassing myself further, I ask that you come back and save me some perspiration."

"You don't mean that," Michael said. "I'm sure you're confident you'll catch up with me eventually."

Lukas Doyle chuckled. "A human lie detector now as well. I'm greatly impressed."

"I aim to please."

"Speaking of please...again, I ask that you come back."

"And if I refuse?"

"Oh, we both know the answer to that, Michael. I'd rather not say on an open line."

Cameron.

"You better not harm her," Michael said.

Lukas Doyle smiled. Michael could feel it over the fiber optic line. "It's such a pleasure working with you, Michael Allan Palmer. You know all of your lines perfectly."

Michael sighed. "How are we going to work this out?"

"Perfectly," Lukas Doyle repeated. "Well, let me tell you exactly how this will be done."

He explained it all, detail by precise detail.

Michael disconnected the call a long moment later.

So this is how it ends?

# FOUR

A large, confusing entanglement of trees and roots. The side of the area facing inland, densely populated with mangroves. The other side, facing toward the Gulf, a small beach of white sand washed ashore by the current. A strong, musty fragrance of vegetation and fish in the hot, sticky air. Swamp.

Michael trudged through waist-deep water crowded with tunicates, fanworms, anemones, and sponges. His skin crawled from the sensation of living things feasting on his neck and back and arms. Nightfall was at best an hour away, but he was grateful for that much as he pressed forward.

The kayak was exactly where Lukas Doyle said it would be: leaned against the trunk of a mangrove tree growing in the land bank about two hundred feet into the mouth of the swamp. Michael sloshed on, his waterlogged pants adding difficulty to the journey, and reached land. He squeezed water out of his pants. Leaned a hand against the mangrove for purchase, frowned a moment later.

Something very wrong.

He screamed and fell away from the mangrove. The trunk was alive with a multitude of small, scuttling crabs. The crooked roots of the tree were gnarled fingers reaching out for him, determined to snatch his freedom away. He blinked his eyes to chase away that vision. Blink, blink, blink.

*Don't let this unnerve you.*

*That's what they want.*

*You're better than them.*

*You've proven it.*

But the inspirational thought did nothing to settle him.

So this is how it ends?

He took a deep breath and made another effort for the kayak, reaching out with one hand to push and topple it over. It plunked down on a bed of mud and bark and shed mangrove leaves. The inside cockpit area appeared undisturbed, relatively clean, so Michael reached out and managed a couple of fingers on the lip of the craft, dragging it, inch by slow inch, toward him.

He noticed the birds then. Nesting herons and egrets in the heavy foliage of the tree. Earlier he'd seen a white ibis and a family of brown pelicans. Alligators.

*Just nature at play.*

*Don't let this unnerve you.*

*That's what they want.*

He took another deep breath and climbed inside the kayak. Used his arms to push it out into the water. He squinted hard against the sun and searched the distance. They'd be a mile in. He was promised that he'd find Cameron alive, well tended to, but he was prepared for the worst.

So why come back? Why not keep traveling the road? Make the Bellatoris show their competence. Force them to be a step ahead for a change. Stay in the wind.

Why come back?

Something Cameron had said: *Because for once in your life, I know you'll do the right thing…*

This was penance. This was the right thing to do. The Bellatoris' quarrel was with him. Cameron was innocent in this mess. Michael's only choice was no choice at all. He had to come back.

He engaged the paddle with the water, set the kayak moving. Birds whistled and flew in and out of the thicket of mangrove trees. Mangrove swamps produced thousands of pounds of organic detritus each and every day, which served as food for bacteria, molds, miniscule crustaceans, larval shrimp, and fish. A dance where every organism had a clear role to play with the environment.

If only life for humans was so settled, so orderly, so defined. But as much as he wanted to stop and think, Michael didn't have the time to contemplate life's inequities. Up ahead he spotted a skiff wading in the water. Merriman, the steroid freak, aboard it.

Michael's heart pounded out a rhythm as he neared. A thick cord of vein stood out in Merriman's neck. His oversized frame looked comical in the little boat. His biceps bulged the sleeves of a light-colored T-shirt. In Michael's mind the oar looked like a pencil in his hand. A Greek god carved out of granite.

"You're a real fuck-up," Merriman snarled.

Voice like concrete.

"Pot calling the kettle black," Michael said, repeating a phrase he'd heard Ridley use hundreds of times. Ridley and everything good about his life was a constant thought out here in the swamp. It gave him strength and belief. Two things he'd need. "You guys couldn't find your thumbs if they were stuck up your assholes."

"Keep talking," Merriman warned.

"Where's Cameron?"

"Around."

Michael sighed. "This is a pointless discussion. You know nothing probably. Where's Lukas? Or Liz even? I need to speak with someone with some say."

Merriman narrowed his eyes, glowered.

Michael smiled, said, "Am I holding you up? You have some shoes to shine or something?"

The blow from the oar flushed Michael out of his kayak and down on his back in the murky swamp water. He quickly scrambled to his feet. Luckily the water there wasn't deep. But he didn't know what lurked beneath the surface. He reached for the kayak, caught another blow in his shoulder. This one from Merriman's fist. The big man out of his skiff and hunkering down on Michael.

"I don't want to fight you," Michael said weakly.

Merriman stepped forward, sloshing swamp water.

Michael took a step back.

Merriman's reach and hand speed were things of wonder. Three quick punches settled on Michael's chin from out of nowhere. He sat down hard on his ass in the water. Scrambled to his feet again. He couldn't talk himself out of this one so he kept silent, raised his hands in surrender.

Merriman smiled and stomped forward another step.

Michael glanced at the low gradient slope of land less than ten feet to his right. Without further thought he took off running in that direction. Just as he reached the land bank a heavy-handed push between the shoulder blades sent him tumbling headfirst, barely avoiding a collision with a mangrove tree. He grimaced against the pain and rolled over in the dirt, too tired to stand again. Merriman casually approached, something near a smile on his face. Michael looked up, squinting.

"Fuck-up," Merriman said.

Michael remained silent, reached around on the ground with the hand behind his back. Closed the hand on something hard and loose from the dirt. Sedimentary rock or something of that sort.

Merriman took another step forward, five feet away at best. Michael moved back on his butt, his back crawling up the side of the tree, hand gripping whatever he had hold of. Even though he was aware of the crabs on the mangrove he didn't flinch away from them. They were the least of his worries. He sat plywood straight, as tense as he'd ever been.

"Say something," Merriman ordered.

Michael swallowed, whispered, "Watch out."

Merriman frowned. "Watch out?"

The words were barely out of his mouth before Michael hurled the ball of whatever at his face. It startled the big man enough to force him backward. He stepped on what he probably thought was a log. It wasn't. It was an alligator.

In Florida, alligators were everywhere and almost always docile. Michael had seen more than one lolling about. It took him several days to lose the inevitable feeling of discomfort in their presence.

But this alligator wasn't docile.

It seized Merriman's leg and dragged him, kicking and clawing, into the brackish water. The big man fought hard but proved no match for the nine-foot alligator. Michael turned away as the lower half of Merriman's body disappeared in the alligator's mouth.

Merriman's tortured screams would haunt Michael for the rest of his life, however long that proved to be. He made it to his feet as they finally died down a long moment later, and brushed the mud from his clothes.

A hungry alligator and a hard rock nearby. Were those things divine intervention? Or plain old dumb luck?

Michael didn't bother trying to decide.

Headed out to retrieve the kayak.

He sat down in it gingerly and listened for the anguished cries of a man being eaten alive by an alligator. Heard nothing, except for the songs of birds nesting in the mangrove trees. Time was a factor, the sky turning a shade somewhere between orange peel and salmon as the sun receded down the horizon. A big factor, time. He didn't want to face the rest of the Bellatoris under the cover of darkness. So he motioned the kayak out into the water again, the muscles in his arms burning from the strain of exertion.

Cotton balls fresh out of the box were more moist than his mouth. Licking his lips and swallowing saliva did little to correct the problem. He frowned at his inability to fix something so simple.

The water splashed beside him and stole his thoughts away from the dry mouth. He refused to even glance in the area of the splash. Better to not know what had decided to keep him company. Better to just chug along. One mile into the swamp. Not a very long distance. Soon this would all be over.

One way or the other.

The kayak glided across the still water. Michael slapped at his face, feeling as though some insect was on him. His hand came back dirtied by mud and nothing else.

He drifted on.

Five minutes. Ten. Approaching fifteen when he spotted something. An airboat butted against the river bank. Cameron tied in some way to the rear cage that housed the boat's propeller.

Cameron alive.

He released a breath he hadn't even been aware he was holding. Paddled the last twenty feet. Easing the kayak next to the airboat. Climbing from the cockpit and running for Cameron. She shook her head furiously and mumbled something that died in the duct tape crisscrossed over her mouth. Michael rushed onboard, climbed over things on the way to the stern of the airboat.

He asked, "Are you okay?" before he had the tape completely worked off of her mouth.

She gasped. "Michael…"

"Where are they?"

A bark of thunder sounded. And then everything turned fuzzy. Splashes of sudden red rain or paint all over Cameron's face. Cameron screaming and wiggling, wide-eyed in terror. A pain in Michael's shoulder that surpassed any he'd experienced before.

"Where are they?" he wondered to himself, and realized he'd said it aloud. The voice disembodied. Not at all his own.

Hot searing pain in his shoulder.

Cameron screaming and crying.

Michael wondering how the sky could be void of clouds despite the thunder from a moment before, the red raindrops on Cameron's face.

Then he looked down. His knees almost buckled at the sight of his ruined shoulder. His shirt shredded. A small chunk of his shoulder missing. Blood on Cameron's face, not paint or rain. The sky growing darker by the second. But not from clouds.

*"Where are they? Where are they?"*

The next pain was a punch to the same shoulder. It knocked him off of his feet, caroming into the metal cage.

Cameron screaming.

Immeasurable pain in his shoulder.

Lukas Doyle stepping onto the boat smiling, a firearm of some kind in his hand. "Don't worry, Michael Allan Palmer, here I am. And don't fret, Liz will be along soon."

Michael chuckled at that, for some reason.

Then his world went completely black.

☙

Something felt heavy and hard inside his chest, distant and disconnected at the same time, as though it belonged to someone else. It took a moment for Michael to realize the hard, heavy thing was his heart. Another moment to test a desire to stand, only to discover his wrists and ankles bound by thick rope expertly tied. He fought through the searing pain in his shoulder and the fog of his memory to glance Cameron's way. Fear and confusion lived in her eyes. She was still tied to the propeller cage. A gray duct tape X covering her mouth once more. Michael squinted at the vision.

"Welcome back, Michael Allan Palmer." Lukas Doyle stepped into view, setting the airboat shifting, a smile on his handsome face. "You left us for awhile. Fainted."

Michael's squint subsided. The fog lifted. "You shot me."

Lukas Doyle smiled. "Twice."

Michael glanced down. A shredded mess, his shoulder. The shirt ruined by a stain the color of communion wine.

"Where's Namako?" he asked, unsure even as those words left his lips why the query existed in his thoughts.

"Where's Merriman?" Lukas Doyle shot back, an edge of severe calm in his tone.

"If I were you, I'd contact the state to send out trappers," Michael said, smiling. "They do that whenever an alligator kills a human. The trapper will kill the alligator in turn."

Lukas Doyle nodded knowingly. "An eye for an eye."

"So you know about Merriman?"

"I know everything, Michael Allan Palmer."

"How are you taking it?"

"I do believe you're about to find out."

"You shot me *and* tied me up. Afraid I'd escape?"

"Ah." All Lukas Doyle said. But there was so much threat in that one syllable.

Better not to antagonize him.

"I'm here," Michael said. "You have me. Now let Cameron go."

Lukas Doyle shook his head. "I think it prudent Mrs. Dias-Santiago stays with us for the duration."

"You son-of-a-bitch."

Lukas frowned playfully. "You knew my mother? Small world."

The airboat shifted again before Michael could respond. Liz Sutherland's heels clicked as she edged near them at the stern. She was wearing a short-sleeve white blouse and a too-short skirt. Stunning woman. Fashionable. The only hint of menace in the pink-knuckled grip of her right hand. Michael swallowed at the sight of the stiletto. Cameron came alive, wriggled next to him.

"Nasty little cocksucker, isn't it?" Lukas Doyle said, noticing Michael's gaze. "And nastier than normal in Liz's hand."

"Let Cameron go," Michael barked. The sudden emotion caused a flash of white hot pain in his shoulder and leg. He gritted his teeth in dismay.

"Careful," Lukas Doyle said.

"Fuck you."

Lukas sighed. "You haven't picked up any Southern colloquialisms? I'm quite bored with your limited communiqués."

Michael calmed his voice. "Let Cameron go. Please."

"All of the trouble you've caused me. The way you've taunted and mocked me the entire way. I'd say Mrs. Dias-Santiago is the spoils of my ultimate victory." He edged near her. Placed the FN 5.57-caliber pistol at her temple. Cameron closed her eyes and wept through the tape. Her body shook. Urine dribbled down her leg.

"Don't," Michael warned.

Lukas sighed. "Liz, cut his throat. I have other business to attend to over here."

Liz edged Michael's way.

"Haven't you taken enough from me?" Michael blurted. "My

job. My freedom. My wife." He breathed deep. "All of my dignity is gone. I've spent the past few days imagining Rachel performing fellatio on you."

"Shut up," Lukas Doyle said. "Liz, cut him."

But she'd stopped moving.

"Do it, Liz."

"What is he talking about, Lukas?" she asked.

"Nothing."

"Having threesomes with my wife and sister-in-law is nothing?" Michael said.

Lukas Doyle glared at him, waving the pistol carelessly. "Shut the fuck up."

"All of this is true, Lukas?" Liz asked.

He turned back to her. "Now is not the time for this."

That quickly tears flooded her eyes. Her knife arm lifted. "When is the time, Lukas?" She moaned. "A threesome?"

"Shit." Lukas placed the pistol in his waistband. "Liz, be professional."

"As you've been?"

"Liz."

"The lothario meets his match," Michael said. "How's that for communiqué, Lukas? *Lothario?*"

"I told you shut up."

"Lukas…" Tears clogging Liz's words.

Lukas moved to her. She attempted a lazy knife swipe. He grabbed her wrist, bent it back. The stiletto clattered on the airboat floor. She attempted a lazy slap with her free hand. Lukas trapped that wrist as well.

"Damn you," she cried.

He pulled her into an embrace. She molded with the curvature of his body. One.

"You love them?" she managed.

"What is love, Liz?"

"Do you love me, Lukas?"

"Shit, Elizabeth, this is ridiculous."

"Do you?"

"Of course he doesn't," Michael said.

Lukas wheeled away from Liz. She stumbled back and gathered herself before falling over the side of the airboat.

"I've had enough of you," Lukas said, taking a hard step toward Michael.

And reaching for his waist. Paralyzed, frowning, confused. By his nakedness. "Where the…"

"Looking for this, Lukas?"

He started a turn toward her. Was halted as an echo of thunder rolled through the swamp. Surprise in his eyes.

Another echo sounded.

Lukas Doyle dropped to his knees, then fell forward like a domino. A good portion of his head splattered as blowback on the airboat.

Liz cried and placed the pistol in her mouth.

"No!" Michael screamed.

A final echo.

She toppled sideways, this time unable to avoid tumbling over the airboat and into the murky water.

Michael closed his eyes.

# CHAPTER FIVE

The call came through later that day. Evening had fallen. Michael had managed, one-armed, to free himself from the rope ties. Had loosed Cameron and hugged her to silence and calm as the airboat swayed. Had maneuvered them silently, again with one arm, in the airboat back to the mouth of the swamp and in the beater Buick for the return to Cameron's home. Her husband away on business still. They stood under a dark sky salted with stars. Cameron's eyes offered the invitation her mouth simply couldn't. Every fiber of Michael's being wanted to accept. The throb that had grown constant in his shoulder momentarily forgotten.

*For once in your life, you'll do the right thing.*

"Describe pain," he whispered to her.

"What?" she said, frowning.

"Pain," he said. "Describe it."

"I don't know that I'd like to, Michael."

He nodded. "Right answer."

"You're leaving?"

"Yes."

"You need medical attention."

"I think the bullet went straight through," he said. "It hurts but I'll be fine for a little while. As soon as I can, I'll have someone attend to it."

"Where will you go?" Cameron asked.

He smiled and kissed her. Left that as their final goodbye.

Certain she was watching him as he made his way down her driveway toward the hundred-dollar beater Buick.

Watching him, that was enough.

For once in your life, you did the right thing.

The call came as he chugged down an interstate, which one exactly not really mattering, his windows down, a hard-earned breeze on his face.

"Hello, Rachel."

She was quiet for a moment. He let her be. Then she said, "You're safe?"

"I am."

"I'm sorry, Michael."

"Me, as well."

They remained silent for a long moment, miles being added to the Buick's odometer.

Michael said, "We're our own worst enemies. I've learned that."

"We are," she agreed.

"*You're* safe?" he asked.

"I'm in contact with the police. I've given several statements through my lawyer. They're parsing through what I've told them. I've told them everything." She paused a beat. "What I know, that is."

Michael nodded, though she couldn't see him. "I appreciate it… if you did it for me, I mean."

"For myself," she whispered.

"Even better," he said.

"Are you coming home?" she asked.

"No," he answered right away.

Her tears came suddenly and fiercely. Her sobs filled his ear. He let her be. Drove on.

"Where will you go?" she asked, many miles later.

"In search of the nearest banyan tree," he said.

"What does that mean, Michael?"

He disconnected without a further word and fed the prepaid phone to the breeze. It clattered to pieces on the roadbed behind him.

Ahead, on the side of the road, a large sign noted the next exit. Michael glanced that way, considered, but kept going.

Freedom allowed him to take any exit he chose.

THE END

# ABOUT THE AUTHOR

Phillip Thomas Duck is the author of several adult and YA novels, including *Counterfeit Wives* and *Dirty South*. He lives in New Jersey with his daughter. He can be contacted at phillwrite@aol.com.